VOYAGEURS

Also by Margaret Elphinstone:

The Incomer
A Sparrow's Flight
Islanders
An Apple From A Tree (stories)
The Sea Road
Hy Brasil

VOYAGEURS

a novel

Margaret Elphinstone

CANONGATE U.S.
New York

First published in Great Britain in 2003 by
Canongate Books Ltd., Edinburgh, Scotland

The publishers gratefully acknowledge subsidy
from the Scottish Arts Council toward the
publication of this volume.

Printed in the United States of America

ISBN 1-84195-549-3

Text design by James Hutcheson

Canongate U.S.
841 Broadway
New York, NY 10003

04 05 06 07 08   10 9 8 7 6 5 4 3 2 1

For Henry

Acknowledgements

I would like to acknowledge the help and hospitality I've received from so many people during this long venture. I can't name them all, but I particularly wish to thank the following: *in Cumberland*: the Friends of Mosedale Meeting; Jocelyn Holland at Warwick-on-Eden. *In Scotland*: Ruth Fisken, Ian Begg and William Ramsay, all of Lochalsh; and Kenneth McManus for the Gaelic; also Tom Furniss, Cathy Kinnear and Helen Reid Thomas. And many thanks to Karen McCrossan, my editor at Canongate. *In Quebec*: Lilloette Naegele, Montreal, and Christine Conciatori of the McCord Museum of Canadian History, Montreal. *In Ontario*: The Friends of Toronto and Yonge Street Meetings, especially Marie Doan, Marilyn Church and Anna Cox at Yonge Street; also Elaine Bishop of Prairie Meeting. Thanks also to John Stevenson at the Canadian Canoe Museum, Peterborough; Barbara Naegele and Roger McDonnell, Ottawa; Alastair and Darlene Baird and family, Pembroke, for the Canadian Voyageur Adventure; Dave Harding at Samuel de Champlain Provincial Park; and Nancy Clark, Thunder Bay. Dianne Graves, historian, assisted in checking the manuscript before it fell under the all-seeing eye of her husband, Donald E. Graves, the well-known historian of the War of 1812.

In Michigan: At Central Michigan University: I thank Steve Holder for allowing me to keep coming back to the English Department, Henry Fulton for suggesting Central Michigan University in the first place, and the staff in the Clarke Historical Library, especially Evelyn Leasher. Thanks also to Lisa Tiger of the Department of Native American Studies, and Ben Ramirez for the Ojibwa translations. I also wish to thank Charmaine Benz and the other staff of the Ziibiwiing Cultural Centre, Mount Pleasant; And many thanks to the following good friends for hospitality, introductions, information and encouragement: Jim Paucquette and Nedra Frodge, Pete and Mary Obuchowski, Ann and Colin Alton, all in Mount Pleasant; Mike Federspiel at Midland; Ann Bardens and Tom McClellan at Interlochen. For hunting, canoeing and bear stories I thank Larry Hilton at Frankfort and Randy Raymond at Clare. Thanks also to Tom and Marje Williams, and Bruce and Chris McAfee, of Bois Blanc Island, and to Michael White, Bois Blanc, for access to his notes.

I'm grateful to my amateur voyageurs: Amanda Haworth Wiklund (second paddle and linguist) and Mike Brown (second paddle etc.)

I also wish to acknowledge the help of the Scottish Arts Council, Central Michigan University, and the Hawthornden International Writers' Retreat, Midlothian. In their various ways they all made it possible for me to write this book.

be supplied

LAKE SUPERIOR

● FORT WILLIAM

SAULT OF SAINT MARY

St. Joseph's Island
Bois Blanc Island
Mackinac Island

Fort
St. Joseph

LAKE HURON

Manitou
Islands
Bear Lake

LAKE MICHIGAN

DETROIT

Fort Joseph

SCALES
British Statute Miles 69½ to a Degree
Common French Leagues 25
German Miles 15

N
W E
S

Québec

River St. Laurence

Ottawa River

Lake
Nipissing

Mattawa
River

French River

Montréal

Georgian
Bay

Kingston

Yonge Street

York

LAKE ONTARIO

Fort George
Niagara

LAKE ERIE

Adapted from the map by John Cary, engraver 1805

EDITOR'S PREFACE

WHEN I FOUND THE MANUSCRIPT, I LITTLE THOUGHT that it would contain such an extraordinary adventure. It had no title page. When I opened the foolscap notebook – which I did carefully, for the leather binding was quite brittle – I only saw closely-written lines of faded brown ink. The script was neat and plain, thank God, though the letters were curiously unformed, as if the writer had been unused to working with a pen. A Lakeland farmer, I supposed – and so indeed it proved – but this was no country tale of life in a quiet backwater, under the shadow of Blencathra. I began to read, and forgot what I was doing, and why I was up there in the dusty attic. I read on, and the words led me over the sea, across a continent, into a wild adventure way beyond anything I've experienced, or that anyone these days is likely to experience, anywhere at all. I took the book back down the ladder with me, and did no more work that day. I finished the tale, but the writer continued to haunt me. What if he'd decided otherwise? He doesn't admit how near to it he came, but reading between the lines, I saw how close we came to a very different ending. And what could possibly have happened then?

I should explain that we bought Highside at the end of

last year, from a farmer called Mark Greenhow. He'd lost his hefted flock to foot and mouth disease – only now do I even begin to understand what that might mean to a man like him – and a year ago he put the farm up for sale. When we came to take measurements, after the sale was complete, Greenhow was taciturn but not obstructive. The place suits us perfectly. There are direct trains from Penrith to London, an airport at Carlisle, and who wants to raise children in London these days? The builders arrived after we moved in, which was not according to plan, but if it hadn't worked out that way I might never have been prowling in the attic on that wet Sunday morning, thinking about my big study that was to run the length of the house, lit by new rooflights, with my work surface directly underneath, and bookshelves all along the back wall. There was no floor yet, just a few loose planks laid over the joists, but in one corner there were thick oak planks nailed down. The end one was loose, and in a moment of idle curiosity I prised it up, and found a little dry box-like space underneath, built in under the eaves. And in it, wrapped in a thin linen sheet, I discovered the manuscript.

I've been busy enough the past few months, but I found time to look into things a little. The records office in the castle at Carlisle was helpful, and so were the local Quakers: there's still a Meeting at Mosedale, and I've got quite interested in it. After I'd talked to one or two people I decided there was no reason why I shouldn't publish the book myself. By this time the first Mark Greenhow had me hooked. Finally I took my courage in my hands and wrote to the present Greenhow. He was cannier than I expected, but with the publisher's help we eventually managed to make a deal.

I've done a reasonable amount of editing. I've modernised the spelling, and made a few obvious corrections.

Greenhow evidently never learned the gentle art of punctuation – except for the copious use of dashes – so I've put that in for him. Luckily his writing was seldom illegible. I've modifed his vocabulary on the rare occasions when it might be offensive to modern ears. On the whole he exhibits a remarkable tolerance for his time, but obviously he could not know the meaning of political correctness. He has attempted to transcribe phrases in French and Ojibwa as he heard them, and sometimes I had to puzzle out a meaning before I could render them coherent. I never heard anyone speak Ojibwa in my life, but my email correspondents were remarkably helpful.

Mark's 'footnotes', in which he took such pride, are actually loose sheets of paper interleaved between the bound pages. I think he'd be pleased with the way I've laid them out on the page. His big foolscap notebook I discovered to be identical to those in which the Caldbeck Monthly Meeting Minutes are written, so he must have bought it from the same supplier.

Otherwise I haven't altered the content. I've cut a good deal of the religious discourse, particularly in the women's letters (these were altogether the hardest parts to edit). Obviously it mattered to the writers at the time; I can't see that it would have any significance for the modern reader. I've added nothing – how could I? – though I must admit there were times when I grew frustrated with Mark. If it had only been Rachel, now . . . But history deals us what it will, and that is that.

There are other questions I can't answer. Why did Mark write the story at all? Did any of his family ever read it? It would have been dynamite if they did. There is a notion among Quakers even now (for I have been doing my homework) concerning the need to speak the truth plainly. Perhaps he felt that he *had* to tell his story – that he had failed to tell the truth for twenty-seven years

– and because he couldn't say it, he wrote it down instead. But this is mere speculation.

Who hid the manuscript in the attic? My guess is it lay there for over a hundred years, for its condition was remarkably pristine, all things considered. Perhaps one of the boys put it there, thinking it shameful, but too important to destroy. Or his wife? Would she do that? Maybe Mark put it there himself. But, again, why? Surely a writer wishes to be read? Perhaps he wrote with a reader in mind – his wife, or one of his sons, perhaps – and when it came to handing it over, he found it couldn't be done. He wouldn't be the first, if that's the way it was.

But I should move out of the way, and let him speak for himself.

M.N.E.
Highside,
January 2003.

CHAPTER I

Sixth Month, 1839

WHERE TO BEGIN? WHEN I LOOK AT THAT FIRST LETTER now, the paper is soft with much folding, and the ink is beginning to turn brown. Aunt Judith has crossed her lines, and her script betrays signs of the moiderment under which she laboured. It is no matter; I have her words by heart, almost, and it is the work of a few moments to transcribe them:

> *From the house of Thomas Nolan*
> *Ste Marie du Sault*
> *Upper Canada*
> *12th day of Ninth Month, 1809*

To my sister Susan at Highside, Mungrisdale, in Cumberland,

This follows within a week of my last letter to thee, my dear sister, and if God wills it the ill news will overtake the good. Little did I think, when I described to thee our voyage from Niagara to York, and thence by the far-flung Quaker Meetings of Upper Canada to the Lake called Huron, where we visited several Indian villages upon the islands, and thence to this far outpost at the rapids of St Mary's, that I should have such terrible news to communicate to thee.

I told thee in my last how the lad got off the sloop, and how when Rachel saved him the Scotchman stopped the fight and got her safe away to the house of a man called Ermatinger until the hue and cry died down, and how he saw us safe back across the river. Would that that were all the story! Oh, my dear sister, what am I to say to thee? She has been so tender a companion, she seemed so clear in the Light, so zealous in our ministry.

Susan, I did not know she was meeting him. He came to our third meeting, and I thought the Truth had reached him. I knew nothing of the gatherings at the Johnston house. I knew there was dancing and singing, for we heard it even at the Nolans' when we lay in our beds at night, but I knew not that our very own ewe lamb was led astray into the wilderness, beguiled by that wolf in sheep's clothing.

What can I say to thee? She left me a note, with her direction. They have gone south into the Michigan Territory, which is a part of the United States, in name anyway, for it is far beyond the settled frontier, peopled only by military outposts, trading stations and savage Indian tribes. The direction she gives is: La Maison de Madame Framboise, Mackinac Island, the Michigan Territory. She says she will be married before a priest at Mackinac. She says it is not possible that we should understand. I do not feel called upon to follow her.

In Peace and with much sorrow,
   Thy loving sister, Judith Scott

It was I that fetched this letter from the receiving office in Keswick, and brought it home to my mother. My heart leapt when the clerk passed me the letter, for we had heard nothing of our travellers for almost a year. (The letter Judith mentions had never reached us, and we had no notion what she meant by the lad from the sloop, and it was the first we had heard of the Scotchman altogether.) My mother was chopping rhubarb at the kitchen table when I came in, and I remember how she slit the wafer open with the sticky knife, not even pausing to wipe it.

Her hands were trembling. A year is a long time, and one cannot help but fear for those called upon to minister in the wilderness.

When our first grief was spent, I wrote to Rachel more than once, but there was never any reply. She was indeed lost to us. About three months after Judith's first letter came, she sent another, enclosing a copy of the Minute that recorded my sister's disownment from our Religious Society. Judith says,

> *Friends here have asked me to send thee this copy of the Minute from our Monthly Meeting here at Yonge Street, disowning thy daughter, my beloved niece Rachel, no longer in unity with us since she was married with a priest, contrary to the rules of our Religious Society, to the Scotchman named Alan Mackenzie, an employee of the North West Company. Thee would know, if thee was familiar with these parts, that the North West enjoys a monopoly of the fur trade from here almost, so I believe, to the Pacific shore, to the detriment of all sober independent traders. Its clerks, like its owners, are mostly Highland Scotchmen, and notorious for their ungodly manner of life. It is more usual, indeed, for them to take women among the Indians, in the heathen fashion, and not to be doing with any kind of marriage at all. How it was that Rachel should have been persuaded to elope by this young man I could not have conceived, had I not met him. But – and perhaps this will be some small comfort to thee in thy distress – I did meet him, on the occasion of the brawl that was fought on the jetty at the Soo, when Rachel . . . but I recounted that incident in my last, and would not have thee pay an extra sixpence for me to repeat myself (assuming that my first letter did reach thee). His conduct on that occasion perhaps explains the predilection shown by Rachel for his society, and indeed I was not myself unmoved by his kind goodwill towards us, although I cannot condone the violent means he used to scatter our adversaries.*

There was little comfort in this, but my parents bore all courageously. Only sometimes my mother would say, 'But why does Rachel not write to us, Mark? Why can she not *write*?' I had no answer to give. We prayed for Rachel every day, and gradually I stopped looking eagerly for a letter every time I went to the Receiving Office in Keswick.

But when the third letter from Aunt Judith came more than a year later, I realised when I read it that I had been living in hope after all. I have that letter before me now:

In the care of Yonge Street Meeting
Beman's Corners
Province of Upper Canada
21ˢᵗ day of Eleventh Month, 1810

To my sister Susan at Highside, Mungrisdale (and my good-brother Caleb Greenhow),

I had thought the letter I had writ thee in eighth month of last year would be the hardest it were ever my ill-fortune to pen. I have not heard from thee again, so cannot even be sure that thee received my last. But – Oh, my poor Susan – the news I have now to relate is infinitely worse than the blow I had to inflict upon thee a twelvemonth since. Our dear daughter was lost to us then, out of unity with us by her own act. But at least we might hope she would find a measure of worldly happiness with the man she had chosen, even though she had cast off her family and her Religious Society, indeed, all that she had ever had, to place herself at his side. But now a circumstance has occurred more appalling than anything we might have conceived of. I enclose the young man's letter to me.

She is lost, Susan! She has vanished beyond the pale of the known world! And yet she lives, perhaps. We cannot know. I can tell thee no more than Alan Mackenzie's letter tells me. Here it is, for what it is worth.

My heart goes out to thee, my dear sister (and to my good brother too). I pray for thee, and remember thee among our Friends in the Meeting here in Yonge Street. If there be any thing I may do to comfort thee, tell me of it, but indeed I know there is nothing. We all mourn her. She was much loved, thee knows, among all the Friends whom we visited. Her ministry was a comfort and a shining light to many. If her fall was great, we must not let it obscure the truth of her witness; she did much good. For myself, I mourn a beloved niece and a courageous travelling companion, one who in the greatest discomfort and adversity could yet make me smile. I miss her. And for thee, who have lost a cherished daughter, the loss is so much more. My thoughts are with thee, sister. I cannot say more, and indeed there is no more space on this sheet.

In Friendship and in Love,
  Judith Scott

It must indeed have been a hard letter to write. Through the open window I hear the little beck that tumbles by our house; having heard it all my life I am seldom aware of it, but sometimes, as now, I am aware of it accompanying my thoughts, its moods changing as mine do.

Alan's letter is quite unlike Judith's. Alan's letters, even under the duress of emotion, are always inscribed in the fairest copperplate – he was a clerk, one must remember, as well as an adventurer – and sometimes (though not, of course, on this occasion) illustrated by neat little pen sketches of such subjects as particularly take his fancy. When I first laid eyes on this letter, I knew nothing of Alan. It seemed to me a cruel letter, and the lovely writing was like a twist of the knife in the wound, that he should be so collected about what he had to say. I hated him – if that be a sin let me confess it – which all goes to show how wrong an impression a scrap of writing can give. It tells thee what thee must know, but there is no reaching the living man through the dead words on the paper. I read Alan's letter when it arrived enclosed in Judith's – in fact it was my task to read it to my parents, and I relished it not – and I learned nothing of Alan in it. I saw a cold man of words who had not even loved my sister, which, if he had done, might begin to excuse what he had done to her.

Alan's letter has travelled further than Judith's. At one time it has got damp. The paper is very soft and like to tear at a touch. I smooth it out very gently. Outside the shower has passed and the spring sun illuminates the page. I glance up, and the grey mist has gone from Grasmoor. The hills look very near. I read Alan's letter to my Aunt Judith once again.

Montreal Michilimackinac Company
Mackinac Island
October 30th, 1810

Dear Mrs Scott,
It is with a sad heart I write. Although I ran away with your niece Rachel it was done with the best will in the world. I loved her, and I would have married her before you all, if your absurd rules had not forbidden it. There was nothing underhand in what we did. I told you that before.

Rachel had a child, but he was born dead. She was not the same after: quite mazed, in fact, so far away in her unhappiness I could not comfort her. We had been trading in the country of the Ottawa, and were on our way north by the lake Michigan. We camped on the south island of Manitou. She wandered off at twilight; it was the way she was at that time. There was no reaching her.

She did not come back. Not that night, nor the next, nor the one after that. It is a big island, but we searched it as well as we could. There were some Indians preparing to leave their summer village and go back to the mainland. They did not have her, I know that, and they helped us to search. There had been no one else ashore so far as I know. People come and go in the summer. There's no way to tell.

We stayed for her as long as we could. Winter was coming, and I could not have kept my voyageurs there any longer. If she were still in the woods she must have perished with cold and hunger by the time we left, but we searched and searched, and I am sure she was not there.

Either she went into the lake herself – she was very unhappy. She was not like herself at all after the child died. It was like living with a stranger – or she was taken. That is all I know. I am very sorry, Mrs Scott, to have to tell you this. We left the island four days ago, and came back into Mackinac last night.

No doubt you will tell her family in England. I know she has a brother, she spoke of him a great deal in our early days – no matter, I am out of your life now.

Alan Mackenzie

The first time I read that letter in this house, my father put his head down on his arms and grat, and my mother with set face said to me, 'Let me see the man's letter.'

I handed her Alan's letter, and looked awkwardly away from my father. I loved him well, but I had never seen him weep, and I did not know what to do other than to ignore it.

'He says he loved her,' my mother said presently. 'Does thee think that what he writes is the truth?'

'That he loved her?'

'Any of it. I know not.' My mother turned away, and drew her arm across her face. 'It is the not knowing. Caleb, how do we bear not knowing?'

I took Alan's letter back, and her control broke. She stretched out both her arms to my father, 'Caleb, Caleb . . .'

I stepped outside and shut the door upon them. They

could comfort one another better than I could, I supposed. There was still a little slairy snow lying in a corner of the garth, and the chickens huddled against the barn door out of the teeth of the wind. I went into the barn and sat down on the edge of the hay where we'd been taking out the winter fodder. I read Judith's letter again, and then Alan's letter, twice. I thought about what my mother said, about not knowing, not ever knowing. I sat and thought so long that a little mouse went back to scuttering in and out over the stone doorstep carrying grains from the floor to her hole behind the haystack. At last a gust of wind sent the barn door banging back against the wall. I roused myself, and realised I was freezing where I sat. But I had thought out what I must do.

My parents were still in the kitchen. My father sat in his place at the head of the table, and my mother, red-eyed but composed, was laying out porridge bowls and bread and cheese for the evening meal. When my father saw me he held out his hand to me. I took it, and said to him, so my mother could hear too, 'Mother's right. At the very least we have to know. Better still, we have to find her. *She was dead and is alive again, she was lost and is found.* We have to believe in that.' My mother had turned away from the fire, the wooden spoon in her hand, and was staring at me. 'I will go and look for her,' I said.

Our Quaker Friends used to say that Rachel should have been the boy, for if she could not find adventure at home she would seek it abroad. I was piqued by the implication that I would have done better with the lass's part, for indeed that was never the case. I was a bold lad enough, but not unbiddable. From an early age I would be out on the fell by myself, and by the time I was twelve years old I had climbed every route on Blencathra that a two-legged creature could possibly attempt, and much of Skiddaw to boot. We had upwards of three hundred hefted sheep on the fell at any one time when I was a lad, and my father used me as shepherd from the time I could well be left alone on the hill. Besides the sheep we had thirty head of cattle in our meadows around Glenderamackin beck, and my mother kept poultry and a couple of pigs along with the dairy. The name Greenhow is well respected in these parts, and our line of the family have lived on this farm since the days of the Valiant Sixty, ay, and for half a dozen generations before that too, in the days when Friends were not, and naught was written down to prove it, but that is what they say.

My fore-elders at Highside were early convinced, for our founding Friend George Fox came to our house late in Fifth Month, 1653, on his way to visit Thomas Bewley at Haltcliff Hall by Gillfoot, where our Monthly Meeting meets now. Mark Greenhow (whose namesake I am), being convinced by George Fox himself, was one of the earliest to testify according to the Light Within, and suffered much for it, being imprisoned in Carlisle jail three times, the term of his natural life being much shortened by his vicissitudes. His son and daughters also lived in the Truth, and received the gift of ministry, travelling in the service of it both in England and Scotland, and at last dying in the faith. When in the early years of the last century the Quaker Meeting House was built at Mosedale, the Greenhows of Highside were among the founders of Mosedale Particular Meeting, and we have been members of that Meeting ever since.

My father was a statesman of Cumberland – that is to say, he owned his own hill farm – and he was an elder of Caldbeck Monthly Meeting, and I in my turn am both these things, and neither the high fells nor our Friends in Meeting are like to condone a life of idleness or ease. I have a sort of fame in these parts for my knowledge of the fells, and that is the only kind of adventure I ever sought. Among Friends these are not, God be thanked, days of great Sufferings, but if witness must be borne I have been there to uphold the Truth, even as my forefathers did in the first days.

But Rachel had always a roving disposition, and if adventure came not to her, why then, she would seek it out for herself. And as for me . . . Let me tell thee this:

My mother kept a flock of white geese in a pen above the rushing beck that flows by our house. In the middle of the pen there stood a young willow that was kept cut back for withies, so there was a place about three foot up like a little house within. When Rachel was just a toddling bairn, she set her heart upon the little house within the withy stems, but she was feart of the geese, and could not get across the clarty yard without one of us to take her. Sometimes my mother or I would let her in, whiles we were feeding the geese and that, but never for long enough. And then one day when no one else was by, she braved the geese, though they were taller than she was, and fierce in their hissing. They chased her and she fell flat on her face in the mud, but she got up again at once, and ran, not for the gate, but for the house in the withies. She climbed up just in time, but the geese were hissing round her, and she dare not get down. She was stuck there two whole hours, and missed her dinner. When we went to look for her, it was I that found her and led her back, for I was six years old and strong withal, and I had a big stick. But – mark this – she was not one whit abashed, nor sorry, only pleased with herself that she had done the thing she dared. She was never one to worry about the way back. I knew, though, from early on, that it was my place to worry about it for her. Rachel expected that of me, and so did my parents; indeed, it is what I expected of myself.

*   *   *

This is the first morning I have devoted to my new purpose. I waited until we were done with the lambing, and it is not yet hay time. The daylight hours are at their longest, which is a consideration with me – I have taken to wearing spectacles for close work now – and my desk is placed so I have all the natural light there is. The truth is that my sons could manage the farm, and the guiding, quite well without me, but I am not yet ready to relinquish more than a little. I've always wished to be a man of letters, but had not the time to pursue my desire, nor was I sure that Friends would think well of it. I've now reached the autumn of my life, and I have two tall sons to bear the burden and heat of a new day. As for the opinion of the Meeting: to be honest, I am less exercised by that than I was wont to be. In short, I care not, so long as I am in unity with them on essential matters. On Second Day and Fifth Day I will dedicate the morning hours to this work, unless pressing matters of business intervene.

I have folded up the four letters again and put them away. I keep all the letters relating to that strange episode in my life in the tortoiseshell box that was Alan's wedding present to me (for he sent me a present, contrary to the rule of our Society, whether I would or no). The box is kept on the mantelshelf in this room, which was the best parlour in my parents' day. Now I keep it more as a study to myself, with my desk in the window, where I may sit and look south across the flank of Souther Fell, over the smoking chimneys of Keswick ten miles to the west, to a gleaming sliver of Derwentwater half-hid by oaks, and the grey hump of Grasmoor beyond. When I was first able to lift mine eyes to the hills, this is what I saw, and I hope my own hills will be the last thing I see on earth before my sight is dimmed for ever. I have crossed a great ocean, and been far into the wilderness. I am rich in memories, but I wish for nothing more now than to dwell in my own place. At least, I would wish that, were it not that Alan . . . the truth is, I would be content even now, were it not for my sister Rachel.

I should be content; even the room in which I sit reflects back to me the blessings of a lifetime. The brocade sofa stands in the same place it occupied when this was my mother's parlour, because sometimes we all sit in here in the evening, and sometimes I have visitors during the day. The picture over the mantelshelf I bought some years ago; it is a view of the jaws of Borrowdale by Francis Towne. He has captured the vibrant colouring of autumn, and the wild sky above it, to admiration, although one cannot deny a touch of romantic licence, as certain Friends have pointed out. My parents had no pictures in the house, and indeed there are some Friends who even now think that such luxuries are not consistent with our practice of simplicity. But I give them the precedent of Thomas Wilkinson, my good friend at Yanwath, who regarded books, pictures and ornamental gardens as all alike gifts of God, and there are many Friends furth of Cumberland who live in a style which we in the heartland of our Society would consider overly lavish.

Be that as it may, the other picture, on the far wall, was brought to me last winter from Upper Canada. It is a watercolour sketch of canoes arriving at the foot of the *Portage des Chats*, with a romantic representation of the falls on the right. The young artist, one William Bartlett, made the sketch when visiting the Falls last summer. He subsequently fell in with Alan in Montreal, being told that Alan might subscribe to a book of engravings Bartlett was making of Upper Canada. Alan bought the painting and charged him to deliver it to me when he returned to England. The young fellow discharged his commission in person, bringing the picture to Highside on his way to Scotland. It was a short dark day at the back end of the year, but in the afternoon the sun set in a cloud of glory beyond Grasmoor, and our artist left his meal to make a pencil sketch of it from our doorstep. He finished painting it the next day, and presented it to my wife, as a mindful return for her hospitality.

I remember the *Portage des Chats* very well. I look at the painting of the great falls, the spray flung from the rocks, the tumbling waters below, all overhung with twisted pines. On the left, in the foreground, I see the reflections in the still water in the little bay at the foot of the portage, the voyageurs unloading the canoes and wading ashore with them. I see the men hurrying up the rocky path, bent double under the immense loads that only a voyageur can lift. I'm glad Alan sent William Bartlett's picture to me. It helps me to remember.

There is also my notebook. Unlike Alan I cannot draw, but I can make pictures with words well enough, and when I think that I was but three or four-and-twenty at the time, I reckon I kept my account well enough. My first plan was to copy the notebook out fair, adding the observations of hindsight as I did so. The notebook is worn and fragile, its green leather binding spoilt by damp and being dried out too fast by wood fires. The ink was never good, and is now almost faded away in places, so that if I had not written the words myself I should be hard put to make out the sense of them. Sometimes I was writing by firelight or twilight, and the script was barely legible when it first flowed from my pen. But on the whole I can read it, though no one else would make anything of it. I talked to my family about my plan, and they said I should not meddle with the words I had once written. When I was a young man I wrote as a young man, and it would be untrue to my earlier self, they said, to alter that. I heeded their advice, and so I am beginning my story afresh. I will use the notebook to guide me, but I will not tamper with the wording of the original, however much I think now it may be improved upon. Twenty-seven years is a long time. Young Mark Greenhow is but a memory; I am not him . . . and yet I am, because sometimes I remember very clearly indeed what it was like to be him.

(I've already digressed too far from that history which it is my sole purpose to recount. I must deal strictly with myself. In future I'll keep any irresistible observations to a footnote, as Gibbon does in his *Histories*. My sons will laugh some day at this stratagem, recognising the need for it all too well. Perhaps it will remind them, in after days, of what their old father was like; I would rather they smiled at the memory than not.)

The tortoiseshell box has a spring lock. I leave the key in, because there is nothing in my life that needs to be hidden. I get up and replace the box on the mantelshelf. I sit at my desk again, my hands clasped in front of me, gazing out of the window while another shower obliterates the hills. I bought this same desk from Thomas de Quincey. (It was made especially to fit his upstairs study in Dove Cottage; he acquired a larger one when he moved to Fox Ghyll.) When I have business to attend to, I sit at my desk with my back to the room, looking out, but when the light fails and the curtains are drawn, I use my father's mahogany resting chair that sits by the hearth. I've built bookshelves in the recesses on each side of the chimney breast. I have upwards of a thousand volumes now, and however many shelves I put in, they seem always to be overflowing. The Friends' Journals were my father's. I buy works of local interest as fast as they appear, which is an expensive hobby, but I think my sons may live to thank me for the investment. The travel books are also my own purchases. All are in English; Alan may mock at me for my linguistic inability, but I have never felt called upon to remedy it further since I came home. I have enough to do out of doors during the daylight, and there is only so much reading a man can do of an evening, when he has a hopeful family to claim his attention besides.

CHAPTER 2

SEVENTH MONTH, 1811. THE BRIG *JANE* LEAPT UP and down against the jetty at Whitehaven, her bare masts tossing against the sky like the horns of an angry bull. I stood within the shelter of the houses at the end of East Strand, and my heart misgave me as I watched. The grey waves were short and choppy, and the wind sliced their tops off in spurts of icy spray. The fishing boats jogged up and down like kittle ponies. Far across the Solway I saw the same Scotch hills that are visible from the back of Blencathra, but with the sea between they looked more wild and lowering than ever I saw them yet.

My uncle kept a chandler's business in Maryport, and he had a share in the *Jane* (for she was built at Peat's Yard in Maryport), so he was able to introduce me to the captain, and arrange my accommodations. I was grateful, for though I'd done business at Maryport, Whitehaven was another world, and I knew enough to know that I was a lamb among wolves, but not so much that I could set about fending for myself to any real purpose. My uncle laments that all our trade is gone to the upstart city of Liverpool, but Whitehaven seemed a busy enough port to my rustic eyes. Our maritime investment was carried on through my uncle: we had a share in the *Friends*, a hundred-ton brig, built in Maryport in the year '03, and it had been my annual task to attend the shareholders' meeting, and to take our dividends to be lodged at Forster's Bank in Penrith. I'd always enjoyed visiting the shipyard on the Ellen River, then strolling along the quayside with my uncle or my cousins, watching the sailors at their work, and meeting the far-travelled captains, getting a whiff of a world that was unimaginably exotic and wholly foreign to me. Twice I'd stayed on in Maryport for First Day and attended the Meeting, and truly I could say that I was among Friends in that place.

In contrast, I'd only twice been in Whitehaven. On my first visit to the coast in '03 my uncle had needed a man to go to Whitehaven with a note about a bill of lading, and being curious about the world as most lads of fifteen are, I offered to ride over. It was a blustery day in Third Month. The war was but newly renewed after the Peace of Amiens, and I could see a couple of frigates beating across the Solway, to defend our harbours no doubt. These were the days when we expected invasion every hour, and indeed there was much unrest among our own young men in Meeting, and controversy among Friends about paying the quotas for the Militia. When I looked upon the great warships in the Solway I felt a stirring in my blood, but it didn't lead me to question the discipline of our Society. I consider 'thou shalt not kill' to be a just law, and I believe that the world would be a better place if men heeded the words they spoke by rote. But at that time I thought little about it; I liked doing more than thinking when I was a lad.

I discharged my errand at Whitehaven, and occupied the later part of the afternoon with wandering along the quayside, looking at the shipping. I'd never been in so great a port before, and I was all eyes, and full of wonder. There was more than a little to shock a country-bred lad:

never had I seen such shipyard taverns, full of language as foul as the stench from the gutters, or such painted barques of frailty coquetting past the tavern doors holding their gaudy skirts out of the mud. Some of them winked at one another and called lewd words at me, kenspeckle as I was in such a place in my broadbrimmed hat and plain coat, so I didn't know where to look. I'd thought to get my ordinary at a harbourside inn where I could look out at the shipping as I ate, but I durst not enter those dark doors, crowded about as they were with seafaring men lounging at the doors with tankards, or even whole bottles, in their hands. They watched me too, or so I thought, and some laid their finger at the side of their nose and caught one another's eye as I passed. With my uncle at Maryport I was proud to be called Quaker, and known for all the probity in business that our name means to the world, but alone as a lad on the docks at Whitehaven I was not proud at all, but simply feart.

Yet never a one of them laid hands on me. I would have passed unscathed through what seemed to me, boy that I was, to be a veritable Sodom. But all of a sudden there was a hue and cry behind me on the quay. When I swung round, it was to see the place emptying like water out of a sieve, the lounging men vanishing away, and the fishermen leaving their nets and fleeing into the dark alleys between the warehouses. Only the painted Jezebels stood their ground, shrieking like cats and blocking the road so I could not see. There was a commotion behind them, shouts and bangs and a crowd jostling. Part of it broke away, and two men, one without his jacket, came tearing past me. I was all amazed. A yellow-haired whore seized me by my coat and shook me. 'Press, tha gommeral, Pressgang! Art tha clean gyte?'

I jumped, but before I could well turn, the blue uniforms were coming in two thin lines, one on the shipward, one on the townward side of the docks, all yelling wildly as they rounded up the men out of the taverns and herded them like gimmers on to the open cobbles. In the thick of it I caught sight of a great red-faced man in a blue coat trimmed with white, wielding a cutlass. His fists were bloody, and a seaman lay at his feet. I would have run, but a tangle of struggling men barred the way townward. To my horror I saw the naval blue again behind the crowd. A sailor with a tarry plait was pushing hard against me, but I could not move. A pressman got to us and twisted his hand inside the fellow's collar, half throttling him, and flinging him hard on to the cobbles. In no time the poor man was trussed like a chicken, hands behind his back. The first fellow was already on me, his mate right after him. I flailed wildly with my fists. I hold our testimony to peace as dear as any: I would turn the other cheek if I could; if a man asked me to walk one mile I would not hesitate to walk with him twain; but to be taken aboard one of those stinking hell-holes misnamed His Majesty's ships, and forced at a rope's end to work towards the destruction and ruin of my fellows, to be hanged without compunction, or starved in irons among the rats, when I refused, as I inevitably must, to take up weapons with intent to hurt another man . . . None of this could I begin to contemplate. And so it was that I fought like a wildcat dragged from its lair, with fists and feet and head and teeth and every ounce of strength I had. And that was not little; I was a big tough lad even at fifteen. I bit one of them, and kicked out at the other. I got him straight in the ballocks so he screamed and fell like an ox. I twisted out of the first fellow's grip in a wrestling turn my cousin John Bristo taught me, leapt over the writhing body of the one lying in the gutter clutching his privates, and I ran like a hare with the hounds after it to the edge of the quay, where I dived straight into the scummy water between two fishing boats. I was weighted down with my winter coat and shoes, but I struck out hard, and came up well clear of the boats.[1] I crossed the harbour and climbed out on all fours on to a slimy beach, foul water pouring off me, then waded through mud over my knees to a wooden ladder. I stood at the foot of it shivering and listening, then went up and cautiously stuck my head over the top. This arm of the jetty was deserted. On the main quay behind me the crowd milled to and fro like a giant jellyfish. No one saw me. I jumped on to the jetty, clumsy in my sodden coat, and ran for a dark alley among the sheltering houses. I dodged down one lane and then another, not stopping till I was out of earshot of the quay entirely. Then I leaned back on a wall, gasping for breath, and looked about me.

I was in the back slums behind the harbour, miscalled Mount Pleasant, at a crossroads of four stinking alleys. A pig rootled among the glore on the little square of ground where the lanes met. I could not tell how much of the stink were the place, or the sliminess that enveloped my clothes and trickled down my neck. My hat was gone, and my hair dripped mucky water into my eyes. It was dank and daggy between the houses, like the bottom of a stagnant well. Little grey children came creeping out to stare at me. They stood round me in a wary half circle, and when I spoke they didn't answer. I heard a man shout, and one of the children whistled. A skeletal dog ran out of one of the lanes. Heavy footsteps echoed between the walls. I pushed aside a child and ran.

All that was eight years ago, and now I was a man grown, and about to board the brig *Jane* and embark on a voyage of my own, such as I had never then dreamed of. The days of the Hot Press were well by. If anyone tried to recruit

---

[1] My father taught me to swim. It's an art as seldom cultivated by Cumberland statesmen as by voyageurs, on the whole, but lads from Mungrisdale are used to go up to a pool under Bannerdale in summer, and egg each other on to feats of daring, jumping in off the rocks.

me now, I could truly say that I was a landed proprietor (for my father had added my name to the title when I came of age) and exempt therefore. To prove my worth I carried a purseful of guineas – thirty-five, to be exact – for the expenses of my journey. Yet I still could not feel easy in Whitehaven. All those years ago I'd escaped from the press gang and ridden back to Maryport on my uncle's cob, letting the wind dry me as I rode. But I could not feel clean again until I'd stripped and flung myself into the freezing sea from a clean sandy beach between the two ports. I remember how I ducked under and swam, even though the seawater was like ice in my ears, and I rubbed myself all over, but still the stench of Whitehaven clung to my hair and my clothes, and indeed the very thought of the place made my gorge rise for many a long day after. And now, as I stood on the jetty once again, considering the clean lines and fresh paint of the *Jane*, I recalled my own part in the fighting, and wondered how much an uneasy conscience might have added to my feeling of abomination. I thought about the Sufferings of the first Friends, and about my ancestor Mark Greenhow wasting away the best years of his life in the dungeons at Carlisle. Would he have turned the other cheek, and been carried resistless aboard that man o' war? Would he have stood before their guns and said 'I will not,' and bowed his head to the execution that would surely follow? That would have been a witness to the Truth, most certainly. But me – I had fought like the very devil, and now I was still alive, and whole, and free, able to look after Rachel, as she had always relied upon me to do.

The second time I had come to Whitehaven was in the year '08, to see Rachel and Judith off on their great journey. Rachel had never been there before, and I could see she revelled in the new sights, the new sounds, the new possibilities of adventure opening up before her. Neither foul smells nor foul language ever had the power to daunt our Rachel. I never saw her shocked, or feart, by anything the world showed her, for all she'd grown up in such a sheltered nook. I remember an Irish whore accosting her as we crossed the quay, taking a fold of Rachel's plain dress and rubbing it between her fingers. 'Could you tell me, is ye a nun, Sister?' she asked. 'Give me a penny then, of thy charity!'

Rachel didn't flinch. 'Nay,' she said, 'I'm no more a nun than thee is. Thee's far from home I think?'

If my father and my aunt had not been Friends, doubtless they'd have dragged Rachel away, but as it was they let her be. Rachel was used to doing what she chose, and she talked to the lass from Sligo a full five minutes, and ended by giving her two pennies from her purse. 'But buy thee a dinner with it, lass,' she said as they parted. 'Thee looks fair starved, and my pennies are not for drink, I tell thee!'

It hadn't been so easy for me to get away – I had no Aunt Judith to sponsor me – and yet remain in unity, After Judith's letter came, I took my concern about my sister to the next Monthly Meeting at Gillfoot. I wanted a letter from them that I could take to Yonge Street, for it must be my first object in Upper Canada to find Judith and get further directions from her, before setting forth into the uncharted wilderness. Only our Friends Joseph Priestman, Joseph Peat and John Nicholson were present at this Monthly Meeting, besides my father and myself. (For Caldbeck Meeting was dwining sadly through all the years of my youth.) It was a daggy day, wet as I have only ever known it in the lee of Blencathra in lambing time. The Meeting House at Gillfoot, which is only opened for our Monthly Meetings, was filled with a dampness that slowly numbed our feet from the earth floor upwards, and crept inside our clothes, while the rain swept between the broken slates overhead, leaking down between the rafters, so that our silent worship was accompanied by a chorus of steady dripping. By the time we ended the silence and proceeded to business my father was coughing deep in his chest, and a drop of rheum sat upon the end of our Clerk's nose, which looked like to fall and mingle with the ink.

It was again decided to put forward the matter of the repair of Gillfoot Meeting House to the following month. Then Joseph Priestman asked me to speak to my Concern. I told them plainly; they listened and looked solemn. Joseph Peat was moved to suggest that the matter should be taken to our Quarterly Meeting at Carlisle, which would have created an unwarrantable delay, for I was wishful to sail this very spring, and to have the summer before me when I arrived in the wilderness. John Nicholson took my point about the need to move with the seasons, and he said that as it was a family concern, surely it was a private matter that could simply be minuted by the Monthly Meeting, but not subject to Friendly discipline. It was not as if I intended, as Judith had with Rachel, to travel within the Ministry. But Joseph Peat stuck to his point, saying that since Rachel had been travelling as companion to a Minister appointed by London Yearly Meeting, the matter concerned all Friends. Moreover, if I, Mark, were to follow her into the wilderness of her transgression, I too would be acting in a manner contrary to the discipline of our Society. I would seem to condone her rashness, and follow her on the path of her ungodliness, beguiled from the straight way by the sinfulness of my sister.

'But,' my father replied, 'Rachel is no longer, sorrow be it to say, in unity with Friends. She is disowned by Yonge Street Monthly Meeting and by this Meeting also, in her absence. She is not in Membership with us, and her fate is no longer the concern of Friends in England or in Upper Canada. Mark's errand is therefore, as our Friend points out, a matter of private charity, the loving care of a brother for a lost sister.'

I think Joseph Peat would have stuck to his point, and prevented me from making my journey in unity with Friends as I desired, had it not been that Joseph Priestman stood aside from his office as Clerk to speak in favour of my purpose. He said that 'if Mark were called into Upper Canada on a matter of business, as it might be in relation to his uncle Isaiah Bristo's maritime interests, then it wouldn't be the concern of any Friend to say to him Yea or Nay. So how should his search for Rachel be different? If Mark conceives it his business to go into Upper Canada on any matter of business whatsoever, so long as it be consistent with the principles of our Society, then 'tis his private and particular Concern. If he were travelling in the Ministry it would be very much our business, as we'd have to furnish him with the means of travel. But he goes at his own expense, and asks nothing of us but our prayers, and a letter of Friendship. Presumably our Friend Joseph would not begrudge him the cost of ink and paper? I see it as our clear duty to send him forth in the care of this meeting, by giving him a Minute for our Friends at Yonge Street, or for any other Meeting where he may visit. For my part I commend his charity towards our poor sister Rachel. I must say in Truth I fear the worst, but if she lives our prayers may help her. We know that she has acted so far in contradiction to the dictates of our society as to marry clandestinely out of the Unity of Friends. But if she lives, she may yet sincerely repent of her backslidings and amend her conduct. If so, she may ask to be received into Membership again, with her husband too, if Friends think them worthy. While any possibility remains that she lives, and that her brother Mark may yet have an opportunity with her, to persuade her back into unity with us, even perhaps to bring her home, should we not commend and support his Concern? *For there is more rejoicing in heaven over one sinner that repenteth, than over ninety and nine just persons that need no repentance.'*

So it was thanks to our Clerk Joseph Priestman that I had the Minute I desired in my knapsack, recommending me to the care of our Friends in Upper Canada, and confirming that I travelled with the blessing of my own Meeting. Without this authority I'd have felt naked as a shorn lamb, setting out into a wilderness of wolves and bears and other predators unknown among my native hills.

I chafed at the delays that followed the Monthly Meeting but they were needful. I stayed until Sixth Month, when the lambs were put to the hill, for my father's cough did not mend that year until all the snow was off the hills (nor was he ever again a hale man in winter from the time that Rachel was lost). He'd not been out on the fell since we'd fetched in the tup, and it was my cousin John Bristo from Portinscale who'd helped me gather the ewes off Blencathra at the back end of the year. After my father and I got soused coming back from the Meeting in Gillfoot in Third Month my father's voice was gone, and his breath was hard to get, coming only in great wheezing gasps that hurt to hear. I had to give him my arm that last part of the road from Mosedale. My mother made him mustard poultices and kept him in by the kitchen fire for five weeks or more, where he had naught to do but nurse the caddy lambs, for all the world, he said, like a doited old granny. So I was out lambing in the fields all hours, with my mother helping me when she had the chance, and young Thomas Carr from Mosedale in the daytime. I taught Thomas all I could, for I was mindful that next winter they would have to manage without me. He was a stout and trustworthy lad even then; he cannot have been more than fourteen when he began with us.[2]

Aside from the lambing we had a dozen cows in calf – this was the year after we bought the Shorthorn bull – and oats to sow, as well as the usual dairy work. I had days to pay back to my cousins at Portinscale, and what with one thing and another I wasn't able to look into the matter of a passage to Upper Canada until spring had turned to early summer. I did no guiding that year. I left a notice at the Royal Oak explaining I was gone for a year or two, and I went over to Greta Hall and explained to Robert Southey that I could not accommodate any of his friends for the next two seasons, but if God saw fit to preserve me I would be back thereafter. He was kind, as I knew he would be, and enquired much after my sister. He offered me ten guineas, which if it had been proffered in charity to me I would instantly have refused, but he asked me to take it to buy any necessary comfort for her, if she should be found, and he said that if I didn't find her alive, then I might bring the sum back to him intact. He reminded me of the occasion when he had called at Highside shortly after he first came to Greta Hall, when he'd followed the Glendaramackin down off Blencathra in the mist, thinking it would take him southward, which of course is not the

---

[2] Thomas and I together built the cottage for him when he married – six months it took us, from first stone to last slate – just where our track joins the Caldbeck road, twenty year ago that would have been, and now he has six bairns living, and three of them full grown forbye. But when I went away he was just a lad, and I was worried about leaving them all, but my cousins and a few of the Friends said they would watch over my family for me when I was gone, and that set my mind at ease a little.

case. He arrived at our house drookit and bemired and entirely lost to direction, and found none at home but Rachel. At thirteen she was a skinny little maid with a thick plait of black hair that reached to her waist at the back. She received Robert Southey with great composure, and brought him in by the fire to dry, and gave him hot milk and bread and cheese. When my father came in she was instructing him in the Advices, for he was always curious about our Society, and never backward in asking questions about it. Later, when my father walked him back around the fell, and set him on the right road to Greta Hall, Robert Southey thanked him for our Quakerly hospitality, and told my father that Rachel had the most beautiful black eyes he had seen outside of Portugal. My father, not being sure what to make of this, repeated the whole to my mother when I was by, but she just tossed her head and made a derisive sound.[3] The next time Robert Southey came my mother watched him closely, but decided that after all she liked him well, and that he had no improper designs upon a tender maiden. Since then he has called at Highside whenever he passes this way, though of late years he goes about but little.

I often visited our Friend Thomas Wilkinson at Yanwath on my way home from the market in Penrith. I remembered how Thomas had shown us a map of North America in his atlas, at the time when Rachel first set out on her travels, and in the latter days of Fifth Month I called

---

[3] Although I come of a longstanding Cumberland family on my father's side, and my mother's father was of the same good Quaker stock, my maternal grandmother was said to be half gypsy, though this was seldom spoken of. The fact is that Rachel and I have our mother's eyes, though in other respects, my mother used to tell me, I am all Greenhow, but not so my sister.

on him, and asked if I might see the map again.[4] This
time, when I looked at the map of North America, I
was appalled by its immensity, and by the great blank
spaces of unexplored land beyond the known frontier.
My heart quailed, but I showed it not. I conned the map
as well as I could, that I might remember the details of
my projected journey. Thomas and I found Quebec, and
the great St Lawrence River, and the five lakes which
Rachel had spoken of, which looked to be each as large
as the Irish Sea, but all fresh water, and surrounded by
a howling wilderness, which the atlas represented only as
an impenetrable blank.

My uncle sent me word at last that he had got a passage
to Quebec for me on the brig *Jane*, that because he was a
shareholder the captain had agreed to give me a cabin berth
for only seven guineas, and that I was to be in Whitehaven
by the fourth day of Seventh Month. I made my final

---

[4] Thomas Wilkinson was an old man, in my eyes, when I first knew him,
and it was from my father that I inherited the friendship. And yet Thomas
and I had much in common, or rather, there was much that I learned from
him, and he was ever kind to me. Unlike certain other Friends, Thomas
never suggested that the climbing of mountains for its own sake should
be regarded as a Vain Sport. On the contrary, he shared my love of the
hills, and although he was much my elder, and in worldly rank greatly
my superior, yet he was a practical farmer too, and always I enjoyed our
discourse. It was Thomas Wilkinson who first encouraged me to read,
and to take issue with the arguments put forth in books. I was never at
school – there was talk at one time of sending me to the Friends' School
in Kendal, but when it came to it I could not be spared from the farm –
but Thomas Wilkinson did his best to make up for the lack in my formal
education. Perhaps he was a strange choice of model for an active lad
in his teens, being always retiring, gentle and patient, but I admired his
erudition, and, raw lad that I was, I did my best to emulate it. Thomas
Wilkinson was distressed by the news of Rachel's loss; he had heard of
her journeyings with interest – I shared her letters with him whenever I
visited Yanwath – for he too had travelled in the ministry when he was
younger, into the wilds of Scotland, where he had climbed one of their
mountains named The Cobbler, and broken the record time of ascent
by half an hour, which showed the Scotch what we men of Cumberland
are made of. But that by the by.

preparations. My mother pressed a little linen bag upon me, to go in my luggage, containing such necessaries as buttons, needle and thread, and a little green glass phial containing laudanum. I protested, for I could not sew, and I'd never been ill in my life. All I got for that was a lesson in stitchery on the spot, but later I had much cause to be grateful for her forethought.

The *Jane* only took half a dozen passengers; she was going out with manufactured trade goods, and reckoned to come back with timber. I think I had some notion in my head that a sea voyage would be a Romantic business; I'd imagined myself alone, confronted by the wild elements. If I was feart at all, it was less of storms and tempests and great seas, but that the French might shoot us to pieces. Indeed Joseph Peat reminded me at Meeting that it was Friendly practice to leave one's affairs in good order and make a will, but I heeded him not, for I had but my share in the farm, and that would go back to my father if I never came home.

CHAPTER 3

THE TRUTH WAS THAT THE SAILORS SAID WE HAD A smooth voyage all the way. In my opinion all smoothness was left behind the wall of Whitehaven harbour. They don't tell thee that at sea nothing stays still: the deck buckets to and fro, often at a ridiculous angle, so a man cannot walk straight, but must needs cling to ropes and bulwarks (which are plentiful and bruisingly hard), and stagger from place to place as best he may. They don't say how the waves gather and swell much higher than thy head, so that thee thinks, every time one comes, that the ship will surely founder, until the grey wall of water disappears beneath the hull, then drops you so thy stomach lurches, nearly tipping the ship right over into the ghastly trough below. I wasn't sick, but I was dogged all the time by an unpleasant queasiness. I could eat the dry biscuits, but the meat was beyond me. I was scunnered by the weevils and cockroaches, which would have troubled me less if my stomach had been composed. At night it was better. As I lay prone in my berth, my eyes closed against the dark, it was more like being rocked in a cradle, and indeed in our little ship on that great ocean I felt as helpless as an infant in its mother's arms. In sleep I succumbed, and yet it was a disquieting sensation of weakness for a young man in his prime.

During the days I found myself a sheltered place upon the aft deck, and wrapped myself in my blanket and wedged myself in there. It was better than the rancid air below, and I need only move when the rain grew to a cloudburst, or if it was dinnertime, or I had to relieve myself. I don't think I prayed. I couldn't read because my head ached; besides, although it didn't always rain it was still grey and damp, and often a great wedge of salt spray crashed over the decks. I cannot bear to see a book mistreated.

At Highside my father had the journal of John Woolman.[1] Woolman's journey across the Atlantic was much worse than mine. In accordance with our testimony of simplicity he insisted upon travelling steerage. I'd wondered if I should do the same, but I couldn't offend my uncle, who'd arranged my berth for me, and to be honest, when I saw how cramped and foisty the ship was, I was glad of the little private space I had. I shared my cabin with a timber merchant who had made this crossing several times. He regaled me with enough stories of disasters at sea to send me home for good, if I'd been in any shape to listen to him. However, he gave me pastilles for my headache, and remarked again – I do not know how many times I'd heard it by the time we disembarked – *that those who would go to sea for pleasure would go to hell for pastime.*

John Woolman, good man that he was, yearned over the plight of the seamen, and laboured tenderly among them that they might recognise the light which is within all men, however low in this world their lot is cast. I yearned over

---

[1] Now shelved on the right hand side of the fireplace in this room, along with a goodly library of works relating to the Society of Friends.

no man, but sat staring up at the white-tipped waves and, each time we rose to the crest, at the far grey space which was neither sky nor sea. There was no horizon, merely a nothingness which surrounded us on every side, so we appeared never to move, for all that the great sails were full and taut above my head, but simply to be suspended in a little world of our own. My senses warred with my reason, and whispered to me that this sea world could never move or change. My notebook is a blank, but for the count of days, which I recorded faithfully, with a double line by First Days to show the weeks. There had not been a day in my life heretofore which deserved no mark but a blank. Life is sweet, and at three-and-twenty, sickened by the endless sea, I first grasped that it is also short, and therefore precious. The present waste induced in me a melacholy I couldn't shake off. So this is eternity, I thought, as my head throbbed, and a rope beat endlessly upon the mast above me – slap slap, slap slap – like a weary heartbeat. And if it were, I thought sullenly, then eternity was a kind of hell. The sailors bent over their work were goblin creatures, the words they tossed to and fro between them over the noisy sea more profane than ever I'd heard in speech of men before, even in Whitehaven.

Yet Woolman spoke the truth: there is that of God even in these seamen, outcasts from the earth, who know not God and malign his name with every phrase they utter. For after a day or so men did stop and speak to me. They offered me rum and tobacco, which they said would stop my sickness. When I refused one lad cried on me, 'To hell wi' thee, tha god-damned son of a poxy whore, thou'rt but a canting Methody. Thee'll be buggered for that.' I knew the accent at once, and said, was he from Cockermouth or thereabout? It turned out his brother had worked for a cousin of mine, a Friend over at Whelpoe, and after that Joshua – for that was his name – forbore to swear when

I was by, and I forbore to mention the principles of our Society, for I could tell he did not wish to hear.[2]

We saw no other vessel for three weeks, but then one foggy morning I woke to a new manner of pitching, and, hoping that we might be in sight of land, I was up and dressed in no time, and struggling up the companion. A thin line of land lay to the west of us, and close to I saw upwards of half a dozen open fishing boats tossing like so many corks on the sea around us. God help the men who earn their bread that way. Joshua, the lad from Cockermouth, was leaning over the gunwale with a couple of other seamen. I staggered over to them, and clutched the rail. They were fishing with a long line – no rod, no bait – just a long line tagged with bright strips of tin, and bare hooks on the end of it. Josh offered me a spell, and I caught six fine cod within a minute. I can claim no skill for that.[3] I never caught so much, pound for pound, in a

---

[2] I should admit, though Friends might well question me on this, that I've never felt the call to minister to any who did not ask. We are known to the world by our plain dress and plain speech; thus we proclaim ourselves. It seemed to me, when I was a lad of fifteen, and my cousin John first took me to the wrestlers' meet in the field by Derwentwater, that it was a courtesy in those country fellows to take no heed of what I wore or how I spoke, and to ask no questions. A young hobbledehoy, as I was then, dreads to be made kenspeckle. And a man stripped for wrestling is just a man; no calling him Quaker then (and indeed, although I learned to wrestle pretty well – and no doubt would still remember how if put to it – I always avoided asking myself if the practice were consistent with the principles of our Society). I've never been a minister in our Meeting, though I've served as elder these twenty years. But I have at times wrestled with the question, whether it be a worse thing to get alongside one's fellow man than to bear witness for the truth in all circumstances. I muddle along for a while. But if I think of such as Woolman, who was ever respectful and forbearing of men as he found them, and yet would not remain silent, knowing that he had truth to impart, I fear that I am no more than half a man, having not the courage of my conviction.

[3] I'm no mean fly fisher. I might have hoped the temptation to Vain Sports would have ceased to afflict me in my older age, but I cannot regret the practice. My private belief is that there are worse evils in the world than this.

day on a Lakeland river as I did in a few seconds off the coast of Newfoundland, but any man could do the same, who had a string and a hook by him, for there are as many fish in those waters as there are pease in a pea soup.

Land.

Had I not crossed the ocean, I would never have thought about land in the way that I do. And yet the first sight of the new continent was grim enough: a cold fog-bound coast with lowering cliffs where the gulls cried like damned souls. Josh told me that seamen fear to be buried at sea because the soul can never find rest. As the body is tossed to and fro and eaten by the fishes, so the soul must wander through the dreary wastes of the world for ever. I told him that was not so, that there is a light within every man that burns as well on sea as land, and neither death nor salt water can extinguish it. He told me that the coast we saw was called Newfoundland, and that none but savages were hardy enough to dwell there, which wasn't hard to believe.

For two days or more we followed an inhospitable coast, broken only by the outpourings of numerous rivers, and always hung over with grey drizzle. We were sailing close-hauled, plunging through grey waters at a forty-five degree angle, which made the simplest tasks a major gymnastic feat. Everything was wet. If this were North America, I thought, I wanted none of it.

I shivered in my damp blanket, and then, suddenly, like a burst of sunshine, I felt rage. I was hugely, furiously angry with Rachel. I forgot I was cold. I forgot to feel sick. I was deluged with memories. I remembered the cradle by the hearth in our kitchen, and the small demon in it who screamed without stopping, while my mother and even my father rocked it and shushed it and sang to it. Now the gulls wheeled over my head and screamed the same screams, mocking me. I would have stopped her screaming;

I would have killed her. When I told my parents that – for I was but three years old, and knew no better – they made us worship together in silence, standing around her cradle. I didn't want to pray. I wanted to seize her by her white blanket and throw her on to the bare flags and shut her red mouth and beat her with my fists until she stopped screaming.

All her life she'd asked me for things. All her life I'd taken what she dealt out. All her life I'd had to accommodate her, to live with her, rescue her, listen to her . . . I cast off my blanket, and lurched across to the gunwale. I held on with numb hands, and stared resentfully at that savage coast to which she'd dragged me. I was sick and cold and – it came to me, as if my blood had suddenly unfrozen in my veins – furiously hungry. As I stared at the troubled water I realised that there were no more white-caps around us. The sea was no longer grey but almost green. I looked up, and the sky was as blue as I had last seen it above Blencathra.

Angry I might be, but I could never help admiring Rachel too. I'd never known a lass less hampered by her petticoats than she. In my young heedlessness I taught her to scale the easier end of Raven Crags, and even took her up Bannerdale. I tucked her frock into her drawers, and showed her how she must only move one hand or foot at a time, and keep her weight against the rock. She couldn't reach as far as I could, and sometimes I had to give her a leg-up, but she could move fast and sure, and was never for a moment feart. 'Twas pity she was not a lad, for never did I feel in so much charity with her as when we were out on the hill. But because she was a maid our wildest adventures had to be kept secret, and as I grew older I realised it was wrong to lead her into such lads' ploys, and so I kept my distance.

That afternoon I did full justice to my dinner at the captain's table. I took the opportunity to ask him if I could see a map. 'A chart,' he said sternly, but he took me to his cabin to have a look.

The chart was a revelation. I pored over it so long that at last the captain left me to it, bidding me not to touch anything. I was too engrossed to be insulted. The wide ocean was of no interest to me: it has no shape. But now I could trace a meaning to our wanderings. I saw how the grim coast was the southern shore of the land of the Little Esquimaux, and how the barren island next to us was shaped like a cloud in the wind, and had a name of its own: Anticosti.[4] The hour I spent studying the captain's chart of the Island of Newfoundland and the Gulf of St Lawrence was a turning point in my journey. For the first time the unknown land had a shape, and a name. I wondered if Rachel had seen such a map when she came here. It might not have interested her, but as for the actual coastline, the reality of the new country: I'm sure she stayed on deck in all weathers and gazed and gazed at it with that silent excitement with which she faced new things, and which I knew so well.

We were out of sight of land again, but now I knew where to look. I sighted Cape Gaspé at the very moment that the man aloft sang out the name. There was a great rock under which the sea had beaten out huge arches, where rainbows shimmered in the spray. After that I began to see little farms, the yellow cornfields ripe for harvest. I was blithe to see that the whole land was not given over to wilderness. People come from all over England to our corner of wilderness here in Cumberland, but they only think they love it because they need have none of it. I farm the land; I have no such romantic notions, and so it was that the little farms of Lower Canada made me feel

---

[4] In the last thirty years there have been a great many maps made of my own country, and I've collected nearly all of them. I love to read them over of a winter evening, when the hills are closed to me.

at home, for all they were as unlike a Lakeland hill farm as chalk from cheese.

The St Lawrence River is so great that we did not see the north shore again until we were almost arrived at Quebec city, though when the weather cleared I saw hills like those at home to the north of us, almost indistinguishable from clouds. I was sick of the confines of the *Jane*, sick of the constant swell and the damp. Put me on land again and I would engage to cross a continent. The last day dragged by. We could see both banks of the river now. We came to a stretch of open water in which above twenty great ships were moored, and little boats plied to and fro between them. Beyond I saw a citadel set on a hill above a precipice. Ever since we'd entered the St Lawrence River there'd been much ado around me setting and re-setting the sails, and now all the men were piped aloft again, and slowly the great sails flapped and furled with tremendous thwacking noises over my head. I heeded them not; my eyes were strained upon the land ahead.

The fort sat on the hilltop like a paper crown; above it the Union Jack streamed in the wind. A city straggled up the spine of the hill. A belltower surmounted by a cross pierced the summer sky. The sun winked against red roofs and made me blink. I saw warehouses, and a street of white houses, three or four storeys high, fronting the harbour. Slowly the gap between ship and shore diminished. All the sails were down; we were barely moving. People were moving on the shore. There was a beach, and a low wharf. A great rattling came from the bowels of the ship. It was the first time I'd heard the anchor lowered. The awful voyage was over.

A cutter rowed out to us, and the Customs men came aboard. As soon as they had the captain's word we carried no infectious disease, the passengers were allowed ashore in a flit boat that was already waiting alongside. When I stepped ashore I was shocked to find the solid ground all tossing and heaving so I could barely stand. I was feart I'd never walk straight again. There were jostling crowds about me, and huge piles of fresh timber, and ox-carts clattering over a cobbled street on iron wheels. The nearest shop was a chandler's; the tarry smell took me straight back to my uncle's warehouse in Maryport. My gorge rose at the stench that rose from the town. It could have been Whitehaven – it was just another port, after all – and yet it was utterly unlike Whitehaven. For the first time in my life I was standing on foreign soil, and I was no longer sure of anything. At least the land was blessedly warm; a heat seemed to rise from the very cobbles to greet me. I shouldered my knapsack and walked dizzily along a street between houses of whitewashed stone.

I came to a square where they were packing up after the day's market. The cobbles were sticky with squashed vegetables and dung, and the last stallholders were loading their leavings into carts. There were two-storey stone houses on three sides, and on the fourth a steeple house with a white spire and wide open doors with people streaming in and out. A signboard on a smart new building opposite, also with open doors and a crowd of motley patrons, proclaimed the Neptune Inn. I felt little reaching hands about my waist; I pushed away a cluster of begging children, but they clung and whined. I cried 'No!' and tried to shove them away, and backed into a chair-mender's stall, where I tripped over a rocking chair. The fellow swore incomprehensibly – but his meaning was plain enough – and shook his fist in my face. The children's hands were over me like mice, searching for the pockets a plain coat does not possess. The glare and the smell and the heat battered against my aching head, and the solid ground seemed to heave worse than ever. The Neptune was not my sort of lodging, but any sanctuary was better than none. I pushed myself free, and stepped within.

The taproom was noisy, full of sailors and merchants, and to my horror I understood not a word that any man said. It was like a bad dream, the Tower of Babel come true, and what was worse, my simple request made no sense to the tapster when I spoke to him. I'd been prepared for strange experiences, but not for this. But thanks be to God, the landlord, when he came, spoke English, though his accent was unlike anything I had ever heard before. The long and the short of it was, I got a clean room with a dormer window that looked out on Place Royale, so I could look down on the covered market stalls and the surging crowd. All day long the place echoed with the cries of the costers, and the rumbling of wheels on the cobbles, and in the evening the Popish chanting from the steeple house was only drowned out by lewd songs and wild carousings in the tap below us. I shared my small room with a silversmith from Bristol, who hoped to find work in Montreal. He was a little quiet fellow, like an under-nourished sparrow, and if I had to have a bedfellow, at least he was clean and sober. It was terribly hot at night, for the roof was metal: there was an ordinance in the town, following several fires, that neither walls nor roofs might be of wood. I believe I was much overcharged for my shot at the inn,[5] but had not the words to argue.

[5] About five years after I left, Alan mentioned in his letter the founding of a Bank at Montreal. Not before time, I replied in my next letter. I've never had trouble casting accounts, but the chaotic mixture of currencies in Upper Canada would have defeated Adam Smith himself. The host at the inn in Quebec gave me my bill in dollars, and when I said I had only English guineas, he said two guineas would be sufficient. Green I might be, but I was never one to be easily fleeced, and I said I'd have none of it. I finally got some dollars from a shady-looking character in the London Coffee House, at a rate of exchange which was still pretty steep, but not risible.

My fellow lodger explained to me that the reason I could not make myself understood was that many people in Quebec city spoke in the French tongue. I should have guessed, I suppose, but my education had dealt little with wars between man and man. My knowledge of what they call the great affairs of the world was sketchy: I'd thought the French had been defeated and driven out of North America long before I was born. It is, of course, contrary to the principles of our Society to align ourselves with any worldly power, but for all that, I am an Englishman born, which is, as I perceive it, the greatest blessing that God can bestow upon a mortal man. Moreover, in all my life I'd heard naught but ill of the French, and indeed, in the day or two in which I wandered the steep streets of Quebec city, I could no more take my eyes off these French people, especially the women and the bairns – I had not somehow thought of them as having women and bairns – than if I had been taken straight into the wilderness and been confronted by so many wolves or bears. Of course I had not then met Loic; how could I know that on his island . . . but I run ahead of myself.

The rock of Quebec is surmounted by a fort; there are batteries on all sides bristling with cannon, and even the civil streets are full of redcoats. I was told that the fortifications, which were much in need of repair, were first made by the French to keep out the wild Indians, and latterly the English, and would perhaps be needed now against the Americans, for the border was only a few leagues to the south of us. But it grieved me to see how it was, even in the wilderness. For where, if not here, might the holy Kingdom of Peace yet be manifested upon this war-torn Earth?

I was astonished that much of Quebec city was given over to the Catholic religion, filled with steeple houses and much chiming of bells, and men in long robes and shrouded women parading the streets so it was like walking into a Raree show. Apart from that I liked the town well enough.[6] I kept wondering what Rachel had made of it; I think the colour and bustle must have pleased her very well. It was built on two levels, and the morning after I arrived I climbed to the upper town, through the city gate, and walked past the fort on to the bare hill. I skirted the precipice above the river, and watched a great raft of tree trunks floating downstream, and on it little figures of men moving about. It passed me by, and I wandered on. There were crickets chirping in the grass, not like our English grasshoppers, but in a massed chorus all around me. At first I wondered what the constant sound could be. When I hear a grasshopper now, it draws me back to North America, where the crickets sing from dawn to dusk all summer long. It was good to smell the earth again; good to have solid ground under my feet. I walked towards a round tower ahead, and when I came up to it I saw it was still a-building, with workmen mixing mortar and pushing wooden barrows up the ramp. I realised what it was. I'd read about these Martello Towers in the Gentleman's Magazine at the Royal Oak. Their rock-solid construction had been much discussed – in the press, I mean, not among Friends – as a marvel of modern engineering, but I never thought to see any so far from England. An old soldier in a shabby red coat, with a folded telescope tucked under

6 Whitehaven is also built on a steep hill with a scarp behind, and it too has an upper and a lower town. Of course it has no fortifications. When Alan and I discussed the point, he scoffed at my comparison, and said that Quebec City, if it were like any city, was the twin of Edinburgh. Both had a citadel set on a rock, and a glorious city clinging to the spine of an ice-cold hill. Both, he said, were civilised European cities, where the art of living was cultivated to the last degree, whereas there was nothing on the west coast of England that matched that description. I forbore to argue (though I was tempted). He never set foot in England, and I had never been in Scotland (nor have I, to this day); I could see no useful object in further debate.

his arm was watching the builders, and – for he was an Englishman – we got to talking.

'War?' he repeated, in answer to my question. 'Of course there'll be war. He pointed south into the blue distance across the river. 'You know what lies down there, young sir? The United States of America! They don't love us and we don't love them. They like putting stars on their flag – Jonathan Yankee doesn't like being outdone, not even by the Milky Way – and I reckon they're hoping the next star's got our name on it. *Quebec*. Oh, ay, they'd like Quebec. Where the hell d'you come from, anyway, if you don't know that?'

'England.'

'Bless you, boy, England's been at war these twenty years!'

'Ay, but with France.' I tried to express some of the confusion that I felt. 'But I didn't realise . . . now I'm here . . . Canada *is* French. Only . . . there are redcoats, just like at home . . . and this tower' – I gestured at the builders in front of us – 'this is a British fort, isn't it?'

'Bless you, boy, where have you been? This ground you're standing on . . . these are the very Plains of Abraham!'

I looked blank.

'For the Lord's sake, where have you been all your life? This is where Wolfe won Canada, when your papa – who damn well ought to have taught you better – was in shortcoats, I make no doubt. You stand on British soil, and should be proud of it!' He looked across the river, muttering, 'Don't they teach them anything these days?'

'But so many people here are French!'[7]

'*I'm* not French. *You're* not French.'

'No.' At least that was certain.

---

[7] I soon learned that the French of Canada are more properly referred to as *Canadiens*.

'*Canada's* not French,' he finished, as if that were some-how a logical conclusion, and to emphasise the point he tapped me on the chest with his telescope.

'No,' I said more doubtfully, while I gazed across the river into the blue haze to the south of us.

The old fellow told me the river was very busy these days, for now that all the ports of Europe were closed to Britain – including the Baltic ports, since Buonaparte set up the blockade in '06 – trade had thriven as never before. The Old Country was desperate for timber, and if Canada had naught else it had trees, thousands of miles of them, stretching away into lands no man had ever seen. As he spoke we watched another of the great log rafts go floating by. 'You'll see plenty more, young fellow, before you get to Montreal.'

I was grateful to the old fellow, for he first put it into my head that I must learn a few phrases in the French tongue, and he took it upon himself to give me my first lesson, up there on the Plains of Abraham, while we watched the boats go by down below on the river.

Next day, when I found the vessel that was to take me to Montreal, I laughed out loud with sheer excitement. For the *Accommodation* was one of the new steamships. When I saw what kind of craft she was, I fairly ran to buy my ticket. I had to wait for a French Madame with a quiverful of bairns who was ahead of me in the queue. For all I knew they were saying the ship was full. My turn came; '*Un ticket, monsieur, s'il vous plaît*. (Alan taught me later that in plain speech I must say *s'il te plaît* but he said he wouldn't be held answerable for the consequences. At the time I speak of I thought it was all one word: *sivooplay*.) The ticket was advertised at nine dollars, and cost me three guineas. They only take twenty passengers but I was in the Lord's hand that day, and there was a place for me.

As we cast off there came a great toot on the whistle,

and a burst of steam from the funnel, as if all the fires of hell were down below a-stoking. Then all at once there was a clank-clank-clank that shook the deck, and when I looked back to the quay there was already a strip of water widening fast. It can be a rough ride up the St Lawrence between Quebec city and Montreal, but all the newness had not yet rubbed off the *Accommodation*. She had neither masts nor sails, but two great paddle wheels amidships. I asked the mate if I could see the wheels from inside, down below, and for a *douceur* he took me down and left me with the engineer. It smelt of woodsmoke in the hold, but it was light enough to see the great engine, and the piston rods going round, all with a great clackety noise, just as loud as the Atlantic wind in the rigging of the *Jane*, only this noise had purpose in it, the kind of rhythm that matches a man's pulse instead of terrifying him out of his wits.[8]

The passage upriver is about sixty hours, including the nights spent at anchor. I said to my new friend the engineer, 'But this is a miracle.' He grinned at me and said, 'You could say so. Neither wind nor tide can stop her!'

I stood on deck and watched the land go by, close to on one bank, a line as faint as the Scotch hills across the Solway on the other. There was no salt in the air; while I was in Quebec city the painful cracks around my fingernails had all but healed. The first evening aboard we had a thunderstorm. I stayed on deck, sheltering from the torrents of rain in the lee of the cabin wall, while the thunder rolled across the sky and forks of lightning rent the sky like the visible wrath of God. Between the thunderclaps I heard the pistons turning below and the scoosh of the

---

[8] I have the specifications of the *Accommodation* jotted down in my notebook; I'm looking at the roughly pencilled figures, and I see myself as if from a great distance: a young fellow all in grey, freshly shaved and trimmed by the barber in Quebec City, but still wearing his farmer's boots and salt-stained coat.

water through the paddle wheels, as if we were caught up in the very chariot of Elisha. In the whiteness of the lightnings I saw a far range of mountains to the north. It was a night full of a wildness that stirred my blood. Rachel would have revelled in it.

The next day, by contrast, I saw a pleasant tended land, with the neat French farms coming right down to the water. Between the farms there were forests and waterfalls, and once a wooded island with towering cliffs, but among the farms these manifestations of the wilderness seemed not so much awful as picturesque. Once a small boat came out to bring fruit and vegetables for the captain's table, these being plentiful in the harvest season. The *habitants* seemed sturdy fellows, though not so hearty as the yeomen of Cumberland. I thought if Rachel's lot had fallen among settlements like these, I could have wished her happy. I sat on deck in the sunshine and read the little packet of letters over again. We had not heard from Rachel herself since she wrote from Yonge Street in Second Month of the year '09. A small aftershock of the rage I'd felt at sea shook me; why did she not write? Why had I bothered to follow her, when she had naught to say to me? The world the letter belonged to seemed to be separated from me by a great chasm. I knew the thrice-crossed words almost by heart – I had had great trouble in deciphering them, especially in the latter part – and they told me nothing:

> *Yonge Street, Upper Canada*
> *3rd day of Third Month, 1809*

To my dear Father and Mother, and to Mark, my brother,

I think of ye, and pray that all is well. At first I looked not back, being overwhelmed by new experiences, and thinking always of our Concern and Ministry for our Friends in North America.

It is almost a full year since I left. John Gill sent on thy dear letters from Philadelphia, and a travelling Friend hath brought them to us here. I was so happy to hear from thee, my dear Mother, and I thank Father and Mark for their messages. I write now because our Friend David Willson is going down to York tomorrow, and will carry this to the Post Office for me.

I told thee in my last how Judith ministered in the Meeting in New York, and how we had a Leading that we should visit the Meetings on the western frontier. So we returned to Baltimore Meeting, which has a Particular Concern to the Indian tribes in the west, where the settlers are yet sparse and the wilderness untamed. It is a wicked thing here in America that too often the Indians are treated like Wild Animals, to be harried and killed, by those who know not that the Light Within shines within every man, even the naked savage, who, through no fault of his, hath never heard the name of God.

In the end we went not to the Meeting at the Wabash River. The Friends dissuaded Judith, saying there was a sudden tumult among the Indians. Word came of a new Prophet among them, who incites them against the settlers, even our Friends. So instead of going by way of the Ohio valley we travelled rather to the north, under the care of Philadelphia Meeting, visiting Meetings as we went. We crossed some mountains called the Alleghenies. The going was very rough, and the journey took upwards of two weeks. The snow was still melting, and the rivers were very swollen at the fords. As we rode – for Philadelphia Friends gave us two sturdy cobs for ourselves, and a man called Daniel to be our escort – we passed wagons with whole families in them, and all their goods, sometimes chickens in a coop, and kettles and axes hanging from the wooden frames. When all were camped at night we sometimes took our opportunity with them, and found them mostly simple godly folk. It's a rough road; I would not like to commit myself wholly to it as these folk have to do. Many Friends have taken this way, for there is much good land in the west for those that have none at home.

About this time we actually met our first real Indians (Iroquois in these parts), but had no opportunity with them. There are not many left in New York, though I believe all this country was once theirs, before the settlers came. The smallpox has decimated their numbers (quite literally, the Friends told us), and many of the survivors have gone away into the far west. Those who remain are much addicted to spirituous liquors, and this has caused a sad degeneration among them. At last we came to a great Lake called Erie, from whence we went downriver to a new Meeting at a place called Niagara. We stayed at Asa Schooley's in Upper Canada (for we crossed the river which is the border with British territory: in these wild places the border between one Temporal State and Another is of no consequence). There is a great Force on the river; our Friends took us to a place where we might gain the best Prospect. Thee would like it well, Mark. If thee can imagine the Falls at Lodore magnified an hundred times, nay five times an hundred, thee has perhaps an inkling of it.

We heard at Niagara that there are several new Meetings established in the Wilderness of Upper Canada. The winters are very bad, and there hath been much hunger and privation among Friends in these remote settlements. When Judith heard this, her heart was wrung for the poor Friends, alone and starving in the great Wilderness. So it was that we visited Meetings at Pelham and Black Creek, and then crossed the Lake called Ontario from Niagara to York, which is the capital city of Upper Canada. We had a rough crossing in a schooner. Judith staid below all the way – I told thee how it was with her in the ship from Whitehaven to Baltimore – but I was up on deck as long as they would let me. I find the white-capped waves, and the sound of the wind in the rigging, to be very exhilarating. If I had been the lad I would have gone to sea, I think: maybe in our own Ship from Maryport. Thee never knows. But then I would not be here in Yonge Street, at the very last outpost in the whole of Upper Canada, and I suppose this is adventure enough, to be doing the Lord's work in the wilderness.

And now I was wanting to describe to thee the settlement here, and the Meeting, and our good Friends who have been our hosts this winter, but it is almost nine o'clock, when David Willson is to come by to fetch my letter. So – I write in haste – I must just tell thee that we have had an opportunity with the Indians who dwell in the forest hereabouts, and they have asked Judith to cross the Lake called Huron to a place they call the Island of the Spirits, where many of them dwell, that we should minister to them there. So when the ice melts, we shall take ship from [the word looks like Pent Anguish – surely not?] ... *But that will be David Willson at the door, and I must not keep him.*

Wrote by thy Friend and loving daughter,
  Rachel

Chapter 4

NINTH MONTH, 1811. OUR JOURNEY ENDED AT MONTREAL:
a city of stone houses like Quebec, but this time set among
wooded islands, with Mount Royal rising behind. No one
on the shore seemed to speak English, but when I said
'North West' I was immediately directed to a warehouse
in St Gabriel Street, just across the road from the wharf.
From there it was easy to find the main Company Offices,
in a high-gabled building with double doors adorned with
an excess of polished brass. A brightly painted shield was
carved above the lintel. I squinted up at it, and made out
a picture of a canoe, with two crosses and a stag's head
arranged beneath it, and beneath all a strange boat that
might have been a canoe with a sail. A tree grew above
the shield, with a little creature at its foot that I took to
be a beaver. I read the legend over it: *perseverance*. I pulled
my hat down hard on my head, adjusted my knapsack on
my shoulders, and went bravely in.

I'd never before been in the counting house of a great
Company. I thought of the small receiving office in
Keswick, or even of the shipping offices of Maryport
or Whitehaven, where Friends' plain clothes spell worth
and honesty in business. In the counting house of the
North West Company in Montreal my plain coat and

broad-brimmed hat brought me nothing but stares, and a few sniggers. When I saw the rows of clerks sitting at their high desks, I quailed inside. The men nearest the door laid down their pens to stare and grin, and frankly listen when the clerk at the front counter asked me my name and business. But whatever I felt, I showed it not, and stepped up to him briskly and looked him in the eye as I stated my errand.

I was told to wait, then passed from the first fellow to another, to whom I had to state my business all over again. He took me upstairs beyond the rows of high desks and stools where the lower sort sat totting up their accounts – I could see the long columns of figures in the ledgers as I was led past – to where the senior clerks sat each one at his own great desk, with piles of papers and ledgers stacked around him. These men were not dressed in the wool and corduroy of the lower clerks, but so much like gentlemen that at first I thought they must be partners in the firm. I had not then seen the magnificence of a North West agent. My guide led me into a small office that looked over the street. In it was a great desk with a white blotter, where a little bald fellow sat writing a letter. 'Mr Mackenzie, sir' – thee may imagine my heart leapt when I heard that, but I was shocked too. Surely Rachel would not have fallen in love with this little grey balding fellow with wire-rimmed spectacles?[1] – 'This . . . gentleman . . .' – I did not like the way he hesitated over the appellation, looking down his nose at me as he did so – 'is seeking a Mr Alan Mackenzie, whom he has reason to believe is an employee of the Company. He . . . says . . . he has come from England in order to have a . . . word . . . with this Mr Mackenzie.'

---

[1] My wife tells me now that spectacles can lend a man a scholarly sort of dignity, which is not unattractive, but at three-and-twenty I had no notion of that.

I didn't like his tone, so I addressed Mackenzie directly. 'Good day to thee. My name is Mark Greenhow. I come from Cumberland in England to seek my brother-in-law, Alan Mackenzie. I understand him to be employed by the North West Company in the far west of Upper Canada.'

The senior clerk looked me over, then held out his hand. 'I grew up in New York State,' he said. 'You're a Quaker, aren't you? First I've met since I came to this country, and that's nearly thirty years ago.'

Truly the hand of the Lord was in it, that my surly guide took me to William Mackenzie out of all the Company agents in that great office. For not only did he search among lists containing more Mackenzies than I'd ever have guessed came out of Scotland, but he enquired among his fellows, until he'd found out everything for me that he could. 'Mind you,' he said, 'If you wait a couple of weeks, maybe three, the first canoes will be coming back, and we'll get the news from Fort William.' I must have looked blank, because he clapped me on the shoulder and laughed. 'You've all to learn, Mr Greenhorn, have you not? The whole of Montreal is waiting for the new season's furs to start coming in. You'll see the canoes arriving at Lachine; fifteen hundred miles they'll have come – you know all our trade is done by canoe?'

'I saw some big canoes on the river.'

'Ay, they're built at Trois Rivières. But you won't see brigades downriver from Lachine, or ships west of Montreal, come to that. The St Lawrence rapids lie between, as you'll see if you ride out that way. As you will, for the canoes are due back at Lachine any day now. That's when we may get news of your brother-in-law. But meanwhile we'll look in the books and see what we can find.'

He was as good as his word. The North West Company first employed Alan Mackenzie as a clerk in the month they record as September, 1803. The following year, in the month they name May, he left with the canoe brigades to go west to Fort William. From there, according to the record, my Alan Mackenzie was sent as clerk to a wintering partner in the country around the Lake Athabasca. He served his apprenticeship there, coming down every winter to Fort William with the furs, and travelling back with trade goods before the rivers froze.

I had no notion of what these names meant. William Mackenzie was the first to open the door a little way and give me a glimpse of the great wilderness beyond the western frontier. But I was more interested in finding out about Alan Mackenzie. For five years he over-wintered in Athabasca, and then in 1809 he vanished from the records. 'He would have been due for Montreal leave . . . Hoping for promotion no doubt . . . Our clerks do their time out west, and naturally they're looking for partnerships . . . And the winterers stay at their posts until they grow too old . . . You could call it a bottleneck, if you take my meaning . . . A bright young clerk wants nothing more than to become a partner, but there are only so many posts to be manned.'

I bethought me of the name Michilimackinac that headed Alan's letter. It was Judith who had told us Alan was in the North West Company. I could not remember the outlandish name, so I took Judith's letter out of my wallet, and unfolded it.

'Michilimackinac! That's it then. If he went to the South West in '09 . . . that'll be when we joined up with Astor's people. God knows what'll happen to that now. Let me see . . .'

'What is Michil . . . Michil . . .'

'You've not heard of Michilimackinac? And yet in London . . . Michilimackinac is the fur trading company based at Mackinac.[2] We don't operate over the border now in our own name, but we still have a major interest.'

'And Mackinac? Is that a Scotch place? Thee must understand, William Mackenzie, that everything thee speaks of is new to me.'

'Ah, well, sir, all I can tell you of Mackinac is hearsay. The British had to leave the island in '96. But me, I was an *hivernant* in the high country – when I say *hivernant*, I mean the gentlemen of our Company who winter west of Fort William, which is the North West rendezvous. You have heard of Lake Superior? No? The wildest and coldest lake of all. I must have been younger than you when I first went out. I joined the company in '91 – there were as many of us Scots as French being hired as clerks by then – I went out from Montreal in May with the canoe brigades – those are the big canoes – *les canots du maître* – which take the trade goods as far as Fort William. Then after Fort William it was into the west in a smaller canoe – *un canot du nord* – to winter in the wild. I was seven years a winterer in the *pays d'en haut*, young man, seven years. Ay, I did my time. Then fifteen hundred miles back again to Montreal. There's just time to do the round trip from here to Fort William between the spring thaw and the fall freeze. I should know; I've done it often enough.

'But you were asking about Mackinac. I was never in Mackinac. Officially it was handed over to the Yankees after the War, but our garrison – you'll note, young man, that I'm a Loyalist – stayed until '96. Then the British had to go. Yes, we had to give up all our garrisons in American territory, and much of the south-west trade went with them. And now we have this new South West Company . . . But who knows . . . Things have changed

[2] He called it Mackinaw, and I amended my own pronunciation thereafter.

at Mackinac . . . In any case, the best furs are up north. Up north where this young fellow Mackenzie of yours has served his time, same as I did, only it seems he went way further north, right into Athabasca country.'

Before I left he took me privily into the agents' Council Chamber. I was struck by the splendour of the polished table with the chairs – one for every agent in the Company – drawn up around it. William Mackenzie showed me a map on the wall, with many spaces in it, that showed the whole territory beyond Upper Canada with the posts of the North West Company, as far as the Pacific Ocean. I could not take in the distances. If it were true that from where we now were in Montreal to Fort William it was fifteen hundred miles, then by the map it was as much again to the territory of Athabasca. This was almost twice the span of the ocean I had crossed. I felt quite giddy. And what was more, this was all done by canoes, and where there was not a river the men must get out and carry the cargo, and the boat itself withal. William Mackenzie showed me the canoe routes that the fur traders took to the far west. He took out a six-inch rule and used it as a pointer, showing me the courses of the rivers, the Outaouais and the Mattawa, the La Vase Portage and the French River, the Lake of the Nippissing, and the great Lake Superior. I looked at the shape of the Lakes, and then at the far west, the rivers and portages, and far-flung outposts of the North West Company in the empty wilderness. 'Truly,' I said to my companion. 'This must be the greatest Company in the world.' He clapped me on the shoulder for that. 'Well said, sir! Well said! Never a doubt of it! Never a doubt!'

He let me look at the map as long as I would, and answered my questions patiently. Then I saw him take out his watch and look at it. I said I'd take my leave.

'Where are you staying, eh? None of your sect in Montreal, unless I'm mistaken . . . You have a lodging?

No? Where's your trunk . . . ? That knapsack is all you've got? That won't get you through the winter. Where are you going now?'

That was how I came to stay at the house of William Mackenzie, who, though no known relation of my brother-in-law, said that Mackenzies were all one clan, and that made us connections somewhere along the line. He said he'd not had the chance to call a Quaker cousin before.

I had the rest of the day to wait until he was ready to go home, which I employed in exploring the city. Not far from the Company offices I came upon a new monument, with scenes of naval battles round its base. It was dedicated to Horatio Nelson, *who terminated his career of naval glory at the memorable battle of Trafalgar on the 21st of Octr 1805 after inculcating by signal a maxim that can never be forgotten by his country – 'England expects every man will do his duty.' This monumental pillar was erected by a subscription of the inhabitants of Montreal in the year 1808.*[3] I knew not what to make of it: Friends in no way condoned the military monuments which were then becoming so prevalent. I was puzzled too because so far I seemed to be about the only Englishman in the place. I wandered through the busy streets, feeling tired and confused, while the jabber of incomprehensible French assaulted my poor ears. The houses of Montreal were built close together, fronting on to narrow streets, but here and there I saw through an arched gateway to an inner courtyard where little scraps of private lives were being enacted: washing left to bleach, two little lasses playing with their dolls, a cat washing itself in a sunny spot among pots of kitchen herbs. I had nowhere private to go, so I walked the length

---

[3] I read recently – it must have been in the *Manchester Guardian* – that there is a proposal to build a similar (but much larger) Memorial column for Horatio Nelson in the new Trafalgar Square in London. This is not how Friends would wish to see their taxes allocated.

of St Paul's Street, until I found myself in a crowded market place where I bought a meat pie and an apple – for it was well past noon – and as I chewed I crossed a bridge and followed a little river inland. In five minutes I'd left the streets behind, and was walking past scattered cottages and fields of ripening vegetables, along an open road that led towards the mountain. The noise of the city died away behind me, and I breathed more freely.

I passed a couple of impressive mansions in modern landscaped grounds, before the road turned to a mountain path, winding between precipices and clinging oaks, and eventually taking me to the summit of Mount Royal. From there I could see I was on an island – one among a multitude – with the huge river curving round its southern shore. An expanse of open water gleamed in the north-west, and I wondered if it could be the lake Ontario I'd seen in Thomas Wilkinson's atlas, but then I remembered the immensity of distance which the map had revealed to me, and realised I had not come half far enough. Away to the south lay distant hills, a vast unknown country. Below me I could see the city, with its red metal roofs and steeplehouse spires, a sharp speck of definition in the hazy wilderness.

I returned reluctantly to the busy streets, but it turned out that William Mackenzie lived in a pleasant modern house with a walled garden, about ten minutes' walk from the city, at the western end of Jean-Baptiste Street. In his elegant dining-room that evening, I did justice to the first home-cooked dinner I'd had for seven weeks: river trout followed by beef dumplings followed by plum duff.

After I'd left him my new friend had taken a wee dander, as he put it, and had a quiet word with one or two fellows from McTavish and McGillivray. 'The North West doesn't operate in Mackinac these days, but we keep our interests there, alongside the Yankees. The old Michilimackinac Company became the South West

Company – what would it be? – a year or so ago. The clerks at the Mackinac house would have been transferred automatically.'

'So Alan Mackenzie's employed by this South West Company now?'

'Yes, but the devil's in it that last year's records . . . well . . . the fact is they hardly exist. Last year the Yankees brought in their damned Non-Intercourse Act. No goods to cross the border. All the trade goods from Montreal last year were held up at Fort St Joseph, on our side of the border from Mackinac. And of course the Indians in the south-west were stuck with the year's furs, and ripe for murder when they couldn't sell them on. Everything was at a standstill. According to the records here in Montreal, all trade stopped. But my informant reckons Alan Mackenzie is still at Mackinac.'

I took a long drink, thinking this over, and savouring the good clean water after my weeks at sea. In the face of my abstinence my host had fairly managed to empty the decanter of what he declared to be a fine Rhineland wine. I didn't like to think how it had come here, when all the ports of Europe were closed. I said as much, and my host winked, and said that Orders in Council were one thing, and Yankee enterprise another, and the one would never take heed of the other, though all the world should go to war for it.

'To war?' I repeated. 'The war with France, thee means? But the Americans – the Yankees – they're not part of that, surely?'

I must have shown my dismay quite plainly. I seemed to have come so far from my own war-impoverished England, to this house of wellbeing and prosperity overlooking the flourishing little colony and busy harbour. William Mackenzie did not live simply, and I'd never before been entertained amidst such ostentatious comfort. His wife was not like the matrons of Cumberland. Although it was a cold night her dress was cut very low, and was of a rich red colour with a sheen on it for all the world like a ripe plum, the kind that splits its skin for very tightness if not harvested quick. She plied me kindly with victuals, commiserating with me on the diet of ship's biscuit and salted pork I'd endured these many weeks. Their family were all away: the daughters married, and the sons working for the Company in the west. It was a peaceful, comfortable house, worn by years of family life, and filled with the grace of many things accomplished. My host said a blessing over our meat in what I take to be the Episcopal fashion; his manner was perfunctory but there was a tenderness in it to which I could find no objection.

Mrs Mackenzie – I was not told her given name – replied to my question with more animation than she had shown all evening. 'War!' she repeated. 'What man is not involved with war! They speak of nothing else. You'll find that out soon enough, Mr Greenhow, if you use your eyes and ears in this city.'

But William Mackenzie leaned forward and tapped his fist on the table to emphasise his words. 'Ah, my lad, you English think only of Napoleon. But I'm telling you there's another war coming. In England they don't see what they don't choose. Not when it's far away over the sea, out of sight and mostly out of mind. You mark my words; there'll be war between the Yankees and the British before the year's out. High time, I say. When the last war ended I was a lad of twelve. My father fell at Green Springs. I was the eldest of the family, and it was my mother and I got the six of us out of the new so-called Republic. We took a ship from New York to the Bay of Fundy – a terrible cold journey that was; my little sister took sick and nearly died of it – then up the St John River to Frederick's Town in an open bateau. We had nothing, and there were thousands like us. We had to fight to get land allotted to us, for I was but a lad, but we got our farm, and we made do, just. I spent my growing up years near Frederick's Town. Then my brother took on the farm, and I came to Montreal and joined the Company. I'm a Loyalist and a North West man. And I tell you that in Canada we want this war; we're ready for it.

'The Company saw it coming long ago, when we lost Michilimackinac and the south-west trade. I'm telling you, if we don't turn and fight, all this land of ours will end up in the Yankee Republic. And not just this land here. The Company has its posts out west from here to the Pacific. Back in England they don't even know there's a frontier out there. But I tell you there is, thousands of miles of it, and the American Fur Company on the other side of it – that's Astor's men – just waiting to move in. God knows what's going on now in Mackinac. Oh yes, laddie, there's going to be a war all right. There's more at stake than shipping rights, though that's all your English papers ever mention. This will be a Company war. The government doesn't know it – Simcoe was the best governor we ever had in Upper Canada, but he's been gone a long time – the English back home don't know it, but the Company knows it. And the Company will win it, when it happens. And mark my words, lad, it'll be soon.'

I was silent while I gathered my thoughts, and then I said, 'Thy words fill me with dismay, friend. I can't believe that war will mend anything, or that anything but evil can come of it. What of the settlers on both sides of thy frontier? What of the wild Indians, who as I understand it have suffered much, and might profit by a Christian example? What of the young men in thy Company, thine own sons even, who love life, and might serve the Company all their days, who may have to die for this? We're in a new country, where all things might be made new. Does thee really wish that it may come to ruin and bloody war?'

My host stood up abruptly. 'Come, lad, this is no talk for the ladies.' (My mother and sister would have had something to say to that, but Mrs Mackenzie just simpered, and laid her napkin on the table.) 'We'll go into the bookroom. There's a deal you must know if you're serious about heading west. I can't have you go in this raw state; it wouldn't be human. Come on through, and if you won't take a glass of port you can watch me have one.'

So it came about that though outwardly it would seem I could have no communion with this man, his way of life and his sentiments being so very far removed from mine, I found such tenderness in him that presently I told him Rachel's story. I made him see why it was that I had to follow my brother-in-law, and find him, wherever he might be, in the far wilderness of this new country.

William Mackenzie blew his nose hard when I had finished, and when I looked at him in the candlelight, I was startled to see that he'd shed several tears. 'It's a sad tale, lad,' he said apologetically, 'and I wish I could see a happy ending to it.' He sighed gustily, and reached for the decanter. 'I wish I could. Truth is, he should never have taken her out there. Never have married her, in fact. There's no place for a white woman in the Company. A man needs a country wife – an Indian to you – it's the system. It wouldn't work any other way. Your Alan Mackenzie should've known that. He did know it. More sorrow to him. He'd been out five years. No, no, let a man have a wife in Montreal, why not? But out there – it's out of the question. There's many a man has one of each, or more, and needs must when the devil drives, I reckon, but to mix up the one and the other, that's going against the whole system. Can't be done. No, no, it's flying against the whole custom of the country. He'd never have kept her, any road.'

'But surely,' I stammered, horrified by his words, 'surely the settlers have wives? Judith's letters talked of women and men, both, at Yonge Street.'

'Ay, but the north-west is a far cry from Yonge Street. Your sister was lost deep in Indian country, a long way from any settlers. Ay, well. There have been cases of women who were kidnapped by the Indians and came back. I've heard of it back in the States. But for all that were found, more than twice as many were lost, I reckon. And not just lost . . . That is to say . . . And now there's like to be a war on . . . Not that the Michigan Territory . . . Your brother-in-law must have his contacts . . . The fur traders and the Indians are natural allies, always have been . . . whereas the settlers . . . My poor young fellow, I feel for you. Are you sure you won't take a small glass of this excellent port? For medicinal purposes? It can be a very present help in times of trouble, I assure you.'

'I thank thee, friend, but no. What was thee about to say about the settlers?'

He leaned back in his leather armchair, and studied his glass reflectively. The drink was a lush purple which winked and blinked in the candlelight. The light from the fire picked out the same deep colour in the Persian hearthrug where I stretched out my feet, clad in borrowed Moroccan slippers, to the blazing log fire. I was sleepy; I realised that in all the weeks at sea I had not once felt quite warm, or quite dry.

My host seemed to be dropping asleep, but he caught himself up on a small snore, and sat up abruptly. 'Settlers, you say?' He loosened his cravat, and reached for the decanter again. 'No, no, laddie. I'm speaking of land way out west where there en't no settlers. Nor should be, that's the long and the short of it. Now if there's a white woman in it, you're talking settlement. A white woman couldn't stand aught else. But the Company don't want settlers.' I watched him pour out another glass. He only spilled a little bit, for all that his manner of speech had broadened to something which I guessed went much further back than his snug bookroom and his Company office. 'Now, we – the Company, that is – we're here to trade, and the Indian is a trader too, always has been. Trade goods for furs . . . Everybody gains. But the settlers . . . Clearing the forest . . . wiping out hunting grounds . . . The way your settler wants his land, no one else can share it. What's more they're all bloody Yankees, your settlers. Damned Yankees down in American territory, and damned Yankees right there in Upper Canada. Bloody Yankees think the whole bang shoot is their god-given country. Simcoe let 'em in, the devil take him – and yet I liked him well. But, God forgive him, he gave the damn Yankees the same deal as the Loyalists in Upper Canada, no questions asked. You Quakers too, settling our frontier – Yankees, too, the whole damn lot of you. Not you, lad, not you. You're an Englishman born, I ken that well, and if I differ from you there, why that's old history, and not to be thought of between us here. Not in this country. No, no, laddie, I like you well, and we'll not think on that.

'Now Upper Canada . . . Our last governor there: Simcoe . . . A fine man, that, a true Loyalist . . . he encouraged the Quakers to come up from the States. Not that I've aught against 'em, laddie. On the contrary; ay, but ye ken I like you folk. Quakers make good settlers, that's a fact. They won't touch the drink, sithee, however tough it gets. Don't need to, they've got their God to keep them going. Out there on the frontier you have to have one or the other. Believe me, you need something, making a farm out of nothing, with the wilderness howling round you and the Indians itching for your scalp. But you Quakers get along with the Indians. The Indian's a fighting man himself, and yet he'll respect a fellow who won't fight because his God says not to ... Sees the courage in it, I guess. But for all that, the settlers, Quakers or no, aren't good news for the Indians ... might not be good news for the Nor'-Westers in the end either, and that's a fact.'

'There are more settlers in the United States than there are here, though?'

'Oh, ay, yes, yes. The Ohio valley ... But the south of the Michigan Territory is all swamp ... the settlers can't go into Michigan ... Plenty of Indian allies there for us ... The Indians love the Company a lot more than they love the American settlers ... Not to say ... the Michigan Territory is over the border, but not settled ... virtually not settled ... Indians friendly ... But your brother-in-law, Alan Mackenzie, he must know; he's been into that country. It's no good us guessing; you'll need to talk to him.'

'That's what I want to do most of all.'

'So you have to find him, eh? Well, I've been thinking on that, laddie. Ay, I've been thinking for you. You can't do anything this winter. You realise that? The canoes will be home in a week or so, and nothing goes west then until the spring. May, when the ice melts, that's when you set out.'

'May? That's Fifth Month next year! I can't kick my heels here till then!'

'Well, laddie, kicking your heels or not is up to you. But I'm telling you, it'll be freezing up north already, and there's no way you can get to Mackinac now until the spring. No one's trying to stop you; it's the dispensh-ation of God. Winter'll be rolling in like a tide any day now, and it won't go out again till May. There's nothing you nor any man can do till then.'

I frowned at him, thinking hard. 'But in Fifth Month – in May – thee could arrange for me to go west with the traders?'

'That's not so easily done as you might think. But I'll put in a word in the right place, for I've a fancy to see you on your way. Tomorrow . . .'

But tomorrow brought different news: Mrs Mackenzie (I never did learn her name so must needs give her the worldly title) was at the door as I came in from a stroll. 'The first brigade is back! Mr Mackenzie sent word that you should take the grey mare, and ride to Lachine. I can give you the direction.'

'Is that where he's gone?' I asked, bewildered.

'Bless you, no! He's seen the canoes come in a hundred times' – this could hardly be so, for they come but once a year, but I let that pass – 'but you should not miss the sight, indeed you should not. The next brigade is due in any time, so they said. You can ride, Mr Greenhow?'

'Of course I can ride!' She was an ignorant old woman, but I was young, and over-quick to take offence. How could she know I'd ride pretty much anything that had a back to sit on, ay, and I was the lad who galloped over Moricombe sands from Skinburness to Cardunnock between the tides, not for a wager, which is against the principles of our Society, but because the wheelwright at Silloth said he would take his oath (for he was not a Friend) that the thing could not be done. That was on my own sweet mare Mollie, and much I missed her, for William's Petal was about the greatest slug I ever crossed, and unwilling even to overtake the empty oxcarts that were already rumbling along the high road to Lachine, raising a dust that covered the hedgerows like untimely snow. For all that, I reached Lachine in time to see the next brigade come in.

I had not in those days visited any of the great manu-
facturing towns of England. I'd never seen so many great
warehouses, or so many manufactories crowded together.
Neither had I seen such a motley collection of folk as
those that thronged the shore road: not only the sorts
of men (and loose women too) a man would find in
Whitehaven, but fellows dressed like Jacobin revolution-
aries[4] in coloured caps and woven sashes, and Indians –
the first I ever saw – who seemed outlandish enough to
me then, dressed as they were in deerskins and moccasins,
all adorned with claws and feathers.

I left the mare in charge of the ostler at the Henley Inn
while I looked round. The town of Lachine fronted on to
a great natural harbour, where two long inlets provided
perfect shelter for any number of craft. There were no
ships, though, only flocks of big canoes drawn up close
together like the hundreds of seals that bask on Solway
shore at this time of year. Clouds of scavenging gulls
cried overhead, and to the west I could see little islands
protecting the harbour mouth.

My first sight of the great *canots du maître* in action
stirred me – and yet I could not know what was to come.
The canoes seemed to slide so easily through the water,
and were brought so swiftly to the shore, where the men
leapt into shallow water and unloaded and beached their
craft in less time than it takes to man a capstan. Every
ship I'd seen before seemed clumsy, ay, even the steamer
that had won my heart on the St Lawrence River. The
paddles moved so fast, all in time, and then when they
came to the shore all stopped as one, and the voyageurs
lifted their paddles and leaped into the shallow water.
The men themselves were as brightly coloured as male

---

[4] I later discovered this to be an unwarrantable assumption which would
have appalled the voyageurs.

chaffinches in springtime. They were little dark fellows, but with great shoulders on them like wrestlers. It was a sight to see them bring the great bales of fur ashore, two at a time – and one alone weighs ninety pounds, William told me – and even more of a sight to see them swing their beaver-hatted *bourgeois* – the Company agent – aloft from his place in the canoe, and dump him dryshod on the shore. Ashore there was as much merriment as at a Penrith fair.[5]

I walked, and I watched, but there was nothing for me to do here. I wasn't used to crowds, and all at once I felt dowy and lonesome. The noise and jostle all about me aroused in me a melancholy which I believe afflicts folk from the great world amidst our quiet grey hills. For me it's the other way around. All of a sudden I could bear Lachine no longer. I went back to the Henley, tipped the ostler, and hotfooted it back to Montreal. William's Petal laid back her ears, and tried to throw me by a sudden stall, but I would have none of it. When she put her mind to it her paces were not so bad. The oxcarts were still trundling westward. I paid no heed. My small victory over William's lazy and overfed mount put new heart into me. By the time

[5] When I went to the fairs with my father, we sold our stock and did what business we had to do, and went home soberly in daylight. But I had also been to the fair twice with my cousin John Bristo and the lads I met at wrestling, and that was another matter altogether. I was once severely eldered by Joseph Priestman, because word reached him I'd wrestled with the Grasmere champion before a public audience. He came to our house with John Nicholson, carrying a minute from London Yearly Meeting of 1795, and read to me solemnly: *In reviewing the answers to that query which respects Vain Sports, we have had good unity with the case of one Quarterly Meeting in noticing . . . the practice of some Members of Hunting and Shooting for diversion. We clearly rank these practices with Vain Sports . . .* My parents were greatly distressed that the Meeting had cause to reprove me, but I protested that I'd never gone hunting in my life, for all that the Caldbeck hounds met almost at our door, and John Peel himself used to hail me when I met them on Blencathra in the winter. I also silently noted that there was no mention of wrestling, and I was not above a specious argument, in those days.

I had Petal stabled and rubbed down (there was a groom somewhere, but I'm a farmer's son, and I needed him not) I felt better, my confidence flowing back like the tide over the Solway mudflats. I was ready to go on.

CHAPTER 5

WILLIAM MACKENZIE OFFERED TO KEEP ME AT HIS house over the winter, which was exceeding kind in him, but I had no fancy to remain idle in Montreal for eight months. When one field lies fallow, it's time to cultivate another. It wasn't too late to get to Yonge Street, and I was beginning to long for the solace of my Society. Before I left home I hadn't passed a day and a night together out of the society of Friends. At first William protested that the distance was greater than I knew, the winter in Upper Canada far worse, the lake would soon be frozen &c &c &c. To distract my mind, perhaps, he insisted that I come and see the new furs unpacked in the warehouses by St Gabriel Street. 'For this is what it's all about, laddie! None of us would be here if it wasn't for this.'

I asked him, as we passed the North West offices in St Gabriel Street, concerning the heraldic emblem above the door, and the picture of the strange canoe at the foot of the shield.

'That?' said William. 'You've never heard of the Flying Canoe, laddie? You've all to learn, have you not? There's more to a canoe than meets the eye. The Flying Canoe takes you to more places than you ever knew existed. Oh, ay, lad, you'll come home a changed man if you go by the Flying Canoe.'

I said nothing; I'd been taught to regard all manner of whimsy as beneath my notice. Moreover, I saw nothing romantic about the fur trade. The stench as we approached the warehouses was appalling. I knew the tannery in Keswick – 'tis where we take our own cattlehide – and I'd passed the tanneries in Penrith, Carlisle and Whitehaven, but never had I encountered anything like the fur depots of the North West Company in Montreal. My gorge rose as we entered, and I was feart for a moment I'd disgrace myself, but as with all things I rapidly became accustomed. There was plenty to distract my mind. Where we came in, the warehouse was piled high with sewn-up canvas bales, unloaded from the oxcarts coming in from Lachine. The road that had taken me less than an hour constituted a day and a half's journey for the lumbering carts with their high-piled loads. Half a dozen fellows were ripping the bales open as they came in, and sorting the furs into piles. This they did with the speed of long practice, while one fellow called out the tally, and the clerk entered the figures in his book. Then a different set of men swept the piles away, to hang them (if damp) and store them ready for tanning. All was done in haste, and it seemed to me that no one fellow saw the same work through to its conclusion, so that I was reminded of nothing so much as ants scurrying about an anthill if one digs it open.

'André! Is that you? Get one of these fellows to bring some pelts over, will you?'

Presently a bent old man in a voyageur shirt and sash came hobbling over. 'You wish to see the pelts, m'sieu?'

'Yes, yes. Show my friend here what we've got.' William swept a pile of notebooks to one end of a battered wooden counter. 'That's right. Spread them out here!'

I recognised the smooth whitey-brown badger pelts

with their distinctive stripes, and the dappled deerskins. I knew the wet-looking otter pelts, gleaming like polished chestnuts, and the soft reddish fox furs. I'd never seen the animal called skunk or the opossum. I was still examining the latter, trying to imagine what kind of beasts they must be, when William said,

'But these are mere bagatelles. Look at this, now, laddie!'

It was a round pelt, so dark brown it was nearly black, the fur thick and smooth, but with a sheen to it almost as bright as the otter's. It came from a squat little animal, for the hide was foursquare, like the badger's, about eighteen inches each way. Its legs lay vertical to the body. The most curious thing about it was its tail, for that was as wide as it was long, a six inch square just like the head at the other end. It had that gleam to it that betokens a water animal. 'Beaver?' I asked.

'Ay, laddie, beaver. Look at this.' William picked up the pelt I'd been looking at and stroked it backwards. The fur was much darker when rubbed the wrong way. Underneath there was a whitish layer, much like the down on a duck. 'See that? That's worth more than gold, laddie. There's currency, in that selfsame hair, goes through this warehouse worth more than all the guineas in the Bank of England, and that's the truth. Give me your hat!'

Surprised, I removed my hat and passed it to him. He rubbed his finger and thumb along the broad brim. 'Ay, laddie, you Quaker folk are just like the rest. One of these little fellows was snared, way up in the north-west, maybe, or dug out of its lodge in the ten-foot snows of a winter the like of which you've never seen. There it was caught and skinned by an Indian savage two thousand miles west of here, brought by sledge to a North West post – I'm assuming it's not Bay goods I'm handling here – then baled up and carried by canoe across more water than would sink Britannia beneath the waves for ever, then shipped from here to London, where it was sent to the manufactory. And all that to get thee thy plain hat, thou honest Quaker!'

I was a little shocked by this. I'd thought our hats were manufactured from English wool, and I said to myself that when I got home I would look into the matter. I was still thinking about it while William conducted me round the rest of the North West Factory. More and more I was missing my own people, before whom I might put the concerns, such as this one, that began to press upon me. I resolved that I'd make my way to Yonge Street without more ado.

I left Lachine two days later, not by canoe, but in one of the river bateaux, which was not near so comfortable as my previous voyage in the *Accommodation*. For days we beat upriver, tacking to and fro as the river wound, while the wind played tricks on us, changing direction – or we did – a dozen times in every hour. I felt sick. I was relieved – but in this I was alone – each time we came to a great rapid, for then the boatmen had to pole the boat through the rapids, with a great clanking of iron poles against the rocks, while the passengers walked along rough trails from which we returned bemired to the thighs, but in my case much refreshed. There were five great rapids on the St Lawrence River; our progress was pretty slow until we got to Prescott. There I was briskly shifted, like so much luggage – and indeed the mails and sundry other bales were flung aboard after me – to a Durham boat, which brought me without further obstacle as far as Kingston. The morning mists chilled my bones and set my nose a-running. We passed islands and rivers, dimly visible in daggy mist; I couldn't have cared less. I never even went ashore at Kingston: there was a big schooner, the *Lord Nelson*, about to sail for York, and I scrambled aboard with the postbags, and we were away within the hour.

We were well into the open lake when the fog lifted at last. A fresh wind rose, a little patch of blue appeared ahead, and within an hour the sky was swept clear and clean. The choppy waves sparkled in the sun, and, chilled and queasy as I was, I couldn't restrain a gasp of delight. This was the sea, though there was no salt in it. There was no horizon, only a distant band of brightness where sky and water met; only far to our right there lay a thin line of land. I had thought to find a continent, and here instead was an ocean. I bethought me of the map in Thomas Wilkinson's study, and remembered the outline of five great lakes, but never could I, brought up within sight of Derwentwater, have conceived of any lake so vast as this. Gulls cried in our wake as they do when they follow the plough in spring, but there was no land to till here, on this fresh ocean at the very edge of the world. I hated the Atlantic, but this inland sea spoke to me of clean water and new possibilities; it seemed untouched as if the hand of the Lord had but this day finished it, and I was filled with new hope.

I only realised when I reached York that the Monthly Meeting named Yonge Street is upwards of twenty-five miles from York itself. I walked the half mile from the fort into the town itself, and inquired for a place to stay the night. I was directed first to Jordan's York Hotel. It looked to be a pleasant house, only there seemed to be some kind of fashionable rout going on, for the place was thronged with carriages full of ladies and gentlemen in evening dress. Several officers of the military were lounging at the door. I withdrew hastily, and asked a passer-by if there were any hostelry nearby that might be a little quieter? He gave me a quick appraising glance. 'You're a Quaker? You'd probably be more comfortable at the Toronto Coffee House.' He took me by the arm and pointed – 'up that way.'

The indifferent words cheered me more than I can describe. For the first time Friends were near. The Toronto Coffee House was in the next street. It seemed full enough to me, but the crowd was less fashionable, and the little slip of a room they gave me at the back of the house was clean and plain, though I was oft awoken in the night by the noise from the Coffee Room below, and the comings and goings from the yard below my window.

I was up betimes next morning, and striding along Yonge Street with my knapsack on my back. Mr Cooper at the Coffee House said I had a day's walk before me, but I couldn't miss the way. He was right; the track had been well cleared through the forest, but underfoot it was not so much a road as a morass, going straight as a die with no regard for the frequent swamps in its way. Sometimes the stretches of black mud are traversed by a path of logs laid side to side, which in Upper Canada they call corduroy, but as often as not the logs were rotted, or floating free, and more treacherous than simple bog. Apparently the old Indian path to the west takes a drier route, keeping to such heights as there are. I was told there would be hills, but I found none, only a long rolling countryside and a dead straight track, so that from the top of each rise one could see the cleared ribbon of track far ahead on to the next rise. William told me that York is distinguished as a capital by its extraordinary distance from anywhere else.

On the road north, however, I met farmers, journeymen and carriers, and twice a straggling band of militia bound for York. Every man going south would stop to ask me, had I news from York? It was the same as in the Coffee House, and in the schooner: the talk was all of war, and rumours of war. Once I was called a bloody turncoat Quaker, and had mud flung at me, and another time a wild-looking fellow held the point of a bayonet at my throat, and ordered me to swear I was a Loyalist. I told him I was an Englishman, and that I would not swear aught for any man. He said he'd supposed me to be a damn Yankee Quaker, and if I was an Englishman he was willing to shake my hand. I shook hands with him, but thought it honest to make clear to him that though I was not a Yankee I was most certainly a Quaker, and that neither force nor the threat of force would move me: I would not take up arms for any cause, nor do hurt to any man.

No one else molested me. It began to grow dusk. I felt small and exposed on the open road. I'm used to a country where I can see out. The forest of Upper Canada is not like an English wood, with its paths and clearings and villages; it's a dense unbroken wilderness, whose compass is beyond measure, and whose depths are unfathomable. As the dark thickened, the trees became a wall of whispering shadows. Night creatures flickered to and fro just beyond the edges of my vision. The going was getting so slow I found myself like to be benighted, but I pressed on through the failing light until I reached the summit at Oak Ridges. Here the forest began to fall away at last, and soon the first farmstead appeared. The clearing was so recently hacked out of the wilderness that the fields were still pocked with stumps. I came to a log cabin built close to the road. A light twinkled at the window; from indoors the fields must already seem to be dark.

I passed more clearings and more cabins, and then I came to a place where the fields were not surrounded by dense forest, but separated from their neighbours by rough-hewn log fences. The harvest was in; the stubble fields looked smooth as a spread blanket. I came to a copse of trees, and just beyond it a house whose windows were filled with lamplight, set back a little from the road. It was so surprising that I stepped up very quietly and looked in the window, standing within the little warm circle of light, feeling the chill of the dark against my back, breathing in the unfamiliar smells of the forest night.

A dozen Friends were gathered on the first three rows of benches. For a moment the Meeting House seemed filled with a heavenly radiance, a Meeting for Worship in the manifest Light of God's presence, but I banished such a flight of fancy still unfledged. In Mosedale we're thrifty folk, and we don't use four great lanterns to light one small Meeting. Our Meeting House is old and damp, built of Lakeland stone, with little windows and oak benches darkened by the years. Here the wood was pale and new, the roof high, and the space below airy and light. There were no dark shadows or unlit corners, no damp streaks on the walls or mouldy patches. Never before, in fact, had I seen so modern and commodious a Meeting House. The floor was of wooden boards, which must be an unconscionable comfort to the feet on winter mornings. The empty benches around the little gathered Meeting could have accommodated upwards of fifty, and that, I realised shortly, was only in the men's Meeting, for, when I peered in the next lit window, I saw I was at the other side of a wooden partition that divided the Meeting House in two, and on this side there were perhaps twenty women in caps and grey cloaks, also gathered in the silence.

I found the door to the Men's Meeting, opened it quietly, and crept to a bench at the back, where I took my place in the gathered Meeting.

At last there was a stirring in the silence. The Clerk set up his desk, and opened the book of minutes. I had no notion why there should be a Meeting for Worship for Business at twilight on Fifth Day, but this was a strange country and perhaps Friends had developed strange practices.

Naturally the Friends were surprised to have a stranger so suddenly appear among them. I explained who I was and handed my Minute from Caldbeck Monthly Meeting to the Clerk, who introduced himself to me as Joseph Doan. He shook my hand and gave me a good welcome. I also shook hands with one David Willson and one Amos Armitage, but it seemed to me that there were other Friends who hung back a little. But Joseph Doan said straight out, 'We pray for thy poor sister. I fear she is lost to thee, but we cannot but love the spirit of compassion which brings thee here. Thee's welcome to our Meeting.' Amos said, 'If we have no means to forward thy concern, at least we can offer thee shelter. Thee can share the comfort of our worship so long as thee desires.'

I thanked them for that, and told him I sought first of all my aunt Judith Scott. David Willson shook his head. 'Our Friend Judith left us almost a year ago. When the letter came telling us that thy sister was lost, Judith fell into a slough of great sorrow, and could in no way feel the hand of the Lord in it. But then the Lord Jesus Christ planted the seed in her heart that she should leave us again, and return to minister among our Friends in Pennsylvania, and from there whithersoever the Lord might send her. She was comforted, and went forth from Yonge Street in Twelfth Month last year. Thomas Armitage took her by sled to York as soon as the road was frozen hard enough.'

That was a blow. I'd counted on speaking to Judith, but to try to follow her into a strange and hostile country would indeed be a wild goose chase. I listened to the Friends in a kind of daze, but presently Amos Armitage said that they were here for a Preparative Meeting (for so they call their Particular Meetings) for Business. He said I might sit quietly among them if I pleased, and when the Meeting was done he would see to my lodging.

I unlaced my gaiters, took off my clarty boots and left them at the door, and returned to my corner, where the little draughts crept around me and pierced my sodden breeks and stockings. I did my best to ignore the grumbling in my belly – for I had eaten naught but cheese and clapbread since I left York – but closed my eyes, and gave sincere thanks to God for bringing me safe through the wilderness this day, unto this remote haven of my own people.

Presently I began to take note of the Meeting. Many Friends felt moved to speak, and that vehemently. If Joseph Priestman had been Clerk, he would have asked Friends to make room between their words for the silence through which the will of God might be revealed. It seemed to me this meeting was sometimes swayed by the opinions of men, and those often contrary, rather than by the leadings of the Spirit which is beyond all human debate or controversy. This can happen anywhere when men are upset by a very pressing concern, but in those days I made less allowance for it.

Joseph Doan was a quiet-spoken grave man, whose words seemed the more precious because they were but few. He stood aside from the Clerk's bench to speak his concern: 'When John Graves Simcoe invited Quakers to settle in Upper Canada, he gave his word that we could live according to our religious principles, including our ancient testimony for peace. He wanted men like us on the frontier, because he knew we could make the wilderness into good farmland, and that we'd live in peace with our Indian neighbours. Those were the terms on which we crossed the border into Upper Canada and settled here. No man has the right to molest us, or to confiscate our goods, or imprison us. It was made clear from the beginning of the settlement that we were not to be subject to war tax or military service. We were led to this place by the Lord God to create our own peace on earth within the wilderness, and we have every right, by civil law as well as by divine guidance, to stand by the principles of our Religious Society.'

A burly Friend with fists like great hams ministered

next: 'Ay, Friend, but is thee going to tell Isaac Brock that? I doubt he'll heed thee; he'll be more mindful of the American army across the lake than a promise made when Yonge Street was a farmer's track.'

A short silence ensued, while Friends sat with bowed heads. I shifted so I was sitting crosslegged on my bench, and could rub my numb feet through my wet stockings. The bench creaked – I'm no lightweight – and I sat very still.

'Friend Joseph is right.' I could not see the face of the Friend who spoke. 'When we were given our contract there wasn't a war in the offing. Just in the last year we've paid nearly three hundred pounds in fines because we won't join the militia. Our farms are small; we can't pay that kind of money. We've already seen eight Friends in prison for not paying. Isaac Brock our new governor is a soldier, and Yonge Street's a military road, like it or not. It wasn't built for settlers; it was built by the government to make a safe route from York to Lake Huron, away from the border. Those of us who live close to the Road barely go a day now without being harassed by militia, or just by fellows going down to York to see what's doing. The soldiers take what they please, and if they don't go their length now, mark my words, they will, if Government condones their ravages upon us. And those who live out of sight of the Road, their time will also come. I know not why the Lord should have sent this trial upon us, just when our fields are cleared of stumps, and our harvests are lasting us right through to next year's growth. I can't believe it's God's will that we should go back to the United States, and have all to carve out of the wilderness again. Some of us grow older, and could not do the work.'

'Our Friend may well find it hard to discern God's will in his present trial.' The speaker was on the elders' bench facing me: the dark, heavy-jowled man who'd told me his name was David Willson. He spoke with a good deal more eloquence than the simple farmers round him. I forgot that I was cold and tired and hungry, and began to be much moved. 'Are we not called,' he said at last, 'to bring forth anew our ancient testimony to peace, and to raise it higher as an ensign to the nations? Is it not the will of God that Yonge Street runs through the very heart of our community? If we are to make the earth a fruitful paradise, if we are to be the children of peace as our Lord desires of us, is it not meet that our light should shine forth to the world as we bear witness against them that persecute us? I say that the road runs through our community so that we may stand by our testimony before the nations of the whole world. For is not this world rent by war from end to end, and delivered thereby into the hand of the Enemy? If our Lord Jesus Christ has sent us here to build his Kingdom of Peace upon earth, here in this place, then this must be our Suffering in the cause of Truth, and our Witness in these times of peril.'

The ensuing silence was broken at last by a hesitant young voice. 'Friends, we talk as if the country were at war. But the war is naught but rumour, apart from the troops going down Yonge Street and causing us distress. As yet there is peace between Upper Canada and the United States. Should we not be praying that there be no war, that this threat will pass away from us? Surely it's not the will of the Lord God of Peace that there be war in the land?'

The next to minister seemed to me to set the last ministries aside, but no doubt it was not meant so. 'It's true that Governor Isaac Brock is a soldier, but Friends, to our certain knowledge and experience, he's a fair man withal, and not hostile to our Society. We can help him by praying that the Lord may show him the right way. I make no doubt that his heart is set upon war, and as far as that goes we can't support him.'

It was quite dark outside the windows now. The silence flowed, and ebbed. A new voice spoke.

'Our Friend is right. We should speak to Isaac Brock, remembering that the true might, the peaceful dominion of the Lord God, is with us and among us. If any man can control the militia, Isaac Brock can. We're already being imprisoned for not paying war tax. The next thing we know, our young men will be seized from their homes. It'll be too late then to start arguing. We ignore the Road at our peril. We'll stand by our testimony of peace until death, if need be, and if we do that the Lord is with us to protect us. The law of our own land ought to protect us too. We must remind the Governor of that before war is declared, and before violent hands are laid upon us. We would be fools to do aught else.'

Ripples of uncertainty spread through the long silence that ensued. Gradually they died away. I recognised the voice of Amos Armitage from the elders' bench: 'Friends, this was the first declaration concerning peace made by those who signed themselves "the harmless and innocent people of God, called Quakers": *Our principle is, and our Practice hath always been, to seek peace and ensue it and to follow after righteousness and the knowledge of God, seeking the good and welfare and doing that which tends to the peace of all. We know that wars and fightings proceed from the lusts of men, out of which lusts the Lord hath redeemed us, and so out of the occasion of war. All bloody principles and practices we, as to our own particulars, do utterly deny, with all outward war and strife and fightings with outward weapons, for any end and under any pretence whatsoever. And this is our testimony to the whole world.'*

The silence gathered. I felt the peace of the Lord like a garment wrapped around, protecting us from the uncharted wilderness without. I leaned back against the wall and shut my eyes. I had walked nearly thirty miles that day, which would have been a small matter in my own country, but here the forest seemed to have thrust its way into my mind, so that when I shut my eyes I saw only the line of trees, the patch of sky above the road, and the shining puddles in the mud. In my mind I still trudged on and on, and when I came back to myself at last Amos Armitage had me by the shoulder and was shaking me. 'Do the elders of Cumberland give a man leave to sleep in Meeting, Friend? But thee has travelled far, and may be forgiven. Come with me, and we shall see what we can do for thee.'

CHAPTER 6

THE NEXT MORNING I WAS SITTING OUTSIDE AMOS Armitage's cabin, scraping the mud off my boots, and thinking about what Amos had said to me at breakfast. He'd been frank about what he saw as the futility of my errand. Rachel was disowned, he said, and therefore out of the care of any Meeting. He respected my concern, however, and even advised me on ways and means. 'But thee needn't go back to Montreal. Thee's already halfway to Mackinac. We know traders who use this road who could help thee on thy way.' I explained about William Mackenzie, and the importance of following up my contacts in the North West Company. He said that the North West Company was concerned only with matters of worldly concern, and it behoved a Friend to keep apart from their militant practices. I tried to make him understand why I must follow the way that the Lord had opened up before me, and in the end I more or less prevailed with him.

He returned just as I was lacing up my damp boots. A young woman was with him. Her grey hood was thrown back. Thick red curls had escaped from under her cap, and stood up like a halo all around her face. I realised I was staring, and I looked down; her plain dress proclaimed her a modest Quaker maid, but the adornments we are born with we must live with as we may, and none can blame us for that.

'This is my niece Clemency Armitage,' Amos said to me. 'She and my nephew Thomas are offering to give thee lodging for the winter.'

Clemency Armitage looked directly at me, and I saw that her cheeks and forehead were pitted with pockmarks; otherwise she'd have been pretty. She said to me, 'Welcome to Yonge Street, Friend. Thy aunt Judith Scott stayed a winter in our house. Thee's very welcome to do the same.'

'This is exceeding kind of thee,' I said.

'We're glad to have thee. Thomas does more than one man's work, and thee looks to be a strong fellow. It would be helpful if thee came with me now, for I have to take the bull back with me.'

I liked her plain speaking, and I was glad to be useful. Since the day I'd boarded the *Jane* I'd too often felt out of my depth, a useless encumbrance to the working men around me. The bull was docile but ill to lead. Clemency Armitage lacked the weight to make him shift, so I led him by the nose, while she urged him with a switch to his flank, which to be honest I think he never noticed. Once we were away from the farm and walking through open fields, the bull walked quietly. I took covert stock of my companion. When we'd met I'd noticed how pale her face was against her fiery hair, but now her scarred cheeks were scarlet after our tussle with the bull. I kept my eyes away from her, and took note of the country. The trees were beginning to turn gold beyond the stubble fields, and the sky was eggshell blue above the wreathing ground mists.

Presently Clemency opened a gate, a simple affair of a loose pole in the rail fence. 'Now we're on our lot,' she told me.

We could walk side by side here across the stubble, which made it possible to converse.

'I see thee had wheat in this field?'

'Yes. We've been growing wheat four years now – second time in this field.'

'Thee's not been here long, then?' I asked. (There have been Greenhows at Highside upwards of three hundred years, they say.)

She counted on her fingers, which made me smile. 'Seven years. The first year we hadn't cleared enough stumps for grain, so we just grew turnips and potatoes.' She kept glancing at me, quite discreetly, but I was much aware of it. 'We bought our first cow, what, four – five – years ago? Obadiah Rogers lends us this fellow' – she slapped the bull on the shoulder. 'We have six cows now, and a fine heifer this year. Thee's a farmer, Friend?'

'Ay.' That sounded over-short, so I added, 'No wheat. We're a hill farm: mainly sheep. A small herd of cattle. We grow a few oats, enough potatoes and hay, and nowadays turnips for winter feed as well. I was noticing the fine turnips here.'

'So thy farm is not like this?'

'No.' I was struggling with a mass of tangled thoughts; this place seemed so alien, so far from anything I knew. And yet things were the same – the great beast that walked between us had the same smell as cattle anywhere, and the tang of the bare fields, the colour of the autumn sky – seemed achingly familiar. I surprised myself by trying to explain to her, which was a thing words could not do, and inside myself I knew it. 'The land here is so flat. Once thee cuts the forest and drains the marsh thee could cultivate every yard of it, I reckon. The sky is so big, but thee can't see out. There's no height of land; there's no rock. Thee can look straight across all thy lands at once, up to the edge of the forest over there, but then – nothing.'

'Thee means "but then – Indian country", Friend. That's the frontier. Thee is standing on the last farm in Upper Canada, thee should know!'

'Are there Indians close by?'

'We've just one family here now. Thee'll be seeing them. They're Mississaugas; their summer village is a few miles further north, by Lake Simcoe. The villages all scatter in winter: each household has its own hunting grounds. If they didn't spread out across the land in winter they'd starve. In winter our Mississauga friends are as close neighbours on the one hand as my uncle Amos is on the other.'

I was startled to think that the Indians were so close. Clemency said they were good neighbours, because they knew well that Friends came in peace. She'd learned a lot from them, she told me, about the wild plants of the forest, and how to use them for medicines, flavourings and so forth. 'When we arrived here,' she told me, 'they came out of the woods with meat for us when we were building our first cabin – that's the byre now – and they watched us fell the first trees when we made our garden.'

'So thee didn't grow up in Upper Canada?'

'Indeed not. I'm an American.'

'But thee's settled . . . thee's British now?'

She shrugged. 'We are Friends.' She let me ponder that, and then she added, 'We recognise no quarrel with any nation. We're American citizens – or so we always thought. We left our families behind over the border, and we're fearing now that we'll never see them more. This is our farm. It cost us dear enough; Thomas would never leave it now.'

I could see a low-pitched log cabin a little way ahead. Smoke blew from the chimney, and I caught the sweet tang of woodsmoke on the air. There was a byre, and a couple of sheds. The garth between was churned to thick mud. Chickens foraged in the ruts; as we approached the cockerel ruffled his fine feathers and announced us with a rousing cock-a-doodle-doo.

'The bull goes in the home field with the cows. I'll open the gate, if thee can let him loose.'

The bull wandered off, snorting, and I fell into step beside her again, coiling the tether neatly as I walked. 'Do thee and thy husband farm this land alone?'

'I have no husband, Friend.'

'I'm sorry.' I blushed like a lass in my embarrassment, but she wasn't looking my way. 'Thee, and thy uncle too, spoke of "Thomas", and I thought . . .'

'Thomas is my brother. Thee'll meet my good-sister Sarah in a moment. Come in!'

The cabin was more spacious within than it looked to be from the outside. It greeted me with a rush of warmth and the combined scents of woodsmoke and new bread. A fire glowed in a huge stone hearth; in the fire there was a bake-kettle with embers banked up round it. The kitchen floor was packed earth, swept very clean, with a rag rug by the hearth. The table was on the right of the door, by a window cut in the wall, so one might peer through the thick glass and see who was coming along the track, even as one sat at meat. There was a spinning wheel in the corner, where the spinner might get the light from the other window, and a dresser piled with crockery against the wall. Above my head were rough-cut rafters where hams of dried meat hung above the hearth, and bunches of herbs and onions. A further door stood half open. I could see a section of board floor; there was a ladder against the partition wall, and a curtained bed place above the inner room.

'Sarah! Is thee there?'

'Here,' came a voice from the bedroom. Sarah, when she emerged, greeted me in a friendly manner. She was little, plump and brown and freckled, and reminded me of a speckledy hen we had at home that used to come in and sit by the hearth. My mother's opinion was that the creature, showing more imagination than most of her kind, thought that she was really a cat. When I got to know Thomas I understood why he had chosen Sarah, for I found him to be an easygoing fellow, who valued comfort at his hearth and snugness in his bed more than vast intelligence or vivacity or argumentation. Whiles I see his point, for all that I made such a very different choice.

It was certainly a more primitive way of life than any I had known, and yet at Highside we live simply enough. The very byre at Yonge Street had started out as a cabin for a family of six – Clemency told me it took but a week to build, for everyone in Yonge Street came to help – and there must have been barely room for all to lie down at night. The new cabin seemed small enough to me, even though there were only the four of us. I had a shakedown by the kitchen fire, and as the winter wore on I was glad to be so close to the warmth, for the floor was draughty. In the end I stayed with them right through till the end of Third Month.

It was a house of deep mourning, as I soon discovered. The typhus had raged through the new settlement two years before, and four of the family had died in it. Thomas and Clemency had lost both their parents and their two sisters within the space of a month. In the face of such loss I knew not what to say, but that my prayers were with them, and they seemed content with that. I was of practical help to them. It was useful to have another man about the place in winter. There were logs to haul and cut, ice to break and water to fetch from under it, and cattle in the byre to feed and water. We did some building work making cattle stalls in one of the outhouses. Thomas and I took the sled on wood trips, and set traps, which sometimes brought us rabbits, and sundry small animals that were strange to me, for the pot. The Armitages were a family long skilled in carpentry, and they'd learned woodland skills as well from their Indian neighbours. I learned a great deal that winter which stood me in good stead.

The forest lapped at the edge of the fields, shut out only by a post and rail fence. On our first night of snow Clemency gave me a bearskin to cover me. I exclaimed at the size and thickness of it.

'It's not as big as some,' said Clemency. 'Thomas shot that one in our own oatfield last year. By harvest time there were two or three of them coming in and helping themselves every evening. He shot this one, and the other two haven't been back.'

'In thy own *field*? But . . . is that not dangerous? Is thee safe in the woods?'

'Nowhere on earth is safe, Friend. But as for bears – they don't usually attack. If thee makes enough noise they keep out of thy way. I met one once when I was picking blueberries. We were both so busy getting our berries that neither of us noticed the other. I think the bear got as big a shock as I did. I just shouted as loud as I could and it went off.'

'Was thee not feart?

'Frightened? Of course I was frightened! But it's true, they hardly ever attack people.'

'And if they do?'

'Then they kill. Thee can't run or climb faster than a bear. If thee keeps still, and prays to God for mercy, then perhaps the bear won't eat thee. But then again, perhaps it will.'

As it got colder, I was glad to roll myself up in my bearskin every night, and glad, too, to think that any lurking bears in the forest were sleeping deeply until springtime. I slept pretty well myself. The brown-black fur was thick and coarse, but surprisingly soft against my shirt. I could have done with a hide like that in daytime. Never had I known such cold. There were days when the heat from the fire seemed to be killed stone dead while the logs yet blazed in front of us. Clemency sewed me a deerskin tunic and a foxfur cap to wear outdoors, and I missed the warmth of them sorely when I had to dress suitably for Meeting. I'd sit on my bench at the back of the Meeting House while the cold came creeping in around the doors and windows, trickling through to my skin wherever it could. The snow fell early, and sometimes it lay right up to the eaves of our cabin. I could in no way walk in it, but Thomas helped me make a pair of snowshoes like the ones they all had. We made the round frames by steaming stems of ash, then I wove the centre part with rawhide, as Clemency showed me, and fixed leather straps to tie them to my boots. I was pleased with my handiwork, but the first time I set out on them I could do nothing but trip over my own feet and fall headlong. It was a day of fine powdery snow, and the sun shone on us in long yellow slanting beams as we chased one another about the clean white yard. I was honestly trying, but my antics made Clemency laugh so hard the tears fell into her shawl and froze there. Then I did get the hang of it, and Thomas ran before me throwing snowballs, which I threw back, and fell again, and caught him, and then we fell together, rolling over and over while the fine snow stuck to us.

Times we were serious enough, and the work got done too. In Twelfth Month Clemency told me what all three of them had known a month or more, which was that her good-sister was in the family way, and of a sickly sort. So more work fell to Clemency after that, while

Thomas and I laboured outside. One icy morning there was a thick layer of ice on the snow, so that every footstep I made knocked a round hole with a loud crunching noise. Days like that it was so freezing clear that one could hear the blow of an axe from nearly a mile away at Amos's cabin. Sometimes there was a sound like a shot from the woods, but they said it was but a branch breaking, or a whole tree splitting apart just from the coldness of it.

Amos was not our nearest neighbour. I'd only been at the farm a few days when the Indian family who were wintering in the forest, a bare mile from our door, came to visit us. We were still sitting at our midday meat, when the door was flung open, and a tall brown-skinned man in fringed deerskins strode in, followed by an old woman and a younger one. The young woman carried a child on her back, and two more children hung back in the doorway and watched us warily, until they took courage and crept up to the table. The tall man roughly pulled out the end of my bench, so I nearly went flying, and sat down next to me without a word.

'Good day, friend,' said Thomas, apparently not startled in the least. 'Is there more broth, Sarah? Bring a bowl for our friend Mesquacosy. And for his family too.'

Mesquacosy's wife and mother-in-law – for so I later discovered them to be – would not sit with us, but took their portions of broth outside into the cold yard. Presently they came in again with the empty bowls, and began to wander about the place, picking up sundry items and exclaiming to each other in their own language. Meanwhile the children eagerly accepted the morsels of food that Clemency picked out for them, crowding up against her chair, and fairly snatching tid-bits of meat and cheese from her hands. When I addressed them directly they looked down shyly and would not, or could not, answer me. The family stayed about an hour and then left as suddenly as they had come, without a word. They left behind five freshly cured rabbitskins and a big bunch of sage which Clemency hung from the rafters. When I went out to the byre that evening to water the beasts I saw the prints of different-sized snowshoes leading away into the darkness of the trees, and I pondered on the strangeness of my new life.

The Indians came again several times after that, and some weeks later, when I was proficient enough on my new snowshoes, Clemency took me with her to their lodge. She kept some of our milk each day (for Clemency had charge of the dairying) for the little boy. The Indians use no milk, but when they saw cow's milk had not the disagreeable effects of other foods upon the little fellow, they were glad to take it. Clemency said this was good, because she and Thomas owed the Indians many favours for their help in past days.

At first the round Indian lodge seemed quite alien, but as I had leisure to look about I saw many things were the same as in our cabin – the dried meat and herbs hanging from the roof, the musket, axe and snowshoes by the door, the iron kettle of stew simmering over the fire. We sat on furs draped over fresh pine boughs. Mesquacosy totally ignored Clemency, but presently passed his long pipe across to me. I don't use tobacco, but in this case I read more into it, so I puffed cautiously, and stifled my coughing as best I could. He seemed pleased with that. We sat in silence, while the women were sorting some herbs on the other side of the fire, using a strange mix of tongues I did not try to follow. Presently my host spoke. I shook my head, uncomprehending. He pointed to the doorway, and spoke again. Then, with less patience, he gave me but one word: *peboon* – *peboon*.

'He says, "It's a hard winter,"' said Clemency, without looking up.

'Ay,' I said. 'It's a hard winter.'

That was the sum of our conversation, but when Clemency finally rolled the herbs she'd been given into a cloth, and stood up to go, I felt content. With most of my neighbours in Mungrisdale the talk would have been much the same. I often remembered this peaceful Indian family in the woods in after days. They had little; some years they come close to starvation, but they have an ease in their own surroundings which perhaps we have lost in our more civilised condition.

It was our custom in the evening for Thomas or I to read aloud while the women took up their work. We had read and talked over the Advices and Queries from Philadelphia (which were much the same as our own Advices and Queries from London Yearly Meeting). We also read over passages from the scriptures (mainly, by common consent, from the New Testament) and Fox's *Journal*, which was all the books they had in the house. I borrowed Woolman's *Journal* from David Willson, for it spoke to my own condition, and I was glad to share the goodness I had got from it before. Twice a copy of the *Upper Canada Gazette* came to us on its way round the community. Amidst its advices to farmers, it brought a page of news of Europe, notably the progress of the war in the Peninsula. I would have been discouraged from reading this at home, but in Upper Canada it felt like a link with my own country, however tenuous, even though I noticed the piece was reprinted from an American newspaper.

In Second Month Amos went down to York, and brought back a letter for Clemency from my Aunt Judith. Clemency read it to us while Thomas sat at the table patching one of his boots, and I sat whittling a porringer, for the one they had was too small to be useful, or so it seemed to me.

Philadelphia
15th day of Eleventh Month, 1811

To my dear Friend and Companion in Christ, Clemency,

When I received thy letter telling me the Lord had brought thee safe home to Yonge Street I was thankful indeed. These are troublous times, and we know not what is to come. These many years we in Great Britain have lived in the shadow of unceasing strife. Even the free Republican government enjoyed by thy own United States was born out of a calamitous and bloody war where outward weapons were used by brother against brother, citizen against citizen, friend against friend. I had thought, though, that on the uninhabited frontier where the world is yet new the Kingdom of Peace, as our Friend William Penn first envisaged it, might yet be possible.

29th Day of Eleventh Month.

News is now come of a terrible battle in the North West Territory fought on the seventh day of this same month, at a river called Tippecanoe, between a prophet of the Shawnee tribe and the governor of the Indiana Territory, one Henry Harrison. I had thought to minister this spring to our Friends at the settlement in the North West, as thee and I wished before, but Friends tell me that it is out of the question. What is worse, Friends say that it would also be unwise to approach the border between the United States and Upper Canada in the present state of unrest. And these same Friends said to me a year ago, 'The only border we acknowledge is that made by solemn treaty with the Indians, between the settled areas of the east, and the hunting territories of the Indians in the far west.' Now it seems that the United States government decrees this border between settler and Indian shall stand no more, and yet on that border which lies between brother and brother, citizen and citizen, friend and friend, across the Great Lakes, there is to be a great gulf fixed as if thee and I, and hundreds of others bound by similar ties of Friendship, unity and kinship, must be summarily separated by strife and bloody war.

With the clamour of such calamitous events around me, I find myself troubled in spirit, even in our gathered Meeting for Worship here in Philadelphia. I am thinking of returning home, but the journey seems a grievous trial (I suffer much at sea) without my first Companion, who was with me before thee, my niece Rachel. She and I set out together – is it only three years ago? – both filled with zeal for the Lord's purpose, seeing always before us our Concern to bring the Comfort of our Ministry in the Lord to our Friends in the New World, and now it is come to this. When I return I must face her mother, my sister Susan. This cannot be put off much longer.

I have long held to the belief that Man is in his essence good, and that any can discover the Light Within. Yet now – can it be possible? – it seems to me to be possible – that His Kingdom may not come, for all the years that may be left to our race on earth. His will may perhaps <u>not</u> be done on earth as it is in heaven. These are terrible thoughts, dear Friend, and perhaps I should not write them to thee. But the paper is good, and I have no more of it if I were to wantonly destroy this one sheet that I have. Were I to do so, thee would have no letter. So let it stand.

In Friendship, and in the bountiful mercy of the Lord to thee and thine,
    Judith Scott

We sat in silence for a time after Clemency finished reading. Sarah said, 'I don't think all this travelling is a good idea; it unsettles people.'

'My heart grieves for Judith,' said Clemency.

'It looks as if thee won't be seeing thy aunt here, then,' said Thomas. 'Does that upset thy plans at all?'

'No,' I said, thinking out loud. 'My mother wrote to Judith to say I was on my way here, but she seems not to have got the letter. I'll go back to Montreal in the spring and see what William Mackenzie's arranged for me.'

'But Amos is right,' said Thomas. 'Thee could go by Georgian Bay and be there sooner.'

'And lose track of Alan Mackenzie again? No, I'll keep my appointment.'

'We'll miss thee sorely,' said Sarah, laying her hands on the bulge under her pinafore, as she often did these days. 'Thee'll miss seeing the little one.'

It would have been unkind to say that I had no mind to be in that small cabin during her confinement, nor to be kept awake by the wailing of an infant all night long[1]. So I kept silent, and so did Clemency, when Sarah and Thomas were saying how much they would miss me when the winter was over, and I had gone away.

---

[1] Indeed, I could not have imagined those sleepless nights with a newborn child to be any worse than they really are.

CHAPTER 7

ON FIRST DAYS AND FOURTH DAYS WE WENT TO Meeting. I found the Meeting House harmonious and filled with Light. The lot had been planted with maple saplings, which divided the Meeting garth from the graveyard. Clemency told me that Judith and Rachel had been there for the tree planting. Judith had ministered about the trees representing the slow growth of peace, being planted, as they were, in a world full of war. Elders expressed concern about the notion of representation, and there had been some little difficulty about that. I caused no such anxiety, for I kept silent in Meeting, and to a large extent without. At Meeting I kept to the place at the back I'd taken on the first evening. Sometimes I used to gaze out of the windows at the line of trees beyond the fields where the unclaimed forest began. When I shut my eyes I'd still see the windows burning green inside my head. There were six plain frame windows (for on First Days the partition between the men's and women's Meeting was drawn up). Each window divided the wilderness into fifteen squares, nine on the lower sash, six on the upper sash, shaped just like the lots into which the land was divided, very square and neat.

On the First Day after my arrival David Willson had

invited me to his house, which lay about five miles east of the Meeting House. He lived in a cabin like the other Friends, but he and his wife had made more of a parlour, with a kitchen behind. David Willson's room had a shelf of theological works in it, and a writing desk and chair. He asked me what I'd thought about the Ministry the first evening I was among them. I'm used to being asked what sense I have of a Meeting, but I never find it an easy question.

'I don't know,' I said. 'I'd never been so long away from Friends as I had that day. I was glad to hear our testimonies – 'twas like coming home.'

'Our testimony of Peace. The Kingdom of Peace.' We were silent for a while. 'What does thee think, Mark? Thee's seen enough of the world in thy travels. Did thee find peace?'

I thought about it for a bit. 'No.'

'*The way of peace they know not, and there is no judgement in their goings.* No, there is no peace in the great world. Where then is our Lord's Kingdom of Peace to be established, Mark? What thinks thee?'

'I know not.' I was about to say that in my own Meeting I was at peace, but then I thought about Joseph Peat, and the bill for the repairs to the roof at Gillfoot Meeting House, which still leaked. I thought about my parents, but then Rachel came into that picture, and the image of peace vanished, as the upside-down hills vanish from a lake when the waters ripple. 'Nowhere on this earth, I think.'

'*We looked for peace and there is no good, and for the time of healing, and beheld trouble.*'

I began to feel indignant. I'd been feeling quite cheerful before we sat down. 'Just now I'm living in a house where there has been trouble and great sorrow,' I said. 'And yet Clemency and Thomas bring peace and healing into that. I think that's as much as anyone can do.'

'And this is why I wished to speak with thee! For now I see clearly that the Ministry that night thee came did indeed speak to thy condition. If the Kingdom of Peace is ever to come on earth, will it not be as a second Eden in the Wilderness? Will it not be in a place far removed from the fightings and wars of the outward world? For are we not a people already set apart, because we have a great work to do in the world?'

'Our fore-elders did a great work,' I said. 'I don't know about now.'

'For ye shall go out with joy, and be led forth with peace: the mountains and the hills shall break forth before ye into singing, and all the trees of the field shall clap their hands.

Instead of the thorn shall come up the fir tree, and instead of the briar shall come up the myrtle tree, and it shall be to the Lord for a name, for an everlasting sign that shall not be cut off.'

When he finished speaking, silence rolled in like the tide, and I let it take me.

'So what does thee think, Friend?' said David Willson at last.

'I was thinking how Daniel Priestman, when he ministers in our Meeting, reminds us that Judaea is a mountainous country just like our own Lakeland, and how thee can tell that very often from the scriptures.' It occurred to me that this wasn't what David Willson wished to hear,[1] although it was the truthful answer to his question. Trying to offer him something relevant, I said – but again it was the wrong reply – 'I don't see the Kingdom of God being quite as flat as Upper Canada.'

Two days later the elders Joseph Doan and Amos

---

[1] Nor was it always what Mosedale elders wished to hear, fifteen minutes into Meeting for Worship every single week, though it didn't trouble me. I believe from sundry remarks my father let fall to my mother, that Daniel Priestman was several times eldered for his repetitions, but to no avail. A kinder man there could not be. He died in '14. I was home in time to attend the Meeting for his funeral.

Armitage came to visit me, partly to accept me into Yonge Street Meeting for as long as I chose to stay, but partly to warn me that David Willson had already been disciplined more than once for his prophetic ministries, and that perhaps I should not allow myself to be led too far. Later I asked Clemency for her opinion. She laughed, and said it was naught to trouble myself over; a prophet seldom had honour in his own country.

'Thee thinks David Willson is a prophet?'

If Clemency ever sat down that winter, it was at her spinning. When the four of us gathered by the fireside in the evening, it was always to the whirr and hum of her spinning wheel. They made their own flax (though not their wool), which seemed to me a marvel of industry.[2] Clemency watched the thread running under her finger as she answered my question, 'I know not. Thy sister Rachel had much discourse with David. The trouble is, he's ministered in Meeting – and this more than once – saying that outward religion, even the Bible itself, speaks not to his condition. Thee can imagine what Friends think of that.'

'But he quoted Isaiah to me!'

'Oh yes, he quotes Isaiah. In no wise does he ignore scripture altogether. Only he says there is no true enlightenment but from the Light that burns within. And this light need have no words to it – it need not resort to any outward scripture – but if it truly burns it will make such a conflagration in the heart it will light every man that comes near to it. And this will be the light of the Kingdom of Peace, in which the days of our innocence will be restored.'

---

[2] My mother always bought linen already made up from Keswick, and my wife now does the same. We sell nearly all our wool at market – it would be a labour beyond all the wise virgins together to spin it all at home – though my wife keeps back what is needful for ourselves. She would take the best, and I would keep only the worst, and she it is that prevails. I have ever a good woollen coat to my back, and my sons the same.

'And we won't have to worry about the price of corn either?'

She chuckled. 'Thee sounds like uncle Amos. But I do wonder – thy sister Rachel listened much to David Willson. She used to repeat his words, saying that outward forms meant nothing, and that we minded too much the petty regulations of our Society. She started reading Leviticus to me – the lists of rules for the Israelites in the desert – and I had to laugh with her. She said surely all rulings concerning temporal matters had their time and place, and once they were outmoded – outgrown, rather – they served only to conceal the true Light, which lighteth every man coming into the world, and so we had not to listen to disciplines from without, but take counsel only with the promptings of our own hearts.'

She looked to see if I had understood the import of her words, and nodded at me. 'Thee sees, doesn't thee?'

'If I were not a Friend I would strangle this man! How many young maids has he talked to in this manner?'

'It's true that women seem to like him well. Some women, I should say. Our women's Meeting too has been much divided. Me, I just think there's enough to worry about. Sometimes I think, well, we've had War, Famine and Pestilence. Must we also be troubled by Specious Controversy?' She grinned suddenly, and I smiled too. 'I shouldn't have said that! Levity is my worst sin!' Her remorse startled me; it was quite genuine. Sometimes I found her lightning changes of mood unrestful. 'I'm serious, Mark. I've been disciplined for it often enough – oh, all my life. Mother would be disappointed in me still. I had a cousin in Catawissa – she and I . . . oh, sometimes in Meeting when we were younger, we would catch one another's eye, and . . . She it was that died of smallpox. Levity is an evil thing, Mark. I pray every day for deliverance from it.'

'It would be a sad world if thee found naught in it to laugh at.'

'I've laughed too much, Friend. God knows, I've been punished for it, and the temptation besets me yet. But Rachel . . .' Her voice trailed away.

'Please,' I said after a moment or two. 'Tell me about Rachel.'

'She was the best friend I ever had.' Her vehemence surprised me. 'I hadn't had a friend – a real friend – since I left Catawissa. I'd never had time to go exploring either, but when Rachel asked, we were allowed whole days by ourselves – on my own I'd never have been allowed. There are Indian paths all over the forest – oh, some days we went miles. It was fall, and we used to come home with full baskets. I guess that's why no one said we were being idle. Mesquacosy's people showed us good places, and what plants and berries to pick. I could talk to them a little, but Rachel was determined to learn their language properly, because she had a concern to minister to the Indians in the west. Somehow she didn't pick up the words as easily as I did. She used to get really frustrated about it, but when we were alone we'd practise saying Indian words together. And we'd talk – we always found plenty to talk about.' She paused, and said abruptly. 'Rachel's very honest. She's about the most honest person I ever met.'

'Did she . . .' I hesitated. 'Did she ever talk about marriage . . . I mean about our Society's testimony on marriage?'

'Thee means, had she any notion of marrying out of the Society back then?' Clemency suddenly stopped being serious and grinned at me, in a way that I would have thought, if I hadn't known her for a modest maid, to be entirely mischievous. 'Maybe thee would be shocked, Friend, to know how maids talk among themselves about such matters. I wouldn't be the one to tell thee!'

I was left with much food for thought. Clemency had known Rachel, as only a woman can know another of her sex. They had shared this hearth, this table. They had slept at night in Clemency's bedloft. Rachel had stayed in this very house, at a time – barely two years ago – when it was filled by a whole family of Armitages, now gone. Clemency's bedloft was separated from the kitchen only by a thin partition and a curtain for a door. Sometimes she wept bitterly in the night, and though the sobs were always stifled I could not help but hear. (It was the same with Thomas and Sarah, but with them it wasn't weeping that I heard). Long hours at night I lay on my pallet by the banked-up fire and thought of how Clemency must feel: what it would be like if I were alone at Highside, while all my family lay in the graveyard at Mosedale.[3]

Thomas and Sarah used to go to bed soon after dusk fell – they were but recently wed, after all – and Clemency and I would talk until long after the tallow dip was burnt out and Clemency had to lay aside her work. We sat at the hearth, and the fire brought out its own colours twice

[3] Of course, my parents do now lie there, but though it was great sorrow at the time, they died in the fullness of years, both having achieved their threescore years and ten plus several years withal, for we Greenhows – and Bristos too – are a tough stock. My great great aunt Agnes Bristo was a hundred and two when she died at Mosedale in my third year, and by no means dwining till the day she died. She never missed Meeting for Worship: she lived less than a quarter of a mile from the Meeting House, and seemingly she often used to tell the children the story of the building of it, which was done when she was a lass fourteen years old. They say she liked to dandle me upon her knee, and indeed I have the faintest recollection of an ancient, dried-up woman who sat rocking, rocking in her chair by the hearth, and of a rag rug at her feet. In my infant mind she had something to do with the Old Testament, but that I cannot now explain. My memory may not be the exact truth. Sometimes we seem to remember what others choose that we should – my mother much desired that I should remember Aunt Agnes, and so I did – but memory itself is a fickle, unreliable will o' the wisp of a creature (not that I place any credence in the phantoms of idle superstition) and can in no way be relied upon as the instrument of Reason or Veracity.

over as it shone on Clemency's hair. In the morning she would come down her ladder all neatly dressed, her curls stowed away under her cap, but there was no mirror in the place, and by evening the cap was all awry, and her wild hair would be standing out all over her head again, like a cloud of flame. One evening late in Twelfth Month we talked about my aunt Judith.

'When I was a little lad I mind Judith coming back from her first travels,' I told her. 'She'd been to Yorkshire and Lincolnshire and Norfolk and Cambridgeshire. I remember reciting the names to myself like a chant inside my head. Years later I saw an atlas in Thomas Wilkinson's house, and he showed me the map of the Counties of England. We hadn't any maps at home. I minded about not knowing clearly where places were, but I'd never seen a map. I didn't know until Thomas Wilkinson showed me his atlas what it was I'd been wanting.

'Judith went all the way to London, I remember, to get a Travelling Minute from the Morning Meeting, to go among Friends in Scotland. We heard that folk there were much tendered by her testimony. I don't think she made any impression on Rachel, though, till she came back from Ireland in '04. That's when aunt Judith came and ministered about the plight of the poor peasantry in Ireland, who – what did she say? It was all written down in the Minute – I mind it now – "lived worse than our English pigs, and in place of an equal society and true religion were enthralled to the stinking corpse of a tyrannous dispensation." Anyway, Rachel's heart was stirred and she wept aloud in Meeting for Worship. I heard her sniffing from right across the room. I was amazed; my sister wasn't the weeping sort.'

'Maybe it's easier for me than for thee to guess what was happening to her. Oh, I don't mean I have more sensibility; I mean thee isn't like a girl in any way.'

'I hope not!'

'I'm sure thee does. Did Rachel and thee talk about it afterwards?'

I tried to find words for Clemency; she was a good listener. Under her questioning I could remember it all very clearly.

'The point is,' Rachel had said to me after that memorable Meeting, 'that Judith knows the Light within exists for everybody. They don't have to know the Bible. They don't have to have heard of Jesus Christ. It makes it fair, doesn't thee understand? It's not fair if thee can only find the truth from the scriptures. What if thee is a poor peasant in Ireland who never learned to read and only has the chance to believe what a hireling priest says to thee? Or what if thee's an Indian savage on the other side of the world? It's no good saying a poor heathen who can't know any better can never enter into Christ's Kingdom. The Kingdom is a real place even if thee hasn't heard of it.'

'I never said anyone couldn't enter anything.' I was annoyed. We were sitting on the sill of the hayloft, the sun full in our faces. I was trying to whittle four wooden rings inside each other, so they would hang together in a chain. I'd made a few with two links, but four was much harder and it wasn't going right. I wished Rachel would leave this kind of talk alone. It was all right as a murmuring background to the real business of life, like hearing the beck flowing past the house, always telling the state of the ground and the weather without me really having to listen to it. But I didn't want to be thrown into the current and have to swim. Moreover, I thought Rachel was showing a typically womanish lack of logic. 'But if the True Light is there to light every man who comes into the world anyway, why bother with all this travelling? Thee can find God's Light within, without being told, whether thee be a wild Indian or a statesman in Mungrisdale. So why can't thee just be left in peace, wherever thee is, without aunt Judith coming to rant at thee?'

She wanted to argue with me, but I jumped down from the hayloft, knowing she wouldn't follow because it was too high for her. To tell the truth, it jarred my bones when I did it, but it gave me back my three years' advantage over her as bandying words could not. I wandered away along the track, kicking stones as I went. I'd never paid much heed to Rachel, but I was used to her. Then suddenly, about two years previously, she had shot up almost as tall as I was, and once her face was on a level with mine she seemed to dispute everything I said. If I tried to argue she would cast up her eyes as if she thought me stupid, and that made me mad. Yet she wouldn't leave me alone. The day she said she'd tell our mother that my cousin John Bristo had taken me to a wrestling match I slapped her face, and she grat. My father spoke to me seriously, saying I was nearly a man grown, and that it ill behoved me to lay violent hands on any, but least of all a young maid, and she my own sister. I couldn't explain to him how her words maddened me, buzzing round my head like midges at milking time. After that things had quietened down. I grew taller than Rachel again, being almost six foot before my eighteenth birthday. I began to be less canaptious with her too, until aunt Judith came back the next time.

I had no words to tell all this to Clemency, but I did say that since Rachel had taken on Judith's enthusiasm, I'd found her much more irritating. 'But then,' I said, 'I never felt the least call to minister. I've never stood up in Meeting, and I don't reckon to either. Rachel's different: the very next First Day after Judith left us in '04, my sister began in ministry. She said the same thing as she'd said to me that day in the hayloft: that the Light within is the gift of all, wherever and whoever they may be, whether they know our Lord Jesus Christ or not. And that makes every man a brother in Christ, whether he be a naked savage in the wilderness or in thrall to a hireling priesthood in a benighted neighbour land. She didn't speak for long, but Friends were much moved by her testimony, even in Mosedale.'[4]

'And was thee moved?'

'No.' That was true, so far as it went. Rachel was never a Friend in Meeting to me. She was just my sister. She had a concern to travel even before Judith came back from Ireland the second time – that would have been in the winter of '07 – and asked Rachel, young as she was, to be her companion in America. But – I said to Clemency, 'Thee may think me very wrong in this' – I knew too much about Rachel to be convinced. I knew she'd never been content in all her life. She always had to be doing, always wanted something different, which she could not find at

---

[4] These days men seem to find much to say in Meeting. We had less ministry when I was a boy; more often than not our worship was entirely silent. I used to find First Day mornings very hard in summer time, when Blencathra was clear of cloud and lay wide open with the whole depth of the blue sky above it. I would sit in Meeting with the sun streaming in at the window on my right hand, and watch the shaft of sunlight on the flagged floor at my feet, as it moved – oh so slowly – from the crack between two flagstones and across the grey stone to the next line. (I have sat on the elders' bench these many years, but I am occasionally aware, even today, how far the sun has travelled in its morning journey across the cracks in the floor. I have observed it for fifty years; I know the time it tells to the very minute.) Long before I could tell the hour, however, I remember looking at the golden line crossing the floor beneath my dangling boots, when my legs were still too short for my feet to touch the floor. Our benches have no backs, and it was very hard, perched at the end of the row, not to fall off when I grew sleepy. One hour, an hour and a half ... I would watch under my half-closed lids to see if the elders were anywhere near shaking hands, and there they would be, immoveable as the currock of grey stones atop Carrick Fell above us. So when aunt Judith descended upon us, in a way I was grateful for the diversion. Even as a child I was aware of a certain resistance in the silence into which her words would fall. I had a notion that the seeds landed not in fruitful soil, or even on stony ground, nor among the choking tares, but that somehow they were falling and falling down a deep dark well and meeting nothing.

home and we could not give. Of course she wanted to get away. In the Society she had her opportunity, because in the ministry travel and adventure is a possibility, even for a young country maid.

Clemency read me more shrewdly than I expected. 'Thee's not impressed by women travelling in the ministry, is thee, Mark?' she said.

'I'm sure that many are called to do great work abroad, men and women both,' I knew I sounded stiffer than I meant, and I didn't like myself.

'But thee finds it hard to believe of thy own sister, perhaps? Can I tell thee how it was with me, when I was companion to Judith Scott?'

'I wish thee would.'

I must have sounded more friendly, for Clemency smiled on me. She laid down her work – for the tallow dip was just beginning to gutter – and came to sit facing me, her hands loosely clasped on the table in front of her.

'I knew I could not replace thy sister in Judith's heart . . .'

I interrupted her. 'Did thee talk to Rachel? Did thee know her mind, before she and Judith went westward?'

'I will tell thee all I can, from the time they first came among us.' Clemency paused, collecting her thoughts. 'They came to Upper Canada from our Friends in Phila-delphia Meeting. I grew up under the care of that Meeting – I was born in Catawissa, on the Susquehanna River – so Rachel had met my relations and Friends from our old Meeting. Judith and Rachel arrived here late one afternoon near the end of Tenth Month – this would have been in '08, I suppose. They came first to uncle Amos's workshop. He was drawing the plans for the new Meeting House. Judith was excited when she saw that. She and Rachel stayed with us – we'd just finished building this house – until the spring. They were there when we dug the first trench for the Meeting House. Nearly everyone came to Meeting that day. Then Judith and Rachel set off north along Yonge Street. When Judith came back the new Meeting House was built.

'When they arrived I wanted to hear everything about my family back in Catawissa. I wish – don't thee tell Thomas this, or anyone else either – I wish uncle Amos had never persuaded us to leave. It fair broke my father's heart clearing the forest here. It had to be done so fast. A farmer doesn't get his title unless he's got five acres ready for cultivation within a year, and built a cabin at least sixteen by twenty feet – that's the byre now – and made a road thirty-three feet wide the whole length of the lot. Friends manage it better than most, because the whole Meeting helps, but even so . . .

'The thing was there was no land for us in Pennsylvania. It was my grandfather's farm, and there were five brothers . . . Also, my mother had been arrested for speaking against slavery in the market place. Bad things happened to us. One night someone put out the eyes of our draught horse. Thomas found him sightless and bleeding the next morning. Uncle Amos had a letter from Timothy Rogers, who founded this Meeting. Timothy said we should make a new land that would flow with milk and honey in the northern wilderness. It seemed to us that the hand of the Lord was in that letter, guiding us into a new land, a place where we might find peace.

'I was sixteen, Mark. I'd lived all my life on the bank of the Susquehanna. At home, when I lay in bed at night I used to hear the river. Thomas and I knew all the boats. We had our cousins to play with, and the other children in Meeting. In Upper Canada we seem to be such a little part of the world, such a small peculiar people. Back in Pennsylvania it was not a strange, out-of-the-way matter to be a Friend. Indeed, to us, those who were not Friends were the ones outside the world – our world. It's only since I came here that I wonder if this is all there is, or will be.

'We came by wagon to Niagara. Then we were nearly shipwrecked on the lake, and after we reached York we had to wait for the summer drought to get another wagon up Yonge Street with our chattels. While we were in York it still seemed to be an adventure, and even when we were building our first cabin here in Yonge Street, the younger ones seemed able to make a play out of it. But I was the eldest girl; I had to help my mother, and it seemed to take all the hours there were just to keep food on the table and clothes on our backs, let alone having to howk out the felled trees and make fences before we could plant. We just got turnips in round the stumps that first year. Thanks to the good Lord we had Friends to help us through. Thee'd never think it now, to see our fields so trig: thee wouldn't begin to realise the labour that went into them. And all for naught. I know Thomas has told thee what happened: how my father died of the typhus two years ago. Rachel had left us again by then. We all caught it, and my two sisters died as well, and after that my mother had it too. I think she really died of grief. When Judith came back, she was not the only one who nursed a broken heart.'

Clemency stopped speaking, and buried her face in her folded arms. I knew not what to do. When my sister was a certain age she was given to bouts of noisy weeping, which has inoculated my sympathies against that kind of feck for all time. Clemency did not weep aloud, but her shoulders shook, and I heard a stifled sob. I was moved to stand up and lay my hand gently upon her shoulder. Her hair had escaped its bands as usual; a thick red curl lay on her shoulder just by my hand. It flashed irrelevantly across my mind that I'd stopped noticing the pockmarks. I knew not if she felt my touch, but presently she sat up and fiercely rubbed her eyes.

'I'm sorry, Friend. It was not so long ago, thee must understand.'

'I understand. Perhaps thee doesn't want to talk any more?'

She shook her head decisively. 'It eases me to talk. But I think it's hard on thee. Thee's not obliged to hear it.'

'No, it's not hard. Go on telling, if thee wishes.'

'Very well, I do wish.' She searched for a handkerchief, then wiped her nose on the back of her hand. 'Well then, Mark, I was like to hate my uncle Amos – which is wicked, I know, for what use is it to kick against the pricks – that he had ever brought us out of our own country and into the howling wilderness of Upper Canada. Judith was distraught too, that ever she had brought thy sister Rachel away from the fair English ground where her lot was cast, and into a temptation that Judith felt she ought to have foreseen – though how she could have done so I know not. That's how it was that Judith and I were one another's comfort here – in this house – for all that grievous winter.

'Last spring she asked me if I'd go with her to the United States. This place was filled with horrors. I was desperate to get away. I felt I'd be going home. Thomas was about to marry Sarah. There was no one left here to miss me. Thee says thee suspects the motives of women who travel in the Ministry. I ask thee if anything we do on this earth is done in utter pureness of heart? God leads us to his purpose sometimes whether we will or no.'

'So when Judith asked thee to be her companion, thee was able to go back to thy home in Philadelphia?'

'Ah, but when I got there I found it wasn't my home any more. Besides, we didn't stay long in Catawissa. We were always on the move, carrying our ministry from Meeting to Meeting. But back in the United States I found myself angry because the Friends seemed not to understand what it was like for us in Upper Canada. They said there would be war, and that as I was an American I'd better not go back. I said to them, "what have wars to do with us?" but the question that was really in my mind was, where did I belong? I never thought I wished to be in Yonge Street, but my parents and my sisters are buried in the graveyard here. I was a child when I came, for all I was sixteen years old. It was breaking in our lot here that made me grow up; that, and the deaths in this house. This place and I know each other pretty well by now.

'But it was Judith I was to tell thee about. We travelled together through Pennsylvania, down into Virginia and the Carolinas. Thee's prejudiced against women travelling, and naturally thee grieves for thy sister. But if thee were a woman, and had aught to say, would thee not wish thy Society to listen to thee? Would thee not be glad that thee could speak what lay on thy heart? Thy sister Rachel was a strength to many. The worst thing that can happen to a woman in this world, I think, is not to be born a Friend.

'I'm concerned for Judith though. Amos told thee how she met another travelling Friend in the Carolinas, and was called to work with her among the Indians. But I was much troubled by the heat, and so we parted. I came home, staying with Friends along the way. I only got back a fortnight before thee came thyself. All through my journey Friends were saying that war was on the way, and trying to dissuade me from crossing the border. It only made me more anxious to get home while I could. I don't know what Judith will do.'

'Stay in the United States until the war is over, I suppose.' I found I did not care very much where Judith was. Clemency's words had struck a chill to my heart, for had not Rachel been lost in American territory? These borders were nothing to me, and the wars over them less than nothing, but a frontier at war might, I supposed, be a significant obstacle. There must be ways round. If Cumberland were at war with Westmorland, I would find fifty ways through, however great the army, and in the great wilderness of North America there must be even more possibilities, once I'd had a chance to survey the territory.

CHAPTER 8

AFTER YONGE STREET, MONTREAL SEEMED LIKE THE very centre of the civilised world. William Mackenzie had become an old friend, his house a haven, albeit a dangerously luxurious one. The snow had melted and the fruit trees were beginning to bud. At Lachine the big *canots du maître* were preparing for their great journey. One bright morning early in Fifth Month I was in O'Sullivan's coffee house near La Place du Marche, five minutes' walk from the Company offices. The place was crowded; I found an empty seat right in the draught from the door, and I ordered a cup of chocolate. What the elders of Mosedale would have said if they had seen me I care not to think. I picked up the only newspaper left on the rack, which turned out to be an American publication, several weeks old, so worn that the columns on the folds were unreadable. At home we did not have newspapers, but sometimes I used to read *The Morning Post* at the Royal Oak in Keswick, not surreptitiously precisely, but aware that certain Friends would decry my concern with military matters.[1] I was reading a report from Washington City concerning the alliance between the British troops in Canada and the wild Indians in the west; I had not realised that fighting was already begun. I have the cutting by me yet:

> ... *notwithstanding the British 'government' disavow the instigation of the savages to hostility against us, yet perhaps there are certain 'persons' in the employ and pay of that government, whose hands are not so clear of the blood of our citizens. It is a fact, sir, that Col. Grant, of the British army, who lately commanded at Amherstberg, did acknowledge (when he was remonstrated with by Governor Hull, in 1807, on the inhuman policy of calling in savages to interfere in the disputes of civilised nations) that the object of himself and the British agents was to engage and retain the savages in their service in the event of war ...*

Suddenly my hat was seized by the brim and tipped off my head. I leaped to my feet and shoved the fellow back.[2] He fell against the waiter. Coffee tipped from a pot all over the table by the window, splattering the white cloth, and the two gentlemen who sat opposite one another in the best seats.

A hue and cry broke out that made me blench, but I

---

[1] Since I was a young man I have lived through twenty years of peace. The world is much changed, and Friends have changed with the world, insofar as men like myself understand the affairs reported in the newspapers to be very much our concern. The elders rebuked me when I took out a subscription to the *Manchester Observer* a few years after Waterloo, but I think I was in the right of it. The *Manchester Guardian* – for so it is now – is less concerned with just reform these days than it was in the twenties, but I still ride over to Keswick for it twice a week, or send the lad. It is six years now since that Act was passed which allows a man to take part in public affairs without taking an oath, which would be contrary to the principles of our Society. I rejoiced to see Joseph Pease take his seat in Parliament, and I care not who knows it.

[2] Such an action was in no way consonant with our Peace Testimony. I'm quite aware of my own backslidings, but I have committed myself to tell the truth, and omit nothing relevant.

wouldn't give ground. I knocked the dent out of the brim of my hat, set it upon my head, and faced them all with folded arms. After all, I could pay my shot like the rest of them, and had as much right to sit in a public place as any man.

One of the coffee-bespattered gentlemen stood up. He was as tall as I was, but old enough to be my father, a high-complexioned gentleman, whether from being much outdoors or from good living I could not tell. He silenced the uproar with the raising of one hand, and explained to me. 'This gentleman objects to you remaining covered, sir, within doors. In all conscience he acted hastily, but we are a civilised nation, and one sees his point, perhaps.'

I was too angry to be bashful. 'It's not the custom of my people to doff a hat to any, save God Almighty, to whom alone do we defer.'

Several people began to argue at once, but he gestured again for silence. 'Well, well. I think you must be Mr Greenhow, from Cumberland. Is that correct?'

Thus it was that I met William McGillivray, the head of the North West Company, disturbing him at his breakfast at the busiest time of year, when the brigades were preparing to set off from Lachine. But if I hadn't done so, I think all the efforts of my friend William Mackenzie on my behalf might have come to naught, for the loading of the canoes is very strictly done, and there is no space given to idle passengers. William had prepared the way for me, certainly, for so it was that my story had got about, but I thought in the days ahead that maybe the hand of God had been in it too, to throw me into the company of William McGillivray himself in such an unexpected manner.

William McGillivray was smooth with the polish of much wealth and a great position. The President of the North West Company has more power in his hand than the Czar of Russia, for he controls his own wealth, and his people prosper under him and therefore like him well.[3] They say the North West, being run entirely by dispossessed Scotch clansmen, is held together by bonds of kinships and loyalty that we Englishmen know nothing of.

I had wit enough to recognise that my errand might stand or fall by this encounter. I've never found it hard to get alongside folk, once I get into conversation. He clearly took an interest in me, or to the oddity of my religious principles. He fixed me with a piercing blue gaze, and questioned me thoroughly, all under the guise of ordinary small talk. He made me sit down at his table, and introduced his companion as a Mr McTavish.

He spoke to the waiter: 'Another pot of coffee, and bring a cup for this gentleman.' He turned to me. 'Mr William Mackenzie has told me somewhat of your affairs, Mr Greenhow. You come from Cumberland, I understand?'

I sat with him less than an hour, and he said nothing of himself, but he seemed to me above all an unhappy man. I learned later that he had been much bereaved, whereat I was sorry, because for all the tales of high-handedness, quarrelling, and the debaucheries of the Beaver Club, I stood in his debt, for he made my way plain before me.

William McGillivray stood up, and shook my hand. 'Come to my house after dinner tomorrow, Mr Greenhow. Say six o'clock. I'll have something for you. Anyone will tell you where I live.'

That was true: St Antoine House was evidently one of the landmarks of the place. As directed, I took the upper Lachine Road out of town, and turned right between impressive gateposts, and followed a long drive up on to the western slopes of Mount Royal. The drive led me

---

[3] At least, I know not how it may be now, for the old North West went down these fifteen years ago, and the Hudson's Bay Company, which bought the old partners out, is altogether a more autocratic institution.

through a park newly landscaped with groves of young trees, past a walled kitchen garden and a formal garden, complete with ornamental pond, which was divided from the estate by a ha-ha, up to a handsome two-storey mansion in the modern style, built of black stone, with an imposing façade and a conservatory and succession houses built to one side. It was bigger than Greta Hall or Thomas Wilkinson's pleasant house at Yanwath (Friend Thomas would have yearned over these gardens, though), but not on the magnificent scale of Dalemain, which I pass so often on my way to Yanwath. A uniformed butler led me to a well-appointed library, where I found William McGillivray at his desk, surrounded by more leather-bound volumes than I had ever thought to have crossed the Atlantic.[4] William McGillivray stood up to shake my hand, and with his own hands set a chair for me.

'Now, Mr Greenhow, to business. My partner William Mackenzie has petitioned the Council that you may be given passage to Sainte Marie du Sault. To be honest, I cannot think that you will find your sister. Women and children are kidnapped occasionally. The population of the Red Man is much depleted by disease these days, which may account for it. They're a brave people, but they die easily. It's a hard thing to face, but if your sister's not dead, she's as good as dead to the world she came from.'

'If she lives, friend, there's that within her which cannot die. I'll find her if I can.'

'I see.' He took a turn or two about the room, while I waited, and then he sat down and faced me frankly. 'Well now. Your brother-in-law Alan Mackenzie was a North West Company employee, but officially we're under no

---

[4] Though I learned later that they publish as many books in the Americas as they do in Europe. In fact they have almost all the accoutrements of civilised living, manufactured on their own territory. Somehow I had not expected that.

obligation to you, for your business with him is entirely domestic. However, the Company is not ungenerous. We don't take passengers in our canoes. A partner may take his servant, however. We have a partner, Hugh Chisholm, going back to Fort William. He says you can travel with him, if you're willing to do the work a servant would have done, as far as the Sault.'

'I'll do whatever's necessary.'

'Good. We can't afford to accommodate a useless man. I should tell you that Alan Mackenzie was clerk to Hugh Chisholm in the Athabasca region before he transferred to the Michilimackinac. Yes,' – for he was watching me closely – 'I thought that would interest you. I'll furnish you with Hugh's direction before you leave. He'll tell you what to bring, and so on.'

'Friend, I am most grateful . . .'

'In a minute. There's one small matter you can do for us in return.' He picked up a sealed paper from his desk. 'This. It's a letter – a small paper – I'd like you to deliver it to Alan Mackenzie, when you find him.'

'I'll willingly do that for thee.'

'Wait. There is that in this letter . . . In short, you must not let it fall into any hands but Alan Mackenzie's. If you find him not, then destroy the papers by fire. And let no man else have sight of it. Is that understood?'

I looked at the letter, then accosted him straightly. 'I must ask thee, friend, if this paper contains any matter pertaining to the coming war? Does it incite Alan, or any other man, to any war or strife or fighting with outward weapons, for any end whatsoever?'

He met my eyes. 'No, it's not about that. Do you want my oath on it?'

'No. Thy word is sufficient.'

McGillivray moved a paperweight on his desk. 'I regret I can't tell you the content of the letter. Suffice it to say that it is important to the Company, and will serve your brother-in-law well. You are a gentleman, sir, and I trust you to enquire no further.'

'Friend, I'm no gentleman; I'm a farmer. But if thee's worried I might read the letter, I give thee my word I will not, just as thee has given thy word that the letter contains no matter contrary to my Society's testimony against all wars.'

He didn't comment on that, but asked me abruptly, 'How many members of your . . . Society . . . do we have in Canada?'

'I know not,' I said, surprised. 'The Friends at Yonge Street are maybe a hundred souls or more, and there are other settlements, for I heard them spoken of. Half a dozen Meetings, perhaps? I think thee might find close on a thousand Quakers, if thee searched this land from end to end.'

'I see.' McGillivray stood up. 'It's been a pleasure to meet you, Mr Greenhow. I hope to see you in Montreal when you come back again. You will come and tell me how you prosper in the west.'

It was not a question, so I didn't answer it, but gave him my hand and thanked him for his help. I put the letter in my breeches pocket, next to my wallet – a plain coat hath no inner pockets – and bade William McGillivray farewell.

My friend William Mackenzie was not as excited about my good fortune as I expected him to be, for all that I owed it to him. Later that evening he took me into his bookroom, and addressed me solemnly. 'Now lookee, lad, I've done my best for you, but there's more in it than you know. I don't want you on my conscience, and faith, I'd be sorry to lose you, for I've grown fond of you. No reason why a Quaker shouldn't join the great North West, either . . . This would be a fine beginning, so long as it don't turn out to be an untimely end . . .'

'I thank thee, friend, but when I've found my sister I want nothing more than to go home.'

'Ay, well, it's early days yet. A sober man – and tha'art always sober, laddie – is always at an advantage in business. And business is what we must come to now. Mr McGillivray gave you a letter to carry to young Alan Mackenzie? Nay, you needn't answer; I ken that he did.'

'Friend, I know quite well that William McGillivray has his own motives. But if thee can tell me aught that will help me – for I'll admit both thy Company and the nature of the country are entirely strange to me – I'd be grateful. The first thing is, I asked William McGillivray, and I'll ask thee the same: is there aught of warmongering in the letter I must carry? For if there's anything whatsoever contrary to my Society's testimony against all wars, then I can't carry it.'

William looked at me sideways. 'Even if you would forfeit all hope of reaching your brother-in-law thereby?'

'Even so. But I wouldn't forfeit all hope. I'd find another way.'

'Good lad. I've not read the letter, but I've talked to McGillivray. I tried to find you a place in the canoes, quite privily, but it got to the ears of the Council, and they wouldn't hear of it. Sadly you're a big lad, and there's no way we could slip you in without leaving behind at least three quarters of your weight in goods, and even if you could wield a paddle no one could take you for a voyageur. I felt bad, for I'd told you to come all the way back to Montreal from Yonge Street, and it looked likely 'twould all be for naught. But then when the brigades came back McGillivray changed his mind all of a sudden – or was it because he met you? – one or the other, most likely a mix of the two – and today he sent for me. Now I cannot tell you all his mind – for one thing I know it not – but I can maybe prime you a little, for what you're going to meet at Mackinac.

'Now mark me well. In the old days the Company controlled all the fur trade in the west, from Athabasca to the Mississippi, and from Mackinac to the mountains. At least, it was never that simple . . . There was always the Hudson's Bay Company . . . the best men can be ill to work with . . . No need to go into that . . . In the good old days, the Yankees had no real interests north or west of St Louis. When you're out there, laddie, you may hear many a tale . . . But understand this: the North West Company now is one and indivisible. Hudson's Bay now . . . you'll have naught to do with that where you're going. All you need to know, lad, is that the North West Company *is* the fur trade in Canada. That is to say the Company *is* Canada, and the Company's interests are the same as Britain's interests, and that's all there is about it.'

'They wouldn't say that in Yonge Street . . .'

'Ay, but we're not in Yonge Street. Mark me well. Our troubles in the south-west began when the Yankees moved in. Did you know that the United States *bought* all the land west of the Mississippi to the sea? Ay, you'll say it can't be done, and you'd be in the right of it, except that it happened. Then – what would it be? – six, seven years back a Yankee expedition reached the Pacific. Now Mr Mackenzie, and Mr Fraser . . . but you needn't concern yourself with all that. The point is that the North West Company couldn't stay in Mackinac, because Mackinac was Yankee territory. So what did we do? The North West couldn't stay, but no reason why there shouldn't be another Canadian company there. And so the Michilimackinac Company was started, to trade in the American North West Territories and into the Mississippi. The Yankees might be hostile to us, but how could they stop us?'

'When thee says "us", thee means that the Michili . . . Michili . . .'

'Michilimackinac.'

'The Michilimackinac Company is the North West Company under a different name?'

'It is – was – a different Company.'

'But perhaps all the shareholders are men of the North West Company?'

'Well, well, laddie, you're more fly to the time of day than I reckoned. Maybe that's just as well. Anyway, your brother-in-law Alan, when he came due for Montreal leave in the summer of 1809, was seconded to the Michilimackinac Company. It's difficult to move from clerk to *hivernant*, so the Company offered him a higher post in the Michilimackinac instead.'

'So he's quite high up in his Company?'

'Well, he got his promotion. Seemingly he fell in with a Hudson's Bay agent up in Athabasca back in '06 or '07. He and the Bay fellow wintered within half a mile of each other. Things got strained, but they came out of it without a fight, and young Mackenzie was commended by his *hivernant* – that's Hugh Chisholm – for his diplomatic handling of the situation. So – wanting to do the lad a good turn, I guess – Chisholm recommended him when they got back to Fort William, and Mackenzie was sent as a senior clerk to the Michilimackinac. Might as well have thrown him into a hornets' nest and be done with it. And then the foolish lad makes his ridiculous marriage . . . Of course, if he'd still been in the North West he'd never have been allowed to take her beyond the Sault. But being down in Mackinac, I suppose he thought he could do as he liked, and no harm would come of it . . . I'm sorry, lad, I don't mean to offend your sensibilities.'

'It would take more than that. Thee speaks of it very much as the Friends in Yonge Street do.'

'So the marriage was objectionable to them too?'

'A Friend may not be married before a priest. My sister was disowned for marrying outside the Society.'

William gave a long low whistle. 'There's more in this than I reckoned.' He gave me that sharp sideways glance I was beginning to recognise. 'But you've not disowned her?'

'She's my own sister.'

'Ay, true, but that's not what I asked.'

'Thee was telling me about the Michilimackinac Company being a nest of hornets.'

'I said Mackinac was a nest of hornets. Very well, the Michilimackinac found itself up against the Yankee traders right from the start – well, that was exactly why we floated the Company, to get upsides with them, so we knew what we were in for. A new American company was on the way up – the American Fur Company it is now. This is the name you'll hear everywhere in Mackinac, laddie – mark it well: Astor. Astor, I said. You mind that name well.'

'Astor.'

'Ay. He comes here to Montreal every year, and stays with old Mr Henry. He's an honoured guest at the Beaver Club; couple of years back he brought his daughter along too. You'd never guess … That man is a weasel in a chicken coop, by my reckoning.

'Anyway, to cut a long story short, eventually a new Company was set up – the South West Company. That happened just after your sister was lost. So our Alan Mackenzie came back across Lake Michigan without her, full of his own grief no doubt, and found that while he was gone trade was worse than ever, and the Americans were doing their best to get all the old North-Westers out of the South West and out of Mackinac.'

'But even so, he stayed in American territory?'

'He's there still. We're not at war yet. The agreement

just now is that the North West doesn't trade south of the American border, and the South West doesn't trade north of it. And for some reason, which to be honest I haven't fully fathomed, it suits McGillivray that you should go and find Alan, and take him this letter.'

I thought it all over for a little while, while the log fire blazed and crackled, and William Mackenzie helped himself to another glass of port. 'So far as I can tell, William McGillivray's interests are in trade, and not in war?'

'Mr McGillivray is a trader, not a soldier. I keep telling you, laddie, the real issue is the border in the far west. Now that's worth going to war for. Fact is, the Company can only operate unhindered in Canadian territory. It's always going to be that way. So we need to establish our Canadian border, once and for all, from Fort William to the Pacific coast. That's what matters. Mackinac will be a dead duck, out of it. The best furs are all up north now anyway.'

'That's what thee thinks. It's not what William McGillivray thinks, is it?'

He darted another sidelong glance at me. 'No, lad, I don't think it is. But he plays his cards close to his chest, Mr McGillivray. He has to. He wouldn't be sending you to Mackinac if he'd given up our interests there. He wouldn't give you a personal letter to carry to a young clerk – one who isn't even in employment with us right now – if there wasn't a reason for it. I just want you to have some idea what you're getting into, seeing as I started you on this track.'

'I thank thee, friend. But I started myself, on my own track. I'll take any road that hath no evil in it, to get where I want.'

CHAPTER 9

I COME TO THE DAYS WHEN I WAS MONSIEUR GREEN-
horn,[1] travelling with the agent Hugh Chisholm and a
dozen voyageurs across the wilderness that covered half
a continent. Hugh dined with us the night before we left.
He was a sandy weather-beaten fellow with a wit so dry
it took me days to learn that I had to take his meanings
aslant if I was to make any sense of what he said. He and
William disposed of several bottles between them, but
the only effect of wine on Hugh was to make him more
whimsical than ever. I can think of no man for whom I
could have acted the role of servant more easily than he.
He gave his orders as if it were all a game, and though he
could be sharp enough in action, I never saw him ruffled
or out of temper, not even when we lay abed too long, and
the voyageurs pulled out our tent poles, which they use
under the cargo in the canoe, so we were left wallowing
in a heap of damp canvas, struggling to make ready.

As for the voyageurs: Jean-Pierre was our *avant*, that is,
our bowsman, who had charge of all the voyageurs, and
Marc our *gouvernail*. (Everyone made much of our shared

---

[1] It was Hugh who gave me this appellation. The voyageurs took it up, but
pronounced it, as near as I can write it, *grin-norrn*. They said it meant, in
their own tongue, *un bleu*.

name. Marc seemed to think that it conferred some sort of responsibility on him, which was to my advantage, for in the canoe he stood with his steering paddle just behind where Hugh and I sat side by side. From there he'd regale me with stories, or simply warn me what was coming next, for which I was at times most grateful.)[2] Jacques was our cook. The other *milieux* were seasoned voyageurs, all but Alban, whose first voyage it was. He was a lad of fourteen, but all the tricks that are played upon novices were played on him and me alike, and so we grew to be comrades, for all the ten years between us.

That first day I found them a drunken, bawdy lot – for it was easy to guess what they were talking about. We left from above the rapids at Lachine, and paddled ten miles or more along the shore of Montreal Island, until we reached the Lake of Two Mountains – Hugh translated the French for me – a choppy stretch of open water longer than Windermere. As we pulled away from Lachine the voyageurs were singing. Little did I know how that song – and many like it – would become woven into the rhythms of my brain. Indeed, even now, as I sit at my desk in my quiet study – Grasmoor is all shrouded today in weeping mists – that same tune comes back to me:

> *En roulant ma boule roulant*
> *En roulant ma boule.*
> *En roulant ma boule roulant*
> *En roulant ma boule.*

The verses are a nonsensical tale about dead ducks – I discovered several of the songs feature this topic; I cannot imagine why – but they have stayed in my head from

---

[2] Marc was horrified that I knew not my own Saint's Day, as he called it. To this day I cannot let the eighth day of Fifth Month pass without holding him in the light particularly. This I know to be a vain superstition in me, but I like to think that if he lives, he may be a little warmed by my remembrances.

that day to this, when so many more weighty topics have vanished in the mists of memory.[3]

Before we finally left Montreal Island, the voyageurs went ashore at the Convent of St Anne, where I understood that some Catholic or pagan rite takes place, to bless them on their way. They were very anxious I should join them in this, but, although Hugh went, and said it would be politic in me to follow his example, I was adamant (which cost me Jacques favour, and possibly that of others; this took several days to remedy) and I waited by the canoes. I was a little feart, not so much of the wilderness ahead but of the strange company I had got myself into. The men might be the worse for a wild night, but today they were dressed like peacocks, in their bright woven sashes and coloured caps. It was I, in my sober grey coat and broadbrim, who was the kenspeckle one.

To compound the temptation of the songs, Hugh had with him a fiddle, and on fair nights he would play to us, and the voyageurs, after fifteen hours of paddling upstream, would up and dance until the fire died down. Then they would suddenly retire under their upturned canoes, roll themselves in their blankets and fall immediately asleep. I could not think the dancing wrong in them;

---

[3] Indeed I have always been given to levity in this respect. As a child I seldom heard a tune, or a song, but if I ever I did, I found there was something about the combination of words and rhythm that imprinted both upon my mind, however much I resisted. We have many tales in Cumberland – though not, of course, told in our household – about the fairies who win folk away from the strait path by the wiles of music, and I can well see the kernel of truth in such legends. The story usually is how a young fellow hears the music, and is enticed away on a strange journey among the fairy people, and when he comes back, many years have gone by and all that he once knew is utterly changed. I would say I've never told my children idle tales, and yet – isn't the burden of my own story, which I have told them over and over (for is it not also the story of their own origin?) a very similar kind of tale? Except, of course, that mine is a true and rational history, in every respect as veracious as memory serves to make it.

they are simple folk, and express their gaiety easily.[4] They are also tough and courageous, and immensely strong. I towered over all of them, and was used to hard work at home, but even so I could only carry half the burden that they took up at every portage along the route.

The first day out of Lachine I felt so cramped I wondered how I'd support the weeks ahead. Our canoe was packed to the gunwales with canvas bales containing all the trade goods William had shown me stacked in the company warehouse – blankets, beads, cloth, ironware, tobacco, and so forth – as well as kegs of liquor and gunpowder, and long boxes filled with muskets. Somehow the voyageurs made their places in among all this. There were no benches, and no legroom either, as far as I was concerned. I passed many a mile, when the water was calm, lying back in my little hole, with my legs up on the bales in front of me, watching the clouds moving overhead, and the forested banks slip past. Somewhere between the first long rapids and *la Chaudière* the voyageurs agreed – I'd been speaking to Marc about it – that I might try my hand with the extra paddle. If I'd had to sit still for five weeks I'd have – no, the plain truth is that I would not have gone mad – but I'd have found it ill to bear. When Marc – for he was the one who could see my efforts – reported with a shrug that I was *pas mal*, they even readjusted the load so I could put my feet to the floor while I paddled, giving me stern warnings not to put my weight on the fragile birchbark skin which was

[4] I know not; I have never resolved this matter of music, or the singing and dancing that accompany it, in my own mind. It seemed to me among the voyageurs, then later among the Indians, that these things brought joy into lives much harder than anything most Friends have to contemplate, and also kept men from fighting by providing a more harmonious outlet for their spirits. Perhaps in the innocency of the world, when civilisation was yet young, such sports were not degenerate. Sometimes I've talked of this with Friends, and I've met with varying responses. As I say, I know not.

all that lay between us and the river. Marc was strict with me until I learned the art of feathering; before I got into the way of it he said it was like having a startled mallard trying to take off beside him. I was a fair pupil. When we finally parted at Sainte Marie du Sault the voyageurs were kind enough to say they'd miss their *voyageur de plus* and even Jacques, who was of a sullen sort, said it would be tough crossing the lake *sans l'aide de cette pousse extra de derrière*.

Hugh thought all this was a fine joke. He spent the quiet hours reading, but I couldn't borrow his books, for they were all in Latin. His favourite was poems by one named Horace. Sometimes he would smile to himself, and translate a passage for me, and occasionally, if he could be bothered, he'd explain the irony to me.

I'd thought that all we had to do was canoe upriver through the day and camp at night. I soon learned better. The Outaouais River proper began with a long stretch of white water – this before we had well set out. We were scarcely in the canoes at all, but had to scramble, heavily-burdened, along a rough trail, while the half-loaded canoes had to be pulled up the rapids with ropes. I'd never seen anything like it; I was expecting every man of ours to be drowned as I watched from the shore, and indeed there are little crosses made here and there along the banks, each marking where a voyageur met his death. Carrying Hugh's tent and personal effects (as well as my own small knapsack and blanket) was my job at the portages.[5] My load was as nothing to the voyageurs, who carry two ninety-pound bales on their backs at a time. Hugh told me many of them die young, and they

---

[5] I gave thanks to God that I had started in the guiding business. I was well used to taking tourists up Skiddaw, and sometimes they had various pic-nics or easels or other nonsense that they must needs have up the mountain with them, so portaging was not an entirely new science to me. Woe betide me if it had been!

suffer much from hernias, and broken backs. Those first rapids were twelve dangerous, weary miles of dragging and portaging. By the end of that day I was beginning to regret that I had committed myself to voyage right up the Outaouais River, for already I'd have been glad never to see it more.

Talking to Hugh, it dawned on me for the first time that our rivers at home are very little, because we have not the hinterland or height of land. The rivers of Upper Canada are a different colour. Our rivers are loud and fast, with ice-coloured water fresh out of the hills. The water runs clear over a grey stone bed; sometimes one sees moss on the stones underwater as clear as if it grew in air. When a road crosses a river, it goes by a solid grey-slate packhorse bridge, wide enough for a cart. The rivers of North America are so great that sometimes, as thee canoes along one bank, thee can't see the other. No roads, no bridges – 'twould be impossible. What we did begin to see was a range of hills ahead and to our right. Whenever I lift up mine eyes to the hills – and this is my first prayer every day of my life – I cannot choose but to glorify God and all his works, most particularly that he created the mountains and hills. My native mountains are – I can say this without prejudice – the most perfectly formed mountains in the whole world, containing within them a great diversity of wildness without immensity. On the North American continent the mountains are on the whole diffuse, and too thickly forested. Alan told me there are mountains in the far west beyond anything I've ever seen, but I have naught to say of that; 'twould be but hearsay.

'Twas not mountains that formed my prayers on that far continent, but rivers. The river was all. I heard it in my dreams at night; before I looked out of our tent in the morning I listened to hear what it had to say to me of the day ahead; its current was the accompaniment to my days; my very thoughts were shaped by the sound of it.

The voyageurs paddle all day because they must. Their strokes are very fast – fifty strokes a minute for hours at a time – and sometimes furious. The profits of the North West Company rest wholly upon their speed, so the Company pays each man 400 livres to spend the best part of the year paddling from Lachine to Fort William and back again. It was not like that for me: I paddled when I chose, and for long hours I gave my blisters a rest. Poor Alban's hands were a mass of bleeding sores until they hardened up. And yet, on the long stretch up to *la Chaudière*, as often as not the men sang at their work, and I have to admit that the tune helped me greatly to get into the rhythm of it. I kept my eyes fixed on Jean-Pierre's back – for every man must follow the *avant* – watching the lift of his arm, and the quick pull back, matching the movement to the song as I tried with all my might to keep time with him:

> *A la Claire fontaine*
> *M'en allant promener,*
> *J'ai trouvé l'eau si belle*
> *Que je m'y suis baigné.*
> *Il y a longtemps que je l'aime*
> *Jamais je ne l'oublierai.*

My paddling muscles grew sore, and then hard. I was lulled into a false sense of growing ease until we reached *la Chaudière*. Just before we came to this cauldron of falling waters we camped opposite a great bluff, where all evening we saw the flickering fires of a loggers' camp on the south bank half a mile away. I hadn't yet seen the force, but all that night I heard it roaring through my dreams like a vengeful beast, and everywhere around us the forest was damp and verdant from the blown spray.

We started on the portage the next morning. When Marc showed me the path I thought he was joking (for the voyageurs' sense of humour was often quite unfathomable). We had to scramble with our loads up rocks as steep as Raven Crags in Mungrisdale. The narrow path was worn down to the rock. The first time I followed Marc to the bluff above the falls I nearly walked over a sheer edge, where the path had been washed away. No one saw. There was a shaking fear in the pit of my stomach, but I didn't let on for shame at my carelessness, for was I not the only mountain-dweller among them?

We got all the bales along that treacherous path, while the hungry waters churned in the depths below. The men jogged along under their loads, over pine roots worn icy-smooth, across moss-covered slippery rocks, as if there were no sheer drop just inches from their passing feet. Then came the canoes. Four men portaged each one, but the path was much too narrow. I was on the downside amidships, being taller. The canoe was a dead weight digging into my right shoulder, and as the other three moved it kept shoving me to the edge. The great bow bumped against a scarred pine – this must have happened many times before – and the whole boat lurched towards me. I braced myself – it was going over – we couldn't hold it – and tried to take the weight across my back. All of a sudden the ground gave way under my left boot. As I slipped I heard my nailed boots scraping. I let the canoe go and threw myself flat against the rock.

The world went slow. The waters roared beneath me, and for an eternity I hung there in the balance. My feet dangled over emptiness. Under my fingers there was naught but wet rock. It sloped so much it was like to tip me off. All that stopped me slipping was the rough wool and the buttons on my coat. I heard a bumping and breaking among the pine boughs – that was the men dragging the canoe away from the edge, stern foremost. Then Marc's voice above me, '*Sacré, Mon Dieu! Arrêtez Marc! Ne bougez pas! Quoique vous fassiez, surtout ne bougez pas!*'

I couldn't have moved. Even when I breathed I seemed to slip a little.

'*Tendez la main! Oui! Oui! Un peu plus! Encore! Bon!*'

Very cautiously I moved my arm upwards. A pair of hands grasped my wrist. '*Et maintenant l'autre!*' I reached up my other hand, and that was grasped also. '*Bon! Bon! Mon Dieu, c'est aussi dur que de pousser un tauteau!*'

Marc and Jacques slowly dragged me clear until I could feel solid earth under my feet. I stood up shakily. We looked at the place where a full yard of the path had slipped into the abyss. The newly exposed rock was white. Bits of earth and little pebbles were still trickling downwards. I was mortified. I, of all men, should have known not to put my weight so near a cornice, path or no path. It was that damned canoe pressing on my shoulder had stopped me thinking – I was swearing inside my head, as I had never sworn before. It was from hearing it all around me, and my own shame.

After *la Chaudière* portage the men retired early, exhausted, as soon as we'd eaten our pease porridge, seasoned, as a reward for our efforts, with an extra ration of salt pork. We could still hear the falls thundering behind us, too near for me to sleep easily tonight, I felt, and so I lingered. Only Jacques, Hugh and I were left alone by the fire. (I never knew men so proficient at making fire out of a strike-a-light and birch bark shavings. No fire could be carried in the canoes, so we had to kindle a new flame every evening.) Jacques watched tomorrow's pease porridge as it simmered in the kettle, and stirred it occasionally with a peeled stick. A myriad lights twinkled in the great river as it swept smoothly past us. The roar of the force five miles away was like endless rain drumming on a slate roof, yet where we were, we were bathed in the calm gold light of evening, like a little kingdom of peace amidst the ragings of the world.

Hugh sat meditatively smoking his pipe. There were ospreys fishing in the river, just like the pair we have on Derwentwater. For the first time – but by no means the last – I was troubled by black flies and mosquitoes, and clouds of small biting flies, bigger than our midges, but just as unpleasant.

'Bear's grease.'

'I beg thy pardon, friend?'

'Pork fat is better than nothing, but bear's grease and skunk oil keep them off as much as anything will. They'll get worse.'

'So all I need do is kill a bear?' I said, swatting the buzzing cloud from round my head.

'I'm sure if I sent you to do it you'd give it your best shot.'

'I've no gun, friend.'

Hugh gave a wry smile. 'I think you were sent into my life for a purpose, Monsieur Greenhorn. Beware the wiles of metaphor! Tell me, have you no gun on principle?'

'Nay, friend. I'd shoot a bear as soon as I'd slaughter a beast for the table, and that I know well how to do. I wouldn't use firearms against a fellow man, nor any kind of outward weapon, come to that.'

'What if the man were about to kill you?' asked Hugh idly.

'Then so be it, but I would reason with him not to, if I could.'

'At fifty yards?' Hugh tapped the ash from the bowl of his pipe, and reached in his pocket for tobacco. 'And what if it were your sister he were about to kill, or worse?'

I had no desire for this argument; besides, I'd been waiting for an opening. 'Did thee know my sister Rachel, friend?'

'If you can't say "sir", I suggest you call me Hugh. "Friend" makes me feel I have obligations, which is uncomfortable. No, I never met your sister, plague take her!' He was tamping down the little twist of tobacco in the bowl of his pipe. 'Saving your presence, but Alan Mackenzie . . . he threw away everything when he ran off with a white girl. I should know; I trained him. He was just a lad when I got him. He lied about his age to get the post; neither his brothers nor I felt it necessary to undeceive the council – but he learned fast. We got along like winking. When I heard what he'd done I thought, that's it, he'll never get back to *le pays d'en haut*. Then I heard she'd gone.' He laid a sliver of birch to the fire, and got himself a little flame. 'What'll you do if you find her? Take her home?'

'I don't know. If I find her I'll talk to her, obviously. It depends what she wants.'

'You won't find her.' There was a pause while Hugh gave all his attention to his pipe. 'But if you do, do young Alan a favour and take her back where she belongs. York, Montreal, England . . . it's immaterial. There's many a wife who's not seen her man for a few years. No harm in that. But keep her away from his work, if you will. You see the sense in that?'

I was puzzled to give him a sensible answer. 'I don't know. It's not our way. Man and wife work together, where I come from. The one wouldn't wish to do without the other.'

'Ah, well, there are ways and ways of having "the other",' said Hugh, and that was the end of our talk for that time.

As we gradually ascended the Outaouais River, I grew used to this new way of life, and fell easily into its rhythms. We seemed to be suspended outside the world, in a place where time was measured entirely in terms of our daily struggle against the flow of the river. Slowly we gained ground, and height. At night we camped in places where the canoes could be unloaded and beached, on soft sand if possible. The camping places were made smooth and the bare roots polished by the feet of many passing voyageurs. Camp was made as speedily as everything else we did: the canoes unloaded, the fire lit, the pease porridge simmering in the kettle, before a tardier soul might say 'Jack Robinson'. The men slept under the canoes on the beach. It was my job to pitch the tent for Hugh on higher ground, and set out his belongings within: his camp bed, his wooden chest, his pewter crockery (the rest of us had wooden utensils), his lamp and writing desk.[6] At night I shared the tent with Hugh. We were woken each dawn by Jean-Pierre calling '*Levez-vous, levez-vous, levez-vous.*' We had to move fast then, *hivernant* and voyageurs alike, for they struck camp in no time (Hugh would say 'and devil take the hindmost'), and we'd be on the move by sun-up. The only stops were for a breakfast of neat spirits (which I declined) and cold pease porridge, and for 'pipes' at intervals. Jean-Pierre would call out '*Allumez*', and every man but myself would take out his tobacco and light up for ten minutes, before Jean-Pierre called out '*Allez, allez, allez*' and off we went again at the same furious pace.

Our arrival at *Les Chats* was not in the least like Bartlett's picture on my wall. It was a wild day: flurries of wind kept catching us broadside, making the last few miles very tricky. At last two islands loomed ahead. I saw white water swirling round them, but the voyageurs headed between the falls into smooth water. A sudden gust caught us just offshore, and we were whirled into the edge of the rapid. In a moment all was spray and confusion. I heard a horrible rending sound under my feet like torn cloth. The canoe lurched: all of a sudden we were in smooth

---

[6] I was much taken with this last, and now I have a similar one myself, with a baize-covered desk top that folds out, and snug compartments for ink, penknife, seals, quills and paper.

water again, paddling wildly. There was water round my ankles. The canoe grounded painfully on a rocky beach. We leapt ashore, unloaded as fast as we could, and carried the canoe on to the island, where the rest of the brigade joined us without mishap. When we turned our canoe over there was a great rent in the birchbark. I found myself thinking foolishly of the boatbuilders' yards in Maryport, where they have everything needful for such an emergency. *Les Chats* could hardly be more different. The portage traverses the island between the two sets of falls, and apart from the voyageurs' camping places and a few trees, there is nothing else at all.

No one seemed anxious, merely vexed. We made camp, and once the fire was going Alban was given the hottest job of melting a lump of resin gum in an iron pot. The upturned canoe was propped up with a forked stick, and Marc and Jean-Pierre leaned over the hull and examined the tear, for all the world like a couple of farmers looking over a gate at a sodden hayfield. I watched Jean-Pierre unroll a length of birchbark, and lay out a length of wattup, which is a twine made of spruce roots. Jean-Pierre cut away the damaged bark, until where the tear had been, there was a long rectangular hole with firm edges. He unrolled the birchbark, and asked me to hold it steady while he pricked holes with an awl, and began to lash the patch in place. It looked so simple, once I knew how; I forgot my anxious vision of the boatbuilder's yard in Maryport, and admired Jean-Pierre's skill. While he worked, we talked about canoes, then while we were waiting for the resin to cool we looked at the patterns painted on the prow, and he showed me how the circle was divided by curving lines into the seasons of human life, '*Alors, pour vous, Marc, le printemps commence juste à devenir l'été. Est-ce que vous avez une demoiselle en Angleterre? Est-ce que vous l'avez beaucoup manquée?*'

I affected not to understand the latter part of this speech. 'Who are the two faces?'

He explained that the face in the stern was always frowning, but the fellow in the bows must always be smiling. There was a story to it that I couldn't follow. But already I surprised myself sometimes by thinking my own thoughts in the French tongue. *Est-ce que vous avez une demoiselle? Est-ce que vous l'avez beaucoup manquée? Quand vous regardez le feu le soir, rappellez-vous la couleur de ses cheveux?*[7]

[7] Just now I got up from my writing, and paced to and fro for a little, stopping at intervals to study my new engraving of *Les Chats* which Alan sent me. Young Caleb was asking me about it the other day, and we had the map out. Caleb has always been more interested than Alan in North America. When I built my canoe at John Bristo's farm at Portinscale (for I keep it on Derwentwater, where it has become as much an eccentricity of the place as the Floating Island or the Singing Stones), it was Caleb who most wanted to come and help, though he was only a little fellow – about eight years old, I think. I got my uncle to buy the American cedarwood for me in Whitehaven. And then I cheated, in a manner of speaking, for I had my wood cut for me at the sawmill in Keswick – I had to stand over them to see that all the parts were rightly measured – and delivered in prepared lengths. We dug out the shape as Loic had taught me, in a corner of the paddock, and built the wooden mould within it. John and I steamed the cedarwood lengths, and lashed the frame together just as they do in Upper Canada, only our twine was not made of spruce root, but bought from the chandler's. It took all our patience, for we had no guide but the rough drawings in my notebook, from which I'd worked out my design. We used oiled canvas instead of birchbark, for though we have birches enough, they are nothing like the size of the Canadian trees – I would have had to denude half the trees in Borrowdale, and instead of resin gum we used tar. My canoe is heavier than it should be, and a little too broad in the beam, so it responds less well to the paddle than Loic's did. I always meant to improve upon it, and make another, but the years go by too quickly. The paddles were done to my specification by a boatbuilder in Maryport. They lack the *je ne sais quoi* of the Indian version, but I cannot tell how to improve them. Various local gentlemen have come canoeing with me. William Wordsworth wrote a poem about the time we paddled to Lodore. Robert Southey's children used to come with us on pic-nics to Derwent Isle, and young Hartley Coleridge borrowed it without my permission, rent a great hole in it, and left it swamped in the shallows. 'Twas lucky I ever found it.

CHAPTER 10

THERE ARE EIGHTEEN PORTAGES ON THE OUTAOUAIS. There are no words in which I can convey the immensity of that river to an English reader. In mist or winter our own hills become dangerous and vast, but from a high edge in the clear light of a summer day all can be encompassed. A man is safe: though the mood of the land may vary, its lineaments are known, and maps can be made. On the Outaouais River I understood for the first time that truly the ways of God are beyond us, for he *hath measured the waters in the hollow of his hand, and meted out heaven with the span*. Our canoes were so little, the river so great, it seemed to me the very angels must be mocking our temerity. And yet we were preserved. Slowly we tracked that endless body of water, forcing our way stroke by stroke against its current. Sometimes the banks were low and far apart so that we seemed adrift on a great lake; other times the land came in high and closed us in, and underneath we felt the deep waters resisting us. In wild weather the shining lakes turned to fierce seas. When the fog came down we were marooned in a treacherous world of changing waters. In rough places the smooth river became a fierce white stranger, roaring over the rocks to meet us, as if daring us to force our way on.

Undaunted, we unloaded at each portage, in stifling heat or driving rain, and carried the whole cargo. Jean-Pierre and Marc took our canoe on their shoulders, helped by a couple of *milieux* when the going was hard. There were as many places again where the canoes had to be partly unloaded and tracked with ropes up the rapids. I began to look for the wooden crosses on the banks wherever the water was white. So we surmounted the islands of the Chenaux, the white rocks of the long Calumet portage, the Morrison rapids and the lake of Allumettes. Then the weather turned on us, and we were *dérangé* – we had to sit out a storm – on a little island the men name Gibraltar, in a place where the Outaouais is wide as a lake. We seemed so far out of the world that all was like a dream. We ate our pease crouched in the lee of the canoe, while the fire under the kettle spat and smouldered in the rain. The men amused themselves by getting me to say sentences in French, whereat they laughed heartily. Hugh and I retired early, the tent being the driest place we could find. I had pitched it at the top of an outcrop above the beach, and when the wind swept through the pines a deluge of water would splatter down on our canvas roof, adding its volume to the steady drumming of the rain.

'Well, well, Mark. Our halcyon days are over, for the time. Do you regret the fleshpots of Old England?'

'I'm used to being on the hill in all weathers.' Since he seemed disposed to talk, I thought I should make the most of it. I couldn't see his face; I was lying on my back looking up into the darkness under our canvas roof. 'William Mackenzie told me Alan had done well in the North West. He said he'd dealt with some trouble with the Hudson's Bay Company.'

'Don't talk to me about the Bay! But yes, that's true enough. I sent Alan up to over-winter at our northern post. Turns out there's an agent from the Bay set up within a mile of him. There's been murder done for less – but that was long ago. Still and all, it was an awkward situation.'

'How did he resolve it?'

'Oh, by the end of the winter they were the best of friends – in a cautious kind of way. Alan had a pack of cards with him; he said they visited now and then and played piquet. The other fellow was an Englishman, not a pig-headed Orkneyman, thank God. But initially it looked as if there might be trouble. Alan had the sense to leave it to Delkalé – that was his woman. Luckily the Bay fellow had a Chipewyan woman too – which is against the rules of the Hudson's Bay Company, though what red-blooded man could take heed of that for twenty years at a stretch? – and she and Delkalé had mothers who were cousins. In short, the men had the common sense to leave it to the women. They spoke to their elders, who arranged to divide the trade without further fuss. It's excellent management, to know when not to interfere. When Alan told me about it I was proud of him. He was scarce eighteen, and one doesn't necessarily look for wise heads on young shoulders.'

I lay rigid, staring into the dark. When I could command my thoughts I said to him, 'Is thee saying that Alan Mackenzie had an Indian wife before he married Rachel?'

'Oh, ay, of course he did. A man can't do without a woman in the *pays d'en haut*. How else would he do the work? He needs a woman to trap and fish and cook, mend his moccasins and make his clothes. You need a woman to keep your tent for you, look after the fire, all that. And in your bed too, of course.'

'And this woman – is she a wife?'

'Oh, ay. *À la façon du pays*, you understand. A country wife. Marriage is easy among the Indians, and divorce too. You're married when you take your girl with her family's blessing, and unmarried just as simply if that's agreed upon.

No marriage before a priest or anything like that. It's not the custom.'

The familiar phrase jarred brutally in that context. 'So when Alan married Rachel he had a wife . . . *à la façon du pays* – already?'

'Had had. They parted when he left Athabasca. Delkalé went back to her tribe. But when she comes into the store she still asks after him, though she has at least two children by now, and a man of her own people.' There was a pause. Hugh said in a different tone, 'You're not worrying about this, are you? It means nothing. It's the way in the North West. When Alan had Delkalé for his wife he'd never heard of your sister. He and Delkalé were never married before a priest. It means nothing.'

For a little while a tumult of thoughts kept me awake, but I slept easily in those days. When I woke a shaft of sunlight had found its way through the tent flap, and there was no sound without but singing birds. I crawled out without waking Hugh. For once I was the first awake. The island was new washed in dew, its colours softened by last night's rain. The fireplace on the beach was a ring of black ashes. The lake shimmered.

My shirt was damp with sweat, and I felt sticky. It felt a long time since I was clean. The island was barely twenty yards wide. The canoes were beached on a stretch of white sand, opposite another pine-topped island fifty yards away. Just below our tent there was another little hidden beach. I jumped down the rocks, stripped and waded in. There were sharp clamshells underfoot; I plunged into icy water.

After the first shock the water felt smooth and milky. As I swam I sent ripples of light circling across the still water. I rounded the point, and heard shouts and piercing whistles from the rocks. My voyageurs had been less sound asleep than I reckoned. As I swam they scrambled over the rocks and watched. I'm a modest fellow, but the cold was getting to me, and I had perforce to walk mother-naked into their midst, for they were all standing round my clothes. They were not slow with ribald observations, which I understood better than I wished. I was still struggling, shivering, into my coat, feeling more like a performing bear in Penrith market place than anything else,[1] when Hugh's furious shout came from above. 'What's going on? 'Tis past dawn and a day lost already! *Allez-y, les gars!*'

Marc prophesied that *je m'enrhumerais*, and told me that if men had been meant to swim they'd be born with webbed feet – *les pattes palmés* – but on the contrary, I was soon warm with paddling. A reservoir of joy welled up inside me, and if I had known how, I could have sung like a voyageur. It was as if God had spread a banquet before us, dazzling our eyes with all the beauty of created things. At the first *pip* I lay back on a bale, watching four eagles soaring over our heads in the blue arch of sky, and I said the verse over in my head: *There be three things which are too wonderful for me: yea four, which I know not: the way of an eagle in the air, the way of a serpent upon a rock, the way of a ship in the midst of the sea and the way of a man with a maid.*

Jean-Pierre cried out '*Allez allez allez.*' My thoughts scattered. I seized my paddle and fell into time as if my life depended on it, but the verse was lodged in my head, thrusting itself into the rhythm of my stroke and mocking me: *which I know NOT; which I know NOT; which I know NOT.*

The north shore, precipitous with small pines clinging

---

[1] I saw one such, when I was a little lad, and it gave me nightmares for many a long day after. The baiting of bears was finally banned four years ago, and indeed I think the law long overdue. We were put on this earth to be the guardians of the beasts of the field, and in no wise unnecessarily to torment them.

to its crags, was closing in on us. We pulled in for breakfast on a long sandy spit on the south side of the river. I'd had an inkling something was up, and no sooner were Alban and I ashore than we were seized, and each one had a noggin of lake water tipped over our heads. 'This is your baptism,' Jean-Pierre said, '*et maintenant vous devenez voyageur!* But first Mark must swear – because he won't get to do it in *les pays d'en haut* – never to kiss a voyageur's wife without her permission!'

'I will not swear,' I said wiping the water out of my eyes. 'But thee has my word that I shall not.'

'*Est-ce qu'on le croît, les gars?*' They were used to me by now, and I realised by their teasing I hadn't offended them. I was thankful, for I was getting to like them well. Hugh offered a *régal* on my behalf, telling me this was a custom that could in no wise be omitted. I reimbursed him a shilling; this is the first and last time in my life I ever exchanged coin for spirituous liquor. Long it lay upon my conscience; I think now that he who makes all forgives all, if so be they are sincerely repentant.

The days passed. So many things I remember ... the dark figures of our voyageurs silhouetted by the fire at night. The scent of resin in the smoke. The pattern of pine branches overhead, and the stars between. Nights full of stars, and strange sounds carried across still water. I mind well how I first heard the call of the loon, and it sounded to me like a lost soul in the wilderness.[2] I remember the howling of wolves in the night forest – but these I never saw until the winter came – and diverse rustlings in the undergrowth. I remember how the chipmunks came foraging right into our tent and even into my pockets, where one of the little pests ate up the

----

[2] When I first saw this great black and white bird on Lake Nippissing, it looked to be not so different from our own Northern Diver, and from all that I could discover its habits seem to be much the same.

last of the ginger biscuits that were my parting gift from William Mackenzie's wife. I remember fiery sunsets as we looked into the empty wilderness ahead of us. I mind pale dawns and *pips*, and the endless paddling through the long heat of summer days. I remember the practised haste of the voyageurs, jog-trotting uphill over rocks and roots with their immense burdens on their backs. I remember climbing to a bluff on the north shore, where Hugh and I looked out to a range of hills far south of us, and how happy I was to see out, for the river curves and climbs but offers no prospect beyond its own banks. I'm used to getting the height of land to see where I am, though there be nothing around me but an infinity of wilderness.

We came to the mouth of the Mattawa – *la petite rivière* – and, if I had thought the Outaouais rapids hard, I soon learned better. We did eleven portages in forty miles, for the Mattawa flows straight down from the watershed. It's a trickier river than the Outaouais altogether, fast-flowing and unpredictable. The country through which we passed reminded me of my native land, much more rugged and open than the featureless miles of forest. One evening we came to yet another portage, where the river ran between huge cliffs. Usually the men like to get the portage behind them, to have a clear start, but we'd been going fifteen hours, and Jean-Pierre called a halt. *Le Talon*, Marc told me, was the worst portage of all. Tomorrow would be soon enough. We beached by a deep brown pool, where we could hear the falls above us. As I ate my pease I watched the reflections of the ripples licking like flames across the bare rock opposite. Spruce and maple trees clung to the cliffs. I caught sight of movement up above. The next thing I knew, a brown body had hurtled into the water, vanishing in a great splash. I jumped to my feet. No one else moved. A sleek black head appeared, and swam to the far shore. A boy climbed out and scuttered away into the woods. There was another huge splash, as the next lad jumped. '*Ah, les garçons!*' Marc held out his bowl for more porridge.

'Who are they?'

'Indians. Nippissings. *Ils sont fous.*'

'*Fous?*'

'Mad,' interpreted Hugh, with his mouth full.

'Oh, but we used to do that,' I said idly. 'Our pool in Bannerdale has a cliff. Not near so high as that. Ours is twenty feet.' I squinted at the rock opposite. A smaller lad was hovering on the brink. I heard shouts and jeers from the other boys hidden in the trees. 'I reckon that'd be about forty feet.'

There was a buzz of talk. I paid no attention; I was thinking about the great shoulder of Blencathra behind Highside, and how if thee crosses the ridge and heads down into Bannerdale, about half a mile from our house, thee comes upon a rocky gorge with rowans clinging to its side. In the hollow of the gorge there's a pool below a waterfall. Thee can step over the beck at the top even when it's in spate – it's not very big – but even so the fall has worn itself a chute on the south bank, and at the top of the chute there's a flat rock to leap from. I've stood there often enough, summoning the courage to jump: the water's always as cold as ice, even in high summer. I've hovered there, looking across at the curve of overhanging rock carved by the beck, and the steep banks all grown over with ferns. I've never failed to jump. A rush of air, the icy plunge – it's deep water; thee can't touch bottom – and then the current catches thee before thee surfaces, and sweeps thee down to the boulders, which is the only place to climb out. The shallow end of the pool is where I learned to swim. I would have been about five.

My sister was forbidden to go near the Glendaramackin pool. Usually she did what she liked anyway, but she didn't dare defy my mother to the extent of going with the lads when they were stripped, and so she couldn't learn to swim. The pool was mine alone. Very occasionally in the height of summer the four of us – my father, my mother, Rachel and me – would walk to Meeting by way of the hill, over the shoulder of Blencathra and down Bannerdale to Mungrisdale, where we picked up our usual road again. It was strange to be out on the hill all washed and brushed for First Day. We'd pass the pool, and it would be like meeting a friend in the road and going by without speaking.

So I lay watching the boys at *Le Talon* Falls, and thinking of my younger self. One of them could do a full somersault before he hit the water. I was getting to know which was which. The little fellow had jumped twice now, but he was scared. I felt sympathetic prickles of tension in my own chest. Jacques gave a piercing whistle, and made me jump. The voyageurs shouted and waved. The Indian boys halted. One jumped, vanished, then his dark head emerged within six feet of us. He grinned at us, treading water. A pantomime of gestures followed, and to my horror I caught the import, just as half a dozen hands grabbed me, took my bowl and spoon, and pulled me to my feet. The lad in the water shouted across to his friends, who burst into shrill catcalls. Hugh said drily, 'I don't think you've much choice, Mark.'

I wouldn't have turned back if I could. Ever since I was a little fellow, and first realised that I was one of a peculiar people, I'd sometimes found it hard to be set apart. Times it seemed that folk thought me less than a man, just because I sought to do the will of God, and abide by the ancient Principles of our Society. I love the Society of Friends; I think it just and good, a Shining Light in an evil world, and I am ever thankful to God that this is my birthright. Never did I wish it otherwise. But times, because I would not fight, nor drink, nor swear, nor speak disrespectfully of women, I felt a belittlement in the eyes of worldly men, which often may not have been so, but only my imagining. But when I felt it, the old Adam would arise in me, as it did now.

I stripped to my drawers – in truth, I shrank more from undressing before them than from the deed itself – and dived into deep water. The Indian lad was already climbing on to the rocks opposite. I followed him into the cover of the trees. There was a little path between the pines. The lad was waiting for me; he beckoned, and led the way up. It was hotter here. Bright butterflies danced in shafts of evening sun. I was aware of my nakedness, the exposed whiteness of my skin, the touch of pine needles brushing against me as I passed. This side of the river was another place altogether. No voyageurs came here. My guide stood on a rock, waiting. He was lithe and dark, a part of this country, and quite at ease: everything, in short, that I was not. I scrambled carefully after him, skinning my knee. Never had I felt so vulnerable.

There were five of them at the top, all in their mid-teens, I guessed. They grinned at me. I smiled shyly back. They stood aside, and gestured for me to go ahead.

It was at least twice as far as the leap at Bannerdale. The crag was sheer, which was something, but there were nasty outcrops to right and left. The pool looked black in the shadows below, very far away. Out of the corner of my eye I saw the canoes, and the bright colours of the voyageurs like little toys. I walked directly to the edge and jumped. There was a rush of air: the plunge sounded right through my body. I breathed out into icy dark, and kicked my way upwards till I burst through into a shower of light.

Once done, I could have done it again – there's an exhilaration that I can't describe – but I let it be, for fear of vainglory. The voyageurs were excessive in their pride and praises, and indeed if there were anything in my strange habits still to be forgiven, the score was paid.

The Indian lads called their farewells across the river and departed. I slept well.

After *Le Talon* the river grew narrower; the rapids got shallower and closer together. The forest turned to wide swamps full of dead trees. By the end we were mostly wading thigh-deep, pushing the canoes through rushing water. One slip and a man could be swept away. We reached Trout Lake, the headwater of the Mattawa. Then came the miserable, mosquito-ridden Mud Portages (this I discovered to be the meaning of *la vase*). Portages is a polite usage: I would describe the place as upwards of five miles of stinking, slimy bog, where the canoes must be propelled among rushes and lily pads, or pushed between banks of willow that slap a man in the face as he passes, while frogs croak mockingly from the marshes round him. The open water, if one could call it that, is created by old beaver dams, but the beavers are gone, and now the voyageurs have to keep the dams in repair, in addition to their other miseries. I came out of La Vase with my face swelled like a fruit pudding with insect bites, and leech scars all down my calves. My boots were permanently soaked through – I didn't have Hugh's privilege of being carried on the shoulders of the voyageurs. I'd given up on stockings, but that was before I realised about the leeches. But the joy of La Vase, which I could not feel until we crossed the last portage and stood looking down on Lake Nippissing, is that it's the watershed. From here on it was downstream all the way.

We crossed Lake Nippissing among treacherous breezes and dancing waters, then fairly flew down the French River – all seventy miles of it – covering more ground in one day than we'd done in the entire haul up the Mattawa. We only portaged twice; everywhere else we ran the rapids. The first time I had my eyes shut, and clung to the gunwale while the canoe twisted about under me like an unbroken colt, and gouts of water hit me in the face. Five Mile Rapids felt like hurtling down an endless chute. Banks of white water crashed down from all sides, even backwards, for all we were meant to be going downstream. Sometimes I thought we were taking off like a bird. I shut my eyes, my stomach lurched and each time as we fell the water hit our underside with a great thump. I got used to the hurly-burly, our forty-foot canoe being tossed about like a shuttlecock, and the rocks sweeping past us like so many wicked teeth waiting to devour us. It was here I lost my broad-brimmed hat, for I had not a spare hand to save it, I was clinging on so tight. There were plenty of crosses along the banks to remind me that even voyageurs were not infallible.

The river ended in a lake of many islands. When we came into open water I gasped: for a moment I forgot all the maps I had seen, in the face of the evidence of my own eyes, and thought we had come through the great continent of North America and stood upon its farther shore. For what lay before me, its waves making endless patterns of light into the distant west, was indubitably an ocean, its waters boundless and bright as the blue sky above us. I said to Hugh, before I could stop myself, 'What is it? Where has thee taken me? Is this Cook's Pacific Ocean?'

Hugh didn't laugh. 'This is Lake Huron,' he said, smiling a little. 'Not even that. This is a little part of Lake Huron, that men name Georgian Bay.'

I shook my head in wonder. The canoe was beginning to dance in the waves, which splashed against its sides with hungry smacking sounds. A fresh wind ruffled my hair, but there was no salt in it. Hugh echoed my thought.

'Smell that – no salt. These are lakes, not oceans. Seas of sweet water.' He leaned over the side, dipped his cup in the next sparkling wave, and offered it to me. 'Drink that! You see? Welcome to our sweetwater seas, Master Greenhorn!'

Just as the light began to fail we met with another brigade come up through Georgian Bay. We all camped in a natural grassy meadow. There was quite a party that night. To tell the truth I couldn't keep away; I'd watched the dancing so many nights I'd learned to like it. Marc and Alban seized me bodily and dragged me into the circle. I couldn't dance, but for an intoxicating moment I felt drawn in. This is an extraordinary thought – nay, blasphemous – but for a wild moment it was like walking into the gathered Meeting and being received.[3] In this place I also encountered my first rattlesnake. I was walking away from the camp through long grass, when I heard a noise at my feet like shaken knucklebones. A great mottled-brown snake slithered past my boots before I had wit to move. I saw the yellowish rings on its tail – just as Marc had described – and I cried out for very terror. Luckily no one heard me but Hugh, who strolled over, pipe in the corner of his mouth, to ask what was the matter. When I told him he laughed, and advised me to take care where I squatted, for 'twould be an undignified way out of the world, to say the least of it.

So the last days flowed by, while we hugged the shore of the Lake Huron. The voyageurs had talked to me about *la cloche* for many miles, and I was expecting some sort of a clock, unlikely though it seemed, but in fact a *cloche* is a bell, and the wonder turned out to be a boulder much like the Bowder Stone in Borrowdale, only this one sounds a deep note when struck.[4] As we crossed the lake many islands hove into sight to the south of us, then drew away

---

[3] This I will erase, lest any child – my unborn grandchildren, perhaps – should ever peruse my manuscript.
[4] When I got home I tried the same experiment on the Bowder Stone, but it hath not the same quality.

behind us. Hugh told me they were called the Islands of the Spirits, and with a great leap of the heart I realised I was looking on the land to which the Lord had summoned Judith and Rachel, when they were in Yonge Street. Hugh said it was true, many displaced Indians had settled there, and it was more than likely they'd be close to starving in winter. As we drew nearer the Sault the weather worsened. To everyone's frustration we were *dérangé* by a little creek for two long days. I wasn't as impatient as the others; there was a confusion growing in my heart that was quite unexpected. In short, I was loath to leave them. I found myself wondering about the lake beyond this one, and the great rendezvous at Fort William, and all the rivers and lakes of the *pays d'en haut* beyond that.

The rain began just as we reached the first channel of the St Mary's River. The voyageurs cursed it, for they like to go ashore to wash and spruce themselves up before a rendezvous, but in this weather the last camp was a dismal, hurried business. As for me, the weather matched my mood. It troubled me not to be soaked to the skin as the rain drummed endless pockmarks into the water, while we paddled onwards into the mists.

CHAPTER 11

THE NORTHWEST COMPANY FACTORY LIES AT THE
foot of the rapids, called the *sault*, of St Mary, on the
north bank of the St Mary's River. Hugh was in the
Company office less than half an hour, and then our
brigade was ready to go through the canal. For at the
Sault the company have built a canal over a mile long,
and there was no tracking to be done either. Instead
the canoes, one by one, were harnessed to a pair of
stout oxen, and our voyageurs had naught to do but
keep the canoes from bumping the sides – the canal is
nine feet wide, big enough for the bateaux that ply the
lakes as well as the canoes – and to enjoy the ride, which
our own crew did, smoking their pipes and calling out
last farewells to me, telling me '*vous comportez en homme
d'honneur parmi les belles femmes de l'Ojibwa!*' At the height
of the canal there is actually a lock. No man who had not
witnessed all the portages of the Outaouais and Mattawa
could appreciate the improvement this little lock – for
it is but thirty-eight feet long, and rises only nine feet –
represents for the men who must work the canoes. After
our brigade went in a gate was lowered behind it. Then
the water was allowed to pour in from the Superior end,
and when it was level with the higher reach, a folding

gate slowly opened at the top of the lock, and the canoes could proceed on their way. I was vastly interested in the whole procedure.[1]

I walked by my canoe as it went through the canal, picking my way over the boards of the towpath, for they were slippery with ox dung. Then I took the shore road, parallel to the canoe course, as my friends set to paddling again. As they drew away the brigade looked very small, for all it had loomed so large in my life. Lake Superior was smooth as a beaver's pelt, with mere kittens' paws wrinkling its surface. I hadn't realised how fast we'd travelled in the canoes, until I found myself ashore and running to keep up. Soon they out-paddled me, and I stood on a point of land while they receded into the wilds of the great Lake Superior. I think I saw a flicker of white, which was Hugh waving his handkerchief to me, being the only man in our canoe with a free hand. He'd have to make do with Alban's services now, until they reached Fort William.

I stopped in the middle of the road, breathing hard, and was suddenly aware of the wilderness at my back.

I'd not been alone for four weeks. I felt bereft, for I'd grown to like my voyageurs very well, but at the same time excitement rose in my chest. Here I was, on a summer

[1] I am better acquainted with our English canals now than I was then. A few years later I invested a small sum in the new Carlisle canal, and I was one of the shareholders who went through on the first boat. Later my elder son Alan and I went on an expedition of pleasure by canal – this would be when he was a lad of ten. We stayed with Friends in Kendal, then took the packet boat from Kendal to Preston, by way of Lancaster, a distance of fifty-seven miles. We went down through eight locks at Tewitfield, and then forty-two straight miles (the longest stretch of unbroken canal in the kingdom) to Preston. There was a tunnel at Hincaster almost quarter of a mile long, a great wonder in itself, but we preferred the locks, and the horses with their uniformed postilion, and the slow unfolding of an unknown countryside as we went by. Alan will be three and twenty this year in Ninth Month, and I have been to Preston several times, ay, and to London Yearly Meeting too, by railway. Thus times change.

afternoon, at one of the furthest outposts of the North American continent, my own man again, on solid land, with an adventure before me that would take me I knew not whither. I was quite alone, as I say, and in a sudden excess of feeling I flisked and ran along that empty road like an unbridled colt, kicking stones and laughing out loud for the sheer joy of being alive.

When I came in sight of the houses I walked more soberly. I picked up my knapsack at the Company office and asked for directions. Thomas Nolan, the man mentioned in Judith's letter, apparently lived on the south side of the rapids. The clerk took me to the factory gate and pointed across the river. On the farther shore, a good mile away, I could make out the specks of houses. The clerk found a man to ferry me over. We crossed above the rapids, so close I felt quite nervous in a frail ten-foot canoe. The whole of Lake Superior seemed to be pouring out around us in a huge stream as wide as the Solway estuary. I could see canoes bobbing in the white water below us. But we got across without mishap, and so it was I first set foot in the United States of America, but if I'd not been told so I'd never have known the difference.

I was directed to a solid two-storey log house set within a high cedar fence. There were cows and chickens in the paddock, and beyond them an enclosed garden. An Ojibwa servant took me in to Mr Nolan. To my surprise I was led into a finely furnished library, where Mr Nolan sat writing at a mahogany desk. He stood up at once, and shook me by the hand. He was something of a dandy, with his embroidered waistcoat and elaborately tied cravat. I must have looked as startled as he did at sight of me. I explained who I was, thinking all the while that this fine fellow seemed an unlikely friend for Rachel and Judith. As if he'd heard my thought, he said, 'You're welcome, sir. 'Twas a sad story altogether. It was my wife who . . .

in short, I could not be persuaded by their religious enthusiasm, but my wife was much moved, and would have it that they must stay with us. Indeed, your aunt and sister were no trouble to us . . . apart, of course, from the unfortunate episode of the young lady's elopement.'

'Did thee know Alan Mackenzie?' I asked him.

'I met him. A very resty gentleman. But the ladies liked him well. In fact my daughter Maddie . . . 'Twas a bad business altogether. But if I can be of assistance, sir, you have only to mention it. You'll stay with us, of course. Let me find my wife.'

To my astonishment – for Nolan was unquestionably a gentleman – his wife was an Ojibwa woman. He introduced her to me without a trace of consciousness. It was if the ground had suddenly grown unstable under my feet, like the heaving and rocking when I stood upon the solid earth at Quebec, that such things could be.

Although Mary Nolan's dress was more or less European, it was embroidered and bedecked with beads in a manner that would have drawn all eyes to her in England, although in this wild place it seemed to me not wholly unattractive. She gave me a bedroom to myself, an extraordinary luxury in those wild parts. It turned out that Thomas Nolan was a Montreal fur trader who'd been at the Sault upwards of twenty years. That evening – and indeed every evening thereafter for the week I stayed there – he talked a great deal about old days in Montreal, and the books he had sent from there, and the friends with whom he corresponded. It was a bad time for trade, he said, since the American embargo last year. He spent most of his time in his study.

His daughter Maddie had been to boarding school in Montreal, and was anxious to let me know it. She wore a white muslin gown, most unsuitable for that country – and for her complexion too – or so it seemed to me, and cut so low in the bosom I had much ado to keep my eyes elsewhere. In the evenings we listened to her playing on her harpsichord (which at home we would have thought ungodly, but I recognised some of the voyageur tunes, and those I liked). She sang well enough – she had learned the art of it at school, but each time she took a deep breath I thought she might burst out of her gown, and that distracted me somewhat from the music. When she was not playing to us, Thomas Nolan read aloud. Only Mary – his wife – was willing to talk to me about Rachel and Judith.

'I am very sorry for you,' she told me. 'I tried to tell your aunt how it was. The young man came here. He said very little, but he looked all the time at your sister. Me, I could see the love between them. But your aunt, she saw it not. I wished to warn her, but she was angry. No one would listen. I could see that Rachel was in great distress of mind, though she tried very much to hide it. Her heart was torn in two, I think. For Rachel . . . I think she is one who feels everything with a great passion. Never would she show a cold heart. Poor girl. I think it was very hard for her. But I was not her mother . . . I was not her kin. What could I do for her? I wish I could tell you where she has gone. But I know not. I have never heard anything more about her.'

Mary Nolan asked me many questions about the Religious Society of Friends. She told me that Rachel and Judith had held a Meeting with her, and she wished that we might do the same. It was the first Meeting I'd attended since I left Yonge Street, and for all that I was the only Member, and only the two of us present, I was comforted by it. It was Mary who looked after the little farm. She kept cows, pigs, chickens and a good vegetable garden. It was good to get my hands in honest soil – I weeded the whole garden in the week I was there, and indeed it needed it. I liked Mary Nolan better than I liked her daughter, which made it hard for me when she said to me, could I perhaps find it in me to love her daughter? For Maddie was hard to please, and wished for nothing more than to go back east. A common fur trader would not do for her, and certainly not an Ojibwa, but an Englishman maybe . . . And then perhaps Maddie would learn the ways of my Society, and set her heart upon less worldly matters.

I explained how I could not marry outside the Society, and when she set about thinking how Maddie might be drawn into Membership, I told her the plain truth, that I could not love her daughter.

'Do you love another girl, then, Mark?'

A lie can be easier than the truth. However, I just said to her plainly, 'No.' I knew she wasn't satisfied, and I was embarrassed. There seemed nothing more to learn about Rachel, so the next day I took my leave, and two of the Nolans' servants ferried me across the Sault. A number of Ojibwa were fishing in the rapids. This time they were standing upright in their tossing canoes, and spearing the fish as they saw them – an incredible feat, it seemed to me. Though as a lad I knew how to guddle a trout (though I would scorn to do that now), I like to do my fishing from firm ground.

When I asked for the South West Company, it turned out to be in the same building as the North West Factory. There my friend the clerk told me that the South West agent, Monsieur Pothier, had just arrived by a fast canoe from Montreal – in fact he'd come in from St Joseph's only the day before. He escorted me to a big office overlooking the canal. A young officer in a scarlet coat stood at the door, apparently taking his leave of somebody within. I heard a voice speaking English in a marked French accent: 'And you will say to Captain Roberts that the Company at the Sault is now gathering its reserves. We hold ourselves in immediate readiness. The captain has but to say the words. *Les voyageurs sont prêts. Il faut frotter ces gens là-bas, joliment. Dis-lui qu'on vient aussitôt qu'il nous appelle.'*

The lad – for he looked to be a good deal younger than I – saluted smartly and stepped back heavily on to my foot. I made way for him quickly. He muttered something which might have been an apology, and strode away.

Toussaint Pothier had an active, youthful air about him, but the expressions that chased one another across his face fell each one of them into deep lines engraved by at least four decades of habit, or so I judged. His desk was piled high with papers, and he received me with considerably less enthusiasm than he'd shown to the young soldier, until I mentioned Alan's name. Immediately I had his attention. I said, 'I have an urgent message for Alan Mackenzie from Montreal. It's important that I find him as soon as possible.'

'Ah, but this is fortunate! Monsieur McGillivray said that I should expect you also. *Vous avez de la chance, monsieur.* Monsieur Mackenzie is this instant at the Sault! This very morning we have met here. *Mais il faut vous dépêcher* – you must hurry. He returned two hours ago to the house of Monsieur Ermatinger, but already as we speak he may be departing. His canoe is at the causeway. Come, everything now is of urgency! *Georges, revenez!'* – this was shouted down the corridor, and a lad appeared immediately – '*Prenez ce monsieur chez Monsieur Ermatinger aussi vite que possible!* Georges will take you to the house of Monsieur Ermatinger, and there I hope you will still find Monsieur Mackenzie. If he has gone already, come back here. Then I will make arrangements for you to follow him directly to Mackinac. *Eh bien, Monsieur, au revoir.* Yes, yes, *je vous en prie*, but now you must go with Georges!'

Georges and I fairly ran down a stony track for about half a mile, until we reached a log house where we pulled up, panting. An Indian woman in a short blue dress was in the garden, hoeing amidst high green corn. Chickens scratched in the dust around the door. There was a sweet smell of woodsmoke in the air, and I could hear the shrill voices of unseen children playing.

Georges spoke to the woman in what I thought at first was French. Unhurriedly she laid down her hoe, and answered him. Georges turned to me. "M'sieu Ermatinger is within, and Alan Mackenzie also, she says.'

'Will thee take me to him?' My voice was steady, but there was a fluttering in my stomach, thinking that after all my travels my quarry was so very near.

Georges nodded. I turned to follow him but to my surprise the woman suddenly spoke directly to me, in English. 'You are the brother of Alan Mackenzie's wife, I think. Is this so?'

I stared at her. 'Thee knows Rachel? Thee knows where she is? Does thee know what happened to her?'

She wasn't a young woman. I had no idea who she was; I assumed she must be a servant of the family. She said, and her accent was so soft I had to listen carefully to catch the words: 'Rachel MacKenzie stayed with us in this house. After the baby died I was afraid for her. She had too many dreams. You've come from over the sea to look for her, have you not?'

She had me mesmerised. 'How did thee know I was her brother?'

'You're of the people in grey, as she was. When I saw that, I looked at you closely. I see her eyes in yours, and much likeness about the mouth. She told me she had a brother, and I remembered. Then you spoke, and I was sure of it.'

'Thee must have known her well.' I could hardly grasp it, that a little something of my sister should so suddenly be vouchsafed to me from such a source. It was as if one of the fruit trees in the garden had spoken to me, or the big rock by the gate.

'No, I did not know her well.' She picked up her hoe. 'Go and find Alan Mackenzie. I've told him he should not give up looking for her. No one else will tell him that.'

'And thee is . . . ?' It occurred to me I might want to find this woman again.

The reply left me all amazed. 'Charlotte Ermatinger.'

I followed Georges, trying to marshal a welter of confused thoughts. A girl was chopping herbs at the table in the kitchen. She said her father had taken Mr Mackenzie to see the site for the new house. So Georges led me by an orchard and a cornfield, back to the river bank, where we could see the whole rapids spread out before us. There was no need to hurry now; Charles Ermatinger and his friend were expected back for supper.

'Who is this Charles Ermatinger, Georges?'

'M'sieu Ermatinger? He is . . .' Georges waved his arms to express the impossibility of explanation. 'He does not work for the Company any more. He is *un marchand indépendent*, he is his own company. And that is not so bad. He has cut down very many trees and made here the biggest farm in the Sault. And now he has so much money that he builds a great house. It is built with stones.'

'Here? I've not seen a stone house.'

'Not yet, m'sieu, not yet. At present it is built with paper and much talk. And now M'sieu Ermatinger arranges that we fight with the Americans. I, Georges, will fight also.'

I looked at him sadly. He was dark, even for a Frenchman. His eyes were alight with an enthusiasm I would never share. The crazy thought flashed through my mind that if I'd come to bear arms by his side I could at this point shake his hand and call him brother, but as it was, a great gulf of misunderstanding would for ever divide us. 'Why must thee fight, Georges? War will beget naught but war. Does thee not know the law of God: Thou shalt not kill?'

'And doesn't *thee* know' – he threw the word back at me mockingly – 'that if we do not fight, the Americans will come here and burn our houses and rape our women, and kill even the little children? They will seize our Company and all the free territory of the west. Does *thee* not know that the Americans come to take away our hunting grounds? They drive us away from the lands where our fathers are buried. They force us from our homes on to land that is no good. Does *thee* not know that there is already a great war in the south, and that by this war our people will live or die, for ever and for ever? Does *thee* not know any of that? And if *thee* does not, I ask *thee*, what right has *thee* to speak so to me?'

I looked at him in puzzlement. 'Thee's right, friend, I'm just arrived here and I know very little. I only know that in no place on this earth can there ever be a good end to war. But – thee's not a Frenchman, then, Georges?'

'Yes, I am French. I am Georges Beauclerc, junior clerk to M'sieu Pothier of the South West Company. And yes, I am not French. I am Abeetung of Sisibakwatominiss, of the Ojibwa people.'

'And the Ojibwa people are preparing to fight the Americans?'

'It is not only the Ojibwa. You know of Tecumseh.'

'No, what is it?'

'*He* is not *it*! Even *thee* must know that. Tecumseh is the great leader of the Shawnee people. Already he is fighting the Americans in Ohio. The Indians will fight together, you understand; otherwise the Americans will take our land and destroy our people, for ever and for ever. And *thee* – *thee* British – *thee* have promised to ally with us. So now does *thee* begin to understand why there must be war?'

'I understand thee. But I too have my people, and our practice is always to seek the way which tends to the peace of all . . .' My own words failed me so I quoted: '*All bloody principles and practices we do utterly deny, with all wars and strife and fighting with outward weapons, for any end whatsoever.* There must be other ways to survive than by violent means, Georges. For God is merciful.'

'If *thee* can swear to that, *thee* has not seen what I have seen. Now, I have said enough. We approach the new house of M'sieu Ermatinger.'

Perhaps Georges had eyes that could see a house made only of 'paper and much talk', but I saw nothing but a flat stretch of river bank, and a thin shingle beach where the waves speedily chased each other into oblivion. Then I caught sight of two men standing side by side on the shore. They were holding a paper between them, and indeed all hands were necessary, for there was a smart breeze down here by the water's edge. One of them must be Alan. Again I felt that fluttering under my ribs. I had thought about finding him for so long. Oddly, now that I had, I was afraid.

They looked up enquiringly as we approached. The short one with greying hair was obviously Charles Ermatinger. The other was a thin young man, very tanned, with a sprinkling of freckles from much sun. He was dressed in the wool coat and corduroy breeches that all Company clerks wear, even in the heat of summer, but his cravat was tied like a gentleman's, and instead of a cap he wore a high-crowned beaver. A hybrid, he seemed, something between a clerk and a Company partner. Certainly he held himself with the assurance of a gentleman, and if his face was weathered and his clothes well-worn, why, that was the way of it with all the Company men who over-winter in the west. I'd imagined him, because I knew he was a Scotchman, to be redhaired and rawboned, but not a bit of it. He was slight and dark, and even on that first meeting I was aware of the pent energy in him, as if he could not stay still for long but must be doing.[2]

'This gentleman wants M'sieu Mackenzie,' said Georges.

Alan looked at me. For all that I had lost my broad-brimmed hat on the French River, and now wore a voyageur's red woollen cap with a tassel ('twas the first coloured garment I'd worn in my life, but as I couldn't see it, I tended to forget I had it on, except when the sun got in my eyes and I missed my hat), my dress was still Quakerly enough. I know not if Alan saw the likeness to Rachel as Charlotte Ermatinger had done. Just as she did, he knew already that I existed. I watched recognition slowly dawn in him, and then I spoke to him plainly. 'Alan, I'm thy brother-in-law, Rachel's brother. I've come from Mungrisdale in Cumberland to find thee, and to find her, if she lives.'

I could see amazement in his face, and a kind of horror, like a man that sees a ghost, and then that passed too. His eyes were neither green nor brown, but that variable colour in between which men call hazel.[3] He held out his hand to me, and said to me in a voice that only shook a little, 'I have

---

[2] Or is all this the knowledge of hindsight? How hard it is to recapture the instant before a momentous change! I wish I had given less space in my notebook to the rapids, and the islands in the St Mary's River, and even the drawing of the winch and tackle on the lock gate, and thought to give my first impression of my brother-in-law. But one thing I did note, and which I recollect well, was that from the moment when I first laid eyes on him I was certain that I'd seen him before. I forgot for a while, because he soon became familiar to me anyway. But whiles the feeling came back to me, and sometimes at night I wondered about it.

[3] It occurs to me now that hazel does indeed change from green to brown and back again as the seasons change; this is not fickleness but merely its nature. That might be read as a parable of my brother-in-law Alan, of whom at that early stage I knew nothing, except that he was implicated as deeply as he could be in the matter that had brought me here, and that I required to know not only all that he had to tell me, but whether or not I could trust him, in word or deed, or in any way at all.

heard of you, of course. You are Mark Greenhow. How do you do?'

The question seemed to me irrelevant, so I ignored it, but I shook his hand heartily. Part of my fear, I realised, was that I should dislike him on sight, recognise him for a rogue and a libertine, and be filled with evil thoughts towards him. It would be easier to walk cheerfully if one were certain of recognising that of God in every man; it was a vast relief to me to find that with Alan it was not difficult. Indeed from that night onwards I was able to add him to the tally of my family in my prayers, and he has retained his place there ever since. I was able in all truth to say to him, 'I am blithe to meet thee, brother.'

'You've come a long way to do so.'

'Ay.'

The silence between us was broken by Charles Ermatinger, who had been occupied in rolling up his plan, but for all that I'd been aware of his eyes upon us. 'I knew your sister, Mr Greenhow. Your family must have suffered greatly. I'm sorry for it.' He turned to Alan. 'Mackenzie, this will change your plans somewhat. If you both wish to stay the night with us, you're welcome.'

Alan was still staring at me as if he couldn't drag his eyes away. 'Tonight?' He sounded dazed. 'That's kind. Except . . . Mr Greenhow . . . Mark . . . what would you? I have to get back to Mackinac. The least I can do is offer you such hospitality as I can command. You must want . . . I don't know. Will you come back to Mackinac with me, sir?'

'Ay.'

'That's best, I suppose . . .' He looked at me doubtfully. 'My business here is a little delicate. If I take you back with me now, can I rely on your discretion? Can you swear you'll forget every detail of our trip, until we go ashore at Mackinac? Because if not, I can't take you.'

'Nay, friend, I'll not swear. As for forgetting, it's not an act of will, so I can't vouch for it.'

Alan smiled. 'I was forgetting. In plain speech, brother Mark, will you please keep silent about anything that happens on our journey from the Sault to Mackinac?'

'Otherwise thee won't take me?'

'Just so.'

I thought it over, while they waited for me. 'I will keep silent, friend, so long as I witness no strife nor conflict with outward weapons, or bodily hurt to any man.'

'Fair enough.'

'But I may live long. Does thee require me to keep silent for ever?'

'That's a hard one.' It was Alan's turn to think a little. 'How about twenty years, and that only if you're in England?'

'Very well, friend. I will be silent for that long, and under that condition.'

He laughed a little ruefully. 'And I believe you, more than I'd believe many a man's oath, brother Mark. Such is the strength of a truthful people!'

The three of us supped on whitefish and cornbread at Charles Ermatinger's house. I would have liked to have had more words with his wife, Charlotte, but she didn't sit with us, although she brought in the food and waited on us. She was silent, and neither of my companions spoke to her. I couldn't break what was evidently the custom of the house.

We sat over our meal a long time. I asked Alan, 'We travel to Mackinac in the dark, do we?'

'It's a full moon, and a clear night.'

Never shall I forget that journey across the river, with the sound of the falls following us, a shining line slowly receding as the current swept us away from the Sault township and into unknown night. The moon was the same midsummer moon that would be shining down on Highside. They would be haymaking by now, I reckoned. I thought of the long hot days in the field, the swish of the scythe and the dry grass falling – I am no mean hand at the scythe, for my father showed me the art of it as soon as I was tall enough – and the chatter of the women as they raised the stooks behind us. We always ate our dinner in the hayfield, in the shade of a hedge, looking across at the hills all bare and shadowless under the noon-day sun. Then back to work until the light started to thicken, and we had to stop because the dew was falling. Of course there were bad years too, when the weather never came right, and in the end we had to bring in the harvest in a scrambling hurry, and the hay was green and some of it spoiled altogether. When I was a little lad the harvests always seemed to be bad, but as I grew older the sun seemed to shine upon us more. I wondered if this year were a good one, and how my parents were faring, and what Thomas Carr was making of my share of the work.

Around the moon the stars shone faintly. I found the Plough: we were heading south, give or take a little. Away from the falls the lake shone clear as glass, as the silence drifted in, broken only by the soft sound of expert paddling. The backs of the voyageurs were dark shapes in front of me, their paddle arms rising and falling in the rhythm that was by now woven into my own dreams too. This was a smaller canoe than the one I'd shared so long with Hugh, a *canot du nord* they call it, but there was so little cargo that I had room enough to stretch my legs out, a luxury unknown on the Outaouais route. At first a black bulk of land rose up on each side of us, but then the left bank fell away, and there was naught but the gleam of open water as far as the eye could reach. On our left the low-lying land went on without interruption. No one spoke or sang. I must have fallen asleep, for when I woke the sky was pale, with a faint tinge of yellow in the east, and for the first time since I left Montreal I felt it cold.

I know not if Alan slept at all, but when I woke, he was looking out across the lake, and munching on a hunk of cornbread. He offered me a bannock and some cold whitefish. 'Better than pease soup, eh, brother Mark?'

'Ay.' I sat up beside him and looked about. There was land on our left, close enough for me to see a white stone beach with stands of pine trees covering all the land behind it. 'What land is this?'

'This is Pekwadinashing.' I must have looked blank, for he grinned. 'St Joseph's Island to you. We have a small message to do here, and maybe a little food and a little sleep, if we're lucky.'

I looked at that featureless forested shore, and burst out 'I wish I had a map!'

He regarded me with interest. 'You like maps? There's a lot they don't tell you. As it happens, that's one desire I can gratify. I've a map at Mackinac you can look at. But we're getting close. Listen!'

I heard the soft plash of the paddles, and a sighing in the pines on the shore. Then a heartbeat rhythm from within the island, still far away. 'What's that?'

'Drums.'

We paddled on. Over the island the sky grew red, then orange. The sun heaved itself over the trees and the lake burst into light. The drums were growing louder. The sun reached us in the boat, and I felt the sudden warmth of it. There was a break in the forest. We were coming to a clearing. I could see smoke. We drew closer, and I saw a wharf. At least a score of big canoes were beached close by. There were little canoes too, some half in, half out of the water. The smoke came from dozens of campfires, with figures moving round them. The drums were beating everywhere. There was a fort at the top of the hill. Under its walls there was a big splash of red. We came alongside. Some of the men around the wharf were voyageurs. A couple were sentries in red coats. Most were Indians. I stared, my heart in my mouth. They were dressed only in breechclouts and leggings. Their bare skin was daubed with black and russet, most of all around the face. Their hair was long; they wore beads and feathers. Worst of all, they were armed. All had knives, some had axes at their belts, and one or two had muskets slung across their shoulders. As for the splash of red up by the fort, I could see now it was a group of soliders, standing at ease against the bastion.

'What is this place?'

Alan caught the sharpness in my tone, for he said, 'We come in peace, brother Mark. The war's not started yet. This is Fort St Joseph. It's a place where traders stop; it's one of our main meeting places. Some live here too. I'm going to take you to the house of one now, a good friend of mine.'

'But this is a fort! This is an army!'

'Yes, it's a fort.' He was getting impatient. 'And the Indian Department has offices here, so the Indians gather here too. It's everything. Will you step ashore, brother Mark?'

Our voyageurs were already ashore, and with the speed I was used to they were unloading food and a kettle and preparing to make a new fireplace among the stones on the beach. I hesitated. The drums were so loud now they seemed to echo in my chest, as if my heart were not my own. Over and above the beat, I could hear a wild howling going to and fro, like men crying to one another across the mountains.

'You can settle in for the day, lads. Get some sleep. We've another night's work before us.' Alan turned to the bowsman, whose face I hadn't seen before, though I'd been watching his back, and the rhythmic twist and pull of his shoulder as he paddled, since first light: an image imprinted on my mind of a voyageur's knitted cap, long black hair hanging loose half way down his back, and a plain trade shirt with the sleeves rolled up to reveal powerful forearms. 'Loic, will you take Mr Greenhow here to Mr Askin's house? Askin won't mind. Tell him – or if he's not there tell someone – to look after Mark today: let him eat, let him sleep. I'll meet you there in an hour or two, brother Mark. I'd get some rest if I were you. I won't be long, I promise.'

He shouldered a canvas haversack and set off through the throng, up the hill towards the battery. I watched him go, frowning.

'Come, m'sieu! Your bag will be safe here. Let me take you to the house of Mr Askin.'

I looked at Loic. Apart from the long hair, he seemed a typical voyageur, dark, tough and sturdy. I knew enough now to recognise that he was as much Indian as French. 'Can thee tell me, friend, what we do here? I thought we were going straight to Mackinac?'

'Mr Mackenzie must speak to Captain Roberts. It won't take long.'

'Captain Roberts . . . is he an officer here?'

'He's the commander of Fort St Joseph.' Loic picked a way through the crowd, sometimes speaking in an unknown tongue to the men we passed. Half a dozen drummers crouched round each drum, singing as they drummed. There were no words that I could hear, only a wild rhythm that rose and fell and made my skin prickle and my spine grow cold. Close to each campfire there was a stack of muskets, barrels pointing skywards. Some of the militia men were grilling fish on twigs over the fire, just the way we do by Derwentwater. Then we were through the crowd, and I was able to fall into step beside Loic. We followed a track along the shore. The sun was well up by now; I could feel the heat against my back. Little waves beat on the shore. Big copper-coloured butterflies flew to and fro. The steady drumming behind us was like the heart of the island beating as it slept under the sun. I took off my coat, and carried it on my arm.

'What has Fort St Joseph to do with the South West Company at Mackinac?'

'The British soldiers built this place when they had to leave Mackinac. Mackinac was given back to the Americans in '96. The British bought this island from the Indians and made a new fort here instead. St Joseph's Island is British. Over there,' – he gestured towards the low line of land to the west of us – 'that's American land. I was only a child, but there was much talk about it at the time.'

'Where does thee come from, Loic?'

'You would call it Bois Blanc.' (I heard him say 'Boblo' but Alan spelt it for me a few days later, when I was bringing my notebook up to date.) 'You will see. It's the next island to Mackinac.'

'In American territory?'

'Yes, though when I was growing up it made no difference. Only now.'

'Thee lives there still?'

'In winter only.' We came to a little wicket gate with a garden of corn and vegetables beyond it. Loic held the gate open for me. 'And you, m'sieu, you've come all this way from England?'

'Ay.'

He stopped me as I was about to go through the gate. 'I knew Rachel, m'sieu. I travelled with them, all the time.'

I stared at him. 'Thee was there when she was lost?'

'Yes, I was there.' The crickets chirruped around us. Stems of raspberry grew almost over the gate. I took hold of one in between its prickles and lifted it out of my way. I could not raise my eyes to his. 'Alan could have done no more, m'sieu,' said Loic. 'We stayed and searched from new moon to full, and back again. The ice was beginning to set. If we'd not left then, it would have been winter. If we'd stayed on South Manitou Island we'd have starved. We had no stores for winter.'

'Loic.'

'Yes, m'sieu?'

'I must go to South Manitou Island. Thee understands that? I've come to find her if I can.'

'I understand why you want to go to South Manitou Island. I think you will not find her.'

I brushed my hand across my face and met his eyes. I could read no expression there at all. 'Thee thinks she must be dead?'

'M'sieu, I don't know. Either she was taken, or she's dead. She couldn't be alive, if she were alone.'

'Taken?'

'Sometimes women are kidnapped. Not only white women. It is a thing which happens sometimes among the Indians.'

I asked him plainly. 'Is thee Indian, Loic?'

'My father is Martin Kerners. My father's father was Loic Kerners of Morbihan. My mother was Ottawa. She came from the south, in the Michigan Territory.'

'And thee thinks that Rachel may have been kidnapped?'

'I tell you, m'sieu, I don't know.' He gestured for me to go through the gate. 'Now I shall take you to the house of Monsieur John Askin. But we can speak again.'

He led me past the garden, and on to a track where some log-framed houses looked east across the lake. We had come right round the little promontory on which the fort was built. There was another big encampment of Indians just along the shore. I struggled with the turmoil of my thoughts. Loic was silent.

At length he stopped at a big log house, two storeys high, knocked on the door, and walked in. I heard him calling out in a language I didn't know, and apparently waiting while someone answered. Then an Indian woman came out with him.

'Monsieur and Madame Askin are not here,' said Loic. 'This woman will give you breakfast, and you can sleep if you like. Alan will come soon.'

It seemed quite dark within at first. Then I saw we were in a plain office, with a desk and chair, and a shelf of ledgers behind it. The board floor was swept and polished. Through an open door I glimpsed a section of a parlour: I could see a chair, and a framed picture on the wall above the hearth, simple indeed, but an extraordinary vision of civilisation to find in this wilderness. We didn't go in. Instead the woman led me through to a kitchen at the back. There was an enamel bowl filled with half washed dishes on the table, and rinsed glasses spread on a cloth to dry. The fire had sunk to glowing embers, which I was glad of, for the place was almost unendurably stuffy, though it was a relief to be out of the sun. The smell, half pleasant, half pungent, I presently identified as a mix of fresh-parched corn and burning sage. There was a pail of fresh water by the door, which was the thing I desired above anything else that might be offered.

Just as Loic was leaving he turned back to me. 'I think you've done right,' he said. 'It's a good thing if a brother looks after his sister, however far she strays. We voyageurs liked her very well. I would help you, if I could.'

CHAPTER 12

'HO, MARK? WAKE UP, MAN! I'M HERE TO TALK TO YOU!'

'I wasn't sleeping.' No point in telling this new brother of mine that I'd gathered the silence to myself, for my heart was troubled, and I felt far from Friends, and far from God also, if the truth be told. I opened my eyes.

Alan was taking off his coat. 'It's hot out there. It's past noon, you know. I trust you're rested.'

'Ay.'

'Well, we have some time now. I'm sorry to have hurried you away from the Sault like that, but this was urgent. I've delivered my message now. We leave at night-fall.'

'Why does thee travel by night?'

'Ah ... These waters are less safe than you know, brother Mark. There was a North West brigade – just five years ago this was – and the Yankee soldiers fired on them as they were coming up the Mackinac Straits. This in peacetime, in a land where trade is supposed to be free.'

'I read in the English newspapers that we've done the same thing to American ships on the high seas.'

'Are you a bloody Jacobin, or what?'

'I'm a peaceable man, friend. I merely made an observation.

Is it normal in these parts for Canadian traders to travel only in darkness?'

'Ah well, there are reasons . . . is this what you wished to talk to me about, brother Mark?'

I sighed. 'I wish that thee and I would talk in friend-ship, Alan.'

'Then maybe we should leave the politics out of it.'

'I don't wish to speak of politics. But even if I'm nothing more than a piece of luggage on this journey, I can't help being luggage with eyes in my head.'

'*Touché*, brother Mark. Now it's my turn to ask you. You came all the way from Cumberland? How did you trace me?'

He listened intently to my story, and said, 'Rachel told me she had a big brother who'd always got her out of scrapes. But I think it's beyond you, or any man, to effect a rescue now.' He paused. ''Twas not for want of trying, you know.'

'I believe thee.'

'You want me to tell you about her? About what hap-pened?' I was noticing as he talked to me the lilt in his voice, as if all his words were poetry. Hugh Chisholm had it too, but not so marked. Alan's English was good; in fact he didn't sound at all like the Scotchmen who come south to sell their cattle at our fairs. But those men are not Highlanders, and that is why I heard such a difference in him.

'Ay. And to make amends, maybe.'

'Amends?' He looked at me quizzically, but I saw that he was wary. 'So what penance have you prepared for me, brother Mark?'

'I'm not the judge of that. I mean only to say that if she's alive, and in this world, I intend to find her, and I can't do that without thee. I don't know the country. Will thee come with me, Alan? Will thee show me the way?'

He flung himself down on the chair opposite me: I'd been enjoying the clean calm of the empty sitting room, and wondering who these Askins were, who lived in this benighted place like Christian Englishmen. 'Are you mad?' demanded Alan. 'Do you think I haven't searched? That I wouldn't have searched the world over, if such a thing were possible? I wouldn't have harmed a hair of her head! There was nothing, I tell you. Nothing. Not a sign. Do you think I haven't been over all this ground before, again and again? Would we ever have come away if there were any sign at all? I tell you there was none. None!'

'Very well,' I said, wishing that he would be calm. 'Perhaps there are no signs. But I have to read that for myself. Perhaps a fresh eye will see more. It can happen.'

'You're mad. You don't know the country. Besides, there's a war on. It's way over in Yankee territory. Man, you know nothing at all. What the devil do you expect me to do?'

'I expect thee to take me to the place where she was lost.' I saw I was getting nowhere with him, and tried to be more persuasive. 'Surely, friend, our hopes are the same. Can't we put our minds together, as brothers should do, and search together?'

'Brothers!' He stared at the window. The glass was thick and greenish, and the sun made patterns in it that cast a streaky light between us. 'I thought you'd be out for my blood. I wouldn't let you kill me, but in fairness – because I admit there are amends to be made – you note that? – I thought in fairness I should let you try, if you desired it.'

'I seek no man's blood. What would it profit me to harm thee? I simply ask thee to help me find Rachel.'

'You couldn't harm me anyway.'

This time I was silent because I was struggling with myself. I could floor him in half a minute if I put my mind to it. There is a great arrogance in men who bear arms, and sometimes I've had to resist the temptation that affords.

'It's out of the question,' said Alan suddenly, as if I'd spoken. 'This war's about to break; you can't go wandering off into the Michigan Territory. The Indians are dangerous – and I mean that. There's been drought two summers running. The corn harvest failed last year and is like to do again. People are starving down there. You didn't know that, did you? And the Yankee law says the Indians aren't allowed to trade with us any more. If you don't get scalped because you're a white man, and the cause of all their troubles, you'll as likely as not be picked up by the Yankees and shot for a spy. You can't do it.'

'I thought the Indians were thy allies?'

'Yes and no. The Indian is his own man. He's fighting a war that's not quite the same as our war. There's ways our interests are the same. The fact is you can't go into Michigan. But I can take you with me to Mackinac. Then you'll see for yourself.'

'I have a letter for thee,' I said, watching him, 'from William McGillivray of the North West Company.'

'From McGillivray! Why the devil didn't you say so before? Where is it?'

I took it from my pocket. 'Thee gave me no chance to be private with thee till now.' He held out his hand for it, but I said, 'William McGillivray gave me his word that this letter had naught to do with wars or strife or fighting with outward weapons for any end whatsoever. I wouldn't have brought it to thee otherwise.'

'I see. Fair enough. May I have my letter?'

I watched him glance at the seal before breaking it. He unfolded the single page and read. His face gave away nothing, which seemed to me unnatural, for I'd noticed that he had a very expressive cast of countenance. He must have read it all at least twice, or else been a singularly poor scholar, which last I did not believe. Eventually he folded up the paper, and slipped it into his haversack, where it lay on the bench beside him.

'So!' he said, as one giving his attention to a new subject. 'Brother Mark! What do you want to do now?' His hostility had evaporated; suddenly he was all animation. 'You're crazy, but I realise you mean what you say. Perhaps I dismissed your plan too quickly, and if I did I'm sorry for it. Remember it's more than two years since I had anything to do with you Quakers.' He paused, 'It's two years since I lost her.'

He was staring at the little bright patch of window again. I waited for him to go on. 'I agree I owe it to you to tell you about it. Is that what you want me to do? To tell you?'

'Ay.'

We sat for some minutes. I hoped that the silence might speak to him, and sure enough, presently he began his story.

'Where to start? I don't feel obliged to tell you how she was won, only how she was lost. You seem to be a gentleman. I wish I could say the same for all your people. It's their fault, not mine, that she was cast out. What do you call it? Disowned. That seems a terrible, cold-hearted notion to me, sir. I'd never disown my sister: not if she ran off with a tinker, or brought home a child to whom she could name no father at all. Not, you understand, that either of these things is in the least likely to happen to my sisters. I'm only saying that my kin are my kin whatever they may say or do, and this disowning seems to me a savage custom. I offered Rachel marriage, and when she was mine I dealt honourably with her. If you, or her father, or any sensible man had been there, I'd have asked for her hand in form. There was no man to ask. I offered her no insult. She was innocent when she agreed to come with me, and so she remained, regarding what I might have been, or done. If your people let women wander the world without protection, leaving them to the mercies of their own ignorance, then you must abide the consequences. I don't have to apologise to you for that.

'When I met her I'd only just arrived at the Sault myself. Before that I was in the north-west. When I got back to Fort William in '09 the partners called me to the Council Chamber. I was hoping it would be to offer me a post of my own, and Montreal leave before that – a winter sleeping in a bed with sheets on it, and the newspapers in a coffee house by a coal fire of a winter morning. I'm no Corinthian; I don't ask much. As it is, I've never been near a Beaver Club dinner, but . . . well, I'm young yet. However, I was partly right: they did offer me promotion, but I didn't get the post I'd hoped for. They were sending me to the Mackinac Company – no mention of Montreal – I was to take up my new post right away. We needed to strengthen our presence at Mackinac – that's just politics – you don't want to hear all that. I'd had to deal with some trouble with the Bay up north – I guess I've learned to talk my way out of things, or into things when necessary. I was flattered they'd picked me for a job that might be a little delicate.

'I laid eyes on your sister a few weeks after I'd started at Mackinac. I come up from Mackinac to the Sault every couple of months or so: I carry the messages between the company posts, you see. You notice my winged heels? I even go up in winter sometimes, when the ice is safe.

'I was walking on the canal towpath with Mr Ermatinger. He came to the Sault the year before I started at Mackinac. I liked him as soon as I met him. He's not in the Company any more, but he's a good man to know. He and his wife keep an open house for folk like me. Ermatinger was telling me about a plan to put another sloop on the upper lake – nothing larger than a bateau can get through the canal;

there's still a hell of a lot of portaging – but never mind that, except it was because we'd been speaking of sloops that we went to look at the one that had just come into the jetty below the rapids. It was the *Francis* – she's often hereabouts – and there was a high old commotion going on around her: a huddle of folk, and a lot of screams and yelling. I know a fight when I see one. My own voyageurs were down there by the canoe. So I upped and ran, with Ermatinger panting after me.

'I pushed through the crowd. Men were struggling for space to use their fists, and women were screaming to get out. A man hurtled on top of me, and I fell against Ermatinger. As the man fought free I saw he was a black fellow, bareheaded and barefoot. That's a rare sight in these parts. He pushed me off as I struggled to get my footing, then shot off like a ragged demon out of hell. A child went flying and began to shriek. The black fellow was away down the towpath. A sailor started after him, but I saw an old Indian fellow stick out his foot, and the sailor fell full length. The black man fled past the sawmill, then leapt off the towpath and vanished behind the fence.

'Ermatinger yelled for order. I pulled a couple of fellows apart and got the jetty cleared. The petty officer was swearing at someone – I heard the words – "And you – you interfering bitch! Clear off! And be damned to you!" I shoved the sailors aside to see who was causing the trouble.

'You know your own sister, I suppose. When I first saw her she'd been in a fight. You can say she'd not used her fists, but she'd bruised her knuckles all right. Her cap was torn off and her hair falling down. Dark hair, with a bit of a curl in it. The collar of her grey gown was ripped open. There was a big red mark on her cheek. She was trying to catch her breath. Her hands were curled into fists, and she was biting her lip, staring at the spot where the black fellow had vanished.

'I was a lost man, brother Mark, from that moment. It was Ermatinger who took charge. "What's this?" he was saying. "Who's the black fellow? Did he assault the lady? What's been happening?"

'A babble of voices answered him in French, Ojibwa and English. He called to a voyageur. "Pierre – you – were you here? Tell me what happened! The rest of you silence!"

'"No," Pierre told us. "It was not like that at all, M'sieu Ermatinger. The black fellow was on the sloop, had been hiding, you must understand, on the sloop. Was down below deck, hidden on the sloop. Had come aboard, in secret, at Fort Detroit maybe, from down south in any case. From the United States. Had come aboard, you understand, without permission, without the knowledge of the captain. The black fellow was apprehended just now, half an hour ago maybe. Had been seen coming ashore, jumping down from the gangplank when he thought there was no guard. And the sailors had come running at once, but the young lady . . . People from the village had been listening, you understand, to the young lady. She was speaking in English. Some understood, and some had come to watch anyway. She spoke with the elders of the tribe, and this was pleasing to them. A small crowd had gathered, and there was some speech and some silence. It was in the silence that the black fellow leapt down from the gangway and began to run. Then the sailors ran after him. The young lady jumped up and flung herself into the fight. She would not let go, and while the one man tried to throw her off, the black fellow fought to be free of the other. Everyone crowded round, to help the one or the other – I know not which – and the rest you saw."

'I was watching Rachel while Pierre spoke. She was getting her breath back. She tucked her torn collar back into the neck of her gown, and pushed her hair out of her eyes. When Pierre stopped she looked directly at Ermatinger and said, "Friend, it is as he says, only I did not fight. I held the sailor merely, so that the man could run away."

'She said that. She's your sister, but it wasn't just a black eye she had afterwards. She'd skinned her knuckles too. I think none the worse of her, either for what she did or what she said. I just wondered why it mattered to her enough to lie. I watched the way she pushed her hair back from her face; her cap was gone and she had nothing to tie it with. I was glad when Ermatinger asked her to come back to his house. I didn't want to let her out of my sight.

'"I will come with thee," she said to him. "I have to find my aunt. We're staying at Thomas Nolan's, on the other side," and she pointed across the strait. "Thee seems to have some authority here. If the stowaway is found, what will happen to him?"

'"This is British territory," Ermatinger said. "And I'm a magistrate here. If the man's a civilian, as I guess he is, there's no reason for anyone to detain him, unless the captain of the *Francis* would like his passage money paid."[1]

'"If he is found, will thee protect him? And if the captain wants money, will thee recompense him, out of the kindness of thy heart?"

---

[1] This incident, and Ermatinger's generous response, caused much stir at the time; there were those that thought the black fellow should have been returned to his owner without more ado. Others said he would have done better to go straight to the Indians, as other fugitives had done. Nowadays, Alan tells me, there is a regular exodus of former slaves from the United States into Upper Canada. I replied to his letter saying I'd heard the subject discussed at London Yearly Meeting, and that Friends were united in offering wholehearted support to the liberated policies of Upper Canada, though we understood that even now complete security of residence was not guaranteed to all citizens, whatever their race, and whatever oppressions they might have fled. Even as I write, we pray daily that the day of equitable justice will yet come.

'Ermatinger raised his brows. "I thought you might be about to offer to pay his fare, since he got off scot-free through your agency?"

'"Perhaps it's thy opportunity to welcome him. If he hears thee's paid his fare, perhaps he'll dare to come into the open. Then thee can give him work and lodging with thy Company."

'Her audacity took my breath away. I wished I could tie back her unruly hair for her. Ermatinger's house is not half a mile from the Huron jetty. By the time we reached it I was already committed to maybe the worst – certainly the most foolish – decision of my life.'

I did not respond directly, but let the silence fill the space between us for a little while. Then I asked him, 'What did happen to the black fellow, does thee know?'

He was astonished. 'Is that all you have to ask? As it happens, I do know. He married an Ojibwa girl and he lives with her people at Mishipikwadina. In the summer he comes back to work at the portaging at the Sault. Ermatinger takes an interest in him.'

We were silent for a while.

'Time is going by, brother Mark. Do you want me to go on?'

'Ay, if thee pleases.'

'I tell it to please *you*. Very well. When they crossed the Sault I crossed too. I escorted them back to Nolan's house, and I stayed with my friends, the Johnstons. I saw her again. She wanted me to find out what happened to the black fellow, and I did, and put in a good word for him too. That pleased her. She said we couldn't meet again after that – that there was nothing more for us to speak about. But then . . . but I said I wouldn't tell you how she was won. 'Tis naught to do with any but her and me. Suffice it to say we did meet again . . . several times. By now it was halfway through September. It was all my post was worth to stay away from Mackinac any longer. There was a schooner at the Sault, and Mrs Scott had arranged their passage back to Penetanguishine, late in the season as it was.

'Oh, yes, I'll admit I did all I could to persuade her. She refused to decide until the last moment. She was packed and ready, but she still didn't say whither she meant to go. It was the evening before she and Mrs Scott were to cross the straits that she finally gave me her word. My voyageurs were camped on the beach. The moon was dark, so we had to wait for the first dawn light. Then we were off – back to Mackinac.

'And then . . . what can I tell you? This was September of '09. The baby was born early in April. The midwife said he couldn't live; I sent a boy to fetch Dr Mitchell but by the time he came it was all over. The midwife called in our neighbour – a devout Catholic woman – and she christened him. I wanted my son christened – a Papist rite was better than none – and Rachel let it be done; I thought she was too ill to care. When Madame blessed the water we thought Rachel was not conscious, but she stirred a little and said, "I want thee to call him Mark." So he was named Mark Alan, and a little after that he died.'

'I am sorry for thy loss, friend.' We were silent for a little. Then I said, 'Thee has not told me how thee and Rachel were married before the priest.'

'Ah. There was a little difficulty about that. There's no priest at Mackinac. There used to be, but after the British took over, the church was misused, and the old priest's house is become a brothel. But I did my best, brother Mark, I did my best. I went to Madame La Framboise – a woman famous on Mackinac for her piety – though mind you . . . but that's another story. La Framboise took a fancy to Rachel, and she'd heard from the Indians that Father Richard was back at L'Arbre Croche for the winter – that's an Ottawa village across the Straits of Mackinac. The good

Father travels among the tribes; sometimes people have to wait years for him to turn up again, but we were lucky. I'm not a Catholic, you understand, but out here you take what you can get. When the Straits froze over there was a party of Indians going back, so we went with them. Sure enough we found Father Richard at the village, and he married us the same day.'

'I see.' Rachel had run away in September. It shouldn't matter to me, who in any case recognised no priestly authority, but I couldn't help asking, 'In what month do the Straits freeze over?'

'Oh,' said Alan, a little too carelessly. 'About December, usually. But you want to hear the rest of the story:

'In May I needed to go into the Michigan Territory before the *hivernants* left their posts for Mackinac. Rachel was better in body by then, but I knew in her mind there were things which weren't right. I was scared. She said she couldn't stay at Mackinac. She said . . .' For the first time in his narrative Alan paused to look for my reaction. Up until then he was like a man speaking to himself, while I kept silent. 'She said if I left her she'd kill herself.'

'That was wrong in her.'

'According to the rules of your Society? I can well believe it. I didn't think her wrong, but I was very troubled. She wasn't like herself. Sometimes I forgot all the joy that had been there when we were married, and sometimes I remembered it and wondered if there was anything in the world I might do that would bring it back. Perhaps I made the wrong decision. It made things worse, certainly. It must be comforting to be a Quaker, and be so sure what is right and what is wrong.'

'Thee maligns me, friend. I'm often not sure at all.'

'You seemed sure enough just now. Anyway, it's the custom to take one's woman when one travels. Only never a white woman: that's unheard of. I didn't know what to do, but I knew adventure came more naturally to Rachel than sewing seams at home with nothing to do but wait. If she'd been that sort of girl she'd never have married me. So the long and the short of it was, I got the right clothes for her, and I took her with me. I knew she wouldn't be much use at first. The Indian women know all that's necessary, and she knew nothing at all. But I thought learning might bring her back to herself a little.

'It was a risk, but sometimes I thought it would work. The voyageurs liked her; if they hadn't we'd have been doomed from the start. They admired her pluck, and they liked her direct way of talking to them. Everything was new to her, but she watched what the men did, and was very quick to learn. She didn't mind if they laughed at her. She'd turn her hand to any work they'd let her do – when she felt well. It was lucky she was a working farmer's daughter and not delicately bred – saving your presence, Mark, but it's the truth. A woman's no use out there if she can't catch a fish or skin a rabbit. Of course she couldn't gather food as the Indian women do, and she was far more inclined to argue. Not that I minded that. But there were times she'd withdraw into herself – just sit and stare at nothing at all. On the water there was nothing she could do. When we reached the posts I had work to do, so I couldn't think about Rachel too much, but as the summer wore on I couldn't help noticing how silent she was, and how unhappy. She never mentioned the baby, but I knew . . . I had reason to know . . . she hadn't got over it, not at all.

'On the way back we were *dérangé* – forced ashore by a gale. We were lucky: we were caught in open water, but we managed to make the Manitou Islands. And so we came to South Manitou.'

The silence grew around us. I sensed peace in it, and so I let it be.

Alan cleared his throat. 'This is the part you want to know about in some detail, isn't it? Do you think I didn't search? I went to just about every Indian village on the Michigan coast, right down to Black River. I asked, and I searched, and I sent the word out, and there was nothing. Nothing, anywhere. There are things I can't know; they don't tell us. I've been working among them these seven years. I know how little I know. Sometimes you think you know, and then you come up against . . . it's a blank wall. What you propose to do – what do you know about it? It's hopeless, I tell you, hopeless.'

I waited for him to go on.

'This is the part you wish to know. We camped on South Manitou Island. We had three canoes, a score of men, and all our furs to bring back to Mackinac. It turned out we were lucky trade had been so poor: if the canoes had been fully loaded . . . As for Rachel – I'd got more and more worried about her . . . Men can live in two worlds at once, and move from one to the other quite easily. They'll have two families, even, in different worlds, and not find it hard. She didn't think of it like that. She was always trying to make connections, judge everything by the same standards. Maybe in the end it broke her heart.

'Oddly enough, to begin with I loved her capacity for silence. At times she'd be very animated, and I liked her to talk to me. But I'd never thought before that a white woman . . . it was restful that she could be around, for hours maybe, and no word said nor any need of one. In my experience, with women of our race there's always talk. I never thought her silence would grow to scare me. And yet she tried very hard to learn Ojibwa, and that helped too. She listened well, I thought at the time.

'I was busy, though. I hadn't had time . . . I thought it was the heat that made her ill. It was a summer like you've never seen in England: hot and humid, day after day, the air so heavy but never a storm came near us. The corn shrivelled in the husk; the springs were dirty; the earth in the camp was baked solid: it burned your bare feet if you trod on it. When it got so hot, she just huddled in the shade of the wilting trees and stared at nothing at all. When it was time to pack up she seemed distracted, almost confused at times. She hardly said a word as we went downriver. She was happier when we were on the open lake. She said she could breathe better. Of course she didn't know . . . no voyageur likes open water.

'It's an exposed coast, and in summer there's usually an onshore breeze driving you on to the shoals if you're not careful. We camped one night by a lagoon, and set out as usual just before dawn. The lake was almost flat calm – it's never quite flat when you're out on it. I swear it breathes – you can always see the rise and fall if you look for it – like an animal asleep. We kept as close to shore as we could. It was hot.

'The weather changed – you get these storms out of nowhere. In less than twenty minutes the waves were four, five feet high. I suppose you're used to the sea? So was I, once. You won't understand the lake. You don't get the long swells you get at sea. Just short waves, high and choppy. A big canoe can get caught on the crest of two of those, and break in half. Just like that. I've seen it happen. The wind was offshore – that's unusual. There was thunder behind us, and then the rain came down like water out of a bucket. The lightning was right on top of it. You can't hold a canoe broadside on to wind and waves. Like it or not, we were being driven out into the lake – even if we could have made the mainland shore the canoes would've been smashed to pieces. But there were the Manitou Islands . . . We signalled to the others – it was already too loud to shout – and changed course. Things eased right away, of course, but it would stop your heart to look back at the following waves. And she was the only one who could look back. The rest of us – me too – were paddling for our lives.

'It was a miracle we raised South Manitou. Visibility wasn't more than half a mile, if that. But we did – we headed for the bay. A *canot du maître* isn't meant for open water. We had to get round the headland and into the bay. It nearly finished us. But then we were pretty much blown onshore. It didn't do the canoes any good. We'd done mighty well, for all that, for none had foundered and we were still together, and on dry land.'

Alan heaved a great sigh. 'I suppose you want me to tell you about the island? The usual camping place is a long beach facing east. Imagine it shaped like a crescent moon – we beached at the top, where we'd be sheltered from the wind. Traders sometimes use the place. The island isn't all that big – maybe a mile across each way – it's all forest, beech and birch and hemlock, and a cedar swamp on the south side. There're no paths, just the dead wood lying, and where the sun gets to the edge of the forest there's the worst poison ivy you've ever seen. It's waist high in places – leaves as big as your hand. You can't go through. The only paths are in the south, where the Indians have a summer village. The voyageurs just use the beach; they don't go inland. We were the only trading folk there.

'There are sandy beaches all round where a canoe could land, even to the west, but there's nowhere to camp that side – too exposed – just high dunes that you'd have to climb atop of to get wood or shelter. No one would camp there, but in fair weather they could land. The only height of land is the dunes. You can't see out from anywhere else – don't I know it! Anything or anyone could hide out in the forest, if they could get past the poison ivy and the flies. If someone knew how to fish and trap he'd manage in the summer. In winter he'd starve, no two ways about it.

'We set up camp and waited for the wind to die down.

We had to repair the canoes – it'd been a rough landing. Our crew caught some pike in a little lake and there was a fight about dividing it – nothing that mattered. Rachel got up and walked away along the beach. When she didn't turn back I ran after her. I grabbed her by the arm and I asked her – yes, to be honest I did say – where the devil was she off to? She said she was just going for a walk; she had to get away for a bit. I said no, it was getting dark. We didn't know the place. She pulled her arm away and said, 'We're on an island. I'll be quite safe.' I made her promise – give her word I mean – that she'd turn back in a minute. She said she'd do that, but she insisted on going, just for a little while. I let her. I said, "Don't be long." That was the last I saw of her. In the twilight her dress was the same colour as the forest; if she'd left the beach I wouldn't have been able to see her anyway.'

He stopped abruptly. His face was turned away from me, still looking at the window. I heard him catch his breath, and I realised there was more grief in him than I'd guessed. I said nothing. He wiped his nose on the back of his hand, and cleared his throat.

'She didn't come back. I walked up and down the beach. The forest was just a curtain of dark. I kept the fire burning. I tended it all night while the men slept: we were all worn out, remember. There was no point trying to go after her in the dark.' I heard him take a breath. 'All nights pass in the end.'

'We searched the island for the best part of a week. I questioned the Indians. Loic was sure they weren't hiding anything. We took a canoe right round the island. We had no more supplies. I had to get the furs back to Mackinac. The men wanted to get home. We left.

'I did what I had to do at Mackinac, and got leave to go back. Loic and I took his Indian canoe, and we came back along the Michigan coast, just the two of us. Have you any idea how large this land is, brother Mark? It was the inshore villages we wanted – bays and rivers – not the open lake. It was like searching for a needle in a bottle of hay. To be honest I knew the result before we started, and I was right: nothing. We found nothing. There was no trace of her, dead or living.'

This time I broke the silence myself. 'What does thee think happened, Alan?'

He gave a despairing kind of shrug, 'How do I know? Maybe she went into the lake. Maybe she did it on purpose, maybe not. The water's deep round the islands. The currents are strong. Maybe she stayed on the island. I don't think so. She had a knife; that was all. Where could she have gone? If there were a canoe, it could only be Indians or voyageurs. Voyageurs would have come to the usual beach. Besides, they'd never steal a woman. They wouldn't want her in their canoe, and then where would they take her? No, it wasn't voyageurs. It wasn't Yankees either; if there'd been an American boat around we'd have heard about it. No, if she was taken, it has to have been by Indians. But news travels fast among the villages, and I had Loic with me, who would hear it all.'

Alan looked directly in my face at last. 'Do you understand what I'm telling you, Mark Greenhow? Do you understand why all hope seemed gone? I realise you think I owe it to you . . . You could hardly have picked a worse time. What is it that you want us to do?'

Chapter 13

THE MOON WAS FITFUL BEHIND SCUDDING CLOUD.
Inky waves slapped against the canoe as we climbed
aboard. One o'clock in the morning seemed an eccentric
time to embark, but Alan's arrangements had ceased to
surprise me. The gusts of wind were strangely mild; at
home our breezes have a bite even in high summer. As
we paddled away the canoe bucked like a fretful pony,
sending bits of spray flying like foam. A chancy night
to go a-voyaging, but I kept mum, and went where I
was bid. We were loaded to the gunwales, so I had to
sit more or less cross-legged. The brigade of canoes that
had been laid up by the jetty that morning was embarking
too. Here and there I could see a flash from a dark
lantern, but once we were afloat all lights were doused
but the moon.

I felt happier than I'd done the previous night. Whatever Alan might be, he'd loved Rachel, and he was not
– I was certain of it – a villain. Sequestered my life may
have been, but a Friend is not necessarily an ill judge of
other men, just because he lives differently. I thought to
myself that as far as domestic virtues went, I would trust
my brother-in-law. As to his other enterprises, I would
not vouch for what he might be up to, even a yard out

of my sight. Or within it, come to that, for what were we doing now, abroad on the wide waters when every honest man was lying a-bed? I let the question rest. The other reason I was happier was that Loic had agreed to give me a paddle. Once again I was at the rear, where I could do least harm, under the eye of the *gouvernail*, but I soon proved I could keep time. I didn't know what we were about; Alan had just said this wild night voyage was 'more convenient'. I put my trust in the Lord and my strength to my paddle; enlightenment would surely come.

How any man could steer a course, with the light so uncertain and the waters so unruly, was beyond me, but our brigade hung together, and pressed onwards. At least, we must have been moving at some speed, at the rate we were paddling, but I saw no landmark by which to measure. At first the wind seemed to be on our right, and the spray came flying into our side of the canoe. Presently it seemed to shift, or maybe we did. At one time the swell got so heavy I was alarmed. We rose so high at each crest that I felt we were tipping backwards, then we seemed to hang poised before we hurtled downwards – that was when I was really feart: it felt as if we'd never rise again, and the next wave would surely swamp us. But after a while that eased off, and when I could look up again I saw that the moon had swung right round so it was no longer on my right but almost dead ahead. We were paddling a path of light directly towards it. The wind dropped and the sky turned pale. I could see a humped silhouette on the horizon, which I guessed was land.

It was quiet enough now to hear a man speak. My brother-in-law's voice came softly from the bows. 'Brother Mark?'

'Ay.'

'Welcome to the United States of America!' I could hear the laugh in his voice. I could read him, as clear as an open book in the bright noonday. This wild adventure – whatever it was we were at – this was the breath of life to him. He was happy, as I was when I stood upon the summit of Helvellyn in deep snow, and saw all the winter fells spread like an ermine cloak around me.[1]

I didn't see the island until we were close up to it. It was long and low, that was all I could tell. We landed among little splashy waves on a sandy beach, and the four *canots du maître* drew in silently beside us. As we jumped into the shallow water and began unloading, a single ray from a dark lantern shone out from one of the canoes.

'Douse that light!' called Alan sharply.

The cargo was all ashore and the canoes beached in no time. The voyageurs took up their burdens, and vanished into the darkness above the beach.

'Are you there, brother Mark?'

'Ay.'

'Come on, then!'

I stumbled after him along a forest path. We didn't go far from the lake; I could still hear the waves on the shore. There was a smell of damp earth and pine. An oblong of light appeared ahead, and when we came close I saw I was looking into an open doorway. Inside, the building was long and low, rounded at the ends, built of birchbark on a frame of sapling trunks lashed together. There were ashes in the cold hearth, but no other sign of habitation. Instead the place was being used as a storehouse. Canvas-covered bales were being stacked high, kegs neatly piled, cases and

---

[1] I walked the Helvellyn ridge from end to end in the snows of First Month, and bivouacked upon Fair Field, just because as far as I knew it had never been done before and everyone said it was impossible. Months later, when I told Alan about that long walk, he was interested, and asked questions, but I realised he didn't understand. I had been involved in no great intrigue, no machinations of war or commerce; I had no comrades and there was no prize. Sometimes, I realised, he found me more foreign to his understanding than I found him.

barrels carefully stowed. A couple of lanterns cast huge crossed shadows.

'Where are we?'

'This is the island of Bois Blanc. We won't be long here. Then I'll take you visiting.'

Once everything was put away Alan led me away along another track. It was getting light. We startled a little herd of white-tailed deer, who bounded away into the forest. Birds were starting to sing in the trees about us; some of their calls had grown familiar to me, but I knew few by name. A dozen questions burned on my tongue, but I uttered none of them. No doubt Alan would speak when he chose. When we came back to the shore the rising sun was glinting on the lake, but we were in shadow, facing north-west. We ducked back under the trees, and came on a clearing sheltered from the shore by barely twenty yards of forest. I saw a hayfield, ripe – more than ripe – for harvesting. Beyond it was a log cabin with many additions built on, and a fenced garden behind. A coil of smoke rose from the chimney. Some mongrel hens and a pig foraged in the mud between the cabin and the shore. On the beach below a canoe lay half in, half out of the water. It looked very like the one that had brought us from the Sault. There was another island across a narrow strait, similar to the one we were on, low-lying and thickly wooded. The place seemed a little haven of habitation in the midst of the waters and the wilderness.

'This is the house of Martin Kerners.'

I followed Alan to the door without replying. He lifted the latch and walked in, and held the door for me to follow.

The cabin was warm and crowded. Three walls were hung with tools and baskets. The usual meats and fishes and herbs hung from the rafters. There were low boxes covered with furs and trade blankets to sit on, and opposite the hearth there was a deal table with benches on each side. Loic was there at the table, and the four voyageurs who'd paddled our canoe from the Sault, all discussing a hearty meal of the inevitable whitefish. Two young Indian women squatted at the hearth, busy cooking bannocks on a griddle.

Loic stood up. *'Bienvenus! Biindigen!* Welcome to my house, m'sieu. Please, will you sit down? Alan, you also. You must be hungry.' He turned to the young women. 'Pakané, *biidaw gondag niniwag waa-kizhebaa 'miijiwaad!'*

The voyageurs moved up to make room for us at the table. One of the young women set out bowls of steaming fish in front of us – 'It is whitefish,' said Loic. *'C'est bon.* You will drink? Water? Is that all? Waase'aaban, *nibi biidaw!'*

The younger girl brought a pitcher of water. She said not a word, but I could not help noting her. For all her dark skin, she seemed to me the most beautiful girl I had ever seen. She couldn't have been above fifteen. She was very slight, her movements quiet and graceful. Like her sister, she wore a trade shirt tied at the waist with a voyageur sash. Her short woollen skirt and coloured leggings were entirely savage, however, and much embroidered with braiding and coloured ribbons, which matched the ribbon in her braided hair. She was all hung about with bead necklaces and earrings. I felt my senses reel – that is the plain truth; I never knew what the expression signified until that moment.

As I sat, outwardly unmoved, I tried to steady my mind. I tried to remind myself that these people were nothing to do with me. I thought of Sarah and Clemency in their grey gowns, and bleached caps and pinafores. With that memory came a sudden vision of red hair brighter than any beads or ribbons, and for no reason at all I was filled with a confusion I could not fathom, as if the blood had rushed to my brain and heated it above the temperature of reasoned thought.

'Thank thee, friend,' I said to the girl, as she set a pitcher of water on the table. She glanced at me, gave a small smile, and looked across at Loic.

'M'sieu, it is the sister of my wife, Waase'aaban. The other, she is my wife. Pakané, *maa bi-izhaan!* M'sieu Mark, you would like to see my son also? He sleeps, but he is here! Look!'

I had seen the flat cradleboards on the backs of women at the Sault, but never so close as this one propped against the stone chimney breast. It looked cruelly hard compared to a cradle, but the small brown face within seemed peaceful enough. A rosary hung from the board, and some woven beads and feathers. The baby already had a fringe of black hair. I knew not what to say – I was not used to a man inviting me to admire his infant – but it was no matter. Loic said, 'His name is Martin; he is called *Biinoojii*. Is he not beautiful; do you not think so?'

'Ay.' I said, but I wasn't telling the exact truth. I thought Loic's wife infinitely more beautiful than her little smudge of a child. She seemed very young – she couldn't have been more than a year or two older than her sister. She was just as gaudily dressed, and just as lissom. I hadn't thought to find anything so exotic in this out of the way homestead, or indeed in Loic's family. I knew not what to make of it, or of myself. Luckily no one took any notice of me. I recovered my complexion and made a hearty meal. By the time I'd finished the voyageurs had departed, to sleep, Loic said. I was feeling quite sleepy myself when the door opened again, and an old white man with a strong look of Loic appeared. His hair was grey, and there were deep wrinkles round his eyes and mouth.

Alan stood up. '*Monsieur Kerners, je suis content de vous voir. Je vous présente Mark Greenhow; c'est le frère de ma femme Rachel.* Brother Mark, this is Martin Kerners.'

Martin Kerners shook my hand civilly, but he, Alan and Loic obviously had other matters to discuss. Plates and mugs were pushed aside, and Alan took some papers out of his haversack. Loic wiped the table with the hem of his shirt, and Alan unfolded his documents and spread them out. I was forgotten for the moment, so I left the house to answer a call of nature. There was no outhouse, only the forest all around. Others had been there before me, and I went further afield, and so it was that some little time elapsed before I returned.

There was no one left in the room but Loic's sister-in-law. She was sitting on her heels by the fire stitching a piece of leather with a length of rawhide, while a big iron kettle simmered over the logs in front of her. She smiled when I came in. I knew not where to sit, but courageously opted for a deerskin-covered box on the other side of the fire. As there seemed to be time, I took off my wet boots and stockings and laid them out to dry, not too close to the heat. My bare feet looked wrinkled and sodden from being damp so long. I began to rub a little life back into my poor toes. The girl seemed as comfortable with silence as I was, and indeed so far as I knew we had no common language. I was wrong about that, for after some minutes had elapsed, she held up her work, and said to me, '*Ne serait-il pas mieux de porter des mocassins, m'sieu?*'

'Ay, – *oui* – *mais je n'ai pas des mocassins, malheureusement.*' I thought for a moment. '*Mes pieds sont trop grands, mademoiselle.*' And I stretched them out to the fire so she could see what I meant.

She seemed to find that funny, for she laughed softly, and went back to her stitching. Her dark head was bent over her work, so I was able to watch her freely. Presently I felt thirsty and went to the table to fetch myself water. Alan had left one of his papers there. It did not look to be a letter, or any private thing. Sometimes to this day I question myself whether it were a wrong thing to do or no, and still I cannot be certain. I couldn't help being curious, and naturally certain questions, ay, and possible answers too, were circling in my brain. But there the thing was, no personal letter but some kind of a list, unfolded on the table for anyone to see. I had not given Alan my word that I would not look about me. I glanced at the girl; she had her back to me. And so I read:

Manifesto of the cargo of four canoes the property of the subscriber bound to the River Missouri and navigated by six men – Viz:

No *1,2,3,4,5,6,7,8,9*	
10,11,12,13,14	*14 bales dry goods*
15,16	*2 barrels sugar*
17	*1 case guns*
18	*1 do. iron goods*
19	*1 do. pipes*
20,21	*2 do. soap*
22,23	*2 barrels salt*
24,25,26,27,28,29	*6 bales tobacco*
30	*1 keg spirits*
31,32	*2 barrels do.*
33	*1 nest tin kettles*
34,35	*2 kegs nails*
36,37	*2 do. liquor*
38,39,40,41,42,43	*6 do. high wine*
44,45	*2 baskets traps*
46,47,48,49,50	*5 bags shot*
51,52	*2 cases do.*
53	*1 keg butter*
54	*1 keg pork*
55,56,57,58	*4 kegs gunpowder*
59	*1 trunk*

Fifty-nine articles of entry and the necessary Provisions, Sea Stores and Agrés for the voyage. Bois Blanc Island. 9th July, 1812. Martin Kerners.

July 9th – that was the ninth day of Seventh Month: three days from now. I hadn't thought Martin Kerners rich enough to own the four canoes. I went back to my place at the hearth, and stared into the fire for a long time, thinking. Waase'aaban was the most undemanding companion possible, yet I was preternaturally aware of her presence. The silence between us grew into one of contentment, the kind a man would like to find at his own hearth. When Pakané came and joined us, and began to suckle Loic's baby, she did nothing to disturb our peace. The two sisters talked a little, and presently Waase'aaban laid down her work, and went out to fetch more wood. When she came back Martin Kerners was with her.

'*Vous ne dormez pas?* – you sleep not? Alan, Loic – all sleep. You sleep not?'

'No.'

Martin sat down. 'You like Waase'aaban? *C'est la sœur de ma belle-fille. Elle est toujours fille non mariée, vous savez.*' He pointed at Waase'aaban. 'No man. She has not yet a man.'

Waase'aaban looked at me and smiled a little. Pakané said something in their own language, and a sharp discussion ensued, in which all three took part. I said firmly, 'Where is Alan Mackenzie? I too would like to sleep now, please.'

'Sleep?' Martin spoke sharply to Waase'aaban, who got to her feet.

'*Venez, m'sieu.*'

I followed her cautiously. She led me into another room – the various additions to the cabin had made it like a warren inside – where there was a raised platform covered with a guddle of furs and blankets. My brother-in-law was curled in a blanket, his head resting on a rolled up beaver pelt. In sleep he looked remarkably innocent, his shirt open at the neck and his dark hair ruffled. The other heap of blankets I took to be Loic. Waase'aaban pointed to the bed, smiled again, and left me. I made myself a little space between Alan and Loic, pulled a spare blanket from under Loic, curled up and closed my eyes.

I woke to Alan's voice. 'Brother Mark. *Mark!* By God, the fellow sleeps like the dead! Mark!'

I sat up. 'Ay?'

'Time to go!'

I rubbed my eyes. There was a little square window of oiled paper sawn out of the wall. As far as I could tell, outside it was still broad day.

'We travel in daylight, do we? Like honest men?'

It was a moment before he answered me. '*Touché*, brother Mark.' It was said without his usual insouciance. I realised I'd touched him on the raw, and noted it. We spoke no more to each other, but said farewell to the Kerners family and repaired to the beach. Our voyageurs already had the canoe afloat. There was no sign of Loic's sister-in-law, or of his wife and son. It was hardly my place to mention them, but when we pushed off I felt a little twinge of regret. I wondered if I would ever come back to Bois Blanc again.

I had all the leg room I could desire this time, and instead of vague shapes in the dark I could see land all round: Bois Blanc behind us, the wooded island across the little strait, and the distinctive humped island dead ahead, which I'd caught a glimpse of under last night's moon. It wasn't far off at all. Alan sat beside me, saying he wanted to see my paddling skills for himself. I was not to be drawn on that subject, so he began telling me what we could see. I wasn't surprised when he pointed to the hump ahead and said, 'Mackinac.'

'Is that a Scottish name?'

He laughed. 'No, it's Ojibwa. Michilimackinac: the Island of the Great Turtle. If I have it correctly the Great Turtle was brought up from the depths of the lake by Gitchi Manitou to become a little island.[2] A blessed little island, on the crossroads of the greatest trade routes in North America. You know of Gitchi Manitou? You shake your head, but I think you do. Better than I do, brother. Your George Fox would have recognised him at once, I believe. You see I've learned something of your sect. But that by the by: you ask me of Mackinac, and as a sober senior clerk of the South West Trading Company, I should keep mum about the Great Turtle, and tell you that Mackinac is a trading post and a military fort. Just now it's in bad trouble. Since the American embargo last year, trade's at a standstill. All the incoming trade used to come by Montreal. Now the border's closed they have to come up from the United States, but that's a tortuous route, and you just can't get the goods.'

'An American military fort?'

'The Yankees have it now, yes indeed. They never took it, mark you. It was built by the British and held by the British, until Jay's Treaty – which betrayed us all – handed it to the Yankees on a plate, along with every other fort we had inside American territory. That was in '96 – before you or I ever set foot in this benighted country. So, as far as we're concerned, yes, it's an American military fort.' Alan chuckled softly. 'Until the

2 Loic told me the correct story in the winter. It was the muskrat who brought up soil from the depths of the lake, when all the animals were in danger of drowning in the Great Flood. Nanubushu sprinkled the soil on the back of the Great Turtle, that through him all might be saved.

war, brother, until the war. Then – well, anything could happen then.'

'Is that the fort?' I asked presently, for a patch of grey wall was now visible at the southern end of the island, atop the hill.

'None other. When you can see the stars and stripes flying over it, you'll know it's less than an hour till dinner time.'

We came ashore on a crowded beach, skirted the Indian village that lines the shore, and walked up to the fort, which stood at the top of a bluff a hundred and fifty feet above the village. The excise office, to which we repaired immediately, was below the cliff. Customs were no mere formality. When we arrived the clerk fetched a senior official, whom Alan introduced to me as a Mr Abbott, and I was thoroughly grilled as to my status, my journey and my reason for travelling. I had naught to fear, for I told him the simple truth. My sister's story was clearly known to him; I think he knew within five minutes that I was exactly what I said I was, but he had the world-weary air of a man used to all kinds of deviations from simplicity and truth.

When Samuel Abbott had done with me he pushed a piece of written paper across the desk to Alan, who knew the form, for he proceeded at once to make a copy in his own hand on a blank sheet of foolscap. That was the third time I'd seen Alan's fair copperplate; he's something of a calligrapher, and prides himself on the aesthetics of all his records, both personal and clerkly. On this occasion, as I sat beside him, I was more struck by the content:

I do solemnly and sincerely swear that the report and mani-fest now delivered by me to the Collector of the District of Michilimackinac contains a full and true account of all the

Cargo which was on board of a canoe at the time of its arrival at the Port of the District aforesaid, and that I know of no smuggling or fraud of any kind respecting the said cargo since its departure from Sainte Marie du Sault. I further swear that there are not to the best of my knowledge and belief on board of the said canoe any goods, wares or merchandise the importation of which into the United States or the Territories thereof is prohibited by law. And I do further swear that if I shall hereafter discover or know of any such goods, wares or merchandise, I will immediately and without delay report the same to the Collector of this District. So help me God.

Alan Mackenzie
   Sworn before me this 7ᵗʰ day of July, 1812

Alan pushed the note back across the desk, and the excise officer added his signature: *Samuel Abbott, Collector*

Alan took the letter back, drew a curly line with a flourish at each end, and wrote on the second half of the paper:

Manifesto of a canoe the property of the South West Company, navigated by six men, bound to Mackinac from Sainte Marie du Sault, and having on board the following cargo—
   Remainder of the necessary Provisions, Sea Stores and Agrés for the return voyage to the Sault. Private letters to be delivered to South West Company officials.

Mackinac 7ᵗʰ July, 1812
   Alan Mackenzie

'Very well, Mr Mackenzie. I'll find you at McGulpin's house as usual, if I need you?'

'Ay, if I'm not at the factory.'

Our business was then concluded, and we stepped outside. Alan turned to me with an easy smile. 'You must be famished, brother Mark. We'll go to the Company factory – you'll need to buy some dollars – and tonight we'll eat at the tavern. You've no objection to that?'

As we walked, I tried to gather my wits and realise I was in another country. There were quite a few American soldiers around to remind me, besides the stars and stripes flapping in the breeze above the fort. (In the eyes of the Lord who made us all no doubt one flag is much the same as another, but I, who had never walked under any foreign flag in all my life, found myself overly aware of the difference.) I had always thought of soldiers in terms of red, but these fellows had blue coats with red collars, and cuffs trimmed with yellow. Like our own soldiers, they had shakoes with polished badges. Some had muskets slung over their shoulders. Besides the soldiers there were voyageurs in scarlet caps and sashes, fur traders in many-caped coats and tall beaver hats, Indians in motley garb – the men in anything from deerskins to discarded uniforms and broad-brimmed beavers, the women in short bright-coloured dresses with embroidered leggings, reminding me of Pakané and Waase'aaban on Bois Blanc. I saw the first white women I'd encountered since Montreal – two young ladies in low-necked gowns and be-ribboned bonnets, carrying parasols. I was very hungry.

McGulpin's house lay to the north of the fort, close under the bluff, beyond some neatly tended vegetable plots. Its own yard was rank and overgrown; foxgloves and nettles almost hid the square windows. The house was usually let to seasonal traders, and normally in the summer it would be fully occupied. This year, Alan said, he had the place to himself, a mark of the strange times we lived in. I had not much expectation of good housekeeping, but the kitchen into which we stepped was swept clean, the fire was laid, and the dresser was laden with a cask of ale, a bread barrel, and a goodly array of pewter vessels, enough to serve a dozen at one time, and indeed the big table and long benches could have accommodated such a number. Two bedrooms opened off the kitchen, and a stair led to a long bedloft. We were but two, and had each our own bedroom downstairs. I found no sheets, but made up my bed with a couple of trade blankets that looked to be moderately clean.

The tavern was as crowded as the George Inn in Penrith on a fair day. If traders were in short supply this year, there were plenty of soldiers to take their place. The best table was taken up by a group of blue-coated officers from the fort. Even the men in civilian dress had muskets propped beside them as they ate. Alan told me these were militiamen, and they'd been in the woods all day at their training, which comforted me not at all. They had some white women with them, who seemed pretty bold in speech and manner to me, but then I'd never met a woman who frequented taverns and such low places, and for all I know they may have been virtuous American wives, perhaps even mothers. Several people hailed Alan when we went in, and two militiamen squeezed up to make room for him. That surprised me; I'd understood from Alan he counted Americans his enemies, but now it seemed this was not so. I listened to their talk: 'twas about a fellow they knew who'd killed the bear that killed him – that is to say, the two bodies had been found together, the one shot and the other mauled to death. I had nothing to say about that, so I ate my fish pie in silence. There were bursts of song from a rowdy group by the kitchen door. Others joined in. Everyone but my neighbours, still engrossed in their bear stories, was listening:

Come, strike the bold anthems, the war dogs are howling,
Already they eagerly snuff up their prey;

The red cloud of war o'er our forest is scowling,
Soft peace spreads her wings, and flies weeping away . . .

I looked round at the flushed faces. At the end of each verse almost everyone raised their tankards and joined in the last line. At Penrith it would have been 'Hearts of Oak', and if my father had been there he would at once have departed from a scene so martial, and led me away with him. But I was alone, and listened to the end:

Your hands, then, dear comrades, round liberty's altar,
United; we swear by the souls of the brave.
Not one from the strong resolution shall falter,
To live independent or sink in the grave.
Then freemen, file up! Lo the blood banners flying:
The high bird of liberty screams in the air,
Beneath her, oppression and liberty dying—
Success to the beaming American Star!

A buzz of talk broke out. I nudged Alan. 'I'm ready to go home. Thee needn't come with me.'
'Are you sure, brother Mark? You know the way?'
'Ay.'
Outside the air was cool and sweet. Beyond the scattered houses the lake lay like a pool of melted silver under the moon. I could hear the faint sound of Indian drums, and in the distance a wild chanting, very unlike the tavern songs, which made my blood run chill. An image came to my mind of the cool wind on the ridges of Blencathra, of the way a mountain range sweeps from peak to peak in lovely curves. Sometimes thee stands on a summit and it's like being in the saddle, looking down at the sweep of a horse's neck, when the ground looks little and far away as thee gallops over it. I thought of other summer evenings, far away, but this was Mackinac. Perhaps in peacetime it

was a place for ordinary folk and their trade, but now the people seemed to be here only to bear arms, in order that they might fight with outward weapons any who came to war against them.

Chapter 14

I LIVED IN AMERICAN MACKINAC NINE DAYS. IT WAS a troubled place to be. The great warehouses of the South West Company, besides all the stores of the independent traders, were empty. No goods had been allowed into the United States from Upper Canada for over a year. 'So Martin Kerners fills his canoes elsewhere?' I asked Alan.

'Hush, Mark, you're too sharp for your own good. Perhaps Martin Kerners has an agent who knows of other sources. There's plenty of trade in the woods if you know where to look for it.'

'So why does Martin Kerners send his . . . agent . . . to Mackinac just now, if it's not where the trade is?'

'Perhaps Monsieur Kerners' agent – the one who knows where to look for trade in the backwoods – can't afford to leave Mackinac right now.'

'This agent expects something to happen here quite soon, then?'

'Hush, brother. Don't even think about it. Now, I'm a free man this evening – no goods, no work. How can I entertain you?'

'If thy business here is done, thee could tell me when we'll set out.'

'Ah, but my business here isn't quite done. But I promise,

as soon as I've dealt with things here, we'll think about our expedition.'

I had to be content with that. I got ready myself, buying a few necessaries at the South West Company store: a good hunting knife, fish-hooks, a tin mug, a billycan, and a canvas haversack like Alan's. I spent most evenings alone at McGulpin's house. The first evening I hardly noticed Alan's absence, because, true to his word, he produced a map for me, the first I'd seen since I'd been in the North West Company council chamber in Montreal. Without a map it had been like seeing through a glass darkly, and all was now made plain. Alan said the map was an old one, and there'd been a good deal of surveying done in the last few years, but I was content.

It was an English-made map, by one John Cary, but it showed the western part of the United States, including a vast green-shaded area which was the Western Territory, which extended east-west from Mackinac to the Mississippi River, and north-south from Lake Superior to Kentucky. Lake Michigan penetrated far into this region; in its waters I found Moneton Is, which I realised must be North and South Manitou Islands. I studied Lake Michigan for a long time before turning to the route of my own journey. There was all of Upper Canada, and there was Canada's northern boundary, the Outaouais River. To my delight every portage was marked, and those on the Mattawa too; the eleven portages on the Mattawa were so close together there was barely room for the script. I examined the approaches to Lake Superior: by St Mary's Falls there was a note: *Here great quantities of Fish – particularly Pickerell, Trout and Whitefish of large size.* I had a brief vision of Thomas Nolan's loaded dinner table. I looked next for Yonge Street in Upper Canada. It wasn't marked, but Gwilimbury, where David Willson dwelt, was written clearly. From there I traced Rachel's travels through Pennsylvania. I couldn't find Catawissa, but there was the Susquehanna River, and there was Genesee. I found Fort Detroit, and Fort George at Niagara; various snatches of talk I'd heard were beginning to make sense. I also discovered, to the north of the Indian Boundary line of 1795, Fort Wayne, to which Friends had prevented aunt Judith from venturing. Next I began to study the areas of the Indian tribes, but the Ojibwa were nowhere to be seen. Later I asked Alan, and he showed me where it said *Chippeway Territory*, right across the northern part of the American western territory, and through Upper Canada. Indian boundaries, he remarked, are not the same as ours. Indeed, the border between Upper Canada and the United States was given more emphasis than anything else on the map: a fat red line was drawn across the middle of each lake and their connecting rivers, all but Lake Michigan, which lay bare of any boundary or settlement. Apart from a quantity of rivers which must have been surveyed at some time, all those shores and islands were shown as untouched wilderness.

The fellow whose room I took had left a few books. I had read no secular literature at all until I came to Mackinac. So I began a lifelong adventure in an unpropitious spirit of apathy, when I took up an exceedingly battered copy of *A History of New York from the Beginning of the World to the End of the Dutch Dynasty* by one Diedrich Knickerbocker. When Alan came home that evening I was halfway through the Creation of the World, and feeling altogether confused, and not a little shocked. Alan explained to me that the account was intended to be witty, and took the trouble to read a passage and expound to me the humour in it. Eventually I grasped it, and all of a sudden I began to laugh out loud at the very audacity of such writing. Alan, much encouraged, continued to read, and whether he laughed at my newly-acquired skill of being amused or at the text, I know not, but we concluded with a very merry evening, and I found myself in more charity with him than ever I had felt before.[1]

Alan told me that the Company agent who used to have my room was an old friend of the author of *A History of New York*. 'I miss Brevoort,' Alan said. 'He was the American Fur Company agent – Mr Astor's representative – last summer. He's gone back to New York; he wasn't a man for the backwoods. But he was the very best of company. Which reminds me, I should

[1] As to this matter of secular writing, I have thought a great deal about it, and at diverse times the elders have seen fit to caution me on the matter. After my sojourn abroad, it occurred to me that I had long known men considered in the world to be great poets, but never read a line of what they wrote. I went into the bookshop in Keswick shortly after my return, and bought a leatherbound volume by William Wordsworth. (Out of loyalty I would have begun with Robert Southey, but this was the Laker season, and they were out of stock). Contrary to Friendly persuasions, poetry is often more plain and direct than common speech: indeed, at its best, simplicity shines through. I opened the volume in the bookshop, and I read:

> Our birth is but a sleep and a forgetting:
> The Soul that rises with us, our life's Star,
> Hath had elsewhere its setting,
> And cometh from afar:
> Not in entire forgetfulness,
> And not in utter nakedness,
> But trailing clouds of glory do we come
> From God, who is our home:
> Heaven lies about us in our infancy!

I was much moved. The following First Day I got up and gave those lines as Ministry. 'Tis the only Ministry I ever gave in all my life, and the elders, knowing not the source, were pleased to approve it. To my lifelong shame I didn't acknowledge my debt; it seemed more politic to be silent. A bad poet is indeed the enemy of plain speech, being obscure and convoluted, seeking to disguise the simple truth merely to impress the credulous with his tricks, but I account William Wordsworth a good poet. He knows his country. My mother was very unhappy when I started bringing secular writings into the house, but agreed to it in the end, so long as I never bought any *novels*, which are narratives woven with untruths and vain inventions, to which I agreed, and I have kept my word.

write him a letter, while I still can. I'll tell him you like Irving's book.'

'I understood that the Americans were *not* thy friends?'

'No, no, that would be most uncivilised. In the South West we're working with Americans all the time. Astor – he owns the American Fur Company – was just as keen to get the embargo lifted as any of us. We thought he'd do it too. He's the richest man in America – in the whole world, some say only who knows but what the Emperor of China . . . but that by the by. Anyway, Astor knows the President personally. But he couldn't reverse the embargo any more than we could. In business I wouldn't trust him an inch – nor he us – that's why we're all bound together in the South West. A marriage of convenience and complete distrust. But the Americans are some of the best men to work with. Especially Brevoort. I miss him.'

During my days on Mackinac I became even more confused about this worldly notion of *allies* and *enemies*. I walked about the island and found everywhere a people similar in every way, so far as I could tell, to those I'd left behind at the Sault. I wandered freely around the outside walls of the fort, and yet for all they knew I could have been any kind of spy. In spite of its impressive situation on the cliff top, when I walked round the back of the fortress I found it quite exposed, where the ground rose behind it towards a little hill. When I mentioned this to Alan he grinned and said, 'Well observed, brother Mark! I didn't think you learned military strategy in your Religious Society.'

'It seemed fairly obvious to me. If I wanted to get in, I'd go round the back.'

Alan replied with a ribald jest which I shall not write. Before I met Alan I had never before heard anyone, even my cousin John, speak so – or not in English, anyway, for I'd grown quite used to the voyageurs. I never responded, and I think on the whole Alan desisted from speaking disrespectfully of women when I was present, but sometimes he forgot.

Word of my presence had spread as fast as it would have done in Mungrisdale if an Indian Chief had appeared in our midst in full war paint and regalia. I was met (and I fear this might not happen if that same Indian Chief appeared on a Lakeland doorstep) with open kindness and a frank curiosity. For my days were not idle. Alan might have deserted me, but I had the direction given to me in aunt Judith's letter. As Alan picked up his hat to leave, the first morning we were at McGulpin's house, I said to him, 'Wait, friend, I have somewhat to ask thee.'

'Won't it wait?'

'No.' I nearly said I'd not come nine hundred miles from Montreal in order to wait, but a show of temper would not aid me. 'Judith Scott says in her letter that Rachel's direction here was the house of Madame La Framboise. Rachel and thee didn't live in this house then?'

'No, I couldn't have brought her here. The place was full of traders – that was back when we had something to trade. You're not seeing Mackinac the way it usually is, brother Mark.'

'So she and thee lived – where?'

'As you say. We rented the little cabin next door to this house. It belongs to our neighbour, Madame La Framboise.'

'Thee means the house with the hollyhocks? The one who was midwife to Rachel? Is she a friend of thine?'

'I told you – she christened my son.' Suddenly his face lightened. He grinned at me. 'A rival, more like. A serious threat to the South West Company – and she a woman, and an Indian at that! Don't look so mystified. Madeleine La Framboise is an independent trader – took over her husband's business after he was shot in front of her eyes down at Grand River a few years back. She was making a mint, too – I don't know how the embargo's hit her. I think her stocking's full enough. When you say a friend – yes, Rachel found a friend in her. After . . . when my son died, she was a true friend. I've not seen her lately. To be honest, she's not pleased with me.'

'Why not?'

'Same reason as you're not, brother.' He was being flippant again, and I knew I could do nothing with him. 'But a man can only wear the willow so long. A shame perhaps, but that's the fact of the matter. *À bientôt!*' And he was gone.

I'd noticed the garden next to McGulpin's every time we'd passed it. Like ours, it was enclosed by a cedar picket fence to keep out straying animals, but there the resemblance ended. The garden of Madame La Framboise looked at first sight wholly English, with hollyhocks and mignonette, marigolds and pansies. Now I opened the gate and went in. The plants were arranged the way my mother – and now my wife – have them, with herbs and salads in among the flowers. The herbs were mostly unfamiliar to me, but I recognised one or two plants I'd seen wild in Upper Canada. Bees buzzed among the lavender. It brought home so close I felt my eyelids prickle, but I wasn't here to shed tears. The cabin was no larger than McGulpin's house, and it too had square glass windows with painted frames, and a proper chimney. I could see curtains trimly looped inside the window. I knocked briskly.

To my surprise a black maid in a print gown opened the door. I gave my name, and asked if Madeleine La Framboise was at home, and she ushered me into a parlour. The table and chairs, and the sofa against the wall, were European. The woven blankets and hangings, and the bearskin hearthrug, were entirely Indian. The floor was not earth, but boarded, and by the sofa there was a carpet.

I had hardly expected such luxury. There was not only money here, but an indefinable quality distilled out of two cultures; I had not thought they could be married so harmoniously. A print of Montreal Island hung over the mantelshelf. I was looking at it when, a voice behind me said, 'Mr Green?'

A tall dark-skinned woman was standing there. I hadn't heard her come in. She was dressed the Indian way, in a quill-embroidered deerskin dress, leggings and moccasins, with no concessions to European fashion whatsoever. Her black hair hung down in two long braids. I was surprised to see grey in it; she held herself like a young woman. In fact everything here surprised me. The maidservant, the comfortable room . . . none of this had led me to expect anyone so uncompromisingly Indian.

'Madeleine La Framboise?' She inclined her head. 'My name is Mark Greenhow. Thee knew my sister Rachel, when she was married to Alan Mackenzie.'

She looked me over dispassionately. 'Yes, I knew Rachel. You'd better sit down, Mr Greenhow.' Her English was perfect, though she had an accent which could have been French or Indian; I didn't know. 'I've been waiting for you to come to me. I was surprised, though, when they told me you were in Mackinac. Rachel said her family had quite cast her off?'

'Perhaps thee misunderstood her. She was disowned by the Religious Society to which we belong, and that must have been a grievous burden. But I – I'm her brother – naught can change that, however much I think her judgement wanting.'

'You've come all the way from England?'

'Ay.' I leaned forward. 'She gave thy name as her direction. I've come to seek her. If there's anything thee can tell me, I beg thee to do so. I've so little to go on, and I don't know the country.'

'You'll never know the country.' She was studying me closely. I met her eyes. 'So Mackenzie brought you here. He has told you his story, *n'est-ce pas?*'

'Ay.'

'You know she was lost a long way south of here? On an island in Lake Michigan. I guess you've no way of getting there.'

'I know all that. Alan told me.'

'He told you that he gave up the search and left, and has never gone back again?'

'Ay.' There was a pause. 'He said she'd never have survived a winter, if she'd still been on South Manitou. He was certain she was not. He searched the island, and then he searched the shores of the lake all round.'

'I know that area far better than Mackenzie ever will.'

'Thee does? And does thee think she's still there? Is it possible?'

'Anything is possible, Mr Greenhow.' She made a restless movement. 'I was born on Grand River. My grandfather was Kewinaquot – Returning Cloud – a chief of the Ottawa people. I winter every year at the rapids on Grand River, among my own people. If Rachel were among the southern Ottawa I would know it.'

'Thee thinks she's dead?'

Madeleine La Framboise crossed herself in the Papist fashion. 'God rest her soul if she is. 'Twas not what I said to you, though. I said I'd have heard if she were among the southern Ottawa. They're my own people. And perhaps I cared more what had happened to her than her husband did. Who can tell?'

'Thee's saying he could have made more search?'

'I say nothing of that, Mr Greenhow. Mackenzie searched from July until the ice came, but that winter he came back to Mackinac. For two years now he's been wholly taken up with espionage, I believe, against my own people.'

'Against the Ottawa?'

'I'm an American citizen, Mr Greenhow.'

'Thee rented a cabin to Alan all the same?'

'I had a cabin to rent, and I rented it. We're in the same trade. I'm an independent, and Mackenzie's allegiance is to the Canadian North West Company – the South West is naught but a temporary alliance between Mr Astor and the Canadians.'

'Temporary? Thee thinks it can't last?'

'Have you heard of the Columbia River?'

'No.'

'Ah, well.' She shrugged in a gesture wholly French. 'The war between the fur companies won't be fought here, Mr Greenhow. It's happening already on the Pacific Coast. That's where it'll be resolved, for good or ill. But that needn't concern us. My business is on Lake Michigan, and so, it seems, is yours.' Her tone suddenly changed. 'I only met your sister once before I left for Grand River. Mackenzie brought her here when they arranged to take the cabin. I came back in the spring. She was with child by then. When I saw her again she had that glamour on her that sometimes comes with pregnancy, if a woman is very happy. When she went into labour it was too soon. I went to see what could be done. It was past preventing. He was a boy: I took one look and saw he couldn't live. I baptised the child: I could do naught else for him, and it was his father's wish. Rachel wasn't fully conscious. She would have died too, but I brought in a *medi* – a skilled woman. Dr Mitchell came – Alan sent for him – but I could have told him Mitchell could do nothing – the baby was already dead, and white men's medicine would soon have sent the mother after him. I cared for Rachel, Mr Greenhow, little though I knew her. I persuaded the *medi* to come to a white man's cabin. Rachel has a look of my own daughter, whom I greatly miss.'

'Thy daughter . . . she is not . . . ?'

'Josette is alive and well.' Madeleine La Framboise crossed herself again. 'She's at school in Montreal. My son also. It wasn't loneliness that led me to befriend Rachel. You're like her in some ways, you know. Not in others.'

'So I'm told. When thee says she's not among the Ottawa – is there anywhere else she could be?'

'The world is wide, Mr Greenhow. I'm no prophet; how can I tell where she may be? On the shores of Lake Michigan you have the Ojibwa, the Menominee, the Potawatomi . . . you have also the fur traders, American, British and native, who travel as far as the Mississippi and possibly even into the Pacific regions by that route. You have also American soldiers, who have been known to patrol the waters of the lake. As I say, Mr Greenhow, the world is very wide.'

'Ay, thee makes it seem so.'

'You give up?'

'No.' I tried to explain to her. 'The world is wide, and if it were like looking for a needle in a bottle of hay, without any clue or guide, then I'd agree it couldn't be done. But I have had clues all along my way. One brought me to thee this day. And I have a guide, the Lord God who is our Father in heaven. He said that not one sparrow would fall to the earth but that he would take heed of it. The very hairs of thy head are numbered. If Rachel is on this earth, then God is with her, and knows where she is. The same God knows my purpose, and if he wills that I find her, he will be my guide.'

'According to your faith be it unto you, Mr Greenhow. But what if it's not the will of God that you should find her?'

'Then I'll have to say, "so be it." I've not reached the end of my road yet.'

I sat with Madeleine La Framboise for over an hour. She said that when she went to her trading post that winter, she'd enquire about Rachel again. That way, she said, I could concentrate on the lands further north, around South Manitou, and next spring we could meet again, and see what we each had been able to find out. I believed her. I thought her sincere in her care for Rachel, and more direct in her dealings than any I had yet enquired of.

I hadn't expected Alan to approve, but he was more vehement than I expected. 'The two-faced bitch! Oh, yes, she did help when the baby died. Yes, she was good to Rachel, I'll grant you that, but only because Rachel reminded her of Josette. If Rachel had … had …' – he sought for a comparison – 'had red hair and freckles, do you think she'd have given a damn! Not she! That woman doesn't act out of charity, Mark. She's a tight-fisted twister, that's what she is. Oh, yes, she pours money into her church. She's given St Anne's more money than your Society has probably ever dreamed of' – he was most certainly wrong about that – 'she talks of nothing but building a new church, and bringing back the bloody Jesuits – even you must know what that means – and everyone's supposed to think she's some kind of saint. Well, I'll tell you this, Brother Abstinence Mark, she woos her precious Ottawa with all kinds of watered-down liquor. She don't care if they drink themselves to death, and she don't care if it's against the law either! She's notorious for it. How do you think a woman like that manages to snatch up all the Michigan trade from under our very noses? Oh, no, she don't keep the rules, not by a long way.'

'I'm not familiar with thy rules. She was compassionate to Rachel, which is what matters to me.'

'Oh, ay, have it your own way. But she's got her knife into me, ever since Rachel's been gone. Perhaps you'll be kind enough to bear that in mind, seeing that we're kin, brother.'

'Ay,' I said, for it was quite true that I bore all this in mind, along with many other things.

It was clear that Alan would give our journey no more thought until he'd dealt with the pressing business that kept him out until all hours. While I waited, I spent my days exploring the island, and talking to anyone who was inclined to pass the time of day – which was most people, because trade was at a standstill, and myself an object of curiosity. Many spoke to me of Rachel, which was my object, but none could tell me anything that might lead me further. During these trips I covered the length and breadth of the island: I reckoned it was little more than a mile or two square. The village and the fort occupied only the southern tip, as I realised on my first day, when I climbed the highest hill, which lay behind the fort. Inland there were a few farms, and groves of pine, maple and basswood. The bluff on which the fort was built circled almost the whole island, and there were many curious rock forms and arches in the limestone cliffs. I was told that some of these places were sacred to the Manitous of the place, and indeed I came upon diverse signs – wreaths, bones and suchlike – that the pagan religions were not wholly abandoned in these parts.

One day I wandered to the far north of the island, where I found a sizeable farm. A wooden farmhouse stood amid fields of maize and wheat, all surrounded by post and rail fences. Though the soil was poor and sandy it had been well dunged. Apart from the view of the lake over the distant trees, I might have been back in Yonge Street. The farmer was on his round; he saw me and came over.

'Michael Dousman.' He held out his hand. 'You must be the Quaker fellow – Mackenzie's brother-in-law.'

I spent a pleasant hour or two in his snug kitchen, and found much in common with him. Like the Friends in Yonge Street, he came from Pennsylvania. He'd come to Mackinac when the Americans got the fort in '96 – which was agreed upon, he said, in '83, but, saving my presence, the English were the arch-procrastinators of the civilised world – and he'd invested in land immediately. It was true about the soil, he agreed, but there were many advantages to being on an island, in terms of 'predators of every kind, four-foot and two-foot'.

'But now?' I asked him boldly. 'Will there be war in Mackinac now, does thee think?'

He frowned. 'Ay, I think it. I don't want it. I'm not the man for bloodshed. I'm a captain in our militia; I'll defend my home if I have to. But if there were any other way, I'd say take it. All folk here want is to get on with our lives. We have all sorts here – Americans, Indians, British – all tribes and conditions of men – all come to trade. Give us back our trade, I say, and don't drag us into any war. But it's too late for that.'

'But isn't the war about this very trade – about the border?'

'Nay, Greenhow. This war was started in London. This war began when your British navy started commandeering American ships and seamen. It started when your government said our country couldn't trade with Europe, except through a British port. In fact, to be honest, this war began in 1776 and hasn't left off yet. It'll end, I guess, when England agrees to treat the United States as a free and independent country. And it'll only end when that day comes.'

I thought of William Mackenzie, and an argument almost rose to my lips. I silenced it, seeing that these were worldly factions with which I had naught to do, the kind of words that led to deeds with outward weapons such as I did utterly deny. And yet it was hard to hear my own country reviled, and I so far away from it. Michael Dousman let the silence be for a while, then he said, 'What breed of cattle do you have then, if your farm is high up in the hills?'

So it was that we parted in charity. Presently I strolled back to the village. My path led through a tall grove of basswood, and the leaves cast a freckled carpet of sun and shadow before my feet. Bright red birds were singing in the trees. In the shade, the noon-day heat was comfortable. My mind had been drifting, but I was suddenly aware there was a tune in my head, and moreover, I was humming it out loud:

> *En roulant ma boule roulant*
> *En roulant ma boule.*
> *En roulant ma boule roulant.*
> *En roulant ma boule.*

I'd never caught myself doing such a thing before. I stopped in the middle of the track and thought about it. I felt in no way degenerate, but, on the contrary, filled with the peace of God as manifested in the beauty of his creation. I examined my mind quite carefully, questioning myself as if I were an elder from my Meeting. There was nothing amiss. I began to walk slowly on, and the words drifted to and fro in the dappled sunshine like a benediction: *there is nothing amiss; there is nothing amiss.*

That evening I wrote a long letter to my parents, trusting in God that it might find its way to them somehow. If it went back to Montreal with the voyageurs in August, it could reach Cumberland before I did, assuming it ever crossed the border to the Sault. When I'd sealed it I sat back and sighed. I still had another sheet of paper, for I'd bought two at the American Fur Company Store that morning. Presently I pulled it towards me and wrote:

To my Friend in Christ, Clemency,

I wrote nothing more for a long time, but sat staring out of the window. Marching footsteps tramped along the baked earth of the lane. A couple of soldiers passed the window; I'd got used to them patrolling the streets by now. I dipped my pen.

> *I write to thee from Mackinac, in the United States, thy own country. Since I left Yonge Street I have met no Friends. Indeed at times I seem very far from all that I . . .*

I paused again. I was tempted to scratch out the last sentence, for it was not my intent to whine to her.

> *. . . that I am accustomed to. Since I have left thee I have learned well how to a paddle a canoe . . .*

(I was wrong about that: to be a spare *milieu* is not to know how to paddle a canoe.)

> *. . . and that pleases me. With thee it must now be approaching harvest; I pray that the Lord may bless thy labours with abundance. It is my hope also that Coltsfoot had an easy travail, and that the calf was a heifer.*
>
> *When I left Montreal, we headed north-west up the Outaouais River . . .*

My pen began to flow more easily. (How I should think that Clemency would be interested in portages, rapids, and canal locks I do not know, but I was a young fellow, grasping at straws in the dark, for all this territory was new to me.) I covered the sheet, but had naught to say that was worth crossing my lines for, so I finished,

Ever thy Friend, in peace,
Mark Greenhow

After I'd sealed it I bethought me that Thomas and Sarah, and indeed the Meeting at Yonge Street, should have been added to my expressions of goodwill, but there was but one stick of sealing wax in the house, and that not mine, so I thought it better to leave things as they were.

CHAPTER 15

TWO DAYS LATER I SAW MICHAEL DOUSMAN AGAIN.
I'd spent another solitary evening (for Alan had been gone
since the previous night), this time reading volume the
second of Gibbon's *The Decline and Fall of the Roman
Empire* (this being the only volume in the house). The
heresies of the early Christian churches were quite new
to me; I had never heard of all these emperors, martyrs
and bishops, nor had I ever conceived that there were
so many unverifiable creeds to quarrel about. In fact my
brain was all of a whirl, but not unpleasantly. I read until
the candles guttered. There was still no sign of Alan, so I
went to bed. I woke suddenly, aware of someone standing
in the room.

'Is anyone there?'

I recognised Dousman's voice, and was wide awake at
once. 'Ay,' I said.

'Greenhow! Of course.' I could just make out where he
was standing at the door.

'Listen, man. The British are here! Don't say anything
– you know my still-house on the south shore?'

'Ay.'

'Go there now! Everyone else has gone. Otherwise –
the British army's mostly Indians. You mustn't be found

here, if they take the island. You know what scalping is? Then go!'

I was scrambling into my breeches. 'Ay. But the American garrison . . . the fort . . .'

'They're not to know. Go quietly. No one will harm you.'

'But . . . Dousman, I don't . . . Thee's American?' For some reason my heart sank within me, to think this man a traitor. And yet, what was it to me?

'Ay.' He came a little nearer. 'There's no time to explain . . . yet I wouldn't wish . . . Greenhow!'

'Ay.'

'Listen, then, quickly! I went over to St Joseph's yesterday. Hanks – the commander at the fort – sent me. Find out what's going on, he said. He's had no orders from Detroit – we've heard nothing. I'm a trader; there's a consignment from Lake Superior I had to see about – that's the truth. Anyway, I can cross the border. So I took my canoe and went last night. We – my man and I – we'd only got to Goose Island – fifteen miles or so from here – it was dark by then – when we ran straight into the British flotilla. I was taken aboard the *Caledonia* to Captain Roberts. I've known those men for years, Greenhow: Pothier, Askin, Johnson, Roberts, Ermatinger. They told me we're at war. Since June 19th, it seems. Pothier brought the news back from Montreal two weeks ago. It's the Indian allies. You understand me? If the British take the fort, there'll be a massacre. I gave my word not to alert the garrison – they told me to come back to warn the village – get everyone to safety. You're the last, Greenhow – I didn't begin at the British agent's house! So go! And fast!'

I was lacing my boots. 'Where's Alan?'

'Mackenzie? Where do you think? That's why Hanks sent me off yesterday – Mackenzie's canoe had gone. They keep a pretty tight watch on that fellow. Now go!'

I was at the door, Dousman close behind me. 'Where's the British army now?'

'Go, I said! Very well . . . at my farm. We landed up north, on my own beach. Two hours ago – you're the last house I've roused. They'll have the cannon brought up by now. Run, Greenhow! To the still-house, mind. If you value your life – and mine – go!'

He slipped past me and vanished down the street. Outside there was a faint glimmer of the dawn to come. Everything was very quiet. Even the birds weren't awake yet. I walked under the lee of the silent fort and into Market Street. There were footsteps behind me: I retreated quietly under the eaves of the Company factory. A family hurried past me – I'd seen the woman before. She and her man were each carrying a child huddled in a shawl. A dog, evidently thinking this was a game, frisked at their heels. They didn't see me; they were hurrying for the still-house. I thought about what it would be like in there, waiting, unable to hear or see, dreading to hear war cries without, and not knowing anything. I heard a child crying, and pattering footsteps. Two women passed me, holding hands with half a dozen running children, all half-dressed. The smallest child was crying as it was pulled along. If I went to the still-house, I'd most likely be the only single man in the place. I could see more people, some weighted with bundles, hurrying through the gloom. The light was growing fast.

The army of British soldiers, traders, voyageurs and their Indian allies, would all be coming along the very track I'd followed from Michael Dousman's farm two days ago. That track came out at the back of the fort, before winding to the shore. I remembered an idle talk I'd had with Alan. I pulled my cap over my ears and began to run, away from the still-house, towards the woods.

When I was exploring the island I'd found a little path behind our house that wound uphill through the trees, by-passing the precipice below the fort. It was quite dark in the wood, but I was used to scrambling over rock. My mind was in turmoil. I was heading towards a bloody conflict between two armies, I who utterly denied any fighting with outward weapons whatsoever. On both sides there were men in whom I'd witnessed, however briefly, a little of that of God, from the anxious young Lieutenant Hanks, whom I'd seen striding down Fort Street with an even younger officer, through to Charles Ermatinger who'd spoken kindly of Rachel. I know not to this day what I thought I could do. But one thing is certain: I could not have stayed away.

I had to come by a long route, for the trees are all cleared away around the fort for fifty yards or more. At last I stood, breathing hard but silently, at the edge of the forest, where I could look out on the flat green field behind the fort. The grass was all covered with dew, shining in the long rays of the rising sun. A jay chattered above my head. The back wall of the fort looked even less daunting than I remembered it. A cannon could fire over it as easily as I could throw an apple over my garden wall.

Slowly the sun rose. A little mist wreathed upwards as the dew began to melt. I shifted my position so I could see up the hill to my right. I saw a flash of light, as if the sun had struck metal. I stared and stared, and saw – or fancied I saw – movement among the trees. Soon I was sure of it. The top of the hill was bare of trees, and I could see people moving up there. The flash of metal came again, and yet again. Though I never studied military tactics in my life, it was easy to guess they were mounting a cannon there, overlooking the fort.

Someone touched my shoulder. I could have jumped out of my skin, and indeed I gave a sort of gasp. It was an Indian warrior, dressed in a breechclout and leggings, his face painted red and black like a demon, all hung about with beads and bones and worse, with a musket over his shoulder, and a long knife in his hand. I had but two seconds for the most fervent prayer of my life, when he said, 'You come now. This is a bad place for you.'

What could I do but follow? The wood where I'd walked a few moments ago was suddenly filled with warriors armed with all manner of outward weapons, crouched or standing motionless beneath the trees. How I had failed to hear them I could not think. (I blamed myself the less later, when I'd learned more of the Indians' ability to go silently in woodland.) I came sinfully close to cursing the blue jay, who I guessed was my betrayer. My captor – if that is what he was – led me back to a little glade where someone had set out beehives, a thing that seemed incongruous in that scene of silent savagery. There was a man in European dress with his back to me. His musket was propped against a tree, while he stood in close confabulation with a feathered warrior. I knew that back. Suddenly rage flared up inside me. I never came so close to striking a man, and yet refrained. All this he had brought on me! Ay, and Rachel, too. I would like to have killed him, and been scalped for it, no doubt, but I held myself in check while my guide whispered to him, and waited his pleasure.

'Mark!' Alan swung round and held me by both arms. To my astonishment he seemed moved to see me. 'Man, don't you realise . . . The Devil! You were within ames ace of being knifed – scalped – you'd be dead by now . . . If they hadn't reported back . . . Most times they only tell you after . . . You were to go to the still-house! Didn't Dousman go to you? I asked him . . . I told him . . .' All this in a frenzied whisper, while the savages looked on.

'Ay, he came,' I said dourly. I couldn't express my fury. There was no point complaining that he'd told me nothing, left me without a word of warning or a by your leave, been as wily in all his dealings with me as a cockatrice, and treated me from beginning to end as if I were no man at all.

'But why did you come here?' He looked at me doubtfully. 'You'll fight with us, after all?'

'No, I will not!'

'Hush!' whispered Alan, and the savages stirred disapprovingly around us. 'No point being angry with me, brother Mark. This is a war you've strayed into. I can't help that.'

'Ay, but thee didn't tell me, did thee? Thee knew war was declared, the very day I met thee, and thee said naught.'

'I was sworn not to, Mark.'

'I've not known thy oath to trouble thee, when not convenient!'

He struck me across the cheek.

There was a moment's silence. The savages had closed around us, silent as ever, watching. I heeded them not. I stepped up to him – oh, shame it is to write it! So far did I then fall! – I twisted him neatly off balance and threw him across my hip. Before he knew I'd moved he was lying sprawled at my feet.

I heard the crash of a cannon shot from the hill behind us. For a moment everything froze. The echo rumbled across the hill. A small breeze shimmered up above; a few leaves fell. All of a sudden a frightful yelling broke out from all sides of the forest. Alan's Indians joined in, in a long-drawn-out howling that froze my blood.

Alan scrambled to his feet. 'By God, it's begun!'

The savages, indiscriminately armed with guns, clubs or tomahawks, were running towards the clearing. I had to see: I followed. Alan was way ahead of me, hurrying through the trees.

Someone touched my shoulder. I didn't jump this time, when I saw the painted face – half-black, half-red, and the glittering eyes looking directly into mine. 'This – you want?'

He held out a musket, the butt towards me. I looked down at it. 'Nay, friend, I will not' – I caught myself up, thinking of the sin that now lay upon me – 'I will not take up any outward weapon.'

'You want?'

'No, friend. I do not want.'

He shrugged, and left me. I ran after him into the sunlight. The scene had changed utterly. The green clearing was filled with men: a wild, parti-coloured army nearly all composed of painted savages, but I could see voyageurs drawn up in rough formation – two hundred and sixty militia, I learned later – and a little body of regular soldiers in a red line below the hill. We were on the far left of the line. The smoke from the cannon still hung in the morning air. I looked towards the fort; the grey wall was bare and blank. Orders were shouted along the British lines. The yelling died away, and ceased. There was a muttering among the savages, then silence. Nothing moved.

Six men detached themselves from the centre of the line. Three were Canadian militia, and three were civilians. The militia captain carried a white flag raised high. They passed quite close to me. I'd seen the captain before, in the factory of the South West Company at the Sault. It was Toussaint Pothier. They walked right up to the gates of the fort. The gate opened a little, and the men went in.

The long silence was tense as a drawn-out scream. The sun climbed higher than ever we see it here. I sorely missed my broad-brimmed hat, and indeed I wished at that moment I looked to be more what I was. I watched Alan, standing a few yards from me. He seemed unmoved, but I noted how his fingers drummed out a silent rhythm on the barrel of his musket – for those who possessed guns had them primed and ready to aim. The savages around me were motionless as Friends in Meeting, but, oh, how utterly different was the quality of their silence! It was like the pent moment between the lightning and the thunder, when the storm is upon one. And here I was exposed on the front line, as if I stood upon the very summit of Skiddaw waiting for the flash that would strike me down. I thought about walking away – it was not any man's place to stop me – but I had it not in me to retreat before them all. So much of a coward was I; it shames me now to tell it. I prayed fervently to God, who seest all things, and forgives all that sincerely repent, that he would guide me. And the Lord put words into my mind, saying, *the thing that hath been, it is that which shall be; and that which is done is that which shall be done: and there is no new thing under the sun.* It came to me that my predicament was one that many had suffered, and yet found a way. I decided that when the charge came I would slip sideways into the wood – for we were on the far left of the line – and watch from there. For the Lord also put it into my mind that everything under the sun has a meaning, and I might yet find a way to serve his purposes, before the day was over.

The sun rose higher yet. At last the gate opened. Toussaint Pothier came out first, still holding the flag of truce aloft. With him came two men in blue uniforms – I recognised Lieutenant Hanks by his stride – and indeed it must have been a long walk up to the hill top. The warriors fell back like the Red Sea parting to make a passage through for the truce party. We watched them climb up the winding path to the plateau where the British gun was placed. They were not gone above twenty minutes before the little group reappeared, and the American officers were escorted under the white flag all the way back to the fort. I'd thought the army would grow restless. The regular soldiers were standing at ease now. It was odd to see how the painted savages, still with their knives and tomahawks unsheathed, waited with an impassivity their more civilised allies were unable to emulate. We could hear the buzz of talk from the soldiers and the voyageurs, but Alan's band of Indians neither moved nor spoke.

There came a thin little sound of fife and drum from inside the walls. The blue-clad soldiers came out, their muskets slung over their shoulders, marching in strict formation with young Lieutenant Hanks at their head. They were pitifully few – fifty-seven, I heard later – to set against two hundred British soldiers, and of Indian warriors twice as many again. The little force of blue uniforms turned sharp left and, still accompanied by their single fife and drum, marched away towards the shore.

A ripple passed along the lines. I looked up at the fort. The flag with its red and white stripes, and its fifteen white stars on a blue sky, was descending the flagpole in little jerks. Our patchwork army sighed, as one man. The flagpole stood white and stark. Another flag rose slowly. It lay limp until the breeze caught it. The Union Jack flared out as the gates below swung wide open.

The cheering, whooping and yelling that then broke out was like Bedlam multiplied a thousand times. The Indians burst into wild war whoops, and the white men threw their hats into the air, and thumped one another on the back, and cried hurrah! as if they had achieved some great thing, when they had but crept through a wood and stood in the sun for a morning. I rejoiced too, because no drop of blood was shed. The Indians would have rushed forward when the gates opened, but their own chiefs restrained them. The voyageurs broke ranks entirely, cheering and singing, carrying their officers shoulder-high as if portaging them to their canoes. Only the red line of soldiers, led by Captain Roberts, kept its ranks. A bugle sounded. The forty-odd regulars advanced, formed a column of threes, and filed into Fort Mackinac.

So ended the only battle I was ever in. I walked away from the riotous rejoicings, over to the western shores of the island, where all was as calm as it must have lain since the beginning of the world. I sat on the shore with my back to Mackinac, looking across at the empty forests on the mainland opposite. I had every reason to give thanks to the Lord and Saviour of us all, and so I did, being moved to remember the words of the Psalm:

As for me, I will call upon God, and the Lord shall save me.

Evening, and morning, and at noon, will I pray, and cry aloud: and he shall hear my voice.

He hath delivered my soul in peace from the battle that was against me.

CHAPTER 16

I WAS BREAKFASTING NEXT MORNING ON GRILLED pickerel, rolls and coffee – the *métis* woman who came each day was a good cook – when to my surprise Alan emerged from the other room. 'I smell coffee,' he said. 'Oh, good: Anne, you can grill me some fish too. I'm devilish hungry. Good morning, brother Mark. I trust you slept well?'

I eyed him warily. 'Ay.' I lied, for I hadn't gone to my bed till past three, and even then my mind was all of a jangle, and I couldn't sleep.

'So.' Alan took his seat opposite me. 'Quite an exciting day, yesterday, didn't you think?'

'Ay.' I buttered a roll lavishly. 'Ay, well, Alan. Thee's had thy battle. Will thee look to our errand now, as thee agreed?'

He smiled. 'I like your style, brother. And yes, I will. But first can we take our breakfast together like gentlemen, as brothers ought to do. Anne! Are there more of those rolls, or has he eaten the lot?'

I looked him in the eye. 'I'm sorry I threw thee, friend. 'Twas ill done; I never wished thee harm.'

'On the contrary, 'twas remarkably well done,' said Alan irritably. 'So much for saying you never fight. You learned that trick somewhere, or I'm a Dutchman.'

'Will thee forgive me?'

'Of course I forgive thee – you, I mean. Here, shake hands.' He reached across the table and I duly shook his hand. 'Now, can we please forget about it?'

I said nothing more until his fish was set in front of him. Anne brought a fresh jug of coffee, and I filled our cups. 'I was out last night,' I told him. 'I saw the Indians dancing.'

'And what did you think of it?'

'Savage,' I said shortly. But in my heart I was very troubled by the way the Indian drums and the dancing had stirred my blood. I had seen dancing before at fairs and such-like, and heard the jingling of fiddles and whistles, but never before had I witnessed a dance that seemed to embody the spirit of war itself – not war as perpetrated by armies and generals, and written about in newspapers, but the spirit of war which sleeps within all men, inciting the unwary to depart from the paths of peace, and go forth like crouching demons to fight and kill. Long after I left the dancing, the drums went on beating, and as I lay sleepless in my bed, they seemed to echo the very rhythm of my heart, awakening a devil within my breast whose presence I had never before suspected. I said aloud, 'Does thee think it right to use these savages in a war between powers that are far away and naught to do with them?'

'Naught? Where had you that idea? This war is all to do with them! This war is fought for their trade, their lands, their existence even! And our interests too, of course. Besides, the Indians aren't children. They have their own wars, always have had. This is nothing compared to the old wars between the Ojibwa and the Sioux. And I'll tell you another thing: take away our guns, artillery, ships . . . take away all our modern armament, and I bet you anything you like who'd be the better warrior. I know what it is

– you've got hold of some notion that North America was a veritable Eden, full of Noble Savages living in a state of Primal Innocence. You think that we live in a degenerate world, and we'd have a happier time altogether if we stripped off our clothes, regurgitated the apple, and emulated our red-skinned allies. I'll wager you've been reading Rousseau, or some such nonsense, haven't you?'

'Nay, friend, I never heard of the fellow. I think we live in a fallen world, 'tis true, and maybe the Indians are less removed from that Garden where the Lord God walked in the cool of the evening, than some Europeans would wish to admit.'

Alan stared at me, his fork halfway to his mouth. 'Mark,' he said eventually, and I realised he was speaking to me seriously for the first time since he'd told me about Rachel, the day we'd dined at John Askin's house on St Joseph's Island. 'Do you know why our soldiers were patrolling the streets of Mackinac all last night? Do you understand why Roberts risked all to send Dousman back and get all the village people safe into the still-house? Do you know why we can't rest until our Indian allies are dispersed and gone safe home? Have you any idea at all what would have happened if we'd fought yesterday's battle and won?'

I caught my breath. Better to know, I thought. 'What would have happened?'

'For a start, every one of those American soldiers would have been killed and scalped. Same with the villagers. There wouldn't be a man alive today, and the women and children would all have been taken, for the Indians need more people, they've lost so many. Every house would have been sacked and burned. You know what Charles Roberts got the chieftains to agree to? These were the terms of surrender: that the fort be handed over to the British without bloodshed, and that the garrison march out with honour. Hanks and all his men are being shipped down to Fort Detroit, on parole not to serve again unless exchanged. Private property on the island to be held sacred; no ships in the harbour to be commandeered. No American citizens to be molested, so long as they take an oath of loyalty to the king. And if they won't – they have a month to leave Mackinac, and take their property with them. That's your degenerate civilisation for you! That's your military despotism! I tell you – this land never saw such terms till now. To the savage mind such tender mercy is utterly unheard of! I saw the dancing too, last night. Impressive, wasn't it?'

'In its way,' I conceded.

'A victory dance. You know how the Indians used to celebrate their victories? By torture. The correct procedure was to torture your prisoners of war to death, in the most imaginative fashion you could possibly devise. You could chop small pieces off them, to begin with – fingers, toes, privates – the women and children found that part especially amusing, I believe – and take it slowly until there was nothing left but a torso – a living torso, you understand. Or you could start by inserting slivers of wood under your victim's fingernails until they slowly peeled away. Or with the eyes . . . All this was quite logical, you understand, because it's a great humiliation to surrender and be taken prisoner. You deserve all you get. These are the rules. You go into battle knowing what the deal is, and you die as you must, or win.'

'When I met thee in the wood yesterday, thee was about to fight alongside these very warriors.'

'Ay, and because we were there, no excesses were committed. But the danger was there – all the time. And you . . . if they hadn't come back with word that you were standing there in the wood, and if the message hadn't been passed along to me . . . You've a fine scalp, brother – good, thick, brown hair: white man's hair. I tell you –

alliance with the Indians – it's playing with fire. Anything might have happened. If Hanks hadn't surrendered . . . if Roberts hadn't held the tribes in check . . . It was very well done, you know. How well done, I think you have no idea of.' He drank down his coffee, and reached for the jug. 'What are you thinking now, brother Mark?'

'I was thinking about Loic, and his baby, and how Pakané and Waase'aaban cooked whitefish for us, and how Waase'aaban said I should have moccasins, and found a bed for me to sleep in. Are not these people thy friends?'

'Of course they're my friends! You misconstrue me, Mark. You've all to learn, in fact, but it's hardly surprising. I keep forgetting you've only just arrived.'

'Nay, I've been with thee nigh on a fortnight, friend. When will we set out for South Manitou?'

He grinned. 'By God, but you're persistent! Brazen too! Do you realise where South Manitou is?'

'Ay. Thee lent me thy map, remember?'

'So I did. It makes no difference to you that our route takes us more than a hundred miles into United States territory?'

'No. I would like to avoid any battles, if I can. Otherwise it's immaterial. We must go wherever Rachel might be.'

Alan said he had to talk to Captain Roberts, now the Commander of Fort Mackinac, before we could arrange anything. I felt it time to take matters into my own hands. I asked Anne, and she said her own brother could paddle me across to Bois Blanc for a dollar. They went there every spring, she told me, for the maple syrup. It turned out she knew the Kerners family well, and was some sort of cousin of Loic's. Her brother Stéphan was a taciturn fellow, or perhaps he had little English. Once we'd set off I couldn't see his face anyway. He was surprised when I said I could take the other paddle, and indeed it was a different feeling in a little Indian canoe, without the bowsman's stroke to follow. I enjoyed it: I could see all the emptiness of the wide waters, but not for long, as Bois Blanc is only a couple of miles from Mackinac village.

Stéphan and I carried the canoe on to the beach, and walked up to Martin Kerners' house. The yard was full of split whitefish laid to dry on rush mats in the sun. Pakané and Waase'aaban were outside, cooking something over a fire in the yard. Biinoojii was in his cradleboard, hanging from a tree; I was reminded of a lullaby my mother used to sing – 'twas the only rhyme she had, I think, certainly the only one she ever sung to us: *Hushaby baby on the tree top* . . . As soon as the women saw us coming they ran to meet us, calling out 'Stéphan, Mark, *Boozhoo, boozhoo! Biindigen!*'

Waase'aaban was more beautiful even than I remembered. She soon left us, but only to fetch the men, it turned out. She was so lithe and quick, her long black braids swinging across her shoulders as she moved. While she was gone we sat in the sun and waited. The mosquitoes here were far worse than on Mackinac. Pakané noticed my discomfort and gave me some grease to smear on my exposed skin. It smelt infinitely worse than the bears' grease the voyageurs had used, but luckily the mosquitoes seemed agreed on that too.

When Loic appeared he was covered with sweat and sawdust, and wore only a breechclout and leggings, and a handkerchief round his forehead. 'Stéphan! *Boozhoo! Que ça fait longtemps qu'on ne c'est pas vu!* M'sieu Mark! I'm glad to see you. Is anything amiss?'

'No, friend. I have somewhat to ask thee, that's all.'

Waase'aaban went back to feeding the fire. They were boiling up strips of basswood bark, Loic explained. He sent Waase'aaban to fetch some twine, so he could show me how the bark fibres from the basswood were woven together. The way she jumped up and ran to do it was entirely childlike, for all that her body was most clearly a woman's. When she came back, Stéphan took the twine from her and demonstrated how even a man as strong as he couldn't break it. Stéphan had clearly left his servant status behind when we left Mackinac. Here, he was a close relative of the family – 'the grandson of Pakané's grandfather's brother', Loic told me – whereas I was a mere acquaintance. Though I was welcomed just as kindly, the conversation was carried on, after the first greetings, entirely in Ojibwa. I'd liked to have known what they said, but I contented myself with watching their faces, especially Waase'aaban's, for hers was by far the most expressive.

Presently Loic said, 'You wish to be private? Come!'

It was dim and stuffy indoors. The fire was banked-up, smouldering at the edges. Loic swept away a pile of dirty wooden platters, and wiped the table with his handkerchief. 'Sit, m'sieu! Here is water. Will you drink? Now, ask! I listen.'

'Loic, I have been at Mackinac two weeks. Today is the nineteenth day of Seventh . . . of July.'

'*Aabita-niibino-giizis*. Yes?'

'Time passes. I need to go to South Manitou Island and see where Rachel was lost. I have to search the shores of Lake Michigan and speak again to the Indians who live there, while they're still in their summer villages. I've barely three months of this season left. I've already been a whole year in Upper Canada. Alan is entirely occupied at Mackinac. I'm willing to pay for a canoe, and a man to take me, if I must go alone. Will thee come with me? Thee knows the place. Thee was there. Thee knew her. I couldn't wish for more.'

To my surprise he was smiling. 'You have not talked to Alan about this?'

'No. I've just waited, till I can wait no more.'

'Alan has not talked to you?'

'About what?'

'M'sieu!' Loic laid his hand on my arm, and he was laughing. 'I am already bespoke! This is why you find me here at home, waiting. There is no trade this year. A man has hired me already to bring my canoe and go to South Manitou! And then to travel the Michigan shore for the rest of the season. For two weeks now I am already hired!'

'Thee means – Alan?'

'But yes, m'sieu! He did not say to you? He told me, very soon there will be war. I am to say nothing; what is it to me? The soldiers will not come to Bois Blanc. No one comes to Bois Blanc. But I listen to Alan, and it is clear that soon there will be war at Mackinac. I care not. So long as there is trade – and at Bois Blanc there will always be a little trade, of some kind – I care not what flag they fly. Alan is very busy. But soon, he says, the business at Mackinac will be done, and then we go. I know this business. Now there is a new flag over the fort. I care not. But I think it means that Alan's business is finished, so we shall go. He, you and I. So I have put all new bark on the canoe, and made packs of food, and already I am waiting for you.'

If Alan had been there I would have been sorely tempted to floor him again, only harder. Luckily he was not. Why had he said nothing? Was it only to tease, or did he not trust me even so far? I was fairly sure it was the former. Never in my life had I had to wrestle with such fury as Alan induced in me – or perhaps that was not the exact truth. I knew of old this heat of rage inside me; I had only hitherto associated it with Rachel, and that not of late years.

'M'sieu, it is of no use to be angry. *Il est comme il*

est. Did he not say to you that he agreed to make this journey?'

'At St Joseph he asked me what I wanted us to do, and I told him. He said – just as thee said – there was no trade this year, so "we might as well go as not." Since then' – I could not keep the chagrin entirely out of my tone – 'he puts me off, and puts me off, and tells me nothing.'

'Perhaps not all his secrets are his own to tell?'

The impropriety of complaining about Alan to Loic had already struck me. 'No matter. I should not have spoken so, friend. Thee has good news for me – the best of news – and I should thank thee.'

'You need not thank. Alan pays me. Also, I wish to go. I told you before, I think, as her brother, you do right. This I told Alan. When you tell him we have talked, I think he will agree to come away very soon. The fort is in British hands now, so he has not that to think about any more. So now that you are here, you will eat with us?'

Instead of fish we had dried bear meat, boiled, which I'd never tasted before. It was a dark, close-grained meat, somewhat tough in the chewing. The men sat at the table while the women waited on us. I never, in all my visits, saw Pakané or Waase'aaban eat. But after the meal was over, I was aware of sundry gigglings from the hearth, and the men were grinning. All the talk had been in Ojibwa, but Loic suddenly said to me in English, 'My wife has a small gift for you, m'sieu.'

Pakané was standing by my chair. I could see Waase'aaban standing rigid by the hearth, her hands pressed to her mouth. Pakané held out the gift, laid across her out-stretched hands. It was a pair of moccasins, made as long in the foot as my own boots, beautifully stitched in rawhide, and ornamented with quill decorations over the seams. There were looped patterns in rawhide stitching around the ankle cuffs, dark leather against light.

'Those will work better than your boots in the canoe,' said Loic.

I knew not what to say. Never in my life had I worn any ornamented garment – I counted not the tassel on my voyageur cap, for once it was on my head I never saw it to think of it – and never had I so much as touched such work as this. Plain Quaker dress was a stand made against the sad luxuries of the so-called great, the corrupt courts and decadent societies of old Europe. It flashed through my mind that, for all their ornamentation, naught could be plainer than these moccasins. Not a penny was spent in the making of them, but every stitch was made in friendship, a simple act of charity if ever there was one.[1] Loic was right: moccasins would be much more practical in the canoe. Marc used to wince every time I stepped into my place, in what he called *tes sales bottes énormes*.

I addressed myself to Pakané. 'I thank thee, friend. 'Tis

---

[1] I believe now that there is no such matter as a simple act of charity. *Charity doth not behave itself unseemly, seeketh not her own, is not easily provoked, thinketh no evil.* A human being may abound in charity, but we are mixed creatures, and in every charitable act I think there is a little of something else. I look back now, and have perhaps more inkling of Waase'aaban's thoughts than I had then, but cannot find it in my heart to condemn any one of them as evil. And if they were not wholly seemly, selfless, disinterested or good, then I have to ask myself, by what standard do I judge? If it be by a measure that meant naught to her, then perhaps it is meaningless even to consider the matter. At the time I thought none of this, but was filled with uncertainty, not only about my parlous situation, but also concerning the unruly promptings of my own heart. There is a passage in Deuteronomy that says what to do *if thou seest among the captives a beautiful woman and hast a desire unto her that thou wouldst have her to thy wife* ... This I see now as an expression of a more primitive understanding, coming from a savage people struggling towards a sense of God. It would surely be an unchristian deed to take a woman from an inferior people and religion, out of the mere lust of one's eyes, knowing that in her eyes thee had done no sin, and suffered no dereliction of one's principles.

exceeding kind in thee. I will use them well.' I turned to Loic. 'Will thee translate?'

'Pakané understands English, only she will not speak. But you can say to her yourself: *G'miigwechiwìgin, nwiijikiwenh*.'

I repeated as best I could, '*G'miigwechiwìgin, nwiijikiwenh*.'

'With moccasins, you have to patch and sew them often,' remarked Loic. 'They do not last for ever.'

Martin Kerners added his mite in a language I could understand. 'For this you need a woman. *Vous avez besoin d'une femme qui prend bien soin de vos mocassins*. This you need.'

Exhorted to do so by all the company, I took off my boots and put on my moccasins – they felt strangely light, almost like being barefoot – while Loic, bending close as I unlaced my boots, whispered in my ear. 'It was not my wife, *en effet*, who did this work.'

I looked up, startled. Waase'aaban was no longer standing by the hearth. She must have slipped away.

After we'd eaten I walked along the shore with Loic and Stéphan. The bay below the Kerners home was shallow for a long way out – we'd nearly grounded on our way in – so the water over the sand was pale green under the sun. We could see Mackinac Island plainly, and the coast of the mainland beyond. It was an excellent place to keep an eye on things. When I said this to Loic he shrugged and smiled. We took a path through the dunes, walking a carpet of silverweed among the juniper bushes. Suddenly the path dived under the trees. The earth was soft with ancient leaves under the maples and giant basswoods that gave the island its name. A mid-day torpor hung in the air. Clouds of mosquitoes hung above the swampy ground on either side. Soon I caught the smell of a human settlement and a tang of smoke. A moment later we were out of the trees, blinking in the sun.

Over a dozen wigwams filled the clearing in front of

us. There was a fireplace in the middle with a shelter over it, where women sat in the shade. Small children were running about; their shrill cries sounded just like the children playing about the green in Mungrisdale; I suppose that children sound the same the world over.

Loic took me to meet the chief, who sat on a log outside his wigwam among a group of men. No one seemed to have any work to do, but admittedly the afternoon was very hot. Loic took a twist of tobacco from his pocket and gave it to the chief, who produced a long pipe. He took his time filling it and lighting it, and after he'd smoked for a while, he passed the pipe back to Loic, who smoked a little, and passed it on to me. I'd learned in Mesquacosy's wigwam at Yonge Street how to breathe the acrid tobacco smoke into my mouth, and expel it a moment or two later as if I'd inhaled, and by the time the sun touched the tips of the trees to the west of us, I had ample cause to be thankful for my skill. Each time it came round, I passed the pipe on as soon as I decently could. I couldn't follow the talk, but I was content to be where I was, watching the men's faces, and the children's play, and the women going to and fro. I realised at one point that Stéphan was telling a story, with graphic descriptions that involved a pantomime of gestures and several different voices. I said softly to Loic, 'Is he telling what's happened on Mackinac?'

'You learn Ojibwa fast, m'sieu! Certainly he is. He is not the first to come, of course, but all points of view are different, and this is what makes a story interesting, is it not?'

Stéphan's recital sparked off an animated discussion. The elderly chief remained impassive, but I noticed how he observed each man closely while he spoke, and I had the impression that he missed nothing. Sometimes when

I glanced at him I found his black eyes resting on me. But if our eyes met he always looked away.[2]

When we reached the shore again little waves were lapping on the sand. Mackinac was fast disappearing into a dark blue haze. 'You will stay the night with us, m'sieu?'

'Ay.' Alan had left me without a word often enough. Now it was my turn. 'Loic!'

'M'sieu?'

'My name is Mark. I belong to a Society where we accept no outward rank or title. We've a long journey before us. Will thee call me by my name?'

'*Oui*, Mark, I will do that.' A moment later he said, 'I have another name too, from my mother's people. It is E-ntaa-jiimid. They named me this because I paddle a canoe very well. It is easier for you to say "Loic", I think. But now I have told you, at least.'

After supper I stood outside the Kerners cabin, letting my eyes adjust to the night. The stars blazed above my head. A soft breeze soughed in the pine trees, and I could hear the waves breaking, always in the same place on that tideless shore. Once I could see clearly enough I walked over to the top of the dunes and lay on my back. The Milky Way was a clear broad road across the arch of heaven. I picked out each constellation, and thought of how those same stars shone down on Highside in Mungrisdale. I could smell resin; the air was still as warm as an English noon. There was a small rustling in the juniper. I got up quickly.

Someone gave a small scream. '*Awenen yaawid aw?*'

---

[2] I gained the impression, then and later, that it's not the Indian custom to hold one another's gaze. At first I thought them indirect in their dealings because of this. But when I got home again, I found the straight gaze of Friends quite intractable, and it was hard to meet their eyes, whereas it had never been hard before.

'It's Mark. Waase'aaban?'

'Oh!'

I could just see a small dark shape, moving away. I spoke before I thought. 'Don't go! *Reviens!*'

The dark shape hovered.

This time I had time to think, and yet ignored it. 'Stay and talk to me a little. *Reste et parle un peu.*'

'*Nin bwanawi! Je ne peux pas!*'

'*Je t'en prie.*'

She hesitated, then sat down more than an arm's length away. I said nothing, but I was filled with an inexplicable glee that I could barely keep hid. I hugged it to myself. If there were aught watching over me just then that cried out 'danger' I heeded it not.[3] I had asked Waase'aaban to talk to me, but for a while neither of us spoke. When we did, it was perforce in French. When that failed us, she found words in her tongue, and I in mine, to supplement, and somehow we found ways of understanding one another. When I think of our talk now, I don't remember it being in a foreign language; I write, therefore, in English, as memory dictates, for all that this must be a trick of the mind.

Presently I asked her if she'd always lived on Bois Blanc.

'No. We always came in spring, for the maple sugar. My mother is from this village here, but my father is from Pawating – this you call Sainte Marie du Sault, only on the south side of the river. My father knew my mother many years ago, because he came every year to this island you call Bois Blanc for the maple syrup harvest. In summer

---

[3] And indeed I think there was nothing; the Lord God who takes heed of the smallest matter among the least of his children cares not for the perils of the world, or the divisions that men have made among themselves. He gave us the instincts that we have; in his eyes we are all neighbours, I believe, and made to love one another accordingly.

we usually live in my father's village at Pawating. The fishing is very good there. My family also sell dried fish to the North West Company factory. At Pawating there are many people.'

'Thee was born there?'

'No, I was born in the fall, when we had gone to our hunting ground. That is where I received my name, from the time when I was born.'

'Why, what does it mean?'

'Waase'aaban? It means – *Waase'aaban* – it is the first light of the day before the sun rises. It is like saying "light all around".'

'I like that. Where is thy hunting ground?'

'It is near the north shore of Lake Michigan. There is a lake there, with a big spring. Here we spend the winter. Two years ago Pakané married Loic and she has stayed here ever since. Now my brother is also married. I don't care for his wife, so last year I decide to come to live with Pakané. Now I have been here one year.'

'And thee'll go on living here with Loic and thy sister?'

'I don't know. After the maple season it's quiet. I don't mind. Perhaps next year I'll go to Pawating. Who knows?'

She asked me about my own home and family. It was difficult to describe so that she could imagine it. Even as I spoke I could see what kind of pictures must be forming in her mind, which were not the truth, but I knew no way of bringing her closer to it.

I hadn't realised that Waase'aaban had met Rachel until she said, 'I knew your sister. She was good. I hope that Nanubushu will send you good dreams so you can find her.'

I asked her to explain what she meant.

'You have not heard of Nanubushu? Truly, you have

not? That is very strange. It is hard also for me to tell you. It is the wrong language, and also the wrong time of year. But I try: Nanubushu is a very powerful Manitou. He was born of an Ojibwa woman and Epingishmook, "of the West". Nanubushu's mother died, and his grandmother took him and taught him everything. The time came for Nanubushu to make his – what do you say – he must go alone and look for his – like a dream, you understand – his dream – and he went west to the land of the Great Mountains. There – I do not tell all this part – he made peace with his father. It is Nanubushu who went through the world and greeted all beings that were made and told each one their name, and so they came to be. But it happened that Nanubushu lost one of his family, one that he loved very much, and so he wandered through the world, always searching. He asked each of the animals and they helped him. And Nanubushu wandered until he came to where the Great Bear was. An evil Manitou was in that place, and said to the Great Bear, "Go and – I have not the word – go and . . . and . . . – like this"' – Waase'aaban's thin hands curled into claws, and she mimed the cruel blows of the Great Bear. 'And the bear did. He came up out of the water and did this thing. But Nanubushu is a very powerful Manitou. As the Great Bear came to kill him he . . . he . . . he changed himself, and the Great Bear said, "How can Nanubushu become like this?" And so Nanubushu went on his way.'

'And did he find the one he sought?' I asked her.

Waase'aaban hesitated. 'The story is too long, I think. If you come in winter you will hear it. But what I am telling you is, Nanubushu is the most powerful one, he created the world and he speaks to all the animals in the world. This is why when we greet one another – or any creature – we say *Boozhoo*, which is part of his name, for he was the first to greet each one, in the beginning of the world. He is Nanubushu, and always he is seeking. And for your sister – I think he is the one who will help you.' There was a pause. 'Do you understand my story? It is a true story, you understand?'

'Ay.' I lied, for I had not understood her in the least.

There was a fire in my head, blazing as brightly as the stars above us. It consumed every rational thought in my brain like so much tinder. Perhaps this is what drunkenness is like, before the flame burns out and it becomes merely sordid. I know not. What I do know is that I took her hand and drew her to me, and she didn't pull away. And that was not all that I did before we parted.

CHAPTER 17

I CAME BACK TO BROILS ENOUGH TO MAKE ME WANT
to turn tail straight back to Bois Blanc. The moment I
walked into McGulpin's house Anne dropped her spoon,
and embraced me tearfully, clutching both my arms with
floury fingers. 'Ah, m'sieu, m'sieu! *Ah mon Dieu! On veut
vous voir immédiatement au fort! Tout le monde vous a cherché!
J'ai dit au lieutenant que vous éttiez allé à Bois Blanc avec
Stéphan, et maintenant tout est devenu encore pire! Que dieu
vous aide, m'sieu!!*'

'Quietly, friend, quietly! It's all right. Here I am. Now
please, *parlez-moi lentement! Répétez, s'il vous plaît!*'

Gradually it came out. I was wanted at the fort because
everyone on the island had been brought in to swear an
oath of allegiance to the British crown. Nearly all the
islanders had done this, but while the oath was being
administered, someone had mentioned me to Captain
Roberts, and told him I'd hired Stéphan to take me across
to Bois Blanc. I'd been expected back the same evening,
and hadn't been seen since. Suspicion was founded upon
the fact that I was a Quaker, and that had led the invading
army to assume that I must be an American – nay, not only
an American, but a subversive one at that.

I calmed Anne as best I could. '*Je resolverai l'affaire*

maintenant, tout de suite! Je vais au fort. Don't worry! I've done nothing wrong – *pas de crime – je suis un sujet du roi d'Angleterre.* We have habeas corpus. *Je vais.*'

She wasn't convinced, but I had no time to waste. For the first time I climbed the ramp up the cliff face to the fort of Mackinac, and reached a guardroom at the gate in the wall.

'Friend, my name is Mark Greenhow. I'm told Charles Roberts wishes to see me at once.'

'*Captain* Roberts to you' – but they jumped up, and called to a sentry within the gates. I was escorted at once into the fort by two soldiers who walked one step behind me, as if I were their prisoner, which was, as I remarked to them civilly, not at all the case.

I was not taken to the commander, but into a long low building. There was a wooden wall inside, and a dark passage beyond. It seemed not like a commander's quarters at all, but I had no chance to argue before I was seized by the arms from behind and thrust into complete darkness. A stout wooden door was slammed behind me, and I heard the bolts shot home.

There was no point in protesting, or banging against the door. Silence would be the better part. I guess it disconcerted them; presently I heard the footsteps go away and the outside door slam shut. After that there was no light at all. I spent a considerable time feeling my way over my new surroundings. I was in a little cell, barely six feet by four, with solid wooden walls and door. The floor was hard-packed earth. I sat down, and took stock of my situation.

My ancestor and namesake was one of the first Friends (he was first convinced, they say, when George Fox came to Mungrisdale in 1653). This Mark Greenhow lay seven years in Carlisle jail, and was never a hale man again, but he was a valiant witness for the Truth through all his sufferings. The Light Within burned ever, though he saw not the light of day in all that time. During the hours I spent locked in my cell on Fort Mackinac I dwelt much upon his example. I thought about all the past Friends who suffered for their witness. I thought about the Meeting at Mosedale, and how I was a member thereof, and how if they knew my present plight they would hold me in that Light which no earthly power can douse.

From that I fell to thinking of my own shortcomings, and indeed there was a grievous weight upon my conscience. Stéphan and I had left Bois Blanc in thick fog. As soon as we'd paddled away from the beach the enchantment of the island had slipped away from me, and in the cold morning I slowly came to view what I had done.

It had come out at some point in our talk that it was Pakané's seventeenth summer. (Loic had been married two years, I knew.) Waase'aaban was her younger sister. I found myself calculating numbers in my head, while a cold sweat soaked my back under my shirt, for all that I was paddling hard. Her seventeenth summer . . . in which case Pakané was sixteen years old. Waase'aaban could not be more than fifteen, and suppose a child was normally nursed for a year (I was assuming that humans are like cows in this respect), then it was unlikely that Waase'aaban would have been conceived before Pakané was a year old. (Alan had told me that Indian families do not breed as profligately as the British poor.) Which would make Waase'aaban fourteen years old. That would figure – she was as slight and light-footed as a child: for all that she had the body of a woman, it must needs be a very young one. I felt a chill emptiness in the pit of my stomach. I thought of the young maids in our Monthly Meeting; at fourteen they were children. I would sooner have cut off my right hand than touch any one of them, I thought, and rightly so.

And yet I could not recollect those nights on the shore of Bois Blanc without a pang of delight, even circumstanced as I now was. But as I caught myself going over past pleasure in my mind, I would again be plunged into despair for the evil I had done. 'Twas the culmination of a desire that had engaged my imagination for – what? – twelve years and more. I'd accepted long ago there was naught I could do to banish lascivious thoughts: if I refused to acknowledge them when waking, they would haunt me the more assiduously in my dreams, and that no man can prevent. I was always convinced that I would marry. Moreover, I couldn't deny that for years past I'd never attended another Meeting, nor visited among Friends, without hoping to find the maid I dreamed of. In my imagination she was lovely, intelligent, virtuous, and at the same most eager to be bedded – in the married state, of course. I can't in truth say that I never looked at a woman who wasn't a Member of our Religious Society, nor that I'd never dreamed of one, sleeping or waking. There'd been more than a touch of wistfulness, too, in that: obviously in my rational moments I could never admit to such imaginings. There's many a pretty girl in Cumberland, but not for such as me.

It is better to marry than to burn; ay, but find me a wife before thee castigates me for being true to my own nature. The Lord God created us, man and woman created he them, in such a manner that a man has no choice but to burn. As I sat in my prison cell, I could not rail against the Lord God, who had created me in his own image, and who was in my present strait my sole defender, but I was never a great apostle of Paul of Tarsus, and if he'd turned up in my cell (in which he would have felt quite at home, I supposed) I'd have been sorely tempted to give him a piece of my mind. But what I couldn't get over, and returned to again and again, was how easily the sin was done. I had thought it such a great matter – the deed itself had seemed separated from all things possible by so great a chasm – and yet, when it came to it, it was the easiest and most natural thing in the world. After her first hesitations, Waase'aaban had been as eager as I was. The impossible thing, I realised now, would have been to have stopped myself. To my utmost shame I had not even tried.

Now, in the darkness of the prison house, I had ample opportunity to repent me. But the terrible thing was I could not. There remained an unholy joy in my heart which I could not quench. *There be three things which are too wonderful for me: yea four, which I know: the way of an eagle in the air, the way of a serpent upon a rock, the way of a ship in the midst of the sea, and the way of a man with a maid.* Three nights I had stayed on Bois Blanc, and in the last two I had acquired memories enough of earthly bliss to last a lifetime – for surely they are with me yet – and without doubt an inward joy enough to take my mind from my present captivity – because in my optimistic moments I doubted not that when Alan came to hear of my plight he would have the decency to come and make them release me.

But no one came, and once again I was plunged into an internal gloom that matched my outward state. I tried to pray, and could not. I began thinking about my father, and what he would say in such a pass as this, and that led me to recall certain passages from Fox's *Journal* and from the Bible that offer comfort to those in adversity. And so I bethought me of Joseph's brothers, lying in prison in far-off Egypt, whence they had only come in order to save their own families from starvation, and how Joseph addressed them, saying, *send one of you, and let him fetch your brother, and ye shall be kept in prison, that your words may be proved, whether there be any truth in you, or else by the life of Pharaoh surely ye are spies.* Thus it was that when the soldiers came again at last, I was prepared for them, and said immediately, 'Friends, I ask thee one thing, which is to fetch my brother Alan Mackenzie, and have him speak to your commander.'

They gave me no answer, but marched me outside. I was very thirsty by this time, and I'd like to have relieved myself, but I had no chance to ask. The sun blinded me, but at least it told me the time. It had been early morning when I came in; now the afternoon was drawing late. I was taken across a wide trampled space into another log building. This one had big windows and open doors. I was marched into a room where a sallow, elderly man in uniform sat at a desk filled with papers, a lieutenant at his side. Another military man was engaged in writing at a desk in the corner. There were two sentries. The only man in civilian clothes stood before the desk with his back to me. My guards shoved me into a corner to wait. I leaned against the wall, for I felt an unaccustomed faintness, and watched the scene unfolding before me.

'Ambrose Davenport, do you still refuse to sign this oath?' Captain Roberts' voice startled me. There was no power or triumph in it. The man sounded utterly exhausted. In contrast, the civilian's voice rang out clear and true: 'No, sir, I will not sign. I was born in America, and am determined, at all hazards, to live and die an American citizen. I will not sign.'

'In that case, Mr Davenport, I have no alternative but to arrest you as a danger to the public peace. You'll leave the island with the United States army, to be returned to American territory at Fort Detroit.'

Alan told me later that Davenport left a farm, a wife and six children, but nothing of that was mentioned now. He was marched away under guard, and I was led to stand before Charles Roberts. Close to, he looked deathly ill, a sickly yellow in colour, and gaunt about the eyes. The lieutenant spoke to him in a subdued mutter.

'Oh, yes. Your name, sir?'

'Mark Greenhow.'

'Citizenship?'

'British.'

'British, eh?' He looked at his lieutenant. 'I understood this fellow was an American?'

More muttering. I waited.

'Then what did we detain him for? ... Bois Blanc ... What of it? ... He came back of his own free will, then? ... Mr Greenhow, how long have you lived at Mackinac?'

'I don't live at Mackinac. I came here from Sainte Marie du Sault less than three weeks ago.'

'You were on Bois Blanc?'

'Yes, I went to see someone about hiring a canoe.'

'Oh, for God's sake!' The man's face was drawn with pain. 'What kind of storm in a teacup is this? Very well, Mr Greenhow, we can end this most quickly if I administer the oath now, and leave you free to go your way.'

'I cannot swear.'

'What?'

'I cannot swear. Our Lord Jesus Christ gave us the commandment "*swear not at all. but let your communication be, Yea, yea; Nay, nay: for whatsoever is more than these cometh of evil*". Therefore I cannot swear.'

'And if I command you to testify to your allegiance to His Britannic Majesty King George?'

'If that is what thee asks, I can tell thee I'm the king's loyal subject.' I was moved to add, 'It's been said to the king himself – not this king, I grant thee – that "*we by those that have tried us are found to be truer in our promises than others by their oaths. That which we speak in the truth of our hearts is more than what they swear.*"'

'That may be so. But what if, as the chief officer of this territory in war-time, I command you now to swear?'

'I cannot swear. And if this territory is now Upper

Canada, I know it to be a law agreed by John Graves Simcoe when he was governor, that members of my Religious Society need not swear the oath of allegiance. And that is the law in England too.'

'So what if I ship you off to Detroit with the other three civilians who won't take the oath?' The man looked like to faint, he seemed so ill.

'Then I will be in God's hand. But as a subject of the king, I would as lief not be forced into a hostile country.' I remembered my contemplations in the prison. 'If thee wishes any man to vouch for me, thee could ask my brother-in-law, Alan Mackenzie.'

'Oh, for God's sake take him away! That accent isn't put on; can't you tell? Why didn't you say who you were at once, Mr Greenhow? I know all about you. Mackenzie was here two days ago. I should have guessed . . . No, no, for God's sake, take him away. And leave him alone, d'you hear? Mr Greenhow, you've no time to waste. Mackenzie's been waiting for you this two days or more. I don't know why you've kept him waiting. Goodbye, sir! For pity's sake, take him away.'

I wasn't sorry to leave the fort. I never entered it again, I'm glad to say. I fairly ran down the ramp and back to McGulpin's house, where to my astonishment I found Alan sitting at the table writing. He was no less surprised to see me than I to see him. It turned out he'd been looking for me everywhere, until it finally occurred to him to ask Anne, who told him I'd gone off with Stéphan. 'You might have told me. I thought you wanted to leave immediately?'

'I'd given up on "immediately", friend. Anyway, here I am. Am I to understand thee's ready to leave?'

'I've been ready for the last two days! Tomorrow, then, brother Mark? Good. D'you want to put the kettle back? I haven't dined yet – Anne broiled a fowl for us, in case you were back. Just let me finish this.'

I put the pot back over the fire and set the pewter dishes on the table. There was white bread in the crock and fresh butter left to cool in a pannikin of water.

'*En roulant ma boule roulant. En roulant ma boule,*' sang Alan, as he sealed his letter, and I realised he was chiming in with my humming. I must learn not to do that before I go home, I thought, and instantly the memory of my greater sin hit me like a kick in the stomach. I felt like one of those days in the hills when one gets all weathers from sleet to heatwave in the space of an afternoon, only this was in my heart, which was infinitely more uncomfortable. One moment I was filled with unaccountable joy, and the next with an awful consciousness of my transgression. Also, I was ravenous.

Alan and I reduced the fowl to a pile of bones, and by the time I'd wiped my plate with the last of the bread, I felt better. In fact the two of us enjoyed the most congenial evening we'd spent together yet. Alan diverted my mind by telling me all the news – I would hardly have recognised him for my elusive and taciturn companion of pre-battle days. Luckily he asked me no questions about my own doings, for I was in no fit state to answer them.

Mackinac was still seething with Indian warriors, Alan said, who'd encamped all round the village and were clearly determined not to shift until adequate gifts had been distributed to them all. Apparently Captain Roberts owed it to John Askin that not a drop of blood, human or animal, had been wantonly spilt. This was unheard of in the aftermath of an Indian battle. Askin had bought a small herd of stirks from the islanders to supply the Indian warriors for the time being. Naturally the islanders were anxious; I remarked that I'd have been worried myself, to find such an army – or any army at all, come to that – bivouacked on the Highside fells. Meanwhile there was another row going on because Captain Roberts had detained some of the American soldiers, who'd been identified either as British citizens or deserters from the British army – I'm not sure which – and was even now impressing them in his all too scanty troops. Roberts wasn't going to have an easy task, ahead of him, said Alan, and he, Alan, was thankful not to stand in his shoes.

That brought us to our own plans. Alan was amused I'd stolen a march on him, and seen Loic. 'So do you want to go over with Stéphan and me tomorrow then, or shall I go and tell Loic, and we'll pick you up here?'

This cast me into such an agony of indecision I nearly gave myself away. Desire conquered reason, after the briefest of struggles. 'I'll come with thee.'

'Good. We can take everything over, in that case. We don't need to come back here.'

Next morning Alan asked me to take his letters to the South West Company Office, while he went to tell Stéphan we were ready to go. Just before we parted, a British infantryman came up and asked if we knew the way to Dr Day's house. 'Indeed yes,' said Alan. 'I hope you're not sick!' He took the young fellow by the arm and pointed. 'Up that way.'

When he turned round I was staring at him with my mouth open. 'Mark? Is anything amiss?'

'I *had* seen thee before!'

'What?'

'Alan, was thee in York last year? Early in Ninth Month?'

'In what?'

'In . . . September. Thee was in York in September, wasn't thee?'

'What makes you think that?' asked Alan cautiously.

'Because I met thee! Outside the hotel! Thee directed me to the Toronto Coffee House!' I took him by the lapels of his coat and fairly shook him. 'None of thy tricks, Alan. Thee can't deny it. I *know*!'

It was his turn to stare at me. 'I don't remember . . . No, no, I'm not denying it! I'm just saying I don't remember *thee* – I mean you.' He laid his hand on my arm. 'It's true, Mark. I was there. I'm sorry. I didn't know you.'

'Nor did I know thee.' I could barely take in the enormity of it . . . nearly a whole year . . . and such a journey . . . and all the time . . . I shook my head. It was neither his fault nor mine; there was nothing to say, in fact.

'Later, I'll tell you about it. I promise.' Alan grinned. 'We're not going to be short of time together, anyway.' He gripped my hand suddenly. 'It's a strange world, brother. I'll see you on the shore.'

I walked slowly on, carrying his letters, feeling all amazed. Many Friends believe that the Lord has his own purpose in everything that befalls us. I'm not so sure; if we have free will, then we bring about our own consequences. Hence the evils of this world, in fact . . . Only in this case I had not chosen anything, being simply ignorant. If I'd met Alan in York last September, and known him then . . . I could not think about it clearly . . . I glanced at the two letters in my hand. Perhaps I should not have read the directions, but I have no doubt the Lord – and Alan too – will forgive me for it. One letter was inscribed to Simon MacKenzie, Agent, Fort William, Indian Territory. The other was to Mrs James Mackenzie, Ardelve, Ross-shire, Scotland, North Britain. That would cost the recipient a pretty penny, I made no doubt. It set me wondering even more about Alan, at all events, and realising how very little I knew of his history.

As we paddled over to Bois Blanc, I began thinking about Waase'aaban. I was very feart, and wished I had not come. When we beached, I felt a fluttering inside that would not be quenched. As we approached the house, I wanted to hurry forward, and yet at the same moment I longed to turn and flee. Stéphan may have had some idea of all this. I am very sure Alan had none. Then Loic was at the top of the beach calling to us, *Boozhoo! Biindigen!* Is it today, then?'

He showed us the canoe, with its new birchbark and strong seams. It was an Indian canoe, bigger than Stéphan's, about sixteen feet, I judged. We took four paddles. The stores were piled ready under a birchbark shelter next to the woodpile. There were two muskets, along with a small keg of powder, a horn of priming powder, and bags of lead and shot. We took three trade blankets, a big square of canvas – no tent, we were to sleep under the canoe – sacks of flour and pease wrapped in oiled canvas to keep them dry, an iron kettle, a small axe, and sundry tools and other items in birchbark containers. As well as his own tools, Loic took rolls of birchbark and spare rawhide for canoe repairs. There was also a bale with tobacco and a bale of beads, traps, axe heads and other trade goods; Alan said we'd surely need presents. Alan didn't take his precious map – he said he knew it by heart, but he had a compass and pocket sundial together in a little wooden box.[1] We laid everything out on the baked earth outside the house, and checked through it. It seemed a great deal to fit into one canoe, with three men as well, but I knew enough about voyageurs by now, and was not surprised when presently the canoe was floating offshore, not too low in the water,

[1] I was much taken with this device, which I often had the use of during our journeying. I bought myself a similar one in Montreal on my way home, and I still take it with me when I walk on the high fells. I find it difficult now to imagine how I ever managed without it. However I think the possession of a mechanical device too often allows a man's innate faculties to fall into disuse. I never dreamed of having either timepiece or compass when I was a lad, and I was never lost or benighted in the hills. Loic, too, had no difficulty with time or direction, and he scorned to use the compass, pleading always that he could not read. I knew that was merely an excuse. I understood his antipathy, but my case was different, for I was in a country where very many of the natural signs were strange to me. Besides, I have a liking for ingenious devices, and so I succumbed to this one. It was a good guinea's worth, and has served me well.

with everything stowed and balanced. We lifted the bow up on to the beach and went ashore again.

In all this time there'd been no sign of Waase'aaban or Pakané. Loic said they'd gone berry picking; it was the blueberry season. He knew where they were, and said he must say goodbye to his wife before he left. 'I'll not be gone above an hour.' He turned to me. 'You come, Mark?'

'Ay.'

I followed him without another word, leaving Alan and Stéphan to speculate as they would.

Loic led me by little paths across the marshes, deep into the heart of the island. We passed brown ponds thick with rushes, surrounded by open clearings full of dead grey stumps. I had crossed the portages of La Vase, so I knew old beaver lakes when I saw them; the water meadows were slowly turning back to forest. A white heron rose into the air each time we came close, only to land further on and be disturbed again. Presently the soil grew sandier and drier. We pushed through bog myrtle and blueberry. And there was Pakané sitting on a bank among the berries, suckling Biinooji. My heart lurched when I saw them; a question entered my mind which I should have asked myself long before. But then I saw Waase'aaban just a few yards away, with berry-stained mouth and hands, filling a birchbark container with blueberries. She jumped up when she saw us, and smiled at me. It was a smile of such innocent delight, just because I had come, that my heart soared. I forgot my sudden fear; I forgot the agonies of guilt and repentance; I forgot that outwardly she was as unlike a Member of the Religious Society of Friends as any girl could well be; I forgot that she was only fourteen and I was twenty-four. I remembered only the two starry nights when we had lain in the dunes, as if we were the only man and woman in the world.

Loic was talking to Pakané, and though I couldn't

understand the words, the effect on Waase'aaban was immediate. 'You go now, Mark?'

'Yes, but I will come back.'

'Before winter?'

'I hope before winter.'

'*Gaa ngoji gdaa-baa-izhaasii*,'[2] she said, very low.

I bent my head to hear her. '*Gaa ngoji gdaa-baa-izhaasii*,' she repeated.

'Please, in French?'

She wouldn't translate, but stood before me, looking at the ground, clasping her hands together.

I clasped my hands over her hands. 'I will come back.'

'*Gaa ngoji gdaa-baa-izhaasii*.'

I gave up trying to speak, but held her hands in mine a moment, then pressed them, and let go.

Loic bent over his son in his cradleboard and kissed him. '*Ka-waabimin nwiidigemaagen, ngwiss!*' He stood up. 'Mark, it is time to go. *Ka-waabimin nwiidigemaagen, Pakané.*'

An hour later we waded into the bay with our loaded canoe. Alan was our bowsman, and I climbed in amidships after him. Loic pushed us out a little further, and swung himself into the stern. '*Allez-y, les gars!*'

'*Allez-y.*'

---

[2] I learned much later this means, 'Thee shouldn't go anywhere.'

CHAPTER 18

THIS WAS WHERE RACHEL WAS LAST SEEN. I STOOD ON the beach at South Manitou in the dawn light, and looked about me. The bay was just as Alan had described it: a mile-long half moon of white sand. The lake was pearl-white, very still. A couple of mallards were swimming parallel to the beach, sending out long dark ripples which spread to the shore, licking my feet with miniature waves. I went on walking slowly, paddling barefoot in inch-deep water where the sand was firmer. The beach shelved gradually, so the water here stayed warm, even though the sun was still lost in a far-off haze. I couldn't see how anyone could walk into the lake and drown: not here. She'd have had to get way from the beach to do that, on to the exposed shore beyond.

It was a good place to walk. I could think at the same time, with nothing to distract my mind but smooth sand and water. The first thing was to visit the Indian village. We'd arrived after dusk the previous evening, but I could see now that Alan was right about the forest. The trees crowded close to the shore. There was a shady clearing at the top of the beach on the north side, made by passing voyageurs, where a small brigade could shelter out a storm behind the birch trees that lined the shore. At this time of year the clearing was a veritable hayfield. The grass was studded with harebells and some bright yellow flowers I didn't know, and orange and black butterflies danced over all. There were clouds of mosquitoes too; in this still weather we'd done much better to camp on the open shore. I'd gone up to the clearing, though, as soon as it got light, and walked slowly round it. From its edges I peered into the forest. At the edges, where it was light, there were huge clumps of poison ivy. In the dim interior great grey beech trunks rose to a canopy so high above my head I felt like one of the crawling insects of the forest floor when I looked up. A huge tree had fallen, letting in a light that turned the leaves above to a shower of green and gold. Below, saplings sprouted from the decaying trunk. From the depths of the wood I could hear the loud knocking of a woodpecker. Yes, Alan was right. She could never have wandered into the trackless forest. She would have had to find a path. The only paths, Alan said, went from the Indian village, where we would go today.

I wandered on, my feet splashing in the shallow water. I asked myself what I'd expected to find. I was born to a country that's bare and open: wild certainly, but if thee can climb, and face the weather, thee can go where thee likes and see where thee's going, on a good day. This flat, sandy country was impenetrable. And yet God created all this, just as he created the hills of Lakeland, on the third day, and he found it good. I said the verse over to myself, but instead of bringing this alien world nearer to my heart, it made the God whom I'd worshipped all my life seem suddenly remote. The ways of God are not comprehensible to us, I knew that well, but it was on the beach at South Manitou that I fully understood that there is infinitely more in the mind of God than I could even begin to conceive. Once, at Mosedale, Joseph Priestman ministered to the effect that we needed to remember that it was God who made man in his own image, and not the other way round. Man, said Joseph, is inclined to the sin of Pride, and what greater Pride could there be than to create a little god in our little image, and to think of the Almighty God, our Creator, who made the heavens and the earth and all that therein is, as someone like ourselves that we could begin to understand?

Certainly when I thought about the interior of South Manitou – and the very heart of the island lay only half a mile to the west of where I stood – I realised that distance is not the only thing that divides us from knowledge. One heart may lie so close against another that they seem to beat as one, and yet the thoughts of that other heart are still alien as the stars. A sudden thought came to me, of that other beach on Bois Blanc, and I felt the tears prickle against my eyes, but I shed them not. I had no answer to the questions in my own heart, and so for the time being I let them lie.

Alan once said to me, had I any idea how large this land was? I thought I had, for did I not cross half a continent to reach this place? The last two weeks, however, had taught me he was right. As the crow – or the gull, rather – might fly, my memory of Alan's map told me we were barely a hundred miles from Mackinac. In the *canot du maître* we'd flown seventy miles down the French River in a day. But then we had a swift current to take us, and the strength of fourteen men. In Loic's Indian canoe, on the open lake, with only three paddlers, the whole world was magnified immeasurably. Loic was our *gouvernail*, and, though I'd never steered a canoe in my life, I was aware of his skill. Often I was very feart; I think he took risks, but if they'd not been justifiable I wouldn't be writing this at my desk in the window at Highside this day.

The first night we had camped at the north point of the peninsula which is the Michigan Territory, close to the burnt out ruins of a substantial fortress, which Loic said was Michilimackinac. That evening Alan regaled me with tales of French wars and Indian massacres at that spot, which kept me from my sleep an hour or more. To be honest, I never slept sound all the time we were in the Michigan Territory, but grew used to sleeping with my ears open, like a dog, for I could never lose the sense of the hostile wilderness at my back, and foes within, four-legged and two-legged, that I knew not, nor wished to know.

We left that dismal ruin before dawn, but that afternoon we camped early, and stayed ashore three full days. I found that ill to bear, for so much time was already wasted, but Loic was adamant, and when we set to again I understood why. We had to paddle several miles due west into open water to get past a long headland with rocky shoals all round it. Even in fair weather it was a desolate, frightening place, for there was no mercy to be had from lake or land, if so be we'd needed it. It was a relief to reach the shelter of a large Ottawa village built on a high bluff further along the coast, marked from the lake by an enormous bent pine tree at the very top of the bluff. The village lay in what looked to be natural meadowland dotted with copses of wild cherry trees, brambles and raspberries. There were gardens of corn, beans and squash, and, just as on Mackinac, long racks of whitefish spread to dry. I said to Loic that the lot of these people had fallen in a fair ground, but he said that was not true, and that the meadowlands were not natural, but had once been settled villages for about fifteen miles along the coast. The French had moved their Jesuit mission here, long before the British came. The British were ill to deal with, and so the Ottawa, who supported the French, had attacked Fort Michilimackinac. A while later a British trader sold a tin box to the Ottawa in exchange for furs. He said the box contained something that would do them great good, but they must not open it until they got home. This they did, and inside the first box they found another box, and within that yet another. They came to the smallest box of all, which was barely an inch long, and opened it. There was naught inside except a little mould. This they passed around, wondering what it could be. Very soon the smallpox broke out among them, and within a few weeks almost all the people had died of it. 'That is why you see the land so empty,' Loic said. 'Forty years ago you would have found naught but the dead unburied, the gardens laid waste, and the rest of the people fled away.'

I hung back. 'Will they wish to see British travellers now, if all this was done to them?'

Loic shrugged. 'The same was done to my people, and here I am. The world – and trade – goes on.'

I could not, however, feel comfortable while we stayed near the village, which Loic said was called in French, *l'Arbre Croche*, the crooked tree. We were accepted with indifference – the village lives by trading with those who pass through the Mackinac Straits – but I was glad to move away. For the first time in my life it seemed less than ideal to have been born an Englishman, and I knew not what to make of that.

After we left the village we ran into bad weather. The lake grew choppy and the mist came down. The view would have been no great loss, for a more wickedly exposed coast I never hope to see. Once the high bluff of l'Arbre Croche disappeared from sight, Loic had naught to steer by but the waves, and the feel of the wind on his cheek. Within minutes the world had closed down to the six-yard radius around us; all I was concerned about was the wave I was on and the one that was coming. It was evening before the mist melted, and we found ourselves about a mile offshore. The land was broken and hilly, the shore still steeply sloping. The water was growing calmer, however, and no harm done.

Alan's map had given me no notion of the roughness of the journey. We reached a break in the coast at last, and came ashore in a natural harbour protected by a thin peninsula, where spring water bubbled up through the soft sands of a little bay. But this was not the unmeasured wilderness I'd been led to expect. There were fishermen mending their nets, just as they do on Solway shore, and children playing in the little waves that broke upon the sand. The smallest ones had smooth brown bodies with round bellies: no sign of hunger or ill-health here, for all I'd heard of failed crops and hungry winters. The bigger boys wore breechcloths, and the girls short dresses of soft deerskin or trade cloth. I never saw so many racks of drying fish as on that beach, so industriously turned and tended by sundry folk, both young and old. We brought our canoe ashore alongside at least a dozen others, and Loic spoke to a couple of fellows who were replacing the birchbark on a big canoe. They sent us into the village, where well-trodden paths criss-crossed between the wigwams, which were grouped around the cooking fires. Behind the wigwams lay well-tilled gardens that any English husbandman would be proud of. The people watched us as we passed. I followed Alan and Loic to a wigwam set a little apart from the others. When I saw it I hung back, for before it someone had planted a carved crucifix in the earth, after the manner of the Papist idolators.

'What is this place?'

'It is for guests,' said Loic, 'Which is you and me, and Alan.'

'Why is there a cross?'

'Because when the priest comes, this is his house.'

I consented to be led within, and to my relief the inside was wholly Ottawa, with skins spread over pine branches for our beds, and an empty birchbark water container at the door. So began a familiar pattern. At each village around the bay – which was fully fifteen miles long – we were treated with incurious courtesy. We gave gifts of tobacco, trade cloth and metal goods, and in return we were well fed on fish and corn, and very often given a place to sleep as well. The elders talked to us in French, although both Alan and Loic could also converse in the Ottawa tongue. I was never sure how much the Indians used French out of politeness to me, or whether the white man's language came naturally to their lips when speaking with strangers. As far as I could understand it, these people were used to trade fish and other natural commodities as far as Mackinac, which they spoke of in much the same terms as we in Mungrisdale speak of Penrith or Carlisle. I got no news of Rachel, but I had plenty to think about, for all my preconceptions were being turned end over end, and I knew not how I should proceed. I had thought of the land beyond the frontier as the map showed it: that is to say, as empty wilderness. I'd expected to find uncut forests tenanted by wild beasts and naked savages. Instead I found neat villages surrounded by gardens, filled with healthy children, and a people wholly preoccupied, or so it seemed to me, with the summer's fishing, and tending their crops of beans, corn and squash. Certainly I heard talk of war – but so I do in England – and very often we heard distant drums in the evening. Sometimes there was more of the savage dancing, and twice we encountered bands of young men painted and armed for war – which is not true of England, or perhaps merely our own manifestations of war and conflict seem less alarming because they are familiar.

We paddled the length of the bay, stopping at several villages, then headed south again. We passed many rivers; later we would follow these inland, or portage our canoe across a spit into an inland lake, each one larger than Windermere. Everywhere there were summer villages, and where the rivers led away into the forest, we always found men fishing where the waters were dreuvy. No one could travel these waterways unseen or unremarked. On this first journey we kept to the shore of Lake Michigan, until we reached a vast bay divided into two by a long peninsula. Later we explored these shores too; for now we traversed the mouth of the bay, where sometimes the water was so shallow among the shoals we had to walk our boat long distances, even when we were far from the shore.

Still we were in inhabited country. I began to think I had been wholly mistaken about the nature of the Michigan Territory, but when at last we came round the point that sheltered the double bay, I looked into a different country altogether. I saw a great headland to the south of us, and way out on the lake two long low islands. The shoreline was a wilderness of steep dunes and blowing sand. The islands looked very far away. When Loic pointed to the islands and said laconically 'Les îles des Manitou', my heart leapt. The north island looked to be the bigger, but from here both were mere shadows cast in the path of the setting sun. That night we camped in a little bay just south of the point, at the top of a grey shingly beach. I walked back to the point in the evening sun, taking Alan's sundial compass, and took a bearing on South Manitou. I have noted it in my book: the time was half past eight, and the island almost due south-west of where I stood. I shut the compass, and went on staring across the lake until the two thin islands were hidden by the dark.

Thereafter the Manitou islands were always in our sight. We kept them on the beam, as we paddled alongside a rugged coast where sandy cliffs fell to a windswept shore. There were no villages, indeed there was no shelter at all except the dead trunks of trees fallen from above as the sand was washed from under them. I expressed some of my disgruntlement, and Loic was quick to sing the praises of that miserable desert, telling me that above the dreary dunes lay a veritable Paradise, where forests of oak and elm, pine and maple were home to every kind of game, the small lakes teemed with fish, and the people were blessed with every gift that the land could provide. Tossing on the lake beneath the barren dunes, I found it hard to take his word for it. In my mind I conjured up images of my own lakes: the wooded islands and lovely curves of Thirlmere, the view south from Derwentwater into the jaws of Borrowdale, the fierce clean lines of the Helvellyn range as it casts its shadow across Ullswater. For the first time I recognised my own country for the veritable Eden that it is. Never before had I thought of it as small, but now it seemed to me like that Paradise on earth which all men dream of and desire. I'd supposed that Garden to be unattainable in a fallen world, but now I saw with new eyes, and knew that the new Jerusalem was already present – had always been, although I saw it not – in that land where my lot was first cast. A great longing came over me, and stayed with me thereafter, like a voice out of the silence which never ceased to call me. I was still determined to search for Rachel, there was still a great tumult in my heart when I thought of Waase'aaban, I was still ready to give all that I had to the daily journey with Alan and Loic, but I longed above all else to be in my own country at Mungrisdale: to be home.

We passed that dour coast at last, and crossed a bay where we could see smoke from a village. We camped in the next bay, where a great maple grove, sheltered from the west by towering dunes, gave on to a small inland lake. There were many paths about the place, and within the grove we found a long hut clad with birchbark, quite deserted. In spring, Loic said, many people would meet here from their winter hunting grounds to harvest the maple sugar. I stood at the edge of the clearing and peered under the tree canopy, while the squirrels chattered at me and the birds cried their warnings. It was late afternoon, and very warm. Even the mosquitoes seemed half asleep. Never had I seen such trees: the biggest roots were as high as my head. I thought of this great forest stretching unbroken from here to the shores of Huron, and of all the unknown lives of birds and beasts and men that it must shelter. This land will always be hidden, I thought; the good God made it, but what lies within can never be revealed, and that is how it should be, and will be until the end of time.

The thought sobered me, but when I repeated it to Alan, as we sat by our campfire on the beach, he said, 'If only that were true. I expect they used to say that about the Ohio River.'

'The settlers will never come into the Michigan Territory,' said Loic, as he laid another stick on the fire. 'The white men say there is too much swamp here. It is not true, of course, but the white men always build their trading posts in a swamp – they seem to choose where the mosquitoes are on purpose – and then they say how bad the land is. They are wrong, *ça va sans dire*, but that is just as well, perhaps.'

From where we sat I could see South Manitou Island more clearly than ever, across the water, which shone green over the sand at our feet and deep blue in the open water beyond. I could see sand dunes at the south end of the island, and a long low greenness. When I swam in the lake that evening, the water was warm and silky, and the island looked so near I could almost have believed I could swim out to it. I woke at dawn to a clearer light. The island was no longer enticing, but cold and blue and far away. But there was no wind to speak of, and the way was open. We were afloat in no time, and slowly, as we paddled, the mainland sank into a faint blue line behind, and still the island looked to be no more than a blue vapour on the horizon. Gradually it took on substance, and after three hours' hard paddling we came into the shelter of the bay on the east side of South Manitou Island. This was the true beginning of our quest – and yet we were almost into Eighth Month – but at last we were here.

I was still lost in thought when I came upon various canals and islands dug in the sand, surrounded by many small footprints. I looked down and smiled, for they reminded me of hours spent damming the beck at Highside when I was a little lad, and of my little Bristo cousins, who lived at Portinscale, and Robert Southey's children playing on the beaches of Derwentwater.

I tried to follow the prints a little way, but the dry sand was all blown about, and they went nowhere. When I looked back the half mile to where our camp was, I could see a trickle of smoke rising vertically. Alan and Loic must be up and about. The clean curve of sand between us was like a sudden invitation. I ran fast, splashing over firm sand, till I reached the camp all damp and out of breath.

'What is it?' Loic looked up from stirring the pease. 'Have you seen something?'

'No.' I sat down, panting. 'I've sat in a canoe too long, that's all. We have a hot breakfast today, do we?'

'Why not? I think we won't travel today. Here's Alan. Will you eat?'

When we'd done Loic banked up the fire with damp wood and last year's sodden leaves.

'So,' said Alan. 'We've told them clearly enough where we are and what we're doing. Shall we go?'

The Ottawa village was beyond where I'd walked that morning. We found marks in the sand dunes where several canoes had been beached in a hollow. Beyond them a path led into the forest. It wound among groves of birch and maple, until it reached a big clearing, made by beavers maybe, with a group of wigwams at the far end. 'This is a summer village,' said Loic. 'People come for the months of fishing, and for berry-picking. They were here when Rachel went away. Since fall and until early summer they are not here. In winter there is no one here, because on an island there are not the big animals to hunt.'

The dogs were already barking as we approached the village. 'No one will be surprised,' said Loic. 'We had our fire in the usual place.' The dogs ran out to meet us, tails held high, followed by a straggling band of children. Loic called out as we came near, '*Boozhoo! Boozhoo! Gii bi-izhaayaang o'ikkidoyaang gi-ogimaa* – we've come to speak to your leader.' In this village they were obviously less used to visitors than they were in the north. The children clustered round us, asking questions. I don't know what Loic said to them, but he made them laugh, and only one or two of the girls hung back shyly. The others jostled round us, chattering like starlings. They accompanied us to some fenced-in gardens. Some women were weeding round the hillocks where the corn grew. Beans twined upwards up the cornstalks, and squash vines covered the earth all round.[1] When they saw us the women left their work and came to the fence. When Loic spoke to them, they pointed to the wigwams. There was some talk, but it was all in the Ottawa tongue. When we walked on, the older woman came with us. She was barefoot like the children, and she too wore a deerskin dress, only hers was embroidered with many beads. A necklace of polished bones hung round her neck. As we walked she fired questions at Loic: as soon as he'd answered one she had another ready. I watched her face, which was that of an old woman, although her hair was still

---

[1] My mother would have liked the Indian gardens. She hated this modern fashion for bare earth between the plants. When my wife began to plant our vegetables the Indian way, in hillocks, my mother was quite ready to experiment. It was the garden that first brought my mother and my wife into friendship. God has been very merciful unto me.

black as a raven's wing, and she walked with an easy stride. She reminded me a little of Madeleine La Framboise.

She led us to the central wigwam, in front of which a big iron kettle hung from a hook over an open fire. A very old woman was sitting on a log, her face turned up to the morning sun, while a younger woman – her daughter, perhaps? – was looking after the simmering pot. A baby crawled over to one of the log benches and hauled himself upright to stare at us with round eyes. I smiled at him, and he smiled back. After some talk Loic said, 'The men went fishing early. We can wait here for them, she says.'

It was peaceful in the morning sun. The fire crackled at our feet. Alan sat on the ground with his back against the log, his feet stretched to the fire, and presently fell asleep. The baby began to grizzle; his grandmother picked him up and fed him corn porridge from a spoon. The other children drifted away. I watched the girls playing a game, squealing like a flock of gulls as they tossed a ball of woven grass to and fro, catching it on a string suspended from two long sticks. The boys had vanished into the woods. The baby's mother brought out a bark bag of flour. She made a dip in it just as the voyageurs did, poured in a little water, and one by one she kneaded little fist-sized loaves. Jacques would have thrown these into the stew, but she impaled each loaf carefully on a stick, and set them around the fire to cook. When they were half done she added a measure of rice[2] and a bunch of herbs to the simmering pot.

The sun was already halfway to noon when the men came back with nets full of fish. I nudged Alan awake and he sprang to his feet. The men stopped short when they saw us. I couldn't tell who was the leader, because they were all dressed for fishing. Alan indicated a tall young man, and

[2] The Indians gather their rice wild from the northern lakes in Ninth Month. It's unlike the East India Company rice we see nowadays, being dark brown in the husk, and much nuttier in flavour.

said quietly, 'That's Nodin. We talked to him before.' Loic spoke, and the young man replied sharply. I watched the quick exchange of words, accompanied by gestures in our direction. Loic translated. 'This is Nodin. He remembers when Alan and I were here two years ago. He thinks there's nothing more to say, but he'll talk to Mark, he says, because I explained you're Rachel's brother, come all the way from your own country to look for her.'

'G'miigwechiwigìn, nwiijikiwenh,' I said.

There was a moment's silence as they all looked at me. Then Nodin burst out laughing, stepped forward and shook me by the hand in the British way, speaking directly to me as he did so. I shook my head, and Loic evidently told him my linguistic abilities were now exhausted, but for all that we sat down in a much friendlier spirit. Alan took tobacco from his leather bag, and Nodin took it, and passed it to the young man on his right to put away.

The women were rapidly gutting and splitting the fish, and tossing them into the pot. A couple of girls were called away from their game, and told to set the baked loaves out on clean rush mats. Nodin called upon Loic to translate some more questions. I answered as best I could, trying to explain where I'd started from and how I'd come on my long journey. The pot of fish was beginning to smell good, for all that I reckoned by this time to have eaten enough whitefish to last me my lifetime. I was glad when it turned out we were expected to share the meal, for reasons both carnal and politic. The young woman – I think she was Nodin's wife – handed out the fish stew in wooden bowls, and the smallest girl carefully gave out wooden spoons with which to eat it. Her sister followed her, bringing round the bread, and then the women retired to the other side of the fire.

We ate in silence. It wasn't until the pipe was filled with a twist of Alan's tobacco, and passed round, that the talk began. I grasped the pronunciation of certain words, particularly 'Tecumseh' and 'Detroit'. Occasionally, when Alan didn't understand either, he nudged Loic, who translated, and in this way I picked up some snippets. Apparently the American General Hull had marched into Upper Canada, but – this is what I understood Alan to say (I found his speech much the easiest to follow) – there was every reason to trust, now that war was openly declared, that General Brock would beat him back to Detroit, especially since the British had taken Mackinac. Nodin was able to tell Alan that the Shawnee chief Tecumseh had defeated another American army in Ohio, and the remnant had already fled back to Detroit. 'It only remains to take Detroit,' said Alan, his eyes blazing.

They all had plenty to say about that, and perhaps Alan's ear was attuned, because there was no translating for a long time. The way the men of the village spoke put me in mind of a Meeting for Worship for Business. Each man had his say and was given due attention, and sometimes there were spaces in between the words. Alan never interrupted these, but he was as alert and bright-eyed as a collie working on the hill.

There was only one point when there seemed to be any argument, and under the cover of raised voices I touched Loic's shoulder. 'What are they saying?'

Loic began to translate for me rapidly as the others spoke. 'This is about a Treaty made five years ago. It is called the Treaty of Detroit. The Ottawa chiefs north-west of Fort Detroit agreed to sell their lands to the United States government. Lewis Cass is the governor of the Michigan Territory – they agreed this eight years ago. Cass has signed this Treaty with the Ottawa. Nidon says what can this mean; what is the Michigan Territory? There are no Americans here, except at the forts at Detroit and Fort Wayne away to the south, and Mackinac by itself in the north, and now Mackinac is once again British. Otherwise, in all this land there are none but the Anishinaabe – we whom you call Indians. In the Treaty the Americans said the Ottawas could still hunt and fish on the lands of their fathers. The chiefs did not wish to sell, but money and other things were promised. But those who signed the Treaty for the United States government have not kept these promises. There is hunger among our people. This is because there has been too much hunting. The traders must have furs, and more furs, and now too many animals are gone. And so the chiefs must sell.

'And now there is trouble. Settlers have come, all around Fort Detroit, and the promises made to the Ottawa are not kept. Some of these men here say the Ottawa at Detroit are fools, and all this is far away. If there is war, it is not our war. Other men here are saying, we have talked to the Ojibwa at Saginaw, and they say the settlers are coming further north, into Ojibwa hunting grounds as well. If we do not fight against the Americans now, our children will live to curse us. Although we are far away, the day may come when it is our hunting grounds that they covet. And what the white man covets, he will take. And so these men say to Alan, yes, we will make our alliance with the British. Your war is our war, and we say yes, we will come to fight.'

'*Alan* is . . . ?' The words died away on my tongue. Had I not known it since the day I met him what he was, and refused to admit the evidence, even when it was clear and plain before my eyes? But if I had admitted to myself what I knew, I wouldn't have been able to compromise. Alan and I wouldn't be here together now, and what slender hope I had of finding Rachel would have been gone for ever. I had no reason to protest; my ignorance had been my own choice.

I turned my attention to Alan, and watched him closely. The talk had changed; Nidon and the man on his right were sharply interrogating Alan, or so it seemed to me, and Alan was talking vehemently, though sometimes stuck for words. When that happened he muttered something low in French for Loic to translate. Very well, so I was the one who was not to understand. I could have interrupted, and confronted him. I chose to wait.

It was almost noon and very hot when Loic nudged me again. 'Now we speak of Rachel.' Nodin was talking, pausing after each statement for Loic to translate for me: 'In winter these people are on the mainland. All the families are scattered, each in its own hunting territory. After your sister was lost the winter came – everyone here left the island. At that time of year there is no news. When they leave their winter hunting territory they go to a place – the place where we camped on the beach two days ago – they all go there every year for their maple syrup harvest. This is the time when there is news from far off. Since Rachel is lost there have been three maple syrup harvests. If Rachel were among their own people she would have come there. Everyone comes to the maple syrup harvest. Each year the story has been told. For three years all the people at the maple syrup harvest have heard it. Each family now knows this story. If there is any news we hear it.'

'And are there many of these maple syrup villages?' I asked.

'*Mais oui*. In all our lands there are such villages.'

When at last the talk and the smoking were done, and we'd taken our leave, Loic went back to our camp, and Alan and I set off along the villagers' path into the forest. 'I said I'd show you where we looked,' he said.

I followed him along a narrow path. The ground under my moccasins was soft with leaf-mould. I could hear a woodpecker again, and sundry calls and screeches of birds. At first we walked among maple, birch and basswood, but presently there were more of the great white cedars, and at last only cedars. When I looked up I saw a roof of huge twisted branches, often broken off or dead, and peeling bark hanging down like a curtain. The canopy seemed to touch the very sky. I laid my hands against a trunk, and gazed up until I felt dizzy. The bark under my hands was dry and flaky. Up above bits of it had come loose and hung down in long filaments. The exposed wood was bright yellow.

After a mile or so we came to a sandy hillock and into blinding sunlight. We climbed up, and were suddenly in open country. Crickets rasped in the thin scrub of willow and juniper, and there were clouds of butterflies among the flowers. I could feel the heat of the sand through my thin moccasins. As we climbed to the top our footsteps crunched through the dried-up grasses. Scoured white tree roots poked through the sand like bones. The dunes were the only high point on the island. I could see down on to the tree canopy, like looking into a strange country. From there I could see North Manitou, and to the east, the high mainland dunes, the low line of the Michigan coast, and a headland jutting out far to the south.

'We canoed all round the island,' said Alan. 'You see how it's sand all round? Here, we'll walk out to the bluff, and you can see the beach below the dunes. I told you before, a canoe could come ashore anywhere, and no one the wiser. We looked for signs where there are beaches – footprints, canoe marks – but anyone who wanted to be secret could hide all that. Then we went to North Manitou' – he pointed. 'We went round that too. No one lives there. It's sacred land – there are graves – Loic would say, strong medicine – many manitous. So we couldn't go beyond the shore.'

'Thee means there are no paths?'

'I mean I wouldn't dare.'

Such an admission, coming from Alan, perplexed me. His courage had never seemed to me to be in question. Another question hovered on my lips, but I didn't ask aloud. Instead, I looked east to the mainland. Only Indians lived there, Loic had said, the Ojibwa and Ottawa. There would be summer villages, like this one on South Manitou, and winter hunting grounds, and maple syrup groves. And apart from that there was just the forest, untouched by man since the day it was created. Only God knew what lay in its depths. Until today I'd thought of Rachel as having vanished into a wilderness beyond all compass. Now I saw that she could not possibly have done so. There was nowhere – at least for a white girl – to go. Either she was among the Indians, or she was dead. Unless someone had carried her away right out of the Michigan Territory . . . but there had been no one. I began to understand how kenspeckle strangers would be, for since we left Mackinac it had fully dawned on me that the place was inhabited. There were eyes to see. An American sloop, or a brigade of *canots du maître*, could not have landed and left South Manitou in summer without Nidon's people being aware of it. Assuming Nidon was speaking the truth – and I had no cause to believe otherwise – she was not among his particular band, or he'd have heard about it. In which case, all we had to do was to visit the Indian bands who regularly travelled in these waters. I was comforted by the logic of my reasoning, and heaved a deep sigh.

But before I could make a plan with Alan, there was the other matter to deal with.

'Alan!'

'Yes?'

'Will thee tell me now what orders William McGillivray gave thee in the letter I brought to thee?'

He had the grace to look guilty, though to be fair, the sin was not his. 'The letter?'

'Ay. Did that letter tell thee to make use of me, and to go among the Indians again, in the Michigan Territory, and say to everyone it was to look for thy wife? Did it tell thee that?'

Alan met my gaze. His eyes were green in the strong sunlight. 'Since you ask me: yes, brother Mark, it did.'

'And under that guise, thy commission is to incite the Indians in Michigan to join with the British army in Upper Canada in fighting the Americans with war and outward weapons, representing to them that such bloody strife will serve their own ends and interests?'

'It wasn't I that told you anything different,' said Alan. 'But in fairness I should say that McGillivray didn't give me that commission.' He sighed. 'I'd better make a clean breast of it. You'll be thinking it's worse than it is. McGillivray's letter is a promise to the Indians. My job is to show it to the chiefs and read it over to them. It clarifies that the trade embargo is an American imposition. It says that if the British – helped by the Indians – drive the Americans out of the North West Territory of the United States, the North West Company will offer the same good terms to traders in the Michigan Territory and the routes to the Mississippi as they did before.' Alan glanced at me. 'You told me McGillivray gave you his oath the letter wasn't about making war. And nor is it – exactly. You look like the avenging angel, brother Mark. I hope you're not going to throw me over this cliff?'

'Loic told me thee was encouraging Nidon and his warriors to come and fight for the British in this war.'

'Mark, you asked me about McGillivray's letter. I've told you about McGillivray's bloody letter! I know you think me perfidious beyond your miserable grey-coated salvation, but I don't tell lies! Here!' He pulled the familiar paper, with its broken seal, from his haversack. 'Read the bloody letter, if you must! But don't call me a liar. Or else you'll go over the cliff. But no – you're too bloody virtuous to fight, but you know a neat trick or two if you want to throw a man, don't you? So I guess it's me that'll go over. Fine! But I'm not a liar!'

'I'll read it later,' I said mildly, for somehow his show of temper had given me the mastery. 'I want thee to tell me now, if it wasn't William McGillivray who ordered thee to incite these people to war and fighting with outward weapons. Alan, who was it?'

'What's that to do with you?'

'Thee knows it's all to do with me.'

'It is not! And if it were, would you have me forsworn? I suppose you'd be glad of it, being above all oaths yourself!'

'I think thee got thy orders in York in Ninth Month last,' I said, watching him closely. 'Maybe thee got them from the general, Isaac Brock. I rather think thee did.' The rigidity of his expression told me all; I knew Alan's cast of countenance pretty well by now. 'Ay, thee was in York to see the governor, for purposes of war. Thee need say no more. But I cannot go further with thee on this business. I'd like thee and Loic to take me across to the mainland, and I'll go my own ways from there.'

'Don't be such a bloody fool!' Alan came away from the edge of the bluff and began pacing up and down, as well as he could in the soft sand. 'You'd be a lamb among wolves! 'Twould be bloody murder, if anything would. No, I can't leave thee – I mean you, damn it!' He stared out at the lake for a bit, and when he turned round the rage had all gone out of him. He grinned at me ruefully. 'I think we're stuck with each other, brother Mark, so we'll just have to thole it as best we may. I'm sorry if I deceived you, but I didn't lie to you, you know. I've been most careful not to.'

'I'm glad of that. But still I cannot travel with thee, while thee incites these people to go to war.'

'This is difficult,' said Alan. 'I'm pledged to others, you understand.'

'Thee also gave thy word to me.'

'Inexorable, aren't you? I haven't broken my word to thee, either, as far as I'm aware.' He sighed again. 'I tell you what, brother Mark. Let's go back to camp and put it to Loic. If we all put our minds to it, I'm sure we can agree on something.'

I thought that over, and found it good. 'I can't change my mind on this. But I trust Loic, so I'll agree to talk with him.'

CHAPTER 19

LOIC SAID, 'ALAN, WHAT DO YOUR PEOPLE DO WHEN two men have a quarrel?'

Alan shrugged. 'These days? Nothing much. Perhaps one challenges the other, and they fight. Mark won't fight. My father fought a duel when he was in the 72nd. The other fellow pinked him; he had the scar on his shoulder to prove it. I've better things to do than fight duels. Or in this brave new world they're more likely go to law, and lose all their money in the courts, and are no better off.'

Loic said, 'Mark, what do your people do when two men have a quarrel?'

I thought about it. 'The elders would come and talk to them. They'd worship together, and the elders would make them resolve their differences. If that didn't work, it would be the concern of the whole Meeting. There might be a Particular Meeting about it. The worst thing that could happen is that one – or both – might be disowned.'

Loic said, 'For the Indians it is much the same. At the worst my mother's people would either fight, and kill, or they would use evil magic against their foe. But we too have elders. Very often they would take up the matter and make the men resolve it. I think this is better, but we have no elders with us. You could ask me to be the judge. I am not an elder, but there is no one else. Otherwise I think you will have to fight, and this Mark will not do; or else part, and this Alan will not do.'

'So we let you arbitrate?' Alan shrugged. 'It's alarmingly like Aesop, but what else is there to do? Go on then, Loic, what's the answer?'

'Wait,' said Loic. 'Mark?'

'Ay.' I realised they hadn't understood this for assent, and added, 'I agree to it.'

'I must think,' said Loic.

Loic's silence seemed to me entirely reasonable. I leaned back on the soft sand and stared into the blue depths of the sky: *The heavens, even the heavens, are the Lord's, but the earth he hath given to the children of men.* I thought of the untrodden forests, and the great cedar swamps that no man yet had looked upon, and it seemed to me that giving the earth to the children of men might not be an unmitigated good. *Whosoever shall say to his brother, Thou fool, shall be in danger of hell fire.* That I could not accept. I could happily have thrown Alan again – though was happier now that I'd refrained – but over the cliff – no, I knew not the rage that could make me do such a thing as that. As for hell fire, that was quite out of my jurisdiction, and when I thought of the merciful God in whom I'd been taught to place my trust from my earliest days, I realised I didn't believe in that kind of hell at all. Besides, I liked Alan well; I could deal with him quite easily without calling down retribution on his head, even if I could. The thought surprised me, and at that moment I knew, whatever Loic decided, that I would be reconciled with my brother, whatever the issues that lay between us.

'I have decided,' said Loic.

Alan sat up and rubbed his eyes. I brushed sand out of my hair with my fingers and waited for Loic to go on.

'We will go on together,' said Loic. 'Mark came this

long way to look for Rachel, and we gave him our word we would do this. And we shall. Our first need is to find Rachel, and everything else comes second to this.

'But Alan has also given his word to the North West Company to give the Michigan Indians promises of trade when the embargo is taken away. He has also given his word to General Brock in York that he would talk to the Indians about the war, and persuade their warriors to go to – well, that has changed a little – to go now to Mackinac – to fight the Americans alongside the British. Alan is fighting for his own people, and for him this work is entirely honourable.

'But Mark has also given his word to his people, that he will not have any part in war or strife, or fightings with outward weapons – those are the words of his bond, I think – and so it would be shameful for him to support Alan in his task. Even to stay quiet and not interfere would shame him.

'Every man on this earth is free to speak as he will, to go where he will, and to act as he will if it's not unlawful in the country where he finds himself. This is the country of the Ottawa. There's no evil power here that'll take away a man's freedom to do these things, though there are certainly people who'll stop him if they don't like it.

'Then his blood is on his own head. So what I say is this: when we go to the villages you'll give each other the freedom to speak as you will, to say whatever you must to whomever you like. No one has the right to deny this to any man. That means that Alan may say what he likes, but all the talk must be translated so that Mark understands. I can do that. And if Mark wishes to gainsay what Alan says, he has the right to do that, and I will translate as much as he needs, so that everyone can hear. This is also more respectful to my people: you let them hear your differences, and then they can make up their own minds. And if you argue too much – why then no one will listen to either of you, and you'll get what you deserve.'

Alan and I looked at each other, and saw in each other's eyes an equal horror. We stared like that for a long moment, and then Alan whispered, 'Oh, Aesop Kerners, what would you!' and began to laugh. I couldn't help smiling at him, and before I knew it I was laughing too. I couldn't help myself, for all the dismay I felt in my heart. For I knew now that I must break my lifelong silence, and begin to speak my mind, and in argumentation too, which was a thing I'd avoided always – or perhaps only since Rachel was born, for my mother used to say I was a clamorous bairn enough, before I learned to hold my peace.

'And now,' said Loic. 'I have a message for Mark. The *mide* of the village has sent for him.'

'Who?'

'This is – I don't know how to describe it – he is a member of the *Midewiwin*. A man of visions, of dreams, with knowledge of many things. Also he understands plants and herbs.'

'Like a priest,' said Alan helpfully.

'I have naught to do with priests.'

'*Not* like a priest,' said Loic. 'That I promise you. I know this much better than Alan, because Father Richard is my priest and sometimes I go to mass, which Alan does not.'

'I'm not a Catholic. There isn't an Episcopal priest west of York, as far as I know. And anyway . . .'

'Alan, thee protests to those who care not. Why has this – this *mide* – sent for me?'

'This he will tell you. I think it must be about Rachel. I can take you there.'

'Now?' I asked, getting up.

The *mide* didn't live in the village, but along a winding path that led to the inland lake. We brushed through rushes, and bright-coloured ducks flapped out of their hiding places and rose, with squawks of protest, as we passed. The *mide*'s lodge lay far enough past the lake to escape the worst of the mosquitoes, in a little glade surrounded by basswood trees, which made the wigwam look small as an anthill, a tiny excrescence of the forest floor. The only sign of life was the smoke rising from the roof. Loic lifted aside the hide curtain and spoke to someone within. Then he turned to me. 'He says I can come too, to translate.'

The wigwam reeked of tobacco. The *mide* sat cross-legged on the other side of the fire. I judged him at first to be very old, but his voice was young, and I have no true sense of what his age might be. His hair was still black. He was much hung about with necklaces of polished bone, bear claws, hair and feathers, and indeed that was all of a piece with his surroundings, for the place was filled with strange objects, half of which had no meaning for me. The bunches of herbs hanging from the roof I could understand, but not the claws and hoofs, the carvings and weavings, the piles of unidentifiable no-things that faded into the darkness like the figments of a frightening dream.

But the long calumet – pipe – I did recognise by now. I took out the twist of tobacco that Loic had told me to bring, and I presented it to the man, who turned it over, sniffed it, broke a piece off and rolled it between finger and thumb, and then nodded his approval. For a time he was busy with the pipe. Loic lit a spill of birchbark and passed it over. Then we smoked for a long time. The second time the pipe came back to me I realised I'd breathed the smoke right in. It filled my lungs with an acrid burning feeling, but I was nowhere near choking. I felt a little dizzy, as if I had overstepped some boundary I'd known nothing of. When a man walks the fells in snow he has to be careful not to tread on the cornices, which look like solid ground, but actually project over the precipices into empty space. I felt as if I was walking on ground which was not there, but I found it not so much frightening in this case as like a dream.

When the old man began to speak I wasn't exactly waiting for him any more – there was no need – and I was content to sit quiet while he and Loic were talking. Then Loic turned to me. 'He says he has waited for you a long time. I explained that the journey was very far, that it had taken you more than a year to come all the way from your own country. He says if you had dawdled any longer it would have been too late. Perhaps it is already too late. You must make haste.'

'Waiting for me? But how? Does he know about Rachel? Surely he didn't know I existed!'

'Oh yes, he has dreamed of you several times – oh, for two years or more, he says.'

'*Dreamed* of me? How can he . . . But does he know anything?'

'Hush, Mark! I am telling you what he knows. Perhaps you do not understand that true wisdom and knowledge come to a wise man in his dreams. This is why white people are not very wise; they don't listen to their dreams. Even my father will admit this. For the Indians . . . we are taught to dream from our first days. A child cannot grow up until he – or she – has dreamed his own dream. Some people can dream what is long past, or what is still to come. Your dreams tell you who you are, and who your guardians are when you have a quest, as you have now. Would you have come all this way, if you hadn't dreamed of this?'

'Ay.' I thought it over. 'Ay, I would have come – I did come – because I was clear in my mind that I should do so. I thought about it when I was awake, not when I was asleep. I said to my parents I'd look for my sister.' I added irritably, 'It would be a lie to say it was because of a dream. It wasn't.'

The old man interrupted, evidently asking what I'd said.

Still annoyed, I watched them talk. Then Loic said, 'He says you are in danger, because you do not listen to your dream. He says if you forget your dream you forget how you will find your sister, and he cannot help you.'

'Forget? But I never knew!'

'Yes, Mark, you did. You said it was not like looking for a needle in a bottle of hay, because you trust in your God, and he knows where Rachel is. So you have said to me you have a guide, and this I have told the *mide*. He says that is very well: you have your Manitou, and by your dreams your Manitou will guide you. I know myself this is true, because Father Richard – he it was who baptised me at St Anne's on Mackinac – used to tell us stories, and the Christian God – who is yours, you say – has always spoken to men in dreams, has he not?'

He was right: examples came flooding into my mind from Old Testament and New. *Your old men shall dream dreams and your young men shall see visions* . . . If any man were guided by his visions in this world, that man was George Fox. Loic had probably never heard of him. And yet . . . and yet . . . Perhaps I was a child of a more secular age than ever I'd thought, even in my own Society. I leaned my elbows on my knees and pressed my fingers to my temples, as if that would help me think. It was hard to be rational, for in my heart I felt deep terror. I told myself it was the reasonable fear of vain superstitions, but it was more than that: I was afraid of the powers of darkness, of witchcraft and evil magic, and of dread phantoms in which I did not even believe. When I was a little lad I had a nightmare about the water scratti that lives in the high tarns. It takes on enticing shapes, then drags men under water to their death. I don't know who told me about the scratti. My parents never lied to us with idle tales of fleys or boggles, but somehow I knew, and moreover I knew that I should not know, the legends of my own country, and

I was more flayt by them than Friends would ever have begun to guess.

The old man was speaking again. 'Now you have remembered the dream,' said Loic.

'What?'

'He says now that you remember the dream, you must seek for the second part of it. She did not drown.'

'*What?*'

'He says, you heard me: she did not drown. If you had not known that, you would not have come so far. You came to this island because you knew this was the place. Here you will remember the second part of the dream, the part that tells you how it is she did not die.'

I shook my head. Unaccountably I felt close to tears, but neither Loic nor the old man would ever see me weep. 'There's nothing to remember.'

They ignored that. The old man was speaking, and Loic was translating rapidly. 'He says, it is two years since he first saw you. In his dream you are blindfold, always blindfold. You are hunting. You are following the tracks of a bear: only, you cannot follow unless you take the bandage from your eyes. He says also, there is blood on the snow. That you will kill. That is how you will find her, if it is not too late. You will kill, or die. When you kill, you must take the tokens and hang them round your neck, for he whom you killed will be your Manitou. He will give his life for you. You must give him thanks and recompense, or you will die. He has spoken.'

In the days that followed I tried hard to erase my meeting with the *mide* from my mind. I wasn't very successful. When I didn't watch my thoughts vigilantly, I'd find they'd gone back to that strange interview in the wigwam and were turning it over and over in my mind. I couldn't stop them, particularly when I was falling asleep. The part about the bear must have got into my dreams, for shreds of memory would haunt me unaccountably in the daytime. Because I was thus pre-occupied the days that followed had an unreal quality to them. I kept having the feeling that I'd been here before, that all this had happened before. I was so troubled by it that I described it to Alan, and he said that he knew exactly what I meant. That comforted me; Alan was entirely sane if not perfectly moral, so if he'd felt it too it could not be madness.

'Does thee believe in these visions?' I asked him.

'Ay,' said Alan.

'Is that all thee can say?'

'I learned it from you,' said Alan. 'Three months in your company, brother, has cured me permanently of guileless chatter, supposing I were given to it before.'

I'd learned that whenever Alan was more than ordinarily facetious he was embarrassed by a serious matter and didn't wish to own it. But it was too important to let him off the hook. 'Thee believes that truth may come in dreams and visions, even the truth of what is yet to come?'

'Ay,' said Alan again. 'I'm not one of your commonsensical Englishmen, any more than Loic is. Hadn't you realised that? Anyway, I'm surprised at you. Rachel told me that the Society of Friends was founded in a welter of prophetic visions. Your George Fox now – what was the phrase she used? *It was opened to me* ... She was all for that sort of thing, your sister. You're not very like her, are you, brother Mark?'

We now began to search the mainland shore, going up the rivers and across the inland lakes, visiting as many villages as we could. At our next encounter with the Indians Alan and I did just as Loic had said, with the result that very soon no one paid any heed to either of us. Instead they launched into what appeared to be a longstanding discussion between their elders and their warriors as to whether or not a war party should set off for Mackinac before everyone left for the rice harvest. 'I don't think they're interested in what we have to say,' I remarked quietly to Alan. He winked at me, and murmured, 'How salutary!'

When I think of the weeks that followed, I realise now that I learned many important things, viz:

First, the Indian lands were no trackless wilderness; on the contrary, we could follow a pattern woven by generations of the people whose land this was. The first Indian path I ever walked was on the far side of the Mattawa at *le Talon* falls. It felt very foreign to me; I wondered now why I hadn't realised that there would be paths everywhere, just as we have. The main roads are lakes and rivers. The Indians have neither carts nor horses, and all the long journeys with heavy cargoes are done by canoe. There's a trade in corn, fish and sugar that has nothing to do with the white man. The villages are linked just as ours are. If Loic had lost a sister in, say, Borrowdale, he'd be a fool to quarter every acre of the high fells for miles around. I'd tell him to enquire in Grange, Rosthwaite, Seathwaite, Stonethwaite and Seatoller, and find out in each place about all the outlying farms. He'd soon pick up the pattern and be able to follow it. There'd be no end to it, of course – from Seatoller he'd be sent on to Buttermere; from Seathwaite over Styhead to Wasdale; from Stonethwaite up by Langstrath into Langdale; from Grange along the lakeside to Portinscale and Bassenthwaite . . . It would be never-ending, but there'd be pattern enough to keep a man from utter hopelessness. I'm niggled when the Lakers call my own country a wilderness. I learned on our journey that I'd had just the same misconception about the Indian lands of the north-west.

Second, Alan and I might have saved our tempers, because our opinions made very little difference to anyone. Nearly everyone we spoke to agreed with me that it would be infinitely preferable to have peace than war. But when I spoke of a world in which there need be no wars nor fightings with outward weapons, the usual reaction was summed up by a woman at one of the villages on the great bay with the long peninsula inside it, where we travelled for many days. She said to me, 'But what were men born for, then? What would you have them do?' When we talked to young men, they listened to Alan. But the question for them wasn't what the war had seemed to be about at Mackinac. Here, the burning issue was the Treaty of Detroit, and the broken promises that had followed the sale of Ottawa lands. We stopped in an Ottawa village where they told us that Detroit had already fallen to the British. Their warriors had already gone to join Tecumseh in Ohio. An elder at the Manistee River said to Alan, 'You don't understand. Once there was no fur trade to Montreal. One day there will again be no fur trade to Montreal. What of it? But if our lands are lost to us, then everything we have is gone for ever.'

Third, I learned enough of the Ottawa tongue to take part in the meetings, instead of being dragged hither and thither like a tailor's dummy. Loic patiently taught me words and phrases as we sat by the campfire in the evening. He didn't laugh at me as my voyageurs had done when they taught me French, but there must have been some entertainment in the task, for presently Alan joined in. This was generous of him, for he whetted my debating skills entirely for use against himself. He said he found the irony diverting.

Fourth, I truly learned how to paddle a canoe. I found out that my weeks as occasional *milieu* in a *canot du maître* had given me strength and skill to paddle the long day through, but taught me nothing of the intricacies of handling an Indian canoe in open water. In good weather Loic let me take a turn as bowsman, and then, once or twice, in his place as steersman. I began to get the feel of wind and water. I learned to change my stroke before we were off course, rather than correct it. I learned to read the lake and the sky, in the same way as I read the land and weather on my own hills. As with any skill, the time came when I didn't have to think about my paddling all the time, but could let the reins hang loose when no immediate danger threatened. And when there was danger, I began to know what we must do, and to adjust my stroke and my weight without being told.

Fifth – and this is the hardest to explain – I learned what it is to walk on the cornice all the time; to have no solid ground under my feet, and to live always in a peril I could not see. Because we looked like traders, and there were only three of us, approaching the villages openly, we met with no overt violence. But there *was* violence, even, I sometimes felt, in the very air we breathed. I walked unarmed, as I'd always done, except once or twice I loaded one of the muskets with shot and went after small game. Alan wasn't going to let me have the gun at all at first – he said, was I sure I was capable of loading it, even, for I might very well kill myself just doing that? I said a trade musket could hardly be so different from the fowling piece I had at home, and when I looked at it I found I was right, except that the musket was heavier, though short in the barrel compared with the military muskets I'd seen at Mackinac. Alan reluctantly handed over his horn, and watched critically while I measured out powder, tore off a strip, and rammed in the shot. I asked for priming powder, and Alan passed me his sling and bag without another word. When I came back to camp an hour later, with a plump duck hanging from my belt, I tried not to look vainglorious. Clearly they'd thought a man who refused to kill his fellows was incapable of firing a straight shot. I thought of the rabbit and pigeon pies my mother makes – and the pigeon is the hardest of all targets, in my opinion – and I said to them, did they think a

Quaker would scorn to have fresh meat to his dinner? A sad undergrown set of folk we'd be, in that case.[1] Whereat they jested somewhat at my expense, but the point was taken.

Sometimes we encountered Indians hung about with the accoutrements of war. It was Alan who told me that the swathes of hair that hung from a warrior's belt were the scalps of his enemies, whereat my blood ran cold. We only once met a full band of warriors, when we landed near a camp with four canoes. The warriors were armed with tomahawks, war clubs, bows and arrows, and some muskets. Alan said the best thing was to walk boldly into their midst, and not act furtively. This we did. It turned out they were on their way south to join Tecumseh, and when Alan announced that we were British, they greeted us as allies, and took gifts of tobacco and, what they coveted more and we durst not refuse, much of our precious powder, lead and shot.

It was not merely that I found myself among a warlike people.[2] I felt danger all around me because I knew I couldn't recognise it even with my eyes wide open.

[1] These days I shoot my beasts through the brain before we butcher them. Most farmers I know still slit the throat in the old way, and so did we, when I was a lad. They say it spoils the flavour to shoot them dead, because the blood cannot run so free, but I think my way is the more merciful. Call me sentimental, if thee will. Death is all about us, in all its forms, and no man can escape it, but I do not believe God gave us dominion over the birds of the air and the beasts of the field in order for us to inflict any pain upon our fellow-creatures that might easily be avoided.
[2] I'd lived nearly all my life among a nation at war. I was used to the sight of redcoats on the street and Royal Naval ships patrolling our shores, from my earliest days. The difference was, I suppose, that I knew a redcoat in the streets of Carlisle was unlikely to fall upon me and slice off my scalp, or, indeed, do me any hurt at all. But then, when I think of the press-gang when I was a lad at Whitehaven, I think now I was in as much danger in my own country (for suppose Buonaparte had invaded in '03?) as I was beyond the settled frontier in the Michigan Territory. Even when no war is declared we are oppressed by the power of arms, for was not Peterloo a massacre perpetrated by our own civil magistrates in times of so-called peace? Perhaps it is only familiarity that gives us the illusion of peace, when there is no peace.

These people were hopelessly foreign to me. Sometimes I thought of Waase'aaban, and my heart misgave me yet again for what I had done. The Indians were unlike me in their religion, their beliefs, their ethics, even their most basic customs. Alan's words about torture had lingered in my mind, but when I repeated them to Loic, he was indignant, and said that no such atrocities had occurred for more than a generation, and that it was not his people, but the Iroquois in the south who were guilty of such devilment. I knew not what to think. And no sooner had I thought how far removed these folk were from the civilisation from which I had come, than I would be startled into recognition: the way they grilled fish, the way a man spoke to his dog, the way the children played hide-and-seek, the way someone would make a joke, and the whole company laugh out loud: all these things and many more, would suddenly cause the great gulf between us to be closed up, just for a moment.

Moreover, these savage people understand silence in the same way as Friends do. They too will sit, sometimes for a long time, with no word spoken, and allow the silence to gather them. Their silence is not different from ours, for were we not all created by the same God? I said this to Loic one evening, and he told me how the stories the priest at St Anne's had taught him fitted in with the stories he'd heard by the fire in winter from his mother's people. 'Sometimes I forget which is which.'

'Tell me one.'

Loic stared into the dying embers of our fire – for it was late – and presently began, as formally as if he were speaking ministry in Meeting. 'In the beginning Gitchi Manitou had a dream. He dreamed, and out of the void he created rock, fire, water and wind. On each one he breathed, and his breath was the breath of life, giving each one its own soul. And Gitchi Manitou saw that this was good. On the next day Gitchi Manitou dreamed the sky, and in it he dreamed the sun and moon and stars, and below the sky the earth. On the next day he dreamed earth, with mountains and valleys, rivers and lakes, forests and islands. On the next day he dreamed trees, grasses, herbs and flowers. He dreamed the fish in the water, the birds and insects in the air, and the four-legged and two-legged animals that walk the earth. Gitchi Manitou saw all this, and saw that it was good. He dreamed the thunder and lightning, wind and rain. He dreamed joy and sorrow, love and hate, fear and courage. When he had dreamed all this he rested, for he saw that it was very good.'

Loic took a stick and poked the embers into a last spurt of life. 'You see? The story is in fact the same.'

'Ay.' I was strangely relieved, and yet perplexed. I thought of Rachel and Judith's concern to minister to the Indians, and of how I'd said to Rachel long ago in the hayloft – in another world, it seemed now – that if the Light was truly revealed to all, then ministry to the less enlightened was a redundancy. It had not occurred to me that the Light Within might prompt similar outward expressions among the heathen. Also, though I knew the first chapter of Genesis by heart, I knew nothing whatsoever of the idolatries and shibboleths of the Catholic faith. Either way, I knew not what to make of Loic's story. 'There are differences,' I said to Loic cautiously.

'Of course. The same story is never told twice, not exactly.'

'Unless it's written down,' said Alan idly.

Loic shrugged. A log shifted, and the little flame vanished. The dark crept in around us, and our talk was gone for that night, like a slate wiped clean.

We had searched the waterways as far as we could, along the coast and inland, as far south as the Muskegon River.

I assumed that Madeleine La Framboise would have kept her promise about sending word among the villages further south; Alan was scathing of my trust in her, but in any case we were running out of time. The summer villages were emptying. We met canoes with whole families aboard on their way north to their rice fields. Skeins of geese tracked across the sky, heading south. Slowly the trees began to lose their green. Loic said that after the rice was harvested the families would scatter to their winter hunting grounds. There had never been any real hope, and now I had to look defeat squarely in the face. At least I could comfort myself that I had tried.

On our way north we stopped at a village at the mouth of a wide brown river. The inhabitants had mostly gone across Lake Michigan to the rice lakes, leaving only the frames of their wigwams. Half a dozen older people had stayed behind, waiting for their families to come back with the winter's supply of rice. They couldn't help us, but they had some furs to trade, which saved us going home empty-handed. We traded away the remnant of our beads and cloth, but refused to part with our last trap or the rest of the powder and shot. The evening was spent smoking the tobacco we'd given them. The men talked a little; Loic didn't bother to translate. We were all sleepy. There was an old woman in the company. She sat bent over the fire across from me. When I looked up I saw an ancient, wizened face, the cheeks fallen in over toothless gums. But her eyes were black and bright, and whenever my glance fell that way I saw her watching me. I don't think she spoke all evening.

That night I dreamed of my great aunt Agnes Bristo, who died when she was a hundred and two years old, and I was a little lad of three. In waking life I'd forgotten that I knew her. Agnes Bristo was a weighty Friend of Mosedale Meeting and had never stirred further from Mungrisdale than Keswick in all the years of her life. But in my dream she walked with a great bear, her hand resting on its neck, as a child might walk with a big dog. And then it was I who was the child, still wet from the water, and my aunt Agnes leading us, and we were walking under the moon on the high dunes of South Manitou Island. Alan's voice spoke in my ear quite clearly, saying 'I would not dare,' and even as he spoke I saw the graves on their high poles, the tattered cloths that bound them streaming in the wind. And I knew that whatever Alan said we had no choice, and this I tried to explain to him. Alan was saying, 'Mark? Mark! What the hell is it? What are you doing, for God's sake?' That part was real. I was awake, and found I'd rolled right up against him, shoving him out from under the canoe.

I was half asleep, and incoherent, but I know I said quite clearly, because they both told me so next morning, 'Not the water. The island. She says go back to South Manitou Island.'

CHAPTER 20

THE MORNING AFTER WE REACHED OUR OLD CAMPSITE on South Manitou, I woke to find a glisky rime over everything in camp. The cold stung my bare feet when I walked down to the lake. There was an end, I thought, to a summer of swimming in the warmest water I'd ever known. I dipped the kettle, and watched the ripples spreading.

When I came back, Alan, still tousled from sleep, was crawling out from under the canoe. Loic knelt by our old fireplace with a strike-a-light in his hand, where he'd made a little pyramid of birchbark among the ashes. I saw he'd laid out a lump of spruce gum resin on a mat, and the pot to melt it in. 'Thee's going to mend the canoe?'

'This morning. Then when we need to go . . . It's very late in the year to be here. We must be ready to get off as soon as we can.'

'It was thee who insisted that we come.'

'It was not I who took so long to listen.' Loic stopped, as there came a sudden wild crying above us. We stood and watched as a long line of geese came out of the north in a straggling V. When they were right above us they broke ranks and circled down quite close. With much honking they vanished among the trees close to

Nidon's village. 'They must go to the wee loch,' said Alan.

'The *mide*'s lake, thee means?' I asked.

'Ay,' said Alan. 'Would you two care for a roast goose to your dinner?'

'*Oui*, only I must work on the canoe.'

'Brother Mark? A little killing with outward weapons today, perhaps?'

When Alan and I walked along the beach, our muskets, horns and gun bags slung over our shoulders, we found the marks of canoes and several prints of moccasins, but when we came to the village it was deserted. Only the sapling frames of the wigwams were still standing, and the empty racks where fish had been dried. A scattering of leaves had blown in over the cold hearths. A shudder ran down my back; the place seemed very empty. Alan was staring into the space between one of the empty frames. 'Mark,' he said quietly. 'Look here.'

The floor of the wigwam was clear of leaves, and the ashes between the stones were soft and white. Alan stepped through the door frame, squatted down and cautiously stirred them with his finger. 'Warm.'

'The canoes are gone.'

'True.' Alan stood up, and wiped his ashy hand on his breeches.

'Let's go to the dunes first,' I said. 'If they left this morning we might still see them.'

'And if we don't see them, either they left last night or not at all, or the sun was in our eyes,' said Alan. 'A fat goose would be more conclusive.'

'I'd rather know we were alone before we fire a shot.' I don't know why I felt so cautious; perhaps all the weeks of pent-up strife around us had come to a head in my imaginings.

'We've already lit a fire,' remarked Alan. 'But I don't

mind. The dunes it is, and let's hope the geese take a siesta after they dine.'

It was warmer in the forest, but even so the air had the tang of autumn in it. We didn't find the same mushrooms that we're used to here, but there were baseberries, crackerberries, wild raisins, and many other berries that I knew not.[1] There was a tangle of homely blackberries at the foot of the dunes, which Alan and I stopped to sample. Before we climbed up the sandy path Alan pulled me back. 'Let me look first.'

The sand was soft, and certainly messed about. Alan frowned. 'There's no telling. Let's go on.'

A sharp breeze met us at the top. I'd forgotten how many hillocks there were, covered by coarse grass and juniper. There was no clear view, either far or near. The lake was dazzling bright. 'Can't see a damned thing,' said Alan. He was getting edgy too: maybe he'd caught it from me.

'Let's walk out to the bluff. We'll see the shore from there.'

'We'll see a hundred yards of it,' grumbled Alan. 'No one in his right mind would land on this side anyway.'

I led the way through the grasses. When I looked back, Alan had stopped and unslung his musket. I went back to him. 'Did thee hear aught?'

---

[1] In Cumberland we have field mushrooms, puffballs and ink-caps, all of which are edible. I also know where to find chanterelles in the woods. My mother showed us the places when we were children, but we keep that information strictly within the family: I have passed it on to my sons accordingly. It surprised me that the Indians made no use of their plethora of fungi, and seemed unable to teach me anything about them. My wife was unfamiliar with either harvesting or cooking mushrooms of any kind, and nervous in the eating of them. This took her many years to overcome, and to this day, when I bring home a feast of fungi, I must perforce turn cook to boot. I have no objection to that, though there are Friends who might be disconcerted to see my handiness with a frying pan and skillet. In the wilderness a man must fend for himself in all ways, and I have never quite forgotten the culinary skills I acquired thereby.

'No.' Alan measured in powder, rammed the ball home, and primed the pan. Then he met my eyes. 'Sorry, brother Mark. Maybe I've got the wind up. Call me a coward if you like. Pass me your musket.'

I unslung the gun, and Alan took it out of my hands. 'Take this.'

I held his gun and watched him loading mine. 'Alan, thee knows I will not . . .'

'Ay, ay, don't tell me again. Just carry it, will you?' He grinned suddenly. 'We might find a sitting goose. You never know your luck.'

I took the loaded gun. Alan carried his across his chest and followed me on to the bluff. We stood about three feet from the edge – the sand was too crumbly to go close – and looked down. There was nothing to be seen either on the sparkling lake or the thin strip of sand below. We turned to go back.

Six warriors stood across our path, armed with knives and tomahawks. Dreadful swathes of human hair hung from their belts. Two wore eagle feathers, and they both had muskets, trained on us.

Alan raised his musket. A shot cracked. Alan cried out. I lunged to save him, too late. I saw him fall. The ground shifted under my feet. I stumbled back, and a plume of sand flew upwards as the cornice gave way and slid down after him.

All I could do was face my foes. The leader lowered his smoking musket. I had a loaded gun in my hand and unstable ground under my feet. I took two steps towards them, away from the cliff.

The leader – he wore a plume of eagle feathers – spoke to me. It sounded like a command. 'What is thee doing?' I asked indignantly, and realised as I did so that I was trembling – not from fear, I think – for I was very angry, and sounded it – but from the shock of Alan's fall. I held myself rigid so he wouldn't see me shake. 'We came here in peace.'

The same command, only louder.

'I came in peace,' I said again. 'Thee has no cause to hurt me.'

They said nothing to each other, but as one man they came a little closer. They had me trapped, and meant, it seemed, to take me whole. I had a loaded gun in my hand, which I knew well how to use, but they heeded it not.

The next moments seemed to pass very slowly: there was time for all the thoughts in the world to go through my head, of the life I had known, and the life that lies beyond all knowing in which I put my faith. But all this was thrust aside: a battle raged inside my head, as it were quite leisurely, although in truth it lasted less than two minutes – for they took their time, as if they were enjoying themselves. *They torture their prisoners of war to death – All bloody principles and practices we do utterly deny – chop small pieces off them – with all outward war and strife – arms, legs, privates – and fightings with outward weapons – until there's nothing left but a torso – for any end whatsoever – insert slivers of wood under their fingernails – under any pretence whatsoever – or with the eyes – and this is our testimony . . . our testimony . . . our testimony . . .*

I half-cocked the gun, and laid it at my feet.

They stood still, and so did I. I've never been so feart in all my life, but I showed it not. I met the eyes of the man who'd shot Alan, and held his gaze.

Then he pointed to me, and said something to his warriors. All my linguistic skills had ebbed away from me, but he repeated the one word several times, addressing it to me. '*Nigigwetagad. Nigigwetagad. Nigigwetagad.*'

Suddenly they turned away. Before I had time to think they'd vanished into the dunes, and I saw no more of them.

I sank down among the prickly grass, and shook like an aspen for the space of a full minute. I didn't begin to make head or tail of it all; I just knew I was feart. But I had to find Alan. I shouldered the gun and began walking along the edge of the dunes, looking for a safe way down. I couldn't see the beach directly below; the overhang was too great. Presently I found a place where the sand sloped steeply, but not so vertically that I wasn't able to slither down. I tried it, and lost my footing almost at once, but the sand was soft, and I slid, as on a scree run, until I reached the bottom. I was standing on a beach full ten feet wide, of firm-packed sand. I didn't like the look of the crumbling slopes above me, but that couldn't be helped. I strode back the way I'd come, scanning the ground ahead.

At first sight he looked like a bundle of clothes someone had dropped. I ran as fast as I could but I seemed so slow it was like a dream. I nearly tripped over his musket, which lay beside him, half buried in the sand. I stood over him. I thought he moved, but it was only my shadow that fell across him. He was all huddled up. I took him by the shoulder to pull him gently back, and felt my hand all sticky. I looked, and it was blood.

Alan's shirt was open at the neck. I slipped my hand inside it; his skin was slippery wet. When I felt the regular beat of his heart I let out a long sigh, and rolled him gently over. Then I ripped his bloodstained shirt open from the neck to the seam, and pulled it off him. He'd been shot high up on his shoulder; it was a nasty hole, and bleeding freely. I bundled the shirt into a pad and held it hard against the wound. Minutes passed. I kept pressing down, and watched his face. He was ashen-pale, but at last his eyelids flickered.

'Alan?'

He moaned a little, which he would not do, I thought, if he were fully conscious.

'Alan!'

The bleeding was slowing down: some of the shirt was still white, and the bloodstains had stopped spreading. 'Alan!'

His eyelids flickered again, and he spoke quite clearly. 'Where the *devil* d'you think you're going?'

'I'm going nowhere,' I said. I was taking the pressure off cautiously. He tried to move away from my hand. 'Keep still!'

'It's not *there*. It's my *leg*.' He sounded like a petulant but sleepy child.

I laid his hand over the blood-soaked dressing. 'Alan! Hold that there, if thee can.'

When I touched his left leg he cried out, and bit his lip. I cut away his breeches with my knife. There was no sign of injury, but the leg lay a little crooked. When I asked if he could move it the pain of trying made him gasp, and bite his lip till the blood came. I'd splinted a dog before, but never a man. I'd seen the barber from Ambleside do it though, when we picked up the fellow that fell over the Striding Edge in mist, the time I went to Grasmere to buy a tup and found myself dragged into a rescue party. I didn't think I'd live to be glad of that miserable day. I felt Alan brace himself, but when I straightened his leg he fainted again, which made it easier. I looked round for a splint. There was nothing on that empty beach which I could use. I picked up my musket and cautiously extracted the ball with my knife. I laid the ramrod alongside Alan's leg and strapped it firmly with my belt and his. Then I packed up the sand as tightly as I could around my handiwork. He was coming round again, and beginning to shiver. I had naught to cover him but my own shirt and breeches, which I took off and tucked around him as best I could.

'Alan! Is thee listening?'

His hands were deadly cold. The beach faced west. I

glanced up. The sun wouldn't strike him for hours yet. 'Alan. I have to leave thee. I'll bring Loic and the canoe. Thee mustn't move. Does thee hear me?'

'Mmm.' He stirred a little, and said thickly, 'Brother Mark.'

I rubbed his cold hands, and let go. 'I'll be as quick as I can.'

For all my haste it was well into the afternoon when we came back. When I came panting into the camp, half-naked and too short of breath to speak, the first thing I saw was Loic bent over the canoe, his hands red with resin putty, and a hole almost a foot square where he'd taken off the damaged birchbark. I never saw a patch put on so fast, but the resin had no time to set. 'It may come off,' said Loic, 'but we'll be close to shore. We'll have to risk it.'

I tied all three blankets in a bundle round the spare paddle. We took the two poles that went under the cargo. I pulled on my other shirt, and tied it round my middle with twine; I had only the one pair of breeks so I couldn't remedy that. We set off, paddling fast, rounding the north coast, and moving slowly – oh so slowly – south under the lowering dunes. I began to think we'd missed him. The distance round the island was vastly longer than the walk across it. At least the sun would be on him now. At last I saw the bluff with its little topknot of twisted pines. We pulled in close. If I hadn't recognised the bluff we'd never have found him; I'd packed the sand close round him till he was hardly visible. He was still flat on his back the way I'd left him, his arms folded across his bloodstained chest. It looked like a bier. I heard Loic's intake of breath. We crouched one on each side of him. Loic made some signs over him that might have been pagan or Popish; I know not. I took Alan's cold hand between my warm ones. 'Alan? Alan?'

'Go to hell,' whispered Alan weakly.

Loic looked at my makeshift splint, and suggested we also strap Alan's legs together while we moved him. With two pairs of hands it was much easier. We made a stretcher round him, rolled him in blankets, half launched the canoe, and lifted him in amidships on the two poles and the extra paddle. It was a desperate journey home, but the birchbark patch had only leaked a little when we got back to our camp, and the blankets took up the water. I could tell Alan was conscious by the deep line between his brows, and the rigidity of his mouth. His shoulder had stopped bleeding. I decided it was better to leave the shirt be than pull the wound open again.

'Loic.'

'*Oui.*'

'His leg will have to be set.'

'*Oui.*'

'Have you ever done this?'

'*Non.*'

I had the phial of laudanum my mother had given me. I'd carried it wrapped in flannel, along with my razor and toothbrush. I gave about a quarter of it to Alan on a spoon, and waited for him to grow sleepy. Loic said, 'We should give him brandy.'

'We have none.'

'I have this.' He reached among his own things and took out a small barrel I'd not seen before.

'Where did thee get that?'

'I brought it, *bien sûr*. It is foolish to travel without.'

'Alan said we'd take no spirits!'

'And I said nothing. He will need it now.'

I couldn't deny it. 'Not with laudanum. But later, yes.' Alan's breathing was changing; the laudanum was taking effect. 'Thee'll need to hold him firmly.'

'Do you know what to do?' asked Loic.

'I know with animals,' I said, 'And what's a man, if not an animal?'

I lied. It was not the same at all. 'Hold him firm. Ready?'

I pulled the leg straight as hard and steadily as I could. Alan lost consciousness at once. I couldn't tell if I'd set the bone right. I could only pray. We cut wooden splints, and bandaged them to him with the last of our trade calico. Presently Alan fell into an uneasy sort of sleep, and began to snore. I'd never known him do so before: either it was the drug, or being laid flat on his back like that.

Loic took a swig of brandy himself. 'Here, Mark!'

'I thank thee, no.'

Loic shrugged, and went back to the canoe. Later, when we were eating our pease – and regretting the goose – we talked about what we should do. 'We can't move him,' I said. 'He must keep still. We can't keep him warm on the water, either. If he gets too cold he'll die.'

'We can't stay here,' said Loic. 'Bad weather is coming. We must get off the island.'

'We can't move him.'

'Then the winter will come, and we will die. We must go home. But I am worried now, because look!' He pointed north-west.

I'd already seen the grey line of cloud rolling in towards us as the day waned. 'The weather's going to break, isn't it?'

'This will be a bad storm.'

He was right. The wind came in at dusk, and rain began to fall in torrents. By that time we'd rebuilt our shelter, dug a channel round it to drain off the rainwater, and weighed the canvas down with extra stones. We spent three nights huddled under our canoe and canvas shelter. Alan took up most of the room, and as the rain drummed on the canoe just above where we crouched, he was at first very cold, and then feverish, which frightened me. An open wound in a beast usually means it has to be shot, but a man must take the death that comes to him, and no help given. Alan wasn't conscious enough to keep quiet – for his courage was indisputable – and after a while he began to talk incoherently in some foreign tongue. I asked Loic what he was saying.

'I don't know,' said Loic. 'It's not any language I know.'

I gave Alan water to drink, piled the blankets over him, and dosed him with the rest of the laudanum to make him sleep. When the laudanum wore off he grew restless, throwing off the blankets and muttering incomprehensibly. I wouldn't let Loic give him brandy because of the fever. We lit a tallow dip in the lantern – we'd managed without using it all through the summer – so I could watch over Alan, but when that burnt out I could do little but feel for the blanket and try to keep it over him. I couldn't hear him because of the rain.

Loic went off before dawn. While I was boiling up water – I managed to make a little fire within our shelter – he came back with a bunch of long brown roots that he said were sarsaparilla. He set about making a poultice; from what he said the plant had the same effect as comfrey. When I sniffed the wound there was no taint of corruption. Perhaps I should have tried to dig the ball out, but I flinched at the very thought, and decided – Dr Day at Mackinac told me later I was right – it was safer to let it be.[2] I cleaned it and used Alan's spare shirt to make a clean bandage.

Loic and I were soon soaked to the skin, as the rain

---

[2] That ball is in Alan yet. I asked in my letter a year or two back if it ever troubled him. He said that, since I asked, his left shoulder was a touch rheumaticky in winter, but not half so bad as his leg, and that otherwise he was pretty hale, and reckoned to make old bones yet.

blew in at both ends of our shelter. We couldn't avoid touching the canvas, which made it leak. Loic mostly sat with his back to us, hugging his knees – Alan had all the blankets – and staring out at the swathes of rain as they swept over us. I'd never nursed a sick person, but I found that if I thought of him as a two-legged animal, rather than another man, it made it easier to do what was needed. I hoped he'd forget the violation; for the moment he was beyond caring.

'We should have moved into the clearing,' I remarked to Loic, after we'd gone out to batten down our canvas for the umpteenth time.

'When?' said Loic.

I'd never known Loic in such surly humour. In the end I asked him right out what was upsetting him.

'Because you're right. It is impossible to get Alan back to Mackinac. We should never have come back to South Manitou island. Unless we have a spell of fine weather, we cannot get home for winter. Even if we do, the lake will already be very cold. Even now it may be too late.'

'Then we'll have to spend the winter here.'

'No, we cannot. If we are here when winter comes we will die. The Indians don't stay. They go where there is hunting. In winter there must be meat.'

'There are deer.'

'How many deer? There is no hunting here. You don't know what it will be like! That is one thing! And there is also my family! What will Pakané be thinking, do you suppose? And my father? I told Pakané – I promised her – I would come back in winter, and now I cannot. She will think me drowned. This is why I am angry, since you ask.'

Rain pelted on the canvas in a sudden cloudburst. I could barely hear myself speak. 'If thee left us on the mainland here, in one of the villages, could thee get home then?'

'The canoe is too big for me to go alone. And after this there will not be many days when the lake is calm enough. And I keep telling you, at this time of year there are no villages. In any case, I said I would go with Alan. I will not leave him. I will not leave either of you. If I leave you now, you will both die. How can I go to *la messe de Noël* with that upon my conscience? I cannot.'

That night I lay awake, huddled in my wet coat, while desperate plans revolved in my head. Alan couldn't be moved. When the storm ended, the water might take days to calm. Tenth Month was almost over, and we were stuck on South Manitou, either with or without six armed and hostile warriors for company. They might, I supposed, fall upon us at any moment and add three scalps to their collection for very little effort. I wouldn't choose a night like this for that, or any other, expedition, myself, but still, it was an uncomfortable thought.

All this – or so it seemed in the dead hours before the day – was my fault. I'd dragged Alan back into a fruitless search for Rachel, who had probably been dead these two years and more, and because I'd done so, Alan now lay close to death himself. And we'd failed. In three months we'd found nothing. Rachel was lost. I should have accepted that when Judith's letter first came. She was lost, and I'd been a fool not to believe it.

The perils of the lake in autumn had been impressed upon me again and again. The water was already too cold to survive an accident, and too cold for an injured man to lie in a canoe. And there was another problem: if Alan had to lie flat – or even sit propped up with his splinted leg stretched out – how then would we load the cargo? It would be madness to leave anything behind, and yet madness to take it all . . . I thought out various schemes for loading our gear, and rejected every one. We'd be down to two paddlers anyway; a badly trimmed boat would make things twice as hard. There was no knowing from one day to the next – nay, from one hour to the next – what weather the winds might bring. The ten miles to the mainland seemed endless leagues away. It was the longest open water we had to cross, but when I thought of the weary miles north to Mackinac, my heart failed me. Besides, we couldn't move Alan. But if we stayed? We had – I laid them out in my mind's eye – less than ten pounds of pease, even less flour, a birchbark container of dried fish, one pound of salt, maybe less. The strips of dried meat were all gone. There were berries in the woods, but how would we preserve them? We could fish if the weather got better, until the ice came. The geese would move on. We had no winter clothes – Alan no longer had even a shirt to his back – though we had furs if we had the means to sew them. We could make shelter. We had guns – I still had to clean the sand out of Alan's musket – but too little powder and lead. The axe was big enough to split kindling, but not to cut logs. No saw, no snowshoes, no sledge, no birchbark . . . If the winter caught up on us, we were dead men. But if we set out . . . and there was a war out there. The Americans might even now be between us and Mackinac, or at Mackinac itself. We hadn't time to be wary . . . I tossed restlessly to and fro.

Then – which was a fatal mistake – I began thinking about Pakané and Waase'aaban, and Loic's promise to Pakané; he wasn't the only one: I'd told Waase'aaban I'd come back. It would be terrible if she were waiting for me, and I did not come. It would also be terrible if she did not wait for me, and I did come. Perhaps it would be worst of all if she did wait for me, and I did come . . . But even as I contemplated the evils resulting from my sin, my baser part began to re-live that sin, even as I first committed it. And it was that memory – not prayer, repentance, nor a considered solution to the problems that beset us – that finally soothed my brain and let me drift into a dreamless sleep.

CHAPTER 21

NOTHING IS EVER SO BAD AS IT SEEMS IN THE DEAD hours before the morning. The storm passed. We moved our camp into the clearing, where the mosquitoes were all gone. We built a shelter, protecting our square of canvas with green cedar saplings and moss with earth packed over it, and we covered the floor with a thick mattress of cedar boughs. We were never so wet again, though more bands of rain came sweeping through. Alan's wound did not putrefy, which is what I'd dreaded, but slowly began to heal. I think his collar bone was broken too, but I durst not meddle any more than I had to, so I let it be. I went out alone, and shot a goose as it flew over the little lake. I had to swim to retrieve it: the water was very shallow, but I sank into mud so deep I couldn't wade. The nights were cold, and day after day Lake Michigan was grey and yeasty, with white-capped waves in the open water. The forest had turned to yellow and gold, all but the sombre cedar groves, which seemed the more dim and chill as the sun sank lower.

The sands of time were running out fast. The fever left Alan very weak, but deprived him of neither wit nor courage. I'd liked him for a long time; it was only now that I learned to respect him. I knew when he was in pain by his silence. There was no more laudanum, so I let Loic dose him with brandy, and we made tisanes of wintergreen, which was better than nothing. As the wound healed I grew more concerned about the broken leg. I made a support for it, and weighted the end. When Alan realised I'd, as he put it, 'ruined all his clothes' he borrowed my needle and thread and sat propped against the support I'd rigged for him, painstakingly sewing up his rent breeches with the kind of huge stitches one sees on the edge of blankets. He was too tired to work at it for more than a few minutes at a time. I gave him my spare shirt, and put off worrying about our lack of winter clothing.

The day came when we woke to a grimin of snow and when I went to fill the kettle I found the lake clear grey, and as flat as a pond. The sky was bright and chill, without a wisp of cloud. I broke the film of ice, and washed my face in freezing water. When I turned to go back with the full kettle, there was Loic at the top of the beach, scanning the horizon.

'What does thee think?'

'I think now, or die,' said Loic.

It was already past dawn. Loic had finished mending the canoe; its birchbark covering was as seaworthy as it could possibly be. We had so little food now that everything fitted. We lifted Alan in amidships with his back against the bales, and one blanket under him and two over him. I'd made a sling for his arm with twine and a handkerchief. I'm sure he neglected to use it when I was not by; by now he could use his left hand almost as well as ever.

We set a course for the great sand dunes the Indians call Sleeping Bear. Slowly the Manitou Islands faded into faint humps on the horizon behind us, and the land ahead took shape. I was in the bow, with only the water in front of me. It was very cold, and very quiet. I fancied I could hear the lake breathing around us, in a long faint rise and fall. Otherwise there was only the rapid swish and dip of the two paddles. We stopped once. I could see that Alan was shivering uncontrollably. There was nothing I could do about it. He took a swig of brandy from Loic; I was doubtful whether it would help for long. I wiped the sweat from my face with my sleeve, dipped my tin cup, and took a long drink of water.

'*Allez allez,*' called Loic from behind me, and we fell into our fast rhythm again. My shoulders ached; we'd been too long ashore. I thought of Marc and Jean-Pierre, Jacques and Alban, doubtless all at home in Montreal by now. With a dozen voyageurs the few miles to the mainland would be nothing on a day like this.

We paddled in past the north point of the dunes, and into the wide bay where we'd camped before. There wasn't much daylight left, so we made a voyageurs' camp in our old place at the edge of the pine trees. Alan was chilled right through, so we built a big fire. The night was still and clear; I thought our luck might hold. I was wrong. When I looked out the next morning, it was snowing.

Our good fire had done its work, though. Just before noon we heard voices. Alan flung aside the sling and reached for his musket. Loic took up the other gun – we kept both loaded at half cock – but it was I that scrambled out of the shelter first. Through the swirling snow I saw three people, clad from head to foot in furs and buckskins. They had no guns, and to my relief the middle one was a woman.

'*Boozhoo,*' I said. '*Biindigen.*'

Loic crawled out after me, and I let him do the talking. 'They say this is their hunting ground – I tell them we had no choice but to come here – I say how we could not leave South Manitou because we have a wounded man – they say we cannot stay here – if we want we can make a camp on the other side of the little lake – I ask if they will trade with us –

they have furs and birchbark – but not food – I say we have furs, we need food – they say they will trade some rice and birchbark for my gun, and half the powder and shot. The fact is, Mark, I think they have many trade furs still from last year's hunting. They've not been able to sell because of the war. That's why they're anxious to trade with us.'

'For thy gun! But we must hunt!'

'We must have clothes and shelter first. I think we have no choice.'

We looked at each other, while snowflakes whirled in the air between us. 'We'd better do it at once, then,' I said.

I listened hard to the rest of the talk, and caught the gist of it. When Loic told me he was going to their lodge now, taking the trade goods, I said, 'Ay, I understood that. Will they help thee carry the things back?'

I lost track of the quick words that followed. 'For the rest of our tobacco they'll bring everything to the place by the little lake. There was a wigwam there before. It's a good place, they say. Then I'll come back and fetch you both.'

'Loic.'

'*Oui?*'

'Thee won't mention that we have another . . . of those?'

'*Je ne suis pas fou!*'

While Loic was gone I gathered wood, while the snow showers came and went. It was a thick wet snow that melted almost as fast as it came. I didn't bother with the little axe, but used my weight and strength to break up dead branches. By the time Loic came back I had a big cache of wood under a shelter of boughs. I set up our trap, and the very first night I caught a porcupine. Beginner's luck, Alan said. I agreed it was true my success owed more to Providence than to my particular skill. I saved the quills carefully and roasted the meat on a wooden spit. Alan, to my surprise, took my rebuke about luck to heart, for he said a grace over our meat in the Episcopalian fashion, giving thanks where it was due.

Loic was gone three days. I was beginning to be anxious, but when he turned up he was pulling an empty sled, and wearing a fur cap, a deerskin tunic with the hair turned inwards, buckskin leggings, mittens, and thick winter moccasins. 'She says they will make you and Alan the same from our furs, if you will trade her your belts with the metal buckles.' Loic hesitated, and I was just thinking that the bargain was too good to be true, when he added, 'And the rest of my brandy.'

'We agreed we would not trade liquor! Alan gave me his word we would not!'

Loic looked at me dispassionately. 'You would rather die?'

I was silent.

'I said you would agree to this,' said Loic quietly, 'but that we would not part with our knives.' The wigwam, he said, was in a good dry place close to a creek, about three miles inland. The Indian family had their lodge about the same distance away in the opposite direction. He'd promised we wouldn't hunt on their side of the lake. Given that we had no choice in the matter, said Loic, they'd been generous with both rice and bark. 'I promised we'd get the sled back two days from now, and that we would take the furs to make your clothes, which she says will soon be ready.'

Forgive us our trespasses, as we forgive them that trespass against us. I could feel a damp chill down my back under my coat, where wet snow had soaked through the wool. Ahead lay far worse cold than that, and far greater hunger than the empty feeling under my belt. I couldn't bring myself to meet Loic's eyes. 'Ay,' I said. 'Very well.'

We took Alan to our new camp on the sled before the first snow melted, and a painful journey it must have been for him. We skirted the maple groves where the Indians had their sugar camp in spring, and headed south. The scrub-covered dunes rose steeply on our right, sheltering us from Lake Michigan, so there was but a thin strip of forest between the sandhills and the inland lake. The site of the old wigwam was on rising ground, where a little creek flowed into the lake. We mended the old frame, and re-lashed the saplings together. Loic showed me how to unroll the fragile birchbark, and lay it round in overlapping layers. We caulked it with moss on the inside, and laid our mattress of pine branches, with the blankets over them. Once we had a roof over our heads, and the fire going within, everything seemed more possible. The little beck ran close by the wigwam – it turned out to be fast-flowing enough never to freeze completely. I used to hear it in my sleep, and dream I was at Highside.

We spent the first weeks exploring the country and getting in all the food we could. It was a short climb – less than two hundred feet, I reckon – to the top of the dunes, and from there I got the lie of the land: to the east the endless miles of rolling forest, still clad in the blazing tatters of its autumn finery; to the west Lake Michigan and the low-lying islands that spattered the water from here to the northern shore, as if someone had thrown a handful of coins across a puddle. As the weeks passed we watched the ice form and settle, until there was a whole landscape between us and the Manitous, sculpted in wild ridges and humps like a silent storm-tossed sea. The dunes themselves were shaped by wind and water even as I watched. I grew to love this shifting desert of sand and ice. At least it was open, like my own hills. But it offered us nothing; our days were perforce spent in the forest searching for food, but whenever I could, even in the depths of winter when the snow lay like a blanket over sand and ice alike, so there was no telling the one from the other any more,

I would still climb the dunes in the teeth of the wind, so as to see out.

But first there was work to be done. Loic said, 'There will be meat all winter, but we cannot live on meat alone: we would be ill. While it is still fall we must gather what we can.'

The berry season was long over, but between the early snows Loic showed me where to gather other foods. All our foraging, and hunting too, was done around the western shores of the inland lake. The lake I discovered to be shaped like a figure of eight, and our end was the smaller part, close up under the dunes, so walking the woods was an endless scramble up and down the sandhills. Wherever a big tree had fallen we could see the bare sand under the thin layer of soil. For all that the place was thickly wooded with beech, maple and hemlock; it seems the great trees of Michigan can grow in earth that would barely support an English cornfield. In the gullies between the sand ridges there were cedar swamps, which became our main hunting grounds, though the going was pretty hard among the deep bogs and rotting wood. The lake shore was often impassable, for the sandy beach was flooded over. One day we walked over to the outlet, which lay in the Indians' hunting grounds, and found the river jammed by floodwood, which accounted for the high level of the lake, but there was naught that we could do about it. Once the lake froze over it was much easier to get about, as the ice became our main highway. Soon the empty white expanse was criss-crossed with paths through the snow made by our passing.

At first, a few filberts were still left on the hazels, but we got much more of the mast of sweet acorns that lay thick under the bur oak. Cooked, they tasted much like potatoes. We dug in the mud of the lake shore for a tuberous root, which we smoke-dried in the wigwam, then boiled in the kettle with our meat, just like the hot-pots my mother used to make. Both earth and water – for there were strange little potatoes to be had on the bulrush roots, though these were pretty much shrivelled away, it being so late in the year – were punishingly cold. However, our need was great, so we gathered every day until everything froze over.

Loic also collected medicines. I was impressed by his knowledge, but he told me he knew very little; he wished now he'd listened better when he was young. He boiled up tamarack bark every day so I could treat Alan's shoulder with it, and certainly the wound healed very cleanly, and the fever never came back. Loic brought in other medicines too, including remedies both for sore gums and ill digestion, which was a good thing, given that we subsisted largely on boiled meat. He'd kept back one twist of tobacco that was his own, and he taught me how to bury a little piece of it in the ground wherever we harvested, by way of thanks to the spirits of that place.

I learned far more about trapping from Loic than I had from Thomas back in Yonge Street. He showed me how to make traps for fishers[1] on fallen tree trunks, and for rabbits among the brush, and the best part of the creek to lay the otter trap. He taught me to look for raccoons sleeping on the deserted squirrels' nests, where we could shoot them down out of the trees. Right up until midwinter we were getting such small game. All the time I was learning how to walk in the forest, how to keep my direction, where to watch for deadfalls, how to be silent and how to be aware of danger. Loic showed me the kind of places where bears made their dens: under piles of brushwood, or among the cedar roots. Sometimes we made the rabbits come out by jumping on the brush piles, and Loic told me how once his father had done that and woken a monstrous black bear

[1] These are somewhat like our own pine martens.

from its winter sleep. I was cautious about the brush piles after that.

Loic made himself a bow from a pine sapling and deergut, and also half a dozen arrows, to make up for the loss of the musket. He cut up one of our tin mugs to make sharp points, and showed me how to use the flight feathers from hawks to balance the arrows and make them fly. He said in some ways the bow was better than a gun, being silent and giving the hunter a second chance, if not more. I went out with the musket sometimes, and wasted too much ball trying to get one of the wild turkeys which gathered in the woods in noisy flocks. At first I was amused by these ungainly farmyard-looking birds with their big black bodies and tiny scarlet heads. I thought at first it would be as easy as shooting a chicken in the yard – not that I'd ever done such a thing – but the fact was I've never encountered such wily birds before or since, and always they eluded me. I did get hares sometimes, but there was no great merit in that, for the first I got were in a thaw, when I caught each of them in their white snow-coats against the darkness of the cedar roots where they crouched, evidently thinking themselves invisible.

Loic shot a turkey with his bow and arrow, and showed me how to use the wing bones to make a turkey call to bring the birds in close. They hear so well, Loic told me, that they can hear if thee flaps the wing feathers against thy leg and let them fall, by way of a decoy. He thought I touched the first one I aimed for, but their feathers were so thick it was hard to bring one down, even if one hit it. He taught me to look for the ridges where the turkeys foraged – they like to get a clear view all round – and how to read the birds by their droppings, and how to creep up close without being seen or heard. I never managed it, and Loic only succeeded once, when I wasn't with him. I couldn't leave the matter alone though – my pride was hurt, I suppose – and still I watched the turkeys, and planned and thought, and all for naught. To add insult to the injury, when turkeys forage for acorns they leave little printed arrows in the soil telling thee exactly which way they're going. I knew where they roosted, too. The flock I had my eye on had chosen a big tree that overhung the lake. I crept down at dusk one night, and waited in the shelter of a cedar trunk, my musket ready primed, until the birds had all flown in. Then I slowly raised the gun, took my time about sighting, and got my bird. It was easily found, a little dark blob on the gleaming ice. So I won, I suppose. I'd like to have hit one flying, but this I never did.

The deer trails were easy to follow. In the middle of the day we often walked quietly through the forest, noticing where the deer had been feeding off bark, or scraping the snow away to get at the undergrowth beneath. Deer are not so different from sheep, and the hunter not so far from the shepherd, when it comes down to it. I wasn't used to the encircling forest, though, and would have been feart of losing myself, even with Alan's compass in my pouch. Loic never asked to see the compass, and yet this part of the Michigan Territory was as strange to him as it was to me. 'If you know what to look for,' he said, when I asked him about it, 'You can read any place. The signs are the same, just the way they're put together is a little different.'

I shot my first deer on a night of full moon. It was easy to find the deer trail even in the half dark under the trees. We crept upwind round the cedar swamp at the end of the lake. When we came out of the trees it was bright as day, and the lake ice shone like polished glass. There was a little icy wind; otherwise all was quiet. I never saw a land so cold, nor yet so alien in its night-time transformation. We might have been the only men on earth. The herd was foraging close to the rushes. I took my time, aimed true, and got my buck. He was a big fellow, and kept us busy a couple of days with the butchering and getting all the meat in strips to dry. We cut the rawhide into long strips for our snowshoes. His antlers had eight tines, and we were able to make sundry items that we needed out of the horn. I reckon the meat from that buck, along with the rice and roots we had, and bits of small game, kept us going a couple of months.

Loic taught me how to fish through the ice on the little lake. When it froze too thick to cut a hole near the bank we walked out to where the ice was thin enough, but as the winter set in, it grew harder to break a hole, for the only tools we had were our knives, the little axe, and a mallet we made from a heavy stone lashed to a wooden handle.

The hardest time we had was around the end of First Month. The snow blew fiercely, and for days at a time we were cooped up in the wigwam. I made a pair of crutches for Alan, which I bound with rawhide. When his shoulder mended enough to use them he soon became adept. Whenever he tried putting weight on the broken leg it hurt him. I'd thought of him as an impatient fellow, but he never expressed any frustration over his hurts, except in jest.

While the weather was so cold Loic and I took turns to stay awake to keep the fire going. I felt like a hibernating animal, as days and nights, sleeping and waking, merged into an endless dozy firelight. But if the day were clear we made the most of it, and the sudden sharpness of the outside air would have me broad awake at once. We had to stir ourselves quickly to make the most of such small gaps in the weather, taking our chance to fetch more wood. But we couldn't hunt or fish; the buck was about finished, and our food was running low.

When we couldn't hunt we talked about it instead. Both Loic and Alan had plenty of stories. We only had a couple of tallow dips for the lantern, which must be kept in case of dire need, so in the dark hours – which was all day when the blizzards came – we had only firelight, and could do little but listen to each other. The very notion of storytelling was new to me. At home we passed our winter evenings in reading from the Bible or Friends' Journals, or considering the Advices from Yearly Meeting and other matters. Or we sat in silence, while my mother and Rachel span or sewed, and I read, or whittled small items out of wood, and my father sat motionless, gazing into the fire, for the only idle hour in his long day.

One night Loic was telling me about bears. 'A bear is not at all like a man,' he said, 'And yet bears are also actually people, or have been people. If you talk to a bear, it is good. It shows him you are not afraid.'

'But I would be afraid,' I pointed out. 'And with good reason, from all thee's told me.'

'*Oui*. But it is also something else. If you go to hunt bear, first you must fast, and then you must sweat – I have told you about this. You can say this is to sweat off your own scent before you hunt. That is true. But that is not all the truth. If you go out as a threat to an animal – to any creature in the world – you must make your peace first. And this you do long before you go to hunt. It is the way you live. When I was growing up I was sent to far-off cousins – my mother's family were dead – so I could learn. Alone I must go into the cedar swamp, and there I must survive. This is how a boy becomes a man. He brings himself close to death. His mind is already on the other side. He must learn how to be in that place. He must be careful how he does this, because perhaps he will get too far to the other side, and not be able to come back. There are spirits round us all the time. In this lodge our own spirits are with us. You believe that, Mark?'

'Ay,' I said. 'I believe that.'

'We have our senses that tell us these things, just as the

animals have. We have them, but we don't use them so well. We must learn. You learn by going into the woods. You go into the woods and you sit down. When you have no interference in your mind you can do this, just going into the woods. You have to face your own death, and not be afraid of dying. Go into the woods and sit down, and think, "I'm part of that." And you know it. Your skin starts crawling. If you find your place and sit there, where there's nothing to distract you, ask for a sign from the spirit world. Ask for your dream. It will come. Always you ask me about the bear, Mark. You can feel him. If you are afraid, you can call on him to help you. If you hunt him, you make your peace with him, and maybe he gives his life for you.'

'No,' I said. 'The first part I believe, but not that.'

'Then why do you always ask? You have dreamed about this again, I think.'

I hesitated. 'It doesn't mean anything. After thee told me about the bear under the brush pile, I dreamed there was a bear in the woodshed at Highside. I had to lead my sister past the door. She was feart; I was pretending not to be. And then it was not a bear at all, but my own dog, Bowder. I laid my hand on his neck, and we walked along together, and I was not feart after all. But it was nothing, only a dream.' I was feeling annoyed with myself for bothering to tell them about it.

'You know that bear,' said Loic. 'I think you will see him when you die.'

'I hope not. I'd rather die in my own country.'

Loic ignored that. 'When you put your finger into that bear's fur and feel his hide and walk with him, then you will be dying. Don't walk too far with that bear. Don't feel that bear's hide and walk with him until you're ready to die.'

'I didn't,' I said, even though the conversation made no sense. 'I just laid my hand on his neck, and it was Bowder.'

We sat in silence for a while. Loic laid fresh wood on the fire, and it spat at us while the flames rose and crackled. 'What are you thinking, brother Mark?' asked Alan idly.

'I was thinking about how Esau came in hungry from his hunting, and sold his birthright for a pottage of lentils. Somehow I'd always had the impression that Jacob was in the right of it. Or at least, I'd never really thought about it.'

'And now you favour Esau?'

'I don't know what I think,' I said, and that at least was true.

'Loic,' said Alan presently. 'Now tell us a story about yourself.'

'Myself?' said Loic in surprise. 'There is little to say about that.'

He was silent for a while; I thought perhaps we were to be disappointed, but I waited patiently.

'This is a story about my father,' said Loic at last. 'My father, Martin Kerners, was at first a voyageur. He came to Mackinac from Montreal. He worked for MacTavish and McGillivray, and afterwards for some other companies. He liked best to be free. One year he went into the south of Lake Michigan and spent the winter there, to trade. Martin Kerners set up his post in the hunting ground of an Ottawa man, who had once been a leader among his people. When this man had been quite young the smallpox came. He had seen terrible things. After the smallpox came there were so few left living that there were none to lay out the dead. When the people died they rotted in the lodges. The stench was terrible. Some of the lodges he burned with fire. Ghosts walked. The two people who were left went away, and after that they never came back to the summer village any more.

'The grandparents of Martin Kerners came from a land called Morbihan, in a country called Bretagne. It was a land like this one, only the sea was salt. You could not drink it. In Morbihan there was a lake, but a little part of it bled into the sea. There were many islands. The islands were the homes of Manitous. The houses of the Manitous were easy to see, being built of stone and sometimes very great. Twice a day the sea came into the lake and went out. When the waters of the sea poured into the lake of Morbihan they came faster than the rapids on the Mattawa River. No boat could ply against them. When the sea went out, where there had been water there was a great plain of mud. From this plain you could harvest a plant called *salichon*, which made every dish taste delicious, such was the power of this herb. There were sand dunes just as there are here. Gorse bushes grew on the sand dunes, also blackberries, raspberries and other berries in the woods, but not all the ones that we have here. There was as much fish as any man could eat. In winter it didn't snow as it does here, but the storms at sea were very dangerous. Men could not fish. If their families were hungry and they went to fish, often they were drowned. There were many widows in Morbihan, and many fatherless children. Such a one was my father's grandmother. She it was who married my father's grandfather, and came with him on a ship with white sails spread to the wind like the wings of a bird, over the great ocean, to the country called Québec.

'In the beginning a saint dwelt in the land of Morbihan, and when she saw how men had to brave the sea, or starve, she took pity on them, and made it her task to watch over them. This she has done ever since. Neither forest nor ocean can divide her from her children, however far they travel. In my grandparents' language her name was Ker Anna. When my people came across the sea to Québec, they brought her with them. But when they came here, they must speak French, and so they called her Sainte Anne. She is here; she watches over the canoes and all the other ships that cross the lakes. She watches over us this winter, and I am happy because of that.

'Martin Kerners remembered his grandfather well, and listened to his stories so that one day he would be able to tell his son. When Martin Kerners went into the land of the Ottawa to trade, he came at last to the lodge of the man who had no people – this is what he is called – because all his people had died of the smallpox. Only his daughter still lived with him. All her family were gone – her mother, her brothers – everyone she had known. She came back from the borders of death, and found only her father still in the world of the living. She bore the marks of her sickness ever after. Some men said that she was ugly, and made the sign against evil when she passed. But she was not ugly, nor evil. She had no magic of that kind – this I know well, for she was my mother – and since only two years ago she is dead. And that is the story of my father, Martin Kerners, whom you know.'

I saw no reason why Loic should say more about himself, but Alan pressed him to do so, and as the weeks passed, he did tell us things now and then. He'd spent most of his early years at the cabin on Bois Blanc; only once did he talk directly about growing up among his mother's people.

'After my twelfth winter they sent me away,' he told us. 'On Bois Blanc my mother taught me all she could, but how can a woman teach a boy to become a man? I mean a man among her people, *vous comprenez*, for I had always my father with me, and so I became a Frenchman, but that is another matter. No man begins to be himself until he has been given his dream. His dream is what he lives for; it is why he is alive. Only among my mother's people could this come to me. Just as Gitchi Manitou had his vision and made it into the world we know, so we must make our own lives in the same way.

'So I went away with my far cousins to a place by Lake Superior where there are very many islands. It came to *Manoominike-giizis* – the moon of the rice harvest. Our rice lake was two days' journey from Lake Superior. It was a long lake, and from it a river flowed yet further into the land. At the rice camp I refused to eat, and though everyone tempted me with food I would not take it. I marked my face with charcoal, and I would not eat. Then my cousins came to me – for they were to me the father and the uncles I did not have – and they took me to an old beaver lake far up the river. On a little island among the reeds they built me a wigwam of withies, and there they left me, and after that I was alone.

'For five days I fasted, while the moon waned in the sky. Never in my life had I lain in a lodge alone. There were no paths – the island was very small – only shallow winding creeks all round, and the river flowing through the heart of the swamp. I made myself a raft of withies and bound it with rushes. I took my knife and cut myself a sort of paddle from an alder stump. In the daytime I explored the lake right down as far as the beaver dams, creeping among the reeds in my little craft. I followed the ways of the ducks and the heron, and sometimes I would disturb a moose standing in the cool water, and it would scramble away with great splashings. But I was not loud like a moose in my comings and goings. No, I was as silent as a moorhen, and even the otters didn't hear that I was there.

'I tried to make a better raft. I paddled to the edge of the forest and cut birch saplings and bound them together, more in the shape of a canoe than my withy raft had been. It was a bad place to be without a real canoe. I felt like a bird with its wing feathers cut off, not to have a canoe. I thought, when I go back, the first thing I shall do is make my own canoe.

'Thinking this, I fell asleep. And now I will tell you a story:

'A long time ago a young man came to Nanubushu's wigwam on Mackinac Island. He found the Manitou smoking his pipe outside in the cool of the evening. The young man laid his gift of tobacco at the feet of Nanubushu, and said to him, "Manitou Nanubushu, I have come far to find you. Will you give me one thing?" Nanubushu looked the young man in the eyes, took the tobacco, and began to fill his pipe.

'So the young man said to Nanubushu, "Only one thing do I ask. I want a canoe of my own, as good as any canoe ever built. Give me a canoe, and the strength to paddle it, so I can go wherever I want in the wide world. This is all I ask."

'Nanubushu took his pipe from his mouth and said, "Fast for three more days, young man, and then go back to your village. Take a gift of tobacco and spread it upon the wide waters. Gather cedarwood and birchbark, spruce root and resin, and for each gift that you take from the forest lay down your gift in return. Take nothing more than you need. And tell your people that you are *E-ntaa-jiimid*" (which is to say, *vous comprenez*, a good paddler). "And now go away, before you ask me for too much!"'

Loic's stories were so unlike anything I'd ever heard that I used to fall asleep with strange images in my mind, and dream wild dreams. But our real troubles hadn't gone away. Not only our food, but also our powder and lead were very low, and for three weeks we'd been unable to hunt. Loic told me about the French priests of old, who boiled up the leather binding of their bibles and ate that, and Alan remarked that whole tribes had survived the winter on naught but skins and bones. They appeared to take the matter lightly, but I was feeling the pinch of hunger for the first time in my life. I have a good appetite – always have had – but even in the bad years of the late '90s we never actually ran short of food at Highside. One evening I watched Alan – for about that time he took over the cooking, saying at least he was fit for that – measure out a little rice into a stock of boiled hide from the buck, and it dawned on me that I was the only one to whom this ache of hunger was anything new. I thought of my boyish appetite in my growing years, and remembered my father rebuking me, saying, 'I think a fourth helping of mutton is more than any man needs,' and feeling ashamed and humiliated. Alan and Loic were both slighter men than I; I found myself wondering where Alan had been when he was thirteen, and what kind of life he had known then.

The day came when we boiled up the last of the lead – it barely filled the ladle – and pressed it into the moulds. There were four balls in each mould. We still had shot, but Second Month was not yet over. There were two months to go, at least, before the lake was open. In two days we'd be out of meat entirely.

'So, we don't use ball for anything but deer now,' said Loic. 'In fact, for anything but a big buck. You will forget the turkeys now, Mark, will you not?'

The next morning was bright and sunny, but my heart was low and I was hungry. I sat on a log in the sun, lashing a split in one of my snowshoes with a length of sinew. The snowshoes weren't as good as the ones I'd made at Yonge Street, for I'd had naught but my pocket knife for whittling, and the boiling pot to steam the wood. I heard nothing, but I caught a sudden movement at the tail of my eye, and looked up.

If thee looks into the eyes of one thee knows will kill thee, thee won't forget. I knew him at once, and the two men with him. I'd last seen him on the dunes of South Manitou island, after he'd shot Alan, whom I regarded as my brother.

I put down my snowshoe, and stood up.

'*Nigigwetagad.*'

They had a fresh-killed buck with them, hung from a length of sapling between two men. I couldn't help it: my eyes were drawn that way, and my desire must have shown in my face.

'*Gibakade na?*'

'Ay,' I said.

'*Nigigwetagad!*' He laughed, and said something I could not follow. I shook my head.

'*Nigigwetagad!*' Then he beckoned to his companions, and they turned away, the dead buck swinging on its pole between them, and disappeared among the trees.

Alan had heard nothing. When I went inside and told him about it he whistled, and said, 'We could have guessed they hadn't gone far. This must be their hunting ground. I don't think their lodge can be close by; we'd have seen them before.'

'The other folk – the ones we traded with – didn't say anything.'

'Why should they? I wonder who he is.'

Alan didn't know the word *Nigigwetagad*. When Loic came back off the ice with the first fresh fish we'd had for weeks, I asked him.

'It means "grey",' said Loic. 'Just the colour: "grey".'

Alan grinned, 'Not much grey about you now, Mark. What'll they say in Meeting when you turn up next winter dressed in skins and rabbit furs?'

'Those warriors will have heard about you,' said Loic, pursuing his own thought. '"The man in grey who will not kill." If they had not heard the story I think you would be dead.'

'So it was worth spending your summer arguing with me in public,' said Alan.

'It would make sense for them,' said Loic. 'The Indians

also have men who are not warriors. There is no dis-respect.'

'That was a fine buck they had,' I said wistfully.

'Be glad it wasn't you, brother Mark.'

The next day dawned icy and bright. I loaded the musket and primed it, put my other three balls in my gun bag, and headed for our lake. I crossed the snow-covered ice, where walking was easy, till I reached a thickly wooded area on the east bank. I hadn't been this way since before midwinter, when we'd collected mast from under the big oaks. The trees were very old, and huge dead branches reached out horizontally over my head. Loic said it was a bad place for deadfalls, but there was no wind. There was a layer of hard frost on the snow. Usually my feet didn't sink in, but in sheltered places the crust broke and I found myself floundering in a couple of feet of soft snow. The deer had mostly run easily over the top, but there was a big fellow who'd broken through the ice here and there just as I was doing.

The trail led me through thickets of saplings growing through deep brush. The deer had made a narrow path, which I followed from tree to tree, ducking under thin branches as I went. I came to a steep bank held together with tree trunks, where the ground had washed away. I was about to grab hold of a branch and swing myself up, but then I thought the herd might be very close, on the far side of the bank maybe. I stopped to check the priming on my gun.

I heard a curious huffing sound, and looked up. Less then fifteen feet away, halfway up the bank, there was a great black bear. I saw its brown eyes fixed on me. It reared on its hind legs like a man, and swatted the air with a huge paw. I saw five long claws like knives. As I raised my gun it dropped on four legs, head lowered. I fell to my knees – I had to get below the head – as it charged. I fired. It didn't stop – it was on me – I rolled down the slope and felt a blow on my back like a falling rock, and a sudden sting like ice. I thought to die. Suddenly I was free. I scrambled to my feet, unsheathing my knife, and ran desperately for the nearest tree. I made it. From the shelter of its trunk I looked behind me. The bear was not two yards away. I dodged back. There could be but one end to this game. I clutched the tree trunk, trying to look both ways at once. I heard that same huffing sound again, and dodged the other way. I peered round the tree. There it was, watching me. Before I'd ducked out of sight it rose on its hind legs again, as tall as I was. For a moment we were both quite still. Then it cried out – a long human moan – a sound of so much sorrow that it pierced right through me, as if my blood were frozen in my veins. The great beast keeled over, and lay still.

I gazed at it for what seemed a great space of time, but it never moved. Very cautiously I left my tree trunk and stood over the body. The mouth was stretched open; I never saw such teeth. Below the head the snow was pink with spreading blood. I looked at the chest below the throat; there was blood in the thick fur. Warily I bent down, and saw the hole where my shot had gone home.

When I was quite sure the beast was dead I fell to my knees in the snow beside its body. My limbs were shaking, and my heart was throbbing in my chest. I fought to get my breath, and then I laid my hand on the thick fur. I was still nervous, for all I knew I'd made my kill. The fur was not entirely black: there were different shades of brown in it as well. It smelt pretty strong. The bear was very big – as big as me – but more compact – heavier. Why had it left its den? It ought not to be here. My back stung. No man could ever have dealt me such a clout. I felt over my shoulder. The deerskin was ripped right open. I looked at my shaking hand and saw blood on it.

I did as Loic had taught me – not the manner of it, but the matter – and gave my Saviour more heartfelt thanks than I had ever done before that it was not I who lay dead on the forest floor. I thanked him that my shot had gone home, and that we had meat now to bring us to the end of winter, and we would not die. And in my prayer I had a consciousness of him whom I addressed which was entirely new to me. Had he not created all things, and given each of his creatures its own nature? For the beasts of the field there is neither right nor wrong; we are what we are. He was not a God of gentleness to me then, but fierce and uncompromising, for all that he had shown me mercy. It was as if he said to me, 'This is the way I made the world, a life for a life, and to each according to his own nature.' I cannot explain it – I seemed to have come to the heart of what I sought. Rachel was not found – I had failed in that – but something quite different had been vouchsafed to me. Extraordinarily, when my prayer was done, I felt at ease.

That was not all that I did. When I told Loic I could not take part in his rituals, he was more upset than I'd ever seen him. He said there were certain things I must do, or revenge would be taken on us all. I thought it over, and it seemed better to let him have his way. If there were nothing in it, what harm could it do? So we boiled the bear's skull clean, and Loic made patterns on it with my ink.[2] He said we should have had colours, but there were none. We hung the skull in the wigwam where its empty eyes looked down on us in the firelight, and in the flicker of the flames it sometimes seemed to move. We

[2] He nearly finished the bottle, which is why I had to cease writing my journal early in Third Month, and was not able to resume the narrative until we got back to Mackinac.

cut the claws out of their fur cases and polished them. Loic strung them on a rawhide cord and hung them below the skull. He burned the last of his tobacco and some sage in a bowl, which he left smoking before the skull as an offering to the spirit of him who had given his life that we might live. I could not think that such practices were in any way consonant with the Principles of my Religious Society, but neither could I explain to myself exactly why they were wrong, and so I let him do it.

CHAPTER 22

IT TOOK US SEVERAL DAYS TO DEAL WITH OUR BEAR. We boiled the meat for a long time, for it was much infested with bloodworms and other parasites. Then we cut the flesh into strips, and spread it on wooden racks to dry. We hung the racks from branches out of reach of animals. The air was so cold again that the meat froze as it dried, without benefit of smoke or salt. Thawed out, it tasted almost as sweet as fresh meat. We made stock from the bones, and ate the marrow. The hide I cured and stretched on a frame, as we did with the small game. Loic had taught me how to use brains for tanning, rubbing them in and scraping the skin clean, so I treated my bearskin the same way. We rendered down the fat for grease, and made more tallow dips. It made life easier to have light again, however little. We needed grease for ourselves too, for with enough fat to eat we quickly regained our strength to withstand the cold.

Loic anointed my back with a lotion of tamarack and sarsaparilla. He said I had five deep wounds, as if I'd been slashed with a razor, from my right shoulder to my waist. It must have been a very glancing blow, he said, or the skin would have been ripped right off. As it was, it was sore for a while, but soon healed pretty well. The scars will be with me till I die.[1]

Third Month came in with a blizzard that kept me broad awake all night, while the wind howled like a whirling banshee. When I touched the frame of our wigwam I could feel it vibrating under my hand, taut as a bowstring. Next morning, when I took the barricade of stakes and deerskins from off the doorway, I was confronted by a solid white wall. Loic and I took turns to dig in that awkward space, and when we got clear the snow was shoulder-high all round us. We dug a path to the meat rack and wood pile, and I made steps up to the surface so we could go abroad in our snowshoes. For two weeks our wigwam was half buried, but that was all to the good, for it hugged us like a blanket, and while we had wood and fat meat we were as snug as hedgehogs in a haystack. I had time to write in my notebook again until I finished the ink. The last passage brings that winter back to me as if it were yesterday.[2]

The draughts creep under the pine boughs and make the fire in the middle roar. As the new logs catch, the bark shrivels and cracks, then drops off in glowing ashes. The red centre of the fire is another country; its colour the very opposite of winter.

[1] When Alan and Caleb were little lads, they embarrassed me by boasting to their friends that their father had nearly been eaten by a bear, and had the scars to prove it. One little fellow – it was James Wilson's son Jeremiah – actually accosted me outside the Meeting House and asked – and this in front of several elders – if he might see the clawmarks of the beast. I reprimanded my boys quite severely after that, but naught but their own advancing years had the power to make them desist.

[2] As it happens, I write this in another blizzard, in First Month, 1840. Wind and snow rage at the windows, just as they did outside our wigwam in the wilds of the Michigan Territory. A sea-coal fire glows in the hearth, and Caleb is lying on the hearthrug reading *The Explorations of Captain James Cook in the Pacific*, being the Journals of James Cook, with a map inset, which I bought in Carlisle some twenty years ago. I look across at that dark downbent head, the intent face flushed by the heat, the chin resting on the hand, the way he rubs his thick woollen stockings halfway

The wind blows flurries of snow down the smoke hole. They whirl like the snowstorm outside, which circles endlessly where the land meets the lake. The new logs are half eaten, grey and lined and glowing. The roar of the fire dies down to a lapping like melted water licking the edges of the ice. A log shifts with a slither and burst of flame. When I look away from it there is only a deep lake of dark; green spots swimming as my eyes move.

When the fire is soft and low there are only the shadows which flicker across the birchbark patterns in the walls. The musket barrel glints in its place against the wall, and so does the iron kettle by the hearth. Light plays across the pale hide stretched on its frame against the wall. It touches the patterns on the bear's skull, but cannot enter the deep sockets of the eyes. I look away to the live faces, warm and ruddy in the firelight. In this light I can't see hunger or dirt, nor cold or pain. I stare into the flames and see them now as a wild orange river. The logs are rocks, and I pick out a route for a phantom canoe through the converging rapids. I sniff my dirty fingers and they smell of ash and resin from handling the logs.

Where the lake meets the shore the snow is blown into a circling blizzard that goes nowhere. When it's dark there's nothing beyond the wigwam but sound and snow. I can't go more than a few feet from the doorway, then I piss in the snow but I can't see that either. I get to the woodstack

---

off his feet with his fidgeting (a habit he acquired as a little lad, and has retained even yet, for all that he's a man grown, and now when he lies in his accustomed place, I see he takes up the whole length of the fur rug). I think to myself with a sense of shock, 'he's only half English,' and I find myself wondering, as I have sometimes done since they were prattling bairns, what really goes on inside his mind, and whether the world he inhabits is more unlike mine than I'm able to imagine. I know not, but I'm glad we're here at home, sheltered by our two-foot-thick stone walls, in this pleasant room with its whitewashed walls and beeswaxed wood, its rugs and pictures, books and furniture. I've never suggested that either of them should go to North America, and they've never mentioned it to me. His mother learned long ago, I think, that the past is gone for ever, and no use repining. It's odd that I should be the one who shrinks from learning the same hard lesson.

through a whirling white world. Up and down, far and near, are obliterated; the few feet to the woodpile is like trying to walk through rapids in spate. I fight to keep my balance. The snow fills my eyes and nose as if it wants to drown me.

On such a day as that I fought my way back to our shelter, and, half blinded by the sudden warmth and firelight, I stumbled against the wall, shaking wet snow over Alan where he lay.

'Steady!' Alan surveyed me critically. '*The way was long, the wind was cold, the Quaker was infirm and old . . .* Pretty wild out there, is it?'

'Ay.' I brushed snow off my fur hat into the fire, which hissed in protest. 'Who said that?' I asked.

'A Scotsman called Walter Scott – well, he said more or less that. In the last ten years he's written three extraordinary poems that took the world by storm – but not the Religious Society of Friends, I don't suppose.'

'Oh, that fellow. Ay, I know him.'

'You do? I thought you didn't read pagan literature?'

'He wasn't a pagan' – I still mistook Alan's remarks from time to time – 'on the contrary, I found him a very pleasant fellow.'

Alan pulled himself upright, and sat staring at me. 'You mean you've *met* him?'

'Ay.'

'You've *met* him! Do you realise he's one of our major living poets?'

'Ay, Robert Southey said that. He was certainly living, I'll grant thee that. We're pretty used to poets, though, where I come from.'

'For God's sake, Mark, is that all you can say? You never mentioned this before. Tell me all about it!'

I was surprised at his excitement, but had no objection

to telling him about it. 'It was Robert Southey that recommended me. I've not told thee about the guiding though. Maybe I should go back to that.'

I thought for a bit, while Loic settled himself down as if expecting me to provide the whole evening's entertainment. Little did he realise this was the first time in my life I'd been asked to tell anyone a story.

'It all began with the ewe's milk cheese,' I began at last. 'My mother kept our dairy from the day she married my father, and now she makes the best cheeses within twenty miles of Penrith.' I swallowed. Just thinking about those cheeses made my mouth water. 'By the time I first remember, we were supplying the gentlemen's houses direct. As a lad that suited me. I delivered the cheeses, and our best butter too, riding one pony and leading the other, to houses around Keswick and to the Royal Oak Inn. That's what first took me to Greta Hall. Sarah Coleridge was in charge of the kitchen then, and she was a bit of a tartar, but she knew we were well to deal with, for everyone in Cumberland knows that Quakers can be trusted.

'That's how I knew Greta Hall pretty well. I'd go into the big kitchen at the back where the family and servants would all be together. Sometimes I'd get a bite there before I went home, for I came in all weather and seasons. They knew they could rely on me.

'The year I turned eighteen I had my first guiding job. It was Ninth Month, and I'd ridden up the lane in the early morning, among brambles covered with gossamer and rowans and bryony all thick with berries. The yard at Greta is at the back of the house, at the top of a steep bank above the beck. The kitchen door and the stables open on to the yard, and Robert Southey's bedroom window is on the floor above. I'd just dismounted when I heard the casement open above me, and there was Robert Southey at the window, his nightcap still on his head, and his razor in his hand.

'"Mark Greenhow, is that you?"

'He could see well that it was I and no other, so I took the question to be a conceit of language merely. I looked up at him and asked, "Is thee wanting me, Robert Southey?"

'"Yes, Greenhow, I am," he said. "I've had a message from Grasmere. Mr Wordsworth is entertaining guests who wish to climb Skiddaw while they're in the country. Miss Wordsworth is indisposed with the toothache, and Mr Wordsworth is afflicted with a melancholy. Neither is inclined to take part in an expedition of pleasure. They ask if I can arrange something, and I thought of you. The gentlemen would be willing to pay for a reliable guide."

'I was flattered that he'd thought of me. I first stood on the summit of Blencathra when I was eight years old, on a day when we could see the hills of Scotland over the sea on the one hand, to the wide west ocean, then south to all the mountains of my own country stretched out before me as the hand of God first shaped them. I said to my father, when he showed me all this, that one day I'd have walked the length of every ridge of those same hills. My father said, "Thy word is thy deed, Mark. What thee says, even so must thee do." And I shall, if God wills that I get home. One day I'll have walked all the hills from Swarthmoor to Caldbeck, and from Gosforth to Shap. That's my country. There are Friends almost everywhere in Lakeland, and even where there are none people will always take a Friend in, because they know we speak the truth and cheat nobody. But that by the by.

'So two days later I was back at Greta Hall. It was a fine clear day, just right for our expedition. The two gentlemen were consigned to my care, and I was given their nuncheon to carry in my knapsack. It weighed enough to keep us on the hill for a week, I reckoned. The stouter gentleman had a lame leg. I was worried about that, but he had an ashplant, and once we got going he walked like a man used to the hills, steady as a shepherd. Robert Southey introduced him to me as Mr Scott – "Mr *Walter* Scott," Robert Southey repeated – but I must have looked blank, for the man laughed, and said with a marked Scotch accent, "You think all the world is interested in literary works, Mr Southey, but indeed, I expect this lad has more poetry in his head than many a scholar. In a land like this, he could hardly avoid it." "Do you read poetry, Mark Greenhow?" Robert Southey asked me, with a queer little twist to his smile. I knew he was thinking that our people read none but the Bible, although there is poetry enough in that. I felt nettled, and told him straightly, "I've read some of Thomas Wilkinson's poems. That's Thomas Wilkinson of Yanwath. He's a friend of my father's."

'The gentlemen glanced at one another, and the Scotchman clapped me on the shoulder. "Well, Mr Greenhow, I'll have some of your Cumbrian ballads out of you before the day is done, I hope."

'We got along very well. The other fellow – Humphrey Davy, he was called – was from Wales – he wasn't a poet – and when we stopped to rest – which they liked to do every hour or so – they each talked about their own hill country. The day couldn't have been better. I got them to the top without any difficulty – some days the hill is so open and easy thee forgets what it can be like – and there wasn't a breath of wind up there. We could sit and spread out our nuncheon as comfortably as if we'd taken a pic-nic to our own back door. Around us all the ranges of Lakeland lay spread out under the sun. But it was the Scotch hills of Galloway that Walter Scott wanted me to name for him. I showed him Criffel, and the one they call Skreel, but that was all I knew.

'He asked me about the Solway shore. He said he'd heard

the tide came in over Solway sands faster than a galloping horse, and I told him that was true, but even so a man might ride across from Skinburness to Cardunnock between one high tide and the next, if his horse were good enough. He asked me if I knew anyone who'd done it, and I said, "Ay, none better." I hope it wasn't vainglorious, but he listened so well that I told him the whole story – how the fellow who sold me our new cart had insisted it couldn't be done. My parents would have been shocked to hear me – but under Walter Scott's enquiring eye I couldn't help it. The excitement of that day came flooding back; I found myself telling him what it was like, with a good horse under me, the line of water gleaming in the west, and the long gallop over the firm flat sands ahead. I told him how a man had to know his path, because of the quicksands. I admit I was gratified by his attention.

'"A wager, was it?" he asked me, his eyes very bright.

'I explained to him that I was a Quaker, and that wagers, along with all other kinds of gambling, were against the principles of our Society. It was merely that the wheelwright said the thing could not be done, and I reckoned that it could, and so I set myself to prove it to him.

'"I thought Quakers did not indulge in Vain Sports either?" he said to me.

'Now that was close to the bone, but he couldn't know it. I tried to explain the difference between a sport undertaken only to indulge the whim and vanity of him that pursued it, and a serious and profitable enterprise. I sensed that he was laughing at me, but it was done with such courteous sympathy that I couldn't take offence. He refrained from asking me what was profitable about risking my life to gallop over Solway Sands, and instead put it to me that, by my reasoning, if profit were a more godly motive than sport, it was a nobler thing to net a salmon than to catch him with a fly. When I looked confounded – for I must have done so – he laughed and said, "I think I have you there, sir."[3]

'I liked him very well, for all that I was no match for him in argument. They were pleased with me too, because Robert Southey recommended more of his friends to hire me when they needed a guide. Then I put up a notice at the Royal Oak, and that brought more work. I'd never had guineas in my hand to spend as I chose before. I've never wanted to live anywhere but Highside, nor to take up any trade other than the farm we had, but it suited me to be a little independent of my parents, and to go about the country more.

'It was as well I had something new to do. Not long after I took Walter Scott up Skiddaw we got news of the victory at Trafalgar. I saw the newspaper – this was in Eleventh Month – when I was waiting in the Royal Oak for our account to be paid. The paper was lined with black because Nelson was dead. They lit a great bonfire on the summit of Skiddaw – I saw the red glow of it against the sky even as I stood in our yard at Highside. A few days later I climbed to the top, and in spite of the swirling cloud about me, the embers of that fire were still warm against my hand. I was feeling – I don't know – angry, and confused, and excited, all at the same time. There was a feeling in the country round about – I'm as much an Englishman as my neighbours, and no coward either – people said things about Friends behind my back, and more than once to my face as well. I felt no meekness in me, only the urge to fight back, and not just with words

---

[3] As a Friend I have no interest in *novels*, and naturally I take no pride in any connection with works of idle fancy, but I have been told that Mr Scott made use of what I told him in a publication he named *Redgauntlet*. Of course I have not read the work, but privately I was not as ill-pleased as perhaps I ought to have been.

either. I can't explain it, but all through that winter I was kicking against the pricks. The other thing that happened was my cousin John Bristo joined the Cumberland Militia. I wasn't at Monthly Meeting when they disowned him, but I was at Meeting for Worship the next First Day, when they read out the minute at the end of Meeting. I never came so near quarrelling with my Society. Instead I took to the hills. I still saw John, though my parents asked me not to, for the time.[4] All through the spring and summer of '06 I kept away from home as much as I could. It threw all the burden of work on my father, but I was in a foul temper, and I cared nothing for that.

'Ever since I was a little lad I was at home on the hill. Now my wanderings took me ever further afield. I found ways where there were no paths, where even the shepherds didn't go. I met a fellow in Wasdale who shared my interest. Together we scaled the Great Gavel from the seaward side. The news of our climb spread around, the way these things do, and the next thing I knew there were Lakers enquiring for me, asking me to take them up the rocks. I never told anyone at Meeting. I let them think I was a plain mountain guide, working occasionally for the likes

[4] John Bristo and I see each other still. He has been out of our Meeting now for thirty-five years. I've had elders speak to me more than once about my continued close acquaintance with one who is no longer in unity with us. I heed them not. John is my cousin and one of my first friends. I would not bring up my sons in a family divided against itself. These days I have the reward of my persistence. I have not changed, but the Society of Friends grows year by year more tolerant of intercourse between Members and those not in unity with us. More and more do Members of our Society take our place in the great world, and indeed concern ourselves with matters that would never have been allowed to impinge upon our Meeting when I was a lad. As the world changes the rights of men are too often eroded, and their grievances grow proportionately greater. Friends' recent concerns about the just needs of men are entirely to be welcomed. There is no place on earth where a people may truly be set apart. Nor do I think the God of all Mercies intended it: for is not that of God in every man, Friend or not, so how then should we not concern ourselves with worldly matters?

of Robert Southey's poetical friends. For myself, I never thought of walking the hills as being in any sense a Vain Sport, but I was beginning to meet a set of fellows who considered scrambling over rocks very much in that light.[5] Mostly they came up from Manchester or thereabouts. I'd thought all city folk were pale, sickly creatures who barely had the use of their legs, let alone a mind to walk upon the high places and know that they were good. I could not truly say, either, that I found their company ill to bear. Anyway, it brought in money, and as I say, that was a new thing for me, and in no way to be despised.'

Next morning the storm was over. I put on my snowshoes and went out to Bear Lake (for thus we'd named our fishing lake). The snow was light and firm, and so cold it creaked under the weight of every step. Freezing air stung my nose and cheeks. I pulled my fur cap as far down over my face as I could. After talking so much all evening it was a relief to head out alone across the frozen lake, while the wind blew the snow off the ice so it looked like smoke puffing in the distance. The sun was so bright it made my eyes water. I never got used to walking over the ice. I felt like Peter on the Lake of Galilee, though glad I had a foot of ice rather than unaided faith to sustain me. I got to the fishing holes I'd made with such difficulty: the branches I'd put to mark them were battered but intact. I broke the new layer of ice with the axe, then settled to the long wait, while the

[5] There was one man in particular who first hired me to take him up Skiddaw. He came again, and paid me double to take him over the Scafells. He had some notion that Scafell was higher than Skiddaw, and insisted that we carry sextants and other instruments by which to prove it. I asked him why it mattered, and he told me about some old fellow in Switzerland who had in his youth climbed to the very summit of Mont Blanc (this being the highest mountain in those parts, apparently), in order to take similar readings, and who thereby set quite a fashion for mountain-climbing in that country. Since then I have taken many such eccentrics into our hills. They are harmless, on the whole.

chill of the ice seeped through the moss linings of my moccasins and numbed my toes. It was a chill way to spend a morning, and we weren't short of food, but always when I came out here I felt my soul expand into the open sky around me. I'd had too much of the dark forests and hidden spaces. I caught one whitefish, and then another. With all the memories stirred by last night's story, I found myself wondering if I would ever get home again.

Thoughts of the past were still running in my mind as we ate our supper. It occurred to me that in all my tale I'd never once mentioned Rachel. Perhaps I was beginning to forget how much of our lives we'd shared. Leaving her out of my story, however unwittingly, was a little like letting her die. I shuddered as a faint chill trickled down my back. Just for a moment I felt I'd betrayed her, but that, I told myself, was a vain superstition; had I not come all this way for her sake alone?

It was snowing again. The fish made an agreeable change, and I was glad I'd got some while I could. I was noticing how Alan had his appetite back, and how the black hollows under his eyes were fading away. I wondered if he ever felt homesick. I suppose it was a mixture of all my drifting thoughts that prompted me to say to him, when we'd finished eating, 'I think it's thy turn now, Alan. Will thee tell us thy story tonight?'

'My story?' Alan whistled. 'All of it, brother Mark? I'm a sick man, you know. The exertion might well be too much for me. Would you ever forgive yourself?'

'We can take it in stages. It's thy turn. We've all told stories.' I looked round for support. 'It is his turn, isn't it, Loic?'

'*Oui*,' said Loic. 'I think it is.'

CHAPTER 23

ALAN CLEARED HIS THROAT. 'I WAS BORN . . . WHAT a tedious beginning . . . I was conceived . . . I have no memory of it. Have you read *Tristram Shandy*? Of course you haven't. Never mind.'

He was silent for a bit, collecting his thoughts. Then he began his story, just as Loic had done, in a surprisingly formal manner, as if storytelling were something set apart: something, moreover, that Alan was well used to.

'I came into the world on the night of the Lammas full moon, in the year 1787, in my grandfather's house at Craig in Lochalsh on the west coast of Scotland. My father had been a soldier, and so was my grandfather before him. I was seven when my grandfather died, but I remember him very well. I have his name. My father went into the 72nd Regiment of Foot – you don't know what that is? – the 72nd is a Highland regiment founded by the chief of Clan Mackenzie. The old chief died a few years before I was born, on his way out to India, and the cousin who inherited – well, he was worse than no good to any of us, as it turned out. My father came out of the army when my grandfather was too old to look after his land. He then married, late in life, my mother Helen Mathieson, who came from over the hill, on the south side of Lochalsh.

'I was the youngest of seven. I have three brothers, three sisters. James followed in my father's footsteps, and became an officer in the 72ⁿᵈ. The old chief had promised him a commission, but he was dead, and his heir wasn't the man to honour an old promise: he honoured naught but what was written down, and my grandfather, and my father too, always held that it was more honourable to trust a man's word than written letters, which could too easily be twisted about and proved false. So the money for James' commission was raised off the estate, and when my father died none of it had been paid off; in fact there were treble the debts to go with it. That's why there was no money for Simon to go into the army, so he went to America instead. And, *ça va sans dire*, when the time came, Tomas and I followed him. But that comes later. Sim went away when I was eleven; I remember my mother weeping as he walked away over the hill. Later, when it came to us younger ones, so much had happened I think all her tears were gone. She lives with my sister Helen now, the one who married back into the Mathiesons and stayed at Ardelve in Lochalsh – at least, I had a letter about a year since, and I suppose they're all there still.

'My father thought of his inheritance in the old way. He held his lands by what we call *duthchas*, which is the bond between a man and his chief, a matter of loyalty which it would be dishonourable to write down. A man's word is sacred; a written paper would be an offence among kin. My grandfather's father fought for his chief in two campaigns, and after the rebellion in 1715 he, along with all our kin, refused rent to the Government. They fought off the soldiers who were sent to make them pay. They paid their rents as usual to Mr Murchison the factor, and he took them every year, for ten years, to the exiled chief in Spain. It was the same after '19: the Commissioners for the Forfeited Estates couldn't sell the Seaforth lands, because they had to admit they couldn't get possession of them. We fought them off each time.

'My father fought for his chief too, only in his day it was a matter of joining the Mackenzie regiment and fighting for pay abroad. My father knew the young chief wasn't like his father. He knew the rents from the land were being used to pay debts far off in England, but he couldn't know until it happened to him – he had no way of knowing – that the bonds of kin, and of service in battle, could ever be betrayed.

'People were leaving our land, and the lands all round about us. Bound for America, mostly, or the big cities in the south if they couldn't afford the passage. It was bad losing tenants, because no tenants means no rents. My grandfather was a tacksman. That means our land – and our holding was smaller than Michael Dousman's place on Mackinac – was divided between all our tenants, who looked to my grandfather for their living, as he looked to them for ours. We never had more than sixty guineas a year from rents, and it was always getting less. The wealth of a nation is in its people: I didn't need to study my book to find out that, for I knew it all too well from my first years, when I watched our wealth, our folk, draining away from us like the tide out of the loch after its turning.

'Our people were our kin. We bore the same name. We never forced anyone to leave Lochalsh. We heard, though, that elsewhere folk were being evicted. They'd burn the roofs over their heads to stop them coming back. Our own chief was doing this, on his island estates. We knew he was head over ears in debt. Even when he inherited, the estate was encumbered. Our turn had to come.

'And yet, when I remember my first days, they're so untouched by shadow that the sun nearly always shines. The hills are clear in the distance, even though the fact is that on most days everything's wet and grey, and the hills are hidden. For a child all things are ordinary; the world is as it is. I didn't know what it was like to have money, or enough to eat in springtime, or not to hear low voices through the cracks in the floor under our mattress, whenever a traveller sat in by the fire below and told the news. It troubled me not at all, though it troubled my mother, that though we were gentlemen's sons we must go barefoot; I'd never tasted fine wines or foreign fruits or sugarplums; why would I feel the want of them? Beef or herring was enough of a treat; most days it was just oatmeal and potatoes and buttermilk, but always, when I was very small, served to us at the oak dining table with a damask cloth laid over it, and set with silver spoons and forks. The silver was gone, though, before I could well wield it. I learned to eat my porridge with a horn spoon.

'My grandfather taught me to read, in English of course, and why would I wish for schooling, when there were books in the house that I might read at will, and stories told by the fire in winter? What else would I wish to know? I was thought to be the bookish one of the family. I was the youngest. I used to get left behind with my sisters when my brothers were out. My grandfather taught me to like books. He used to sit in the sun in the parlour window, looking out over the loch, and I used to climb up on to the windowsill and gaze out at the Applecross hills while he read to me. He left a small library when he died; I don't suppose anyone looks at it now. The books were mostly English, and those I grew to know nearly by heart. *Robinson Crusoe* was my favourite. I had to read it covertly, for although my grandfather purchased it (he had written on the flyleaf *Alan Mackenzie, bought at the recommendation of Peter Hill, Creech's bookshop, Edinburgh, March* 1777), my father would have none of it, declaring that the author was a treacherous southron, whose machinations had been the first cause of the evils which would yet be the ruin of us all.

'My father gave my other favourite short shrift too. It was called *The Pilgrim's Progress*, and although it had overmuch preaching in it, there were also the monsters, travels and adventures, in which I delighted, but my father said the writer was as fanatical as a Galloway Covenanter, and I would do better to leave him on the shelf where he would get the dusty ending he deserved. The last books my grandfather ever bought were sent up from Edinburgh the very week he died. They lay in a pile on the end of a shelf until, years later, I took them down and dusted them. I cut the pages of Buchanan's *Travels in the Western Hebrides* and read it aloud to my family, until my father seized the book from my hand and hurled it out of the window. Mr Buchanan hated tacksmen, that was for sure. I heard later that the man was much given to fornication, and the tacksmen of Harris dealt with him accordingly. But it seemed wrong that such baseless calumnies should be set in print and published for all the world to read. Later I retrieved the book from the mud, wiped it clean, and pressed it flat again under Mr Johnson's dictionary, because however misguided the content, a book is a precious object and should not be mistreated.

'The French books, of which there were half a dozen, were more of a struggle, but Tomas used to make me translate Rabelais in the privacy of our bedchamber. Some of the Latin and Greek might have served his purpose better, but they were beyond my comprehension. There aren't any books in our language. We did have Macpherson's lay of Ossian, but my grandfather had written in his own hand upon the title page that he doubted the veracity of the translations.

'There's an island below our house where herons nest in the pine trees. I remember the sound the herons make at nesting time. In our language we call them *skriagh* – like the sound they make. We used to set otter traps on the island. That's how I first learned to dress pelts, but little did I think then that pelts were to make my fortune, as they will – not yet, brother Mark, I grant you – but as they will.

'I never saw your country, Mark, so I don't know what comparisons you're making. You said there are no roads here. If your idea of a road is the Wade road to 'inburgh, or Yonge Street perhaps, then we had none eith. And yet there are broad highways through every glen, the ways the cattle go down to Crieff. If those aren't roads, I don't know what a road is.

'Sometimes *le pays d'en haut* looks to me like home. It has lakes and islands and rocks. Michigan is just sand. My country was – is – full of rocky hills with lochans in between. You have to get up high to see where you are. Eagles nest on the crags. We used to climb up and throw down their nests: they prey on the young stock. There's a path round to the west, and that's the way the ponies come up to the peats, and the cattle too – we put them on the hill in spring, so we can use the fields for crops. Even now I could name all the places to you, but it wouldn't mean anything; you don't know.

'I left home at midsummer, when the sun was setting behind the Applecross hills. I saw that gold light again, with the long shadows stretched across the rocks, when I got to *le pays d'en haut*. There are no real evenings as far south as this. Anyway, I walked along the path by the loch. I looked at the heron island a long time, until the midges sent me running. I headed for the crags and climbed up fast, up on to the ridge.

'If you stand on the edge of the crags you see our stone house right below. It looks across Loch Carron. Our boats are on the beach. It's too shallow for anything big, but just round the headland there's one of the best harbours on the west coast. Ships moor there sometimes. You see the infield dotted with tenants' cabins, just like wigwams only made with stone and turf. You see cattle and crops, and all the little holdings sewn together by stone dykes. The line of the infield sweeps across the hillside like the cut of a knife, dividing green fields from crags and heather.

'The highest hill on our land is called Beinn Raimh. That last day I ran all the way around the lochans and over the crags to the top. There was still snow on the far mountains, but where I was the ground was bright with little flowers; you could smell the grass and hear the pipits whistling. The lochans were blue in the sun, except for Loch a' Ghlinne Dhuirch in the shadow of the hill, which was the colour of slate. I could see the cattle grazing on Carn na Sean-chreag. You can't see our land from Beinn Raimh, it's hidden below the crags.

'The sea lies to the west of us, and a big island. The island of Skye is all Macleods and Macdonalds. I never went there but once, when I went with Simon to Kylerhea about some cattle. The cattle from Skye come across to Glenelg at droving time. There are other islands too. My grandfather taught me their names, and after he died I had Tomas to remind me. From our crags you can see the Black Cuillin on Skye, and a little to the right of it, the smooth curves of the Red Cuillin. The Cuillin is sharp and sheer like no ridge you ever saw – it looks uncanny, when you can see it at all: blue under a summer sky, or a dark outline against the setting sun. I wanted to go there. I wanted to touch the rock and feel that it was real. But I never did.

'We used to fish on summer evenings, especially at mackerel time. The islands at the mouth of Loch Carron are summer grazing. You can get plenty of fish round there with a handline. I could tell you the names of every family on the shores of Loch Carron, and how we were related to each one. But I'll spare you that, brother Mark.

'I was afraid of my father. He had enough to be angry

about. All that he had was slipping away like the tide, and there was nothing he could do to hold it back. When he came home from the wars, everything cost money, where no money had been needed before. The year I turned four the harvest failed. We couldn't sell our cattle. The tenants were starving, and no rents came in. My father took his sword to Edinburgh and sold it, along with the candlesticks and my grandmother's silver teapot, just to buy meal for ourselves and the indoor servants. There was none to spare for the tenantry, barring the widows and orphans who could not be forgot. We ate nettle broth and limpets from the shore that year, but the shellfish made me sick. I've never eaten them again. Once a shoal of herring came right into the loch. I remember – it's one of the first memories I have – how the men took out all the boats and filled them to the gunwales. No one need have been hungry again, except that we had no salt – there was never enough salt, because of the tax – and so the fish rotted and had to be thrown back to the sea for the stink they made, so after just a few days we were all as hungry as before.

'Then came the war with France. Prices began to go up. We had butter and eggs and herring to sell. There was the fair at Ardelve twice a year, and sometimes we went to the fairs at Glenelg as well. I remember the music and dancing at the fairs; it wasn't all bad, not at all. We were sending cattle down to Crieff again, and that was good, but we lost too many men off the land when the recruiting sergeant came up from Bernera. Whenever we made a recover, we were always struck down again. My father was an obstinate man; he was determined to hold on.

'People were leaving the country too fast. The government was trying to stop it by getting folk off their farms and making them work for money. It was a bad business, though, because the money went into the hands of those who never laboured for it, and to work like a slave at the kelp or the fish is not the same as holding your own bit land from a man of your own name that you can trust. My father thought of his chief as kin, right to the end, but my brothers never did. They were right, because kin was no longer honoured above money, and money was honoured above all.

'When I was nine or ten a Mr Knox came to our house to talk to my father about the good anchorage in the next bay. He came from the Society for the Recovery of Fisheries. He wanted to build a fishing station, with a built town like ones he told us about down south. My mother and Sim wanted it; my father wouldn't listen. After Mr Knox had gone my parents quarrelled. That was when I first heard my mother say out loud that we could not stay on our land, and live. She said my father should buy into the new fishing town for the children's sake. She meant us: Sim, Tomas, my sisters, and me, James being away at the wars, but always sending his pay back home.

'We were always afraid, long before Mr Knox came, that the chief would have the land cleared for sheep in Lochalsh; after all, he'd done it elsewhere. He didn't though, because the news came – I was big enough by then to mind it well – that Lochalsh was sold to an Elgin man, a Mr Innes – who'd bought on the expectation of clearing the glens for sheep. He started right away, as soon as he'd got the papers for the land. Sim was away by then, gone to America. My sister Helen was married to our second cousin on my mother's side, and gone to Balmacara, but when they were thrown out they came back to the new fishing town for a bit. Now they live in Ardelve. Mary married a MacRae from Glenshiel. When they were moved away they went to Glasgow, which is a city as big as Montreal, so I've heard. I don't know what family Mary has. But back then my sisters were only just wed, and it was just Ann and Tomas and I left living at home.

'When the new century came in we had a bonfire on the shore, and another on the crags above, and there were fires lit on the Applecross hills. My cousin Rob the fiddler came over, and we had a – a party, you would call it – the way I never saw again until I reached Kamanistiquia – they call it Fort William now – on Lake Superior. If I try I can see each face in my mind now, as clear as if it were this very night gone, our tenants and neighbours and family and all of us. All gone now, all scattered.

'We had snow after that. My father used to cough at night, on and on, keeping us awake through the thin partition. A week or so into the new century he got the pneumonia, and just before Lent he died. He was fifty-eight. I was twelve.

'James was in India with his regiment. The rest of us talked about what we should do. My mother wanted to keep the land going until James should come back from the wars to claim it. Tomas said that was a lost cause. He said we should buy a share in one of the new herring busses at the fishing station. My mother said she didn't believe in a town which was naught but a drawing on paper; there'd been too many promises made and too few kept. The land had been ours for twelve generations, and she would hold it for James, as my father would have wished, if it was the last thing she did in this world. Tomas said, how would she do that, with the rents fallen by half, and two more families leaving us this very springtime? He and I knew enough about boats, more than the tenantry, at any rate, and we should go together and speak to Mr Innes before others got in before us. My mother said, no, Alan would stand by his family and hold the land until James came home. I sat there, with hot words about my future flying to and fro over my head, when my sister Ann, who'd been as silent as I up until then, suddenly said coolly, "Why don't you ask him? What do you want to do, Alan?"

'No one had ever asked me before what I wanted to do. I looked at her and I think my mouth fell open. The words came out before I knew I'd thought them. "I want to go to Edinburgh and work in Mr Creech's bookshop."

'They stared at me as if I had grown two extra heads. "Do what?" "What's that?" "*Edinburgh?*" "Who is Mr Creech?" "A shop?"

'"Grandfather bought his books there. He writes it on the flyleaf, with the date. A shop, with books in. People go there. They read books, and talk about them. Grandfather told me."

'I'd never argued with my family before. It was as if, my father being gone, I suddenly discovered that I had a voice. When I was little, and knelt on the windowseat while my grandfather sat looking out over the loch with his plaid over his knees and his spectacles perched on the end of his nose, he would look up sometimes from the book he'd been reading to me and ask me what I thought. I don't remember what I said except once, when I asked if Mr Johnson had been the fattest man ever to go over Mam Ratachan, and could Grandfather and I go ourselves and dance upon Dun Caan? That amused him, and afterwards it was like a secret between us. If ever Dun Caan was mentioned, he'd look at me and wink, and say, "Our day will come, eh, Alan?" None of the others ever troubled to ask what we meant by that.

'But Ann stood up for me now. "Why shouldn't he go to Edinburgh?" she kept saying. "If our uncle's still there, why shouldn't Alan go to him, and at least he can ask? If there's nothing in it, he can always come home again."

'My father's brother, with whom my grandfather had stayed whenever he was in Edinburgh, was a schoolmaster in the city. There had long been a coolness between him and my father, because he'd changed to the established religion in order to attend the University in Edinburgh.

My family were all Episcopalian, which was illegal when I was young, because of the Penal Laws. It was allowed by the time I'm telling of, but that's why my uncle Alan first went over to the kirk, and my father never forgave him for it. Not having heard of his death, we had no reason to suppose he was not still living.

'And so I went down to Falkirk with the brother of one of our tenants, who was a drover. It was a long, slow journey – we did no more than twelve miles on a good day – for cattle must feed and sleep, much more than a man. It was the first long journey I ever made, and prepared me well for *le pays d'en haut* – for the Highlands are *un pays d'en haut* of their own, and the drovers not so different from *les voyageurs*. They take what shelter they can and sleep in the wild, they live on porridge – there's not so much difference between oats and pease, hot or cold – they do their own work and speak their own tongue and sing their own songs, and people who live in houses and sleep every night in their own beds know nothing about it. I was used to the cattle, of course, and I don't think I was a burden to Ian Mhor, for all that I was in no way bred to the droving life. We had about two hundred head of cattle, mostly from Skye, but a good few from Lochalsh as well, and four of us to drive them. Through Glenshiel and Glenloyne we went, then east over the Corrieairack Pass. When I stood on the top of the pass and saw all the Highland hills around me I realised my own country was much greater than I'd ever understood, for all I'd looked at my grandfather's map often enough – but there are things maps don't tell you, and what you see from the *bealach* of the Corrieairack is one of those things.

'By the time we came to Drumochter there were hundreds of beasts on the road before us: it was as great a migration as the caribou herds in Athabasca, only all contrived by men. The signs are the same though – a road through the hills fifty yards wide, where grass and heather are churned to mud and peat bog, and the grazing places bare and mucky for miles around. Everything's coated in peaty sludge, beasts and men alike, and sometimes it's raining so much you can barely squint through it to see where you're putting your feet. And other days it's like heaven up there, with the larks singing and all the blue hills around you.

'We got to Wade's bridge at Aberfeldy, where we had to wait all day for our turn to cross the Tay, and soon after that I was looking down for the first time on the green Lowlands. We kept to the high ground as much as we could, over the Ochils and into Falkirk. There I parted from Ian Mhor, not without fear, for I'd never seen anything like Falkirk Tryst, and I was overwhelmed by the noise all about me and the crowds – for men and beasts would be shoving against each other, right up close, all the time – and Ian Mhor had told me to watch my purse and keep my wits about me, and I'd never had to go on in such a way as that before. I fairly wanted to run. But I didn't. I walked out of there, my money and dignity alike intact, and set off on the dusty post road to Edinburgh.

'I can't explain to you how different it all was. When a stage coach passed me, with four horses to pull it and half a dozen passengers sitting on the roof, I fairly stopped and gaped. No one accosted me on the road, but I had trouble buying food at the inns. I'd thought my English was fluent – I could read anything I had a mind to, both aloud and to myself – but no one seemed to understand me, and as for what they said back to me, it could have been ancient Hebrew for all I could tell. Sometimes they were short with me, and occasionally they were kind, but by the time I reached Edinburgh I'd learned one thing – that in this land I was not only a stranger, but about as welcome among them as a stray dog. Before Falkirk I had a pretty good opinion of myself – was I not a gentleman's son, well-born and well-bred, and yet tough enough to work and sleep out on the open hill among the drovers? But when I picked a hot pie from a stall at the market in Linlithgow – with every intention of paying for it, you understand – the fellow swore at me for a thief, and they would have set on me, but I dropped the pie and took to my heels, and never stopped running until I was out of the city gate. To be honest with you, when I was far enough away to feel safe, I climbed through the dusty hedgerow and into a cornfield, where I just sat down and cried. If I could have gone back to Ian Mhor and asked him to take me home again, I would have done so, but for my own honour I couldn't turn back. I slept under a hedge that night rather than ask for shelter, and when I walked into Edinburgh I was dirty and hungry, and knew not where to go. I found myself among great houses six storeys high or more, all built huddled together on the sides of a hill, with hundreds of alleyways and steep stairs between. Sure enough, there was the castle at one end and the palace at the other, just as my grandfather had described to me, but what use was either to me?

'In the High Street of Edinburgh my luck turned. The place was full of Highlanders, so I could ask the way in my own tongue, and the first lad I spoke to knew the address I had – it was a close just off the Canongate, he said. He led me to the very spot. To my dismay it was a great towering tenement, so high I couldn't count how many storeys from the narrow wynd. The alley was filthy with slops and dark as a dungeon. I wished I'd never come, but the lad asked the woman in the cookshop on the ground floor – little did I know then what a friend she was to be to me – and she said Alan Mackenzie was not home yet, but he lived on the fifth floor, and if I wanted to sit on the step and wait for him he would be back before long. I gave the lad one of my pennies, and spent another on a slice of bread and meat from the cookshop.

'And there,' said Alan, 'We can leave me. I've had enough of myself for one long evening.'

'But tomorrow you go on,' said Loic. 'I have never heard a story like this before. You have never said these things.'

'Of course not. Things have to be pretty desperate before one starts on one's life story. Goodnight!' Alan rolled over, his back to the light, and said no more.

I too had never heard such a story before. I'd expected to find North America foreign, and indeed it was, but Alan's story disconcerted me, because it was equally strange, and yet so close to home. I knew dealers who came down from Falkirk Tryst each year to the markets in Carlisle and Penrith. I was familiar with the black cattle from up north; I'd talked to Scotch drovers before now. But the country they came from – the world Alan had described to me – all that seemed far more remote to me, now, than the lands of the Ottawa in which we dwelt.

The next evening I was outside the wigwam wiping our mugs and bowls in clean snow. The storm had subsided. All life seemed to be suspended in the windless night. I heard a branch crack. When I breathed in, the freezing air tingled my nose and burned inside my chest like fire. The stars blazed above my head like chips of ice. God made this night exceedingly beautiful, I thought, but if he had done all this for men, he would not have made it too cold for them to stop and look. I ducked under the curtain of deerskins, and went back inside.

'Here's Mark,' said Loic. 'So now, Alan, you can tell us of your father's brother, Alan Mackenzie, in Edinburgh.'

Alan lay back against a bale, his striped trade blanket huddled round him. 'If my uncle Alan were here now,' he said, 'He would say, "This all seems exceeding odd to me." He wouldn't like it.'

'Go on,' I said, after a pause. 'Thee can't stop there.'

Alan sighed. 'My uncle Alan? What's he to thee, or I to Hecuba? Very well, if you insist: he asked very little of life, and would be astonished that you wanted to hear a story about him. Sometimes – not very often – he'd get drunk at the tavern down the wynd, or, if he were in a different mood and hadn't drunk his money away, he liked to go to a coffee house and read the newspaper, but he couldn't afford that every day. If he were here he wouldn't mind the cold, or the dirt, or the discomfort – he was used to all that – but he'd miss the folk going by. Not his friends – he didn't have friends – he used to say friends were an expensive commodity, and very seldom gave value for money – he was a cynic, my uncle. A man of considerable wit, however, but not in a way either of you would understand.'

I was unaccountably irritated by that. 'Hugh Chisholm is like that too, and I understood him.' Honesty impelled me to add, 'Once I got used to him.'

'You wouldn't understand my uncle,' said Alan firmly. 'He wouldn't let you. You belong in different worlds entirely, and you'll never meet him.'

'Then tell the story,' said Loic. 'That is what stories are for.'

'Oh, very well,' said Alan crossly, but I knew quite well he wanted to go on. 'I lived nearly two years with my uncle Alan. I was happy. He had no money; he once told me that was why he'd never married. We had a bare little room on the fifth floor of the tenement. When we could afford it we used to eat our dinner at the Half Way House – that was the tavern just down the steps from our front door. For a country lad that was something of an education. The only food uncle Alan cooked on our own fire was porridge, which we had cold for breakfast, a cold slice wrapped in a paper for mid-day, and sometimes (for a treat) hot before bedtime on a winter's night. I went to school. Because my uncle was one of the masters I got a place at the Royal High School. I learned to tell lies, to fight, to keep my religion secret, and to speak Lowland Scots. (No one spoke my language, and they used to laugh at the literary English I'd learned from my grandfather. They didn't listen to what I said; they were just waiting to imitate my accent.) In class I learned Latin and Greek mostly, and mathematics. The other lads I didn't care for, but I was out to learn everything I could.

'One of the first things I did when I reached the city was to seek out Mr Creech's bookshop by the luckenbooths, just up the High Street from our close mouth. At home I'd been allowed to read what I liked, but after my grandfather died there were no new books. At Creech's there were all the books in the world, or so it seemed to me, and journals, and, what I had never seen before in my life, a newspaper every day with that day's date upon it. I had never thought of news from the wide world as happening in the present before, and suddenly I became aware that Lochalsh was not the centre of the world, that the life I'd lived was not the measure of all things and made to last forever. I'd heard all my life that the best times were over, in the past, and that I was born too late. I'd been taught that the future was a place of fear and foreboding. In Mr Creech's bookshop I learned for the first time that there were other worlds, that they too were changing, and that every world was inhabited by beings like myself who thought their way was the right way, just as I did. I began to think about change without so much fear, more as a matter of interest.

'Peace was declared on Tomas's eighteenth birthday. My mother had a letter from Sim the same year; he'd left the state of New York and gone to Montreal, where he'd got a clerkship in the North West Company. (The letter was two years old; Sim had been in *le pays d'en haut* two winters by the time we got it.) He said there were several of our name in the Company, and that there'd be a place for Tomas too, if Tomas wished to join him.

'Tomas is a good brother. He walked all the way to Edinburgh when the letter came, to suggest that I go with him. Oddly enough it was uncle Alan who insisted. He – mild man that he was – positively ranted at me, saying did I wish to live in poverty all my life, to struggle for my living, to lose the girl I loved, and come to a chilly old age and doubtless a lonely death? Did I realise there was no money for me to go to University, and even if there were, an education would not necessarily save me? I looked at him in alarm; certainly it was a grisly picture he set before me. Between the two of them they had me persuaded. Tomas and I took the long road home together, across the Forth from Queensferry, over the farmlands of Fife and Perthshire, across the Corriearrack and into the familiar hills.

'We sailed from Fort William – our Scottish Fort William – in Lochaber on July 2nd, 1802. I've never forgotten that date. Nor have I forgotten the date we landed in Quebec: September 15th, 1802. Our ship was called *Friends of John Saltcoats*. There were two other ships: the *Jean of Irvine* and the *Helen of Saltcoats*; we were supposed to travel in convoy but the *Jean* and the *Helen* left us behind almost as soon as we were out of the islands. The charter was arranged by a second cousin of my mother's, Archibald Macmillan.

'When we got to Montreal Sim was wintering out west, but he'd asked a friend of his, Hugh Chisholm, who had Montreal leave, to look out for us. Sim gave Hugh enough money to get board and lodging for Tomas, but of course he hadn't been expecting me. Hugh was like a brother to us: he got us a room in the house where he lodged, and advanced us money for my board. Tomas got a berth as clerk with the Company, and started paying Hugh back at once, but Hugh took this notion into his head that I must go on with my schooling. I rebelled – I wanted nothing better than to work for the North West too – but Hugh was adamant, and as he held the purse-strings at that point, he won. There's no High School in Montreal, just the Catholic schools. So I found myself huddled over the fire in Hugh's sitting room, construing my Caesar and Cicero, and solving what seemed to me to be quite unnecessary problems in Euclid. We read Xenophon in Greek, and after that Thucydides. All I remember now is *thalassa, thalassa*. I don't know if I'll ever see the sea again – I mean the real sea. I read Hugh's English books too – Hume and Gibbon that winter, and Cook's voyages. I found novels on Hugh's shelves as well: my grandfather hadn't had Smollett, or Fielding, or Cervantes. It was the coldest winter I'd ever known. The snow was five-feet thick outside our door. I got my first snowshoes, and I learned to use them on the slopes of Mount Royal. It was up there that Hugh taught Tomas and me how to do dead reckonings, and survey with a compass. I didn't miss being with lads my own age. In fact, once I'd fairly settled down, I was as happy as a grig.

'When Hugh went back to Fort William in May, Tomas went with him. I didn't see either of them until I got to Fort William a year later. I started as a very junior clerk at the Company offices, and lived in our rooms by myself. I was proud to be on my own and earning my living. I worked my way slowly through the list of books that Hugh left for me: Locke, Reid, Adam Smith. Each time I got to the end of a section, I'd reward myself with another story from the *Arabian Nights*. Apart from that, I was learning a fairly pragmatic view of love from Catullus, Ovid and Apuleius, green youth that I was. Most evenings I spent reading. I knew some lads from the office – I wasn't unsocial – but I'd never been alone before, and I liked it.

'In the spring of '04 I left with the brigades. I was still only seventeen, but neither my brothers nor Hugh were there to gainsay me when the fellow asked how old I was. I got to Kamanistiquia for the rendezvous in July. (They changed the name to Fort William a few years later, in honour of William McGillivray, but naught else is different.) It was as busy as the Tryst at Falkirk, but this time I wasn't a frightened lad; I was a man among my own folk. For my own folk is what they were – Highlanders almost to a man, apart from the *engagés* – *les voyageurs* – and they were easy to deal with; my French was pretty fluent before I left Montreal. And it wasn't cattle we were dealing with, but furs. Kamanistiquia is where the *hivernants* bring the furs in from all over *le pays d'en haut*, and the brigades from Montreal bring in the trade goods in exchange. But we're all one Company. There's no buying and selling, just processing and re-packing the goods, and just as much revelry and banqueting as a thousand honest traders can fit into a fortnight. The Company was what my own kin should have been to me, but weren't – like the old days that I grew up hearing about, when all that Seaforth had was ours, and we were his – like the days before the Rebellions, which were hearsay even to my grandfather. And maybe it was never like that at all, not even in the clans – for who knows now? Anyway, at Kamanistiquia we belonged to no one but the Company, and any man might make his fortune if he could, whether he were born to it or no.

'I found Tomas and Hugh right away, and my other brother Sim arrived a couple of days after my brigade got in – I hadn't seen him for ten years and we made quite a night of it. So that was me: in my own place at last, no longer a lad waiting to grow up, but who and where I wished to be more than anything else on earth. I was happy as a king – if kings are happy, which I doubt. But that's the fact of the matter: since I joined the North West Company I've never wished for one moment to be anywhere than where I was – that includes the tough times too – and that's the honest truth. Hugh asked the Council if he could have me for clerk, so when the rendezvous was over I said farewell to my brothers for another year, and went with Hugh up to Athabasca.

'As soon as I got to *le pays d'en haut*, I knew this was where I wanted to be. I remember when I used to look west across the sea to the Cuillin, right on the edge of the world, with only the sun setting into the sea beyond them. I never got there, and I've not got to the edge of the world either. But when I was in Athabasca I knew I was *there* – I can't explain it to you – whatever it was that lay west beyond the Cuillin, when I used to look at it from Craig – the place that I wanted to be. The first winter was terrible – far worse than this. I used to go by sled – out there where the sky is so huge you can't imagine it – so much sky, and the empty space around you. I used to look around me at all the great white barrenness of it, and think to myself, "This is *it*." And it was, for me. The North will kill you if you stop paying attention to it for one moment – it's like a white bear stalking you, always after you, and waiting for your blood, and if it doesn't kill you dead it gets you another way. Even if I went back to Lochalsh now – and I never will – I'd be homesick all my life. You think my leg bothers me because of the pain, don't you? I couldn't give a damn about that – not now – it's what it might do to me that worries me. I never wanted to be sent down here. I wanted my promotion – oh, yes, I wanted that – but only so as I could get back *there*, and be my own agent. That's what I want – a partner's share in the North West, and a post up north. But not if I'm crippled – not then . . .'

'You won't be crippled,' said Loic. 'Your leg gets better each day. You will limp a little, perhaps. But, because of Mark, you will walk – and run, I think – quite well.'

'It's true that the setting worked,' I said. 'If I'd known thee was feart for that, I could have told thee weeks ago.'

Alan looked at me, half-embarrassed, half-suspicious. 'You'd swear to that, brother Mark?'

'No. But thee has my word for it.' I hesitated; there were more reasons than one for changing the subject. 'Thee had an Indian wife, I think, in Athabasca?'

'Ah. Hugh told you that?'

'Ay.'

Alan glanced my way again. 'I did her no harm, brother Mark. I have never – wittingly, at least – done any woman harm.'

I said to him, as I never could have done a year ago, 'I believe thee.' I did not bother to add my thoughts about harm done unwittingly, and whether a man should be held guilty of a sin that is entirely invisible to his own conscience. Indeed, I know not what I could have said, for in my own mind the question is not resolved to this very day.

In the weeks that followed, Alan, now that his tongue was loosed, told us many more stories about the far north, and the Chippewyan people among whom he had lived, and the many things they had taught him about their barren northern land. But he never mentioned his domestic life again, and I never asked him. He believed what I said about his leg – and indeed I'd spoken with more confidence than I felt in my heart. But it seemed to do the trick; a weight of anxiety was lifted from him, and from that day he mended fast, until he was walking almost as well as ever. His melancholy, though, seemed to have transferred itself to me, as if I had taken on the burden of it. We had failed to find Rachel. Clearly Alan, as soon as he was free of this war, would go back to *le pays d'en haut*, and find himself a wife among the people of the country he had chosen, a woman who would serve him better in the life he loved than my sister would ever have been able to do. I should never have interfered in his life. I had helped him not at all; on the contrary, I'd come near to destroying him. And my sister Rachel, as I should have known, was lost forever.

CHAPTER 24

THE DAY THE WARRIORS CAME BACK, WE'D JUST brought the canoe up to our wigwam so we could start repairing it for spring. They took no notice at all of Alan or Loic. They were armed as before, but their muskets were slung harmlessly across their shoulders. The one who'd addressed me before came right up to me, and said again, '*Nigigwetagad.*'

'Ay?'

He spoke too fast, and the Ottawa tongue was beyond me anyway, so I held up my hand. 'Will thee let my friend translate?'

Loic watched the man warily as he interpreted. 'He says, "So you have lived another winter."'

'Ay.'

'He says, "You have lived so long, what will you do with all this life that is given to you?"'

'Tell him I seek my sister Rachel.'

It was clear that the answer concerned Alan. Alan didn't flinch when he was pointed out, but stood stolidly, leaning on his crutch.

'He says, you say what he knows already. He says, "Why do you travel among the Ottawa with this man?"'

'This man is the husband of my sister who is lost.'

'He says, "This man has come to make trouble among my people. This man incites us to an alliance with the British." He says, "We have heard what he has to say many times before. For generations his people have made use of us. They drag us into their wars and persuade us to fight for them. We know what happens. Sometimes white people come as enemies, and make war on us. Sometimes they say they are allies, and they bring worse evil than our enemies. If it were not for you, *Nigigwetagad*, I would have killed this man. It would be better for us if there were none like him. It would be better if there were no white people in our country at all, if you had stayed in your own place, and not come to our lands in order to rob and murder and steal, and entice us with promises that do not last."'

'Say to him, "He is my brother, my sister's husband, and he is a good man. I love him well."' I kept my eyes away from Alan as I said that, and waited for the reply.

'He says, "What is that to me? I came to speak to you, *Nigigwetagad*. You killed a bear in my hunting ground this winter."'

'Ay.'

'"And because you did that, you lived."'

'Ay.'

'"Did you give thanks for the life that was given that you might live? Did you make the proper offerings?"' Loic went on speaking rapidly, then turned to me again. 'I told him that I showed you, and you did everything that you ought.'

The man was speaking again, and Loic translated, 'He says, "There is no reason why I, or any of my people, should help you, *Nigigwetagad*. You have no right to hunt on my lands, and yet you came, and you took what you wanted, and now it is spring, and you have lived. You owe me something, and I owe you nothing. Yet I do as I will. Your sister is not far away. Do you wish to take her?"'

I felt Alan's startled movement as if it were my own. I think our thoughts were never so close as in that moment, and yet I could not look at him. 'Ay,' I said quietly. 'Tell him that is what I wish.'

'He says, "Then come."'

Dazed as I was, I had to think. 'Ask him, "Is it far?"'

'He says, "One day, two days, maybe. He will lend you a guide."'

'Just me?'

The answer was a single word. 'Yes, just you,' interpreted Loic.

'Tell him I'm ready.'

But it was Loic who delayed us for a moment. He said something I couldn't follow, and disappeared into the wigwam. While he was gone, Alan said suddenly, 'You'd better take the musket, brother Mark.'

There was that in his voice I'd never heard before – bitterness, perhaps, or shame – an emotion I'd never seen in him, for all we'd lived so close for the best part of a year. 'No,' I said. 'Thee and Loic will need it. Besides, if I were not *Nigigwetagad*, I wouldn't be going. So that is who I will be.' I touched him awkwardly on the shoulder. 'I'll do my best, Alan.'

He took my hand – he was not as reticent as I – and gripped it. He didn't look at me. I was still too much amazed to be jubilant, and I supposed he felt the same. Only later did I realise how much I must have shamed him. At the time I thought his flippancy unseemly, so little did I understand him even yet. 'I know that, brother Mark. And we will wait, like docile wives, for your return. I have naught to do but thank thee, I suppose.'

I went into the wigwam, and emptied my journal

and other small items out of my knapsack. My purse, unopened for half a year, lay at the bottom. After a moment's hesitation I left it in, and stuffed the knapsack with such trade goods as we had left – cloth and beads, mostly. Loic was beside me. He took down the string of bear claws, which he'd hung under the skull. He followed me outside and put it in my hands. 'Take them, Mark. Hang them round your neck, as I told you.'

'No, that I can't do!'

'Mark, I tell you to do this. If it means nothing to you, how can it hurt you?'

There was no time to explain to him. I took the string and hung it about my neck. My hunting knife was already at my belt. I turned to the warriors who stood watching. 'I'm ready.'

To my surprise, my guide was not one of the warriors, nor, indeed, any man at all. We'd gone less than a mile when we came to a little glade among the cedars, where the snow had melted in patches. The exposed grass was brown as if it had been scorched. There was a fallen tree trunk at the far end, and when we came close I saw that a woman was sitting curled up in the crook of it. Her deerskin dress was the same colour as the cedar bark, and I could have walked right by without noticing her. She jumped down as we approached, and took up a deerskin bag which she swung on to her shoulder. She was taller than Waase'aaban, but she had some of Waase'aaban's easy grace. She glanced at me, then listened to what the leader of the band said to her. They both turned to me. He gestured towards her, and held up a hand to me, as if in farewell.

'Is she to be my guide?'

Of course they didn't understand. I watched them vanish into the shadow of the trees. When I looked round my companion was looking at me seriously, but without any fear, apparently, of being thus left alone with a stranger, and a white man at that.

'So what now?' I asked her, not so much expecting a reply, as feeling that I must speak.

She beckoned, and I followed.

For two days she led me ever further into the forest of Michigan. At first we walked on thick snow, but that grew less, until the patches of dirty snow alternated with a soft carpet of wet pine needles and rotted leaves. There was a path all the way, but without my guide I'd have lost sight of it time and again, for it was faint, and the snow patches were untrodden. Yet we seldom had to push our way through saplings or undergrowth, or duck our heads under overhanging branches. We walked under winter birches, where the lichen hung down in curtains from the bare branches, and the twigs were just taking on the purple sheen of new buds. The trees echoed with birdsong. Bright-coloured birds darted to and fro, some familiar chaffinches, tits and sparrows, and some – and these the least plain, it seemed – quite unknown to me. There were more tracks in the snowy patches than I was used to at the lake shore. The deer tracks were larger, too; several times we saw little bands of does which bounded off into the thickets when they heard us. We crossed swamps where our footsteps crackled through ice and freezing water. We skirted a big lake where the ice had melted at the edges, so we were forced to follow the shore, my companion walking easily, while I slipped and slid on the icy rocks in my moccasined feet.

Once we stopped at a creek high with meltwater, and squatted side by side to drink. Before she stood up again I pointed to my own chest, and said. 'Mark. *Nin Mark. Aaniin ezhinikaazoyan?*'

Her smile lit up her face. 'Waubagone,' she told me, and added a sentence I couldn't follow.

'*Daga ikidon, miinawaa*,' I said, as Loic had taught me.

She obligingly repeated what she'd said. After that we managed to converse a little sometimes, though I was never entirely sure if I were making sense.

Just as dusk was falling on the first day she halted at the foot of a giant fir tree, led me round the side of it and vanished. For a moment I thought myself bewitched, led by a will o' the wisp that was swallowed up into its own element with the coming of dark, leaving me eternally benighted – for I could never have found my own way out. Then I heard her call, and saw the split in the huge trunk. I could barely squeeze my way through but, once inside, the hollow of the tree was dry and snug, as wide across as our own wigwam. Others had bivouacked here before us, for there were cedar boughs already spread across the floor. They were hardly needed: the ground was soft as a sponge with ancient bark and wood dust.

I sat down, and leaned against the trunk. The light was thickening fast. Waubagone brought out dried meat with berries in it, which could have tasted worse. I offered her water from my flask, but she shook her head, and went away. Presently she came back with fresh water in a birchbark container, so we weren't short, though I never did discover the source of it.

By the time we'd eaten it was almost too dark to see. '*Nibaan!*' Waubagone suited the action to the word, and curled up on the cedar boughs on the far side of our shelter, with her back to me.

Obediently I lay down in my corner, said a brief prayer, and composed myself to sleep.

I was cold in the night, and when I did sleep at last I woke late, thinking I was back in the wigwam with Alan and Loic, but then I remembered, and sat up and looked about me. Waubagone had gone. I was a little anxious, but before long she returned with more water.

We shared that, and more of the meat. Waubagone stood up. '*Bi-wiijiiwishin!*'

We walked as silently as on the day before. Presently the path grew wider. We came to a place where four roads met, and after that we were following a veritable track between stands of birch and maple. I'd never seen such maples; when I stretched my arms around a trunk I could barely reach halfway. I could feel the heat of the sun on my back, and the air was full of the smell of new growth. Somewhere on my right a thrush began to sing, the same mellow, liquid tune we hear from the thrushes that nest in the blackthorn by the gate at Highside. My heart quickened at the sound, and I stopped to listen.

'A throssel,' I said.

Waubagone looked at me and smiled. '*Opitchi*,' she told me, and I smiled back.

It was not long after that that I caught the sweet whiff of woodsmoke. 'Are we nearly there?'

She said something I couldn't follow, and then repeated one word several times, slowly. '*Sisibakwat, Sisibakwat.*'

We were among tall maples. The sweetish smell grew stronger. Then I saw trees with wooden troughs fixed against their trunks, and realised where I must be. 'This is a maple syrup village?'

Waubagone beckoned me over to the trees, and I saw how little spouts of cedar wood were driven into the trees, so that watery sap dripped out into the troughs. She signed for me to put my finger under the flow and taste. It was like the sugar-water people use to wean infants.

I followed her onwards, until we reached a clearing where there was a single great lodge, with walls of rushes and a birchbark roof. Racks of freshly caught fish were drying in the sun. Smoke rose from the lodge, and with it I breathed in a rich toffee smell that made me think of nothing so much as my mother's baking days when I was a little lad at Highside, when I used to be allowed to scrape the bowls and lick the wooden spoon. I could hear dogs barking and children shouting, and then someone calling us from under the trees. A girl came running to meet Waubagone. Three or four women came to the door of the lodge. Suddenly Waubagone, whom I'd thought of as so silent, was laughing and talking, no doubt describing our journey to them. An older woman came over and interrupted her, and in a loud, firm voice she asked a single question. A sudden silence fell. Waubagone turned to me. '*Bi-wiijiiwishin!*'

The door of the lodge was wide, and the curtain of matting was tied back. I could see the glow of a long fire inside, through a thick mist of steam and smoke, and the rush of heat from within brought with it the rich smell of boiling sugar. I wasn't invited in: the woman indicated a cedar log bench at the door, and I obediently sat down. The others went back into the lodge, but Waubagone and the older woman walked away into the maple grove. I knew I should have had tobacco to give, but we'd had none left, so I'd come empty-handed. I was torn between anticipation and wild hope about Rachel, and awareness of my own empty belly. I'd had nothing but a few strips of dried meat for two active days, and I couldn't stop thinking about toffee.

'*Nigigwetagad!*' I looked up. One of the girls had come outside again, and was holding out a wooden bowl.

I took it gratefully. '*G'miigwechiwigin, nwiijikiwenh,*' I said.

She laughed, and clapped her hands together in appreciation of my linguistic skill, which was more than kind of her, I thought, for I was angry with myself for being so ill-prepared when it was vital to communicate. The food was fresh trout cooked with corn, and very good. The ice must have melted hereabouts, I thought, for the men to be doing so much fishing. When I'd scraped the bowl there was nothing to do but wait.

My patience was not tried much longer. I saw Waubagone coming towards me. With her were three women, one with a cradleboard on her back, and another with a toddling bairn carried on her hip. They came halfway across the clearing. Then the woman with the bairn left the others and came towards me.

I stood up slowly. She was wearing a deerskin tunic that reached to her knees, over a trade shirt, and fringed leggings over winter moccasins. Her braided hair fell down her back, just like any other young woman. She was a little shorter than the girl who'd brought me here, and much paler. The child, who was not pale at all, but brown as a fledgling wren, looked at me unblinkingly from under a fringe of thick black hair.

I went slowly towards her. We stood about five feet apart, and I looked into her eyes.

'Rachel?'

I thought she tried to speak, but no words came. I saw her swallow. Then she said, in a kind of hoarse whisper, as she looked at me with a terror I'd never seen in her before in all our lives, 'Is it . . . Mark?'

'Ay.'

If she'd been the sister I knew, her face would have crumpled up then, and she'd have hurled herself, sobbing, into my arms. It had happened before. This Rachel stood frozen, staring at me as if she was seeing a ghost, and trying to refute the evidence of her own eyes.

'Ay,' I said again. 'It's me. I've come to fetch thee home.'

'Mark,' she said hoarsely, as if she were asking herself a question. Then, '*Mark!*'

'Ay. It's me.' Something had to happen. At least we could both speak English, or so I hoped. 'Is this thy bairn?'

I asked her gently. I felt like I was coaxing an unbroken colt towards the halter. If I'd had sugar in my pocket, I daresay I'd have held it out to her on my spread palm.

Then she did begin to cry, but not the way she used to do. She made no sound, but I saw her tears falling. 'Is it my bairn!' she repeated. 'Thee asks me that!'

'Ay,' I said. 'It seems a reasonable question.'

'Thee *is* Mark.' That time I did hear her sob. 'Thee *is*.'

'Ay.' I wasn't sure what to do next. 'Does he have a name?'

'She,' said Rachel, and sniffed. I knew that sniff. It brought her back to me so much I felt my own tears rise. 'Thee's right, she is mine. Her name is Zhawenjigewin. I won't leave her, Mark.'

It wasn't worded as an appeal, but I caught a note of desperation in it. 'No,' I said. 'I see that.' I looked at the little girl, as if she were a riddle I were called upon to solve.

'It means the same in English,' said Rachel suddenly.

'Oh?'

'Zhawenjigewin. Thee can say it in English. Clemency.'

'Clemency,' I repeated numbly. 'Ay well, Rachel, thee'd better get ready, if we're to bring her home. It's a long journey.'

'Mark.' Two tears rolled down her cheeks and dripped off her chin. She made no move to wipe them away. 'Thee's just the same. Mark. Isn't thee?'

'Ay, but thee needn't greet for that.'

'But thee must see . . . how can I go home? . . . Where in the world could I go now?'

'Rachel,' I said. 'Alan is close by. He's hurt; he couldn't walk so far to find thee.' (That was not the whole truth, but it was true in fact, and seemed more politic.) 'We came to look for thee, and for that he was injured. I left him waiting for thee.'

'I won't leave my child.'

'Have I asked thee to?'

'But Alan . . .'

I couldn't in honesty finish the sentence for her. 'There's only one way to find out,' I said. 'If it seems that Alan and thee must part, I shall take thee home.'

'Home!' I thought then she'd break down. If she'd been alone I think I'd have taken her in my arms, but the bairn made that awkward. I didn't want to frighten it. 'Home! Thee knows I can't go home! Am I not disowned?'

'Ay,' I said. 'But not by me, nor thy father and mother.' I was struck by an afterthought. 'The little maid is not disowned.'[1]

---

[1] I said this in all sincerity, but it would have been a moot point. If Clemency had come to Highside, where her grandparents were in unity, I think, discounting her mother, she would have been accepted into birthright Membership under their guardianship. Legitimacy of birth would not have been an issue; being the offspring of parents who were married before a priest would have created more difficulty. My sister would have presented a more intransigent problem than her child. If Rachel had expressed sincere repentance for her backsliding, and a firm intent to mend her way of life, and if she had given a written statement to that effect to Monthly Meeting, I think after a time her plea would have been accepted, and she restored to unity. I cannot imagine that Rachel would have submitted easily to the process.

When I was at London Yearly Meeting I was almost moved to put forward my concern about our Testimony on marriage. Over the years I have seen so many good men and women lost from Membership of our Society because they chose to marry one who was not in Membership with us, which marriage must perforce be carried out before a priest. As I grow older the conviction grows on me that if our beloved Society is to survive in this fast-changing world, we must not cast out such Members from the fold. A way must be found to accommodate them, for very often these are convinced Friends, whose fault is only that they marry where they love. If this be sin, then who among us would desire to cast one stone? I say I was almost moved. The truth is that London Yearly Meeting daunted me somewhat: I had never been so far from home (except when I was in North America) and the place was full of southerners, who have much to say for themselves, and I found I could not speak.

Tentatively I held out my hand. Suddenly Rachel brushed the tears from her face with an impatient gesture I knew well, and turned away. I watched her disappear into the lodge.

I became aware of the women watching us. The older woman followed Rachel into the dark interior. There was nothing to do but wait. I paced to and fro under the maple trees – I was far too anxious to be still – and watched the sap dripping into the troughs. The dogs and children followed me at a little distance, watching warily. When I turned back towards the lodge a group of men were standing between me and the door. As I walked towards them they watched me gravely. No one moved or spoke. I stopped about six feet from them. '*Boozhoo,*' I said cautiously.

I don't know what would have happened, but just then Waubagone came out of the lodge with the older woman, who was evidently an elder among them, for she talked to the men, and they seemed to listen respectfully. But then there was some kind of argument. As far as I could make out, a couple of the young men were speaking quite forcefully to a tall warrior – I knew he must be a man of note by his eagle feathers – who seemed to be the leader. But another, older man, seemed to disagree with them. I couldn't tell who the leader favoured; he seemed impatient with both parties. I'd had enough. I interrupted them all, and said as firmly as I could in French, '*Messieurs! Je cherche ma sœur. Je la trouve. Je la prend chez nous!*'

The Lord was good to me; one of the men who had held aloof until now tapped the leader on the shoulder, and after a little discussion between them, he spoke to me in halting French. I had trouble understanding his accent, but the gist was clear enough. They – or some among them – said that Rachel was theirs, and disputed my right to take her away. My heart sank. Then I remembered the gifts that I had brought. I opened my knapsack and laid out the lengths of cloth and ropes of bead. I wished I had more, but at least the women came out to look over what there was.

It seemed not to be enough. '*Asemaa*,' said Waubagone, and then more emphatically: '*Asemaa!*'

I spread my hands helplessly. 'I have no more tobacco.'

The leader spoke, and there was a ring of finality about his words as he turned away. One of the young men shot me a look of scorn as he turned to follow.

I pushed in front of him and stood before the leader. He frowned at me, but I was past fearing. All I had left was my purse, and there was little enough in it, only the ten guineas which I could not spend in Mackinac, in spite of my needs, because they'd been given to me by Robert Southey as a gift to Rachel, if ever I should find her. I untied the leather string, and shook the gold coins on to my palm. I saw I had the man's attention. I held my hand out to him. The ten coins gleamed in the sunlight. 'I have brought thee this gift,' I said loudly and clearly, although not one among them could understand a word I said. 'It comes from one of my own people. My sister gave him food and shelter when she was a little lass, and he was lost on the hill. I have brought this gold all the way from Greta Hall in Keswick, and used it for no other purpose because it was given for her. So now it is thine, and I will take her.'

Though the words can have made no sense to him, he must have understood me by my tone. He wasn't frowning now, but he was watching me gravely. After a moment's hesitation he held out his hand, palm upwards. One of the young men seized him by the shoulder, and said something vehement, but the leader brushed him aside, and looked at me. I met his eyes, and some instinct I did not know

I had, told me to act with all the ceremony of which I was capable. I picked up the gold coins, one by one, and transferred them from my palm to his. When they lay in a neat circle in his left palm, I held out my right hand. He looked down at it, puzzled, and the man who knew a little French whispered something in his ear. The leader held out his right hand, and I solemnly shook his hand to seal our bargain.

Then the leader spoke sharply to the group around him, and in a moment all dispersed. The younger men went into the lodge, followed by Waubagone and the old woman, and I was left alone.

I kept my eyes on the door of the lodge. I waited a long time, and began to be very fearful. At last the skins were pushed back, and I saw Rachel coming towards me. She was without the baby, a small tense figure, braced as if for confrontation. My heart misgave me. It had never crossed my mind that after my long journey, and all my successful bargaining, she might refuse to come with me. The thoughts rushed through my mind: what would I say to Alan? To my parents? What could I possibly do to insist? When Rachel's mind was made up, she never budged. I waited apprehensively.

She didn't waste words. She came up to me and said, 'I will come. We will both come. They say I have no choice. If I had ... I don't know ... I don't know ... *Mark!*' Her control broke suddenly. She threw herself against my chest, weeping, and I hugged her in my arms. She smelt of maple sugar and woodsmoke. Her face was buried in my coat; she clung to me like one possessed. I said the sort of things one says to a frightened puppy. I don't know if she listened, but she stopped suddenly, and held herself away from me, gripping my arms. 'Mark. Thee came. Thee *came*. I have to tell thee: I *dreamed* it. I dreamed thee would come. Again and again I dreamed it. I made myself stop, because I knew it was impossible. But thee *came*.'

'Ay.'

'Thee *came*.'

'Ay, we've established that. Where's the bairn? Is thee ready to go now?'

'No.' She looked down. 'I'll come . . . but I can't just leave . . . Tomorrow.'

'Why may we not depart today?'

She hesitated. 'I can't tell thee. I'll tell thee later. I must . . . Will thee wait for me, Mark? Will thee wait one day?'

'It's been a bit more than a day. It won't make much difference now.'

She never told me what it was she had to do. In the end I agreed to go back the two hours' walk to the hollow tree, and wait for her there. I found my way quite easily: the track was clear back to the turning, and thereafter Waubagone and I had left our footprints here and there in snow and mud. I stayed the night alone, and in the long silence of the dark my fears subsided. I wouldn't feel quite safe until I had her back to Mackinac, but there was a joy growing in my heart, as gradually I began to believe in it, that I had found her, that I had succeeded in what I set out to do.

Halfway through the next morning they came: Rachel, with Clemency-Zhawenjigewin on her back, and Waubagone. The baby looked at me with bright eyes, and made bab-bling noises.

'She can't talk yet?' I asked Rachel, for the ways of infants were little known to me.

'She says, "ma-ma". And "da-da-da".'

'Ay, that's a start, I suppose.'

In fact the child had more to say than any of us on the journey through the forest. Sometimes she slept, and sometimes she babbled and crooned, and sometimes she gazed with wide eyes at the sunlight that shafted through the trees about us. I offered to carry her, but Rachel refused to hand her over, and Waubagone, when Rachel said something about it to her, looked at me in astonishment. We had to stop at intervals for the child to nurse, and be cleaned up. While all that was going on I sat a little space apart and occupied myself with my own thoughts, which were mostly concerned with what our journey home would be like, with a woman and a baby in the canoe as well. I wondered if Alan would be fit to paddle. He certainly couldn't sit for hours with his legs tucked under him. I could apply my mind to the material problems. The emotional ones I could not face, but they hung at the back of my mind like a lowering storm that closed in nearer with every step we took. Finally it was right over us. We came out by the creek, and walked along the path trodden out by Alan, Loic and me, into our own clearing.

They'd lit a fire outside, and were sitting side by side on a log eating their dinner in the evening sun. The pot had been taken off the heat, but still simmered at their feet. I saw them for a second before they saw us, and, most unexpectedly, a wave of grief swept over me, for all the days we'd spent together, just the three of us, that were now ended. I'd spent my time struggling and longing for this moment, the time when our long task would be accomplished, and I might go home. But now that it had come, I was acutely aware of the thing that I was losing, which, in that little moment, I knew would never come again.[2]

They saw us, and Loic jumped up. Alan reached for his ashplant, and got slowly to his feet. I stood back,

[2] I was right; it never has.

and let Rachel walk towards him on her own. Of course, I realised, they'd both had time to prepare themselves. The small matter that Alan wouldn't have expected was Clemency-Zhawenjigewin. But there I wronged him: Alan wasn't stupid. He knew what would happen to a captive woman; he would have thought of this. I saw him look at the baby, and instantly comprehend. What I didn't know – I'd had plenty of time to consider it – was what he'd do.

'Rachel,' said Alan. He sounded diffident, but he held out both his hands.

She didn't take them. 'Her name is Zhawenjigewin,' she said without preamble. I knew that truculent defiance. It was the way Rachel always faced trouble, refusing to compromise, as if deliberately inviting more. 'She's my daughter.'

If I'd been Alan I'd have been tempted to strike her.

After a long moment Alan said, 'And you're my wife. We were married before a priest. In law that makes her mine also.'

'She isn't thine,' said Rachel flatly. She had no need to state the fact. Clemency-Zhawenjigewin was clearly neither two years old nor white. I saw that Rachel, reverting to her old self, was determined to behave badly. I couldn't bear it. I turned my back on them, and gave my sister up for lost.

Alan said, 'I know that. Do you . . . Are you asking me to leave you?'

'Leave me?' repeated Rachel. 'Thee left me long ago, I think. So how can thee leave me now?'

'Rachel . . .' Alan stopped, and brushed his hand across his forehead. 'I don't want . . . We've come so far . . . You're my wife. I didn't leave you. I came to find you.'

'Mark found me.'

'That's enough!' I flinched – I'd had Alan's anger come

my way, once – but Rachel never quailed. 'For Christ's sake, woman, is that all you can say! After all that . . . you'd be better served if I . . . You're married to me, by God! *You* left *me*! I told you . . . Oh, for God's sake!' He looked at her in exasperation, and gave a twisted smile. ''Twas not what I meant to say, Rachel. I've had enough time to think, God knows. I'll say to you what I planned to say, whether you choose or not: we were married before a priest. In law that makes your child mine. If you come back to me, there's no other way for it to be.'

'Does thee mean that?' asked Rachel slowly. She seemed so cold, but I, who knew her best, saw the naked grief in her eyes. She looked more like one bereaved than one restored. Why she should torture herself – and Alan too – in this fashion was quite beyond me.

'Yes,' said Alan baldly. He paused. 'But I can't call her Zhawenjigewin. She'll have to have an English name.'

'She has one,' snapped Rachel. 'Clemency.'

'Then bring her in,' said Alan, and limped over to the wigwam. He held back the hide over the door. 'Won't you . . . Can we speak about this privately? Please? Rachel?'

Rachel hesitated for a moment. Then she swung Clemency off her back, and shifted her on to her hip. She walked slowly over to the wigwam, recalcitrance writ large in every step she took, ducked under the doorway, and disappeared inside. Alan followed her, and the hide fell into place behind them.

Loic and I looked at each other. Waubagone was still standing there, waiting patiently. 'Are you hungry?' asked Loic. 'We made plenty, hoping you'd be back.'

Waubagone left as soon as she had eaten. The only gift I had for her was a couple of bears' claws, but she seemed pleased with those. Loic and I sat on by the fire. We talked a little, but mostly we just watched the logs crackle, and the sun go down behind the trees. Loic told me how he'd shot a doe the day I'd left them. We should be all right, he said, now that spring was coming. In a few weeks we'd be able to go home. At the thought of home we relapsed into silence, each of us thinking his own thoughts.

'Loic?' I said at last.

'*Oui?*'

'Nidon said . . . everyone has said, all the time, that if Rachel were among the Ottawa in the Michigan Territory, they would have heard about it.'

'I have been thinking that too. It is quite true, they would have heard. So we were not to be told, *en effet*. I have been trying to remember the things that were said, exactly. I doubt if anyone has lied to us. Waubagone says the warriors you met on South Manitou are going away now that spring has come. They go to join Tecumseh.'

'Thee thinks it was because of them we were not to be told?'

'Rachel was taken from Alan,' said Loic. 'She was returned, not to Alan, but to you.'

'I don't understand.'

'*Oui*, Mark, you understand quite well, if you think about it. Would you welcome a stranger coming into your own country, inciting men to war? I think not. You like your own ways best, do you not? It is the same here. Perhaps Rachel, when she is used to being among us again, will be able to explain it to you more.'

Rachel, it turned out, was not willing to explain anything. I found our winter quarters far less peaceful now that she was with us. She didn't say much, but her presence was unrestful, as it had always been. I was shocked at my own resentment. It wasn't the first time in my life that Rachel had come in as the unwanted fourth. Perhaps she told Alan more than she told me, but they had very little opportunity to be private together, for fine weather in March seldom lasts for long, and we spent many days crammed together inside the wigwam. Rachel interrupted the easy flow of silence and story to which we'd grown accustomed, and she didn't make up for it by telling us any stories of her own. In fact she was singularly unforthcoming. Alan never seemed to be irritated. He said little, but very often I caught his eyes resting upon her, and what I read in them told me he still loved her. I couldn't see what she'd done to deserve it. But then my part in this was done, and the sooner I could go back to my own life the better.

It was her silences that were the worst. Alan, Loic and I were not inclined to prattle needlessly; we had grown used to our own easy silences, just as we'd grown used to our evenings of desultory talk and occasional stories. Rachel's silences were not like that. They had a gowry, brooding quality, which cast a tension over us all, even Loic. The first time that she got up abruptly from her place by the fire, and walked off towards Bear Lake, we were left looking at one another, uncertain what we had done, or said, that might have upset her.

I got up to follow.

'Leave her,' said Alan curtly, without looking up.

'Alan, 'twas how she was lost before!'

'Ay,' said Alan. 'Do you think you need to tell me that?'

'The Indians are back in the maple village by the lake here,' I reminded him. 'There's no saying that she may meet them. On purpose even.'

'And if she does?' said Alan. 'Who am I to stop her? Besides,' he pointed out, with a faint grin, 'We have a hostage, brother Mark.'

I'd forgotten about Clemency-Zhawenjigewin, who was sleeping peacefully inside the wigwam. Alan was cleverer than I was. I sat down.

Rachel did come back just as it grew dark. But if anything – or nothing at all – happened to upset her or displease her, she'd walk away without a word, which seemed to me inconsiderate, to say the least, in the light of what had gone before. But sometimes I was actually relieved to see her go, her presence often being wretchedly oppressive to us all. Her Maker knew what was in her mind, no doubt, but for mere mortal men her inexplicable melancholy was a sad trial. I would have thought she would be filled with joy that she was back among her own, but joy seemed to be the furthest state from her condition. I could not help thinking her ungrateful, and was peeved accordingly. We were not happy with each other, but then, I began to ask myself, had we ever been?

Loic said, when he and I were working on the canoe together, 'I think she is sad for what she has left. You did not see the man?'

'What man?'

He looked at me as if I were a particularly obtuse small child. 'Her man, Mark. Zhawenjigewin has a father, does she not?'

'I know nothing of him,' I said stiffly.

'That is a pity,' observed Loic. 'If you, her own brother, cannot speak to her, then she is lonely indeed, I think.'

'*Lonely?* But she is back among her own people. She has her husband again!'

'It would be better if she could talk to you, I think.'

'Talk about what?'

'What she cannot say to Alan.'

I gave up. Rachel presented me with enough riddles without Loic offering more. 'If thee passes me that spruce root,' I said pointedly, 'I can lash the gunwale here.'

My little niece was easier company. She was blate at first, and fretful if her mother was not immediately at hand. Soon we grew used to one another. I kept the bears' claws round my neck because she liked to play with them. She preferred Alan, because he sang to her for as long as she desired it: all the old voyageur songs I'd learned on my journey west, and other, more plaintive, songs in his own Scotch language, which I'd never heard him utter before, except when he was very sick, and knew not what he spoke. But Clemency seemed to understand it well enough, and, what was a blessing to us all, the songs often had the power to make her fall asleep, when nothing else would do the trick.

My opportunity came when Rachel said she'd like to come up the dunes with me. There was a brisk wind at the top. Our eyes watered as we gazed across the shining icefields to the distant Manitous. 'The ice is like clouds,' said Rachel, 'like looking down on the cloud over Borrowdale from the top of Skiddaw.' She gave a little chuckle, the way she used to do when something pleased her very much. 'I'd like to walk on it.'

''Twould be too slippery for thee.' I glanced at her sideways; it was the first time I'd seen her smile since she was found. I seized my chance. 'Rachel, will thee not tell me what happened, just this once? I give thee my word I'll never ask thee again, if thee tells me now.'

Her face clouded over. She went on staring at South Manitou, a little frown between her eyes. I let the silence be, and at last she spoke. 'I suppose I could have fought. I can fight. They were five or six, and I was but one, and a woman at that. I don't *think* I could have helped it.'

'I'm sure thee couldn't help it,' I said, when the silence seemed to grow too long.

'I died to the world I came from,' she said eventually. 'Or so I thought. For ever and ever. I thought of myself as dead. My old self, that is, because when I grew accustomed, I found I *was* still myself. Deep inside, I mean, for in every other way I was someone else. I was a different woman in another life. God gives us life, and we have to take our strength in our hands and live it, whatever he sends. I tried to do that, according to his will. I did my best to learn – I tried to be brave – and God rewarded me. I changed. I was a different woman: a woman who could still be happy sometimes, even though she had no past. I *am* that woman, Mark. I don't wish to die again.'

'Of course thee isn't going to die!' Such talk seemed to me morbid, and yet Rachel was a woman of robust mind, and I hoped to encourage her.

She sighed. 'Oh, Mark!' But after a moment she went on, 'In the eyes of God I belong to no one but myself.'

'That's true enough.'

'And yet I'm capable of love, Mark. I don't know what thee thinks love is like. I don't think thee and I would ever agree about that. But I can love.'

And that was all I could get out of her.[3] I felt more in charity with her when we were scrambling over the dunes. She was as sure-footed as ever, a fast runner, for a lass, and daring with it. I think we always did best together when there were no words.

*   *   *

[3] To this day I do not know exactly what happened. Conjecture is easy enough; one could say that it's fairly obvious how she was taken. One can only surmise who may have been responsible, and why they did it. I suspect that over time Rachel confided more to Alan about her life among the Ottawa. There were references in one or two of his letters that made me suspect he knew more of her story than he told. I have one of his letters by me now, dated February (as he puts it), 1814, wherein he writes, 'I don't care to trespass upon her loyalty, although the object of it is not entirely plain. She insists that – in her words – *nothing was taken that was not owed*. I don't say I understand, but I can only respect her silence, since I have no means to break it.' Rachel's letters never referred to the matter again.

I never told my parents that Clemency was not Alan's child. I didn't lie; merely, I didn't allow the question to arise. Moreover, what they believed was true, because in Alan's own mind Clemency was his daughter, and as far as I know he has never wavered from the opinion he gave when he first laid eyes on her, either in word or deed.

When Loic and I walked over to Lake Michigan early in Fourth Month, there was still mottled ice as far as the eye could see, but it was breaking up fast. Icy waves lapped the shore with a whispering sound like the wind through summer leaves. Further out, the jagged ice ridges were worn smooth by the waves until they looked like nothing so much as cream poured over a steamed pudding. We kept a close eye on the lake as the days grew warmer. The ice on our own little lake was beginning to melt, so we could set the net at night. We were trapping more game too, so we didn't go hungry. The Ottawa came back to their maple sugar camp by Bear Lake. Although we never saw the men whose hunting ground this was, we were surprised one day by a visit from Nidon and the other men from the South Manitou village, for this was their maple sugar camp too.

When Nidon saw Rachel his eyes widened, but the Ottawa are an impassive people before strangers. When she'd gone away, we men talked very little, but sat before the wigwam and smoked. Loic mentioned presently that I'd bought Rachel back from the people that had taken her. Nidon looked across at me. We met each other's eyes, and no words were said. I don't think he'd lied to me before, but simply held his peace.

We parted as friends, and when he realised we had no more tobacco he gave us two big rolls of it. Recklessly – for spring seemed very near – Loic and I gave our own trade blankets in return, and slept in furs thereafter. We enjoyed having neighbours in the maple sugar village after the long solitude of winter. When the breeze blew our way, it bore the heavy sweet smell of boiling sugar, and filled my heart with memories of baking days at Highside. The children were curious, and egged one another on to visit us, and on still days we could hear the voices from the maple grove, and the sound of drumming in the evenings.

But Rachel kept herself aloof, and when Nidon and the others came over for a smoke in the evenings, she always hid away in the wigwam. I didn't think she was frightened; it was something else. I went so far as to ask her about it, but all I got was the answer she'd given me all her life: 'Doesn't thee understand *anything*?' I said to her – and the words seemed stale on my tongue, I'd spoken them so often before, 'How can I understand if thee won't tell me?' At which she sighed, and walked away from me.

Oddly enough, now that the day of our departure drew near, I felt in no hurry to leave. I was almost sorrowful. The weather was mild enough now for me to climb the dunes every day, and I'd look out over the shifting icefields, and watch the far blue line of open water creep gradually nearer. On windy days Lake Michigan was filled with the noise of breaking ice, rattling and cracking as it moved. Then all of a sudden the days – though not the nights – were hot, and we shed our smelly furs at last, and went bare-chested in the fresh heat of the sun as the Indians do. Now, instead of pools of water among the icefields, there were islands of ice in the blue waters. Rafts of ducks began to appear, sitting on the ice or floating in the free waters. The ice on Bear Lake broke up into segments, and our winter paths were drowned.

We didn't want to take any risks with a fully loaded canoe, so it wasn't until a week into Fifth Month that we finally broke up our winter camp. We left the rolled up birchbark, the snowshoes, and some other tools we'd made, just inside the frame of the wigwam. The absurd thought crossed my mind that the correct thing to do would be to leave a note. That made Alan laugh, but Loic said seriously that Nidon and the others would read our message without any difficulty. And so we pushed off into the freezing waters of Lake Michigan, carefully skirting the remaining rafts of ice when we encountered them. As we got further north we found more ice, and indeed we had to wait at L'Arbre Croche for several days, for there were still miles of broken ice clogging up the Straits. At Sleeping Bear I would never have guessed it would be so bad at Mackinac, though Alan and Loic had warned me.

We travelled in easy stages, for we had a full load, and Alan was pretty weak at first. It was hard for him to sit in such a way that he could paddle, so I kept my place as bowsman. Rachel and the child sat on the floor of the canoe, where we made a sheltered hollow for them among the bales. The weather was kind, and sky and water stayed blue and bright. The onshore breeze merely played with us, never threatening to fling us back on to that inhospitable shore. We met no one until we got to the village at L'Arbre Croche. The summer villages along the shore were empty; everyone was still inland at the maple groves. There were times when we even fell into a holiday mood, as if we were merely cruising for pleasure close to home.

On one such day I heard Rachel say – for I had my back to her, being bowsman – 'Mark, does thee mind that day we went on the barge right to the end of Derwentwater? And they fired the cannon under Lodore crags, and it echoed back and forth from Cat Bells to Castle Rigg for hours and hours?'

'Not hours and hours. A minute or so, if that.'

'But thee minds it?'

'Ay, I mind it.'[4] I laughed, and called back to her – for

[4] It was the only half-holiday we ever took, I think – my father, my mother, Rachel and I – all at once. It was so contrary to our usual practice that I cannot conceive now how such a trip ever came about. It was hardly my parents' practice to join the summer Lakers at their vain ploys. I can only think that Rachel desired to go, and would not let the matter rest until she had persuaded us all to accompany her. There is no other way it could have happened.

I had to keep my eyes on the waters ahead – 'That was the day thee pushed Jamie Wilson off the jetty on Lord's Island, because he guillotined thy doll.'

'' Twas *not* that day. The barge didn't land on any islands. Thee's thinking of when we took a pic-nic to Lord's Island after the hay harvest, in uncle John's big rowing boat. Father and Mother weren't there the time Jamie fell in.'

'Ay, but thee did push the poor lad off the jetty, all the same.'

'Ay, and so would thee have done, if it were thy baby had its head wrenched off!'

I laughed again. For the time being we were happy. At night we made voyageur camps along the shore. I remember a night when I stood under the pines and looked up through their canopy to the stars slowly pricking out. A nightjar sang from the darkening thickets while a small wind stirred the branches, and brushed my face with cool fingers. A pair of loons were calling back and forth across the lake, each like an echo of the other. I looked down at our camping place on the beach, and saw four familiar figures – three big, one very little – silhouetted against the red glow of the fire. I heard the flames crackle, and two – no three – voices singing:

> *Derrière chez nous, y'a-t-un étang,*
> *En roulant ma boule.*
> *Derrière chez nous, y'a-t-un étang,*
> *En roulant ma boule.*
> *Trois beaux canards s'en vont baignant,*
> *En roulant ma boule roulant.*
> *En roulant ma boule.*

I found myself thinking of Hugh, and Marc and Jean-Pierre, and Alan and Loic, and the time left, which was so swiftly running out. I thought about how I found Rachel, because it was not like looking for a needle in a bottle of hay after all, and about the little maid who had not been born when I set out from England. I found the words of the first psalm I ever learned going through my head . . . *for my cup runneth over. Surely Goodness and Mercy shall follow me all the days of my life: and I will dwell in the house of the Lord for ever.* Then – I know not why it was, except that many things had happened – in general I am not easily overset – I leaned against one of the pine trees – it smelt of bark and resin just like the pines at Highside – and fairly grat like a bairn.

CHAPTER 25

OUR CANOE ENDED ITS LONG JOURNEY WHEN LOIC
and I drifted gently onto the Kerners beach at Bois Blanc.
The brief glimpse of Mackinac had left me dazed, and
Loic's sudden urgency infected me. It had taken us a bare
half-hour to get Alan and Rachel ashore, and carry their
gear up to McGulpin's house. Even in that short time I
felt overwhelmed by the noise, the press of people, the
strangers passing to and fro. And yet less than a year
ago Mackinac had seemed to me a desert outpost. I had
no time to think of the extraordinary change in my own
appearance, or indeed of anything but Loic's need for
haste. I think Rachel was upset when I announced that
I couldn't stay. It must have been even stranger for her
to be back in Mackinac. I realise, looking back, that she
may have needed me. Obviously neither she nor Alan had
expected me to go off immediately with Loic. If Alan had
ever guessed my feelings about Waase'aaban, I imagined
he'd have forgotten about it by now. Anyway, my task was
done; I couldn't help Rachel rebuild her life. Alan seemed
to know how to deal with her better than I ever had.

At Bois Blanc Loic didn't wait to unload the canoe. We
beached it half out of the water, then Loic leapt up the bank
and ran towards the cabin without looking back. I followed

him more slowly. He flung the door wide open and rushed inside, shouting. I saw someone coming from the garden. It was the old man: he was half-running, calling as he came. Loic came out and ran straight to his father and embraced him. Martin hugged him, then kissed him many times on both cheeks. My own father loves me well, but if he ever kissed me it must have been before I have any conscious memory. Martin Kerners knew no such reticence. He held Loic by both arms, talking fast.

When they turned to me at last, Martin greeted me with formal courtesy, while the tears still ran freely down his cheeks. I thought for a moment something terrible had happened, for I couldn't follow their rapid French. I looked at Loic. But Loic was smiling broadly. 'Pakané is at the village. Her mother is back for the summer already. Now I go! You come, Mark?'

All of a sudden I was feart. If the two sisters had been at the house, that would have been one thing, for the Kerners' cabin at least belonged to a world I recognised. I suppose by now I ought to have felt at home in an Indian village, but if I could have avoided going there now I would have done. Her mother ... It had never occurred to me that Waase'aaban had a mother. I associated Waase'aaban with Loic and Martin and Pakané and Biinoojii, not with an unknown Ojibwa family. I thought of what I had done to Waase'aaban, not with the carnal pleasure that the memory had engendered all these months, but with a shock of guilt which, indeed, I should have felt long before. Her mother ... I'd been taught what was right – I had no excuse at all – but I'd allowed myself to ignore it.

'Come!' said Loic, and began to run.

I had no choice, having got so far. I panted after him – he was a good deal fleeter than I was, and he didn't wait. We pounded along the shore path, into the woods and through the pine trees. I tripped on a root and fell headlong. By the time I'd picked myself up Loic was out of sight. Anyway, I didn't want to burst in among them like a charging bull. I walked soberly, and got my breath back. A film of green lay over the ground. The willow buds were open, and under the trees there were clumps of tall white flowers, pale and clean-looking, like exotic daffodils.

Before I reached the village I saw a little group of people on the path. I came closer. One of them was Pakané, her face full of joy, and her hand on Loic's shoulder. And there was Loic, holding a little boy up high, and laughing in his face.

'See him!' called Loic as I came up. 'See my son! He is not Biinoojii any more. Now he is Martin. He is a proper boy! Here is the new Biinoojii! Here is our new little one!'

I looked, and there behind Pakané was Waase'aaban, as dark and beautiful as I remembered her. She was smiling, and when Loic spoke she turned her back, so Loic and I could look at the baby she carried in its cradleboard.

I saw a little puckered face, very new, and a fringe of black hair.

In those few seconds I lived a lifetime – a lifetime of repentance, uncertainty and pride. I felt like a man falling down a deep dark well, his whole world wiped away in a single moment. And yet the future was in it too: a future of possession, of delight, of a millstone round my neck that would drown me in the uttermost parts of the sea. I knew in that moment that I would never go home again.

Then I heard Loic's joyful exclamations, which hadn't ceased, only I'd not been listening. 'See! The winter was not wasted! She has made me another son! Biinoojii! Martin and Biinoojii! Give him to me! Let me take him!'

Waase'aaban wriggled out of the straps of the cradleboard as Loic grasped it. She turned round, watching Loic hold the small face very close to his own. He shifted the cradleboard into the crook of his arm, and drew Pakané towards him with his other hand. She was holding Martin on her hip. The little boy leaned forward and touched his brother's face.

'*Doucement, doucement,*' said Loic. 'Don't pinch him. I think now we go home, eh?'

He swung Pakané round, and thus entwined, they began to walk away.

I looked at Waase'aaban. In that moment I knew not whether relief or disappointment were uppermost in my heart. Away from her, I'd sometimes panicked at the thought of this impossible entanglement. When I saw her, I knew all things were possible. She was not a Quaker maid, but there was no reason why she should not become one. If I could cross an ocean, why then, so could she. I could make her understand and accept the principles of my Society, and there need be no cause for disownment. I found it possible – which I hadn't done before – to think of her at Highside. Friends are already a peculiar people; never have we conformed to the shibboleths of an unjust world. We believe that there is that of God equally in every human soul. Why then should outward differences matter? In the eyes of a just and merciful God such things are nothing, and less than nothing. I held out my hands to her.

A little quiver ran through her. She wasn't smiling now. She looked at me doubtfully, and half reached out towards me, then snatched her hand away.

Oddly enough that settled all my doubts. I'd come here more than half fearing her advances. Now that she made none, I could think of nothing except how to coax her back.

'Waase'aaban? *Qu'est-ce que c'est?*'

She shook her head, and looked so sorrowful she seemed like to cry, but no tears fell.

'*Je t'en prie*,' I said, and meant it.

She came a little nearer. '*Ce n'est pas possible* ...' She stopped, and looked down.

I took her hands. '*Oui, c'est possible. Je t'aime*, Waase'aaban. I told you I would come back, did I not?'

I hadn't noticed anyone approach us, but suddenly I was seized by the shoulder and pulled roughly back. I swung round; it was no man who thus molested me, but a woman, no taller than Waase'aaban, though maybe twice as old. I didn't know what she was saying to me, but the meaning was plain enough, and loud enough, too, to bring Loic and Pakané hurrying back. Pakané instantly began to argue with the newcomer; I had no idea what was happening. I tugged Loic's sleeve. 'What is it? What is she saying?'

But everyone was speaking at once. The little boy began to wail. Pakané – I didn't know she had it in her – shouted above them all, '*Anwaataan! Anwaataan!*' Then she spoke quietly to the older woman: '*Eya, Ninga, Mii ya'aw Mark*,' followed by a spate of words I couldn't follow. Then she told me in French, with grave dignity, 'This is my mother, Mark. Her name is Beedaubun. She is very angry with Martin and Loic, and with me also, because when my sister came to live with us we did not look after her properly. Waase'aaban was able to go abroad at night as she liked. My mother says if we lived in a proper house, and not the cabin of a white man, this could not have happened. It is a dangerous thing for a young girl to sleep away from her family. My mother says you have seduced Waase'aaban, and this was very wrong of you, to treat her daughter without respect, and bring shame upon our family because of what you did.'

I looked at Beedaubun, and at Pakané and Loic, all regarding me seriously. Waase'aaban stood before her mother, with her eyes lowered and her fists clenched tightly against her chest. If it had been the whole of

London Yearly Meeting of Friends surrounding me, I could not have felt more shamed. Beedaubun began to speak again, more gently this time. I read a sorrowful scorn in her face, which made me wish the ground beneath my feet might open and swallow me up. Naturally it did nothing of the kind. When Beedaubun finished speaking Waase'aaban broke into impassioned protest, but I cut across her and spoke to her mother in such words as I could find, both French and Ojibwa, whatever came to mind.

'It was wrong,' I said. 'But not without respect. I have come back. I have come to marry Waase'aaban, if she is willing.'

I caught the gist of the reply, and even as her mother spoke, Pakané gave me the same words in French. 'To marry her! Oh, yes, we know about your kind of marriage. You will take her for a while, and when it suits you, you will leave her, with children perhaps, to fend for herself. When you have taken her away from her own people, and used her as you wish, then you will go away, and she will be left. That is your English kind of marriage, I think!'

'No!' Loic broke in for the first time. 'Not Mark. Mark would not do that! You give him no chance. You don't know him! Why should he be a worse husband for Waase'aaban than I am for Pakané?'

'Are you an Englishman, Loic?'

'Of course I am not, but—'

Pakané took a breath, and tried to catch up with the torrent of words. 'My mother says to Loic, "No, you are not English! You are of our people, and you are Martin Kerners' son also, who lives always on Bois Blanc. Martin Kerners is a fool. He threw my daughter at the feet of this man, without respect for her virginity or regard for my shame. But at least Martin Kerners is a Frenchman, not like this man here, and that means he will stay among us and have some regard to his family."'

'My father is not a fool!' Loic cut in. 'He thought – we both thought – we were serving Waase'aaban well. Mark is a good man. He has money too. His father has his own farm, and—'

'She says, "But no! And no, and no and no!" She says, "Tell me then, who is this Mark? Where does he come from? Will he live always on Bois Blanc, and look after Waase'aaban, and be a father to her children? No, I can tell you now – he will not! Even if he takes her to Mackinac, and marries her before the white man's priest, he will leave her when it suits him. And therefore I say he cannot have her, whether he says he marries her or no. She is not his!"'

'That's not true!' cried Loic. I saw Waase'aaban's eyelids flicker. Had she not expected Loic to defend me either? 'His word is sacred to him, as it is to us. In this he is not like white men. His people marry our way: they put no trust in oaths made before a priest. They do what we do: they take each other by the agreement of their families and with respect for one another. To break that bond would be as shameful to him as it would be to me, or to my father-in-law when he was alive. I have talked to Mark a great deal, about many things. I would not be shamed – in fact I would be glad – to call him brother. I swear to you this is the truth!'

Beedaubun replied with blazing scorn, and Pakané translated rapidly, 'My mother asks whether you will stay here with Waase'aaban always, and not leave her daughter when it suits you to go home?'

'Tell her,' I said, 'That when I go home to England, Waase'aaban shall come with me. If I marry her, I will never leave her.'

Loic interpreted this time, obviously saying a good deal

more than I had said. I could see it was to no avail, even before he translated bluntly, 'She says, if you take Waase'aaban to England, she will die.'

'Die? Why should she die? I'll look after her!'

Pakané took over: 'She says, "Have you power over death, young man, to be able to say that?" She says, "If you take my daughter across the great ocean, out of the world where she belongs, she will die. Waase'aaban will stay among her own people, and if you will not stay too, then you must leave her now, forever." She says, "Why must Waase'aaban be taken away from her people? Why not you? If you loved her beyond life, you would stay and live among her people. But you do not love her that much. No man loves that much, and if he did, he would be a fool, because to leave your own people and become what you are not – it cannot be done," she says.'

Loic said suddenly. 'I don't know. None of us know. But Waase'aaban has not spoken. What does she say about it? Waase'aaban, do you wish to marry him?'

Waase'aaban looked at her mother, and at me, and pressed her lips together. The answer, when it came, was so low I hardly heard it. '*Oui.*'

'Then will you go to England with him? Will you go to his home?'

I thought she looked at me beseechingly, but I knew not what to say. Then she whispered, 'Forever?'

I looked from her to Pakané, who said, 'She means: never to come home any more?'

They were all quite still, waiting for my reply. Waase'-aaban's mother put her hands on her child's shoulders, not so much possessively, I thought, as offering comfort. I saw Waase'aaban's shoulders relax a little in acceptance. I looked at them, mother and daughter standing together, both looking at me with eyes full of anguish. Just for a moment I saw the striking likeness between them, which was more a trick of expression than a similarity of feature. I looked at Waase'aaban, and a flickering love was rekindled in my heart, as if our time together had been but yesterday. Then I thought about the vast distance back to Montreal, and the river journey to Quebec, and the endless weeks of the Atlantic crossing beyond that. I thought of my home at Mungrisdale, of my parents, of our Meeting at Mosedale, and what Waase'aaban would have to become, in order to belong among us. There was nothing I could say but the truth. 'Ay,' I said hoarsely. 'It would be forever. Never to come home any more.'

'She will die! If you do that to her, she will die!'

'Waase'aaban?' asked Pakané softly.

Waase'aaban looked at me sadly, and I saw her answer in her eyes before she spoke. '*Non.*'

Then she pressed her hands against her eyes for a moment, before she fled from us all, running like a child, out of the circle of adults and away into the woods, where she quickly disappeared from sight.

It was Beedaubun who broke the silence.

'She says, "What have you done to my daughter, white man?"'

I had naught to say. But I looked at Loic, and asked him in English. 'What will happen to Waase'aaban now? I would not ruin her!'

'Ruin?' repeated Loic, as if that were somehow the wrong question. 'How do you mean, "ruin"? She lives. She will live.'

'But if I've shamed her, and her people know it?'

They talked rapidly among themselves, then Loic said to me, 'Who among us has never been shamed? Waase'aaban is young, and there is no child. It is her brother who would feel most shame, and he hasn't yet arrived in Bois Blanc. Any day now he will come. I think you must be gone by then, Mark. No one has told him that a white man has lain with his sister. Probably they will not; he's not a man to accept being shamed before his face. I don't think anyone will try. Otherwise it is not such a great matter. She will marry; she will have children, and all will be forgotten.'

'Is thee telling me the truth? I have thy word? For it wouldn't be true among my people.'

'It is true here.'

What more could I have said to them? I watched them talking among themselves, and then the whole family set off along the path to the Kerners' cabin. I would not go with them, but called to Loic, who came back to me, carrying his son Martin.

'I will go,' I said. 'Can I take the canoe?'

He didn't try to persuade me against it, but merely said, 'My father's small canoe would be better. You'll find it on the beach, by the path. The paddle is underneath.' He gripped my arm. 'I'm sorry it happened like this, Mark.'

'Ay,' I said. 'I'm sorry too. Will thee say my *adieux* to thy family, Loic? I will see thee, will I not?'

'*Oui*. I shall come to Mackinac.' He gave a wry smile. 'For Alan must give me my wages, I think. I will see you then, Mark.'

I found the canoe, but I didn't launch it immediately. Instead I sat alone a little further along the shore. In the place where Waase'aaban and I had spent those two nights there was now a carpet of little purple irises, each flower made as delicately as if it were the only one in the world. I picked one, and sat pulling it apart, while I gazed across to where the turtle's back of Mackinac lay humped across the horizon. I don't know how long I sat there before she came. I half hoped she would; I had no reason to suppose she might, or else I must in decency have gone away at once.

'Mark?' Although I was not entirely surprised, I jumped, for I'd never heard her approach.

'Ay.'

She came and sat down about six feet from me. She'd been crying, I could tell. 'You are truly going back to England?'

'Ay.'

'*Adieu, Marc!*' She stood up.

I reached out my hand. 'No, wait!'

'For what?'

I lowered my hand. 'For nothing, I suppose.' She stood poised, about to leave me.

'Waase'aaban!'

'*Oui?*'

I was on my feet then, and had her in my arms. She was slighter than I remembered, her body taut with tension. I know not what I said to her – or I choose not to remember – but she gave way, and heard me. I did her no hurt at all, but it was an hour or more before we parted, and that for the last time. I let her know I loved her, for that was the truth, and that I had never meant to hurt her, for that was true too, so far as it went. At last she said she must go. I watched her slip away among the willow shrubs, and then I saw her no more.[1]

From the moment that I climbed out of Martin's canoe at Mackinac and carried it ashore, I felt I'd come back too soon. It was like being woken up from the middle of a dream, when thee knows that the end of the dream is the vital part, even as it vaporises into the mists of

---

[1] This was my last visit to Bois Blanc. I last had news through Loic ten years ago, when Alan met him at Sainte Marie du Sault. Waase'aaban, Loic said, had married an Ojibwa from the Huron shore of Michigan very soon after I left. After the Treaty of Saginaw was signed, which ceded nearly half the lands of Michigan to the United States Government, her husband chose to leave his own country, and take his family into the Ojibwa territory west of Fort William, far beyond the rapacious purchases of the white man. That would have been in the spring of '20, the year after the signing. And that was the last Loic had heard of Waase'aaban, at the time.

unconsciousness. Dusk was already falling. I heaved the canoe on to my shoulders, and carried it on the yoke all the way to McGulpin's house, where I laid it near the door. I was lifting my hand to the latch when I heard Alan hirpling up the street behind me.

'Mark! Mark! Have you heard the news?' He grabbed me by the shoulder and shook me. 'The Michigan Territory is ours! Ours since last year! What do you think of that?'

It was weeks since I'd given a thought to Alan's orders from General Brock, or to the letter I'd carried from William McGillivray. Over the winter I'd come to certain conclusions of my own, which made Alan's mission seem to me largely irrelevant. 'How can that be?' I said aloud. 'We never saw any white men in Michigan at all. I don't see how either nation can lay claim to it.'

'There was a battle at the Raisin River. We took the Yankees by surprise, thanks to our Ottawa allies. So you see, I didn't fail completely; some of those allies must have been our recruits.' He peered into my face in the growing dusk. 'Say something, Mark! What are you thinking?'

'*Thy* recruits,' I corrected him. 'If Michigan is in British hands, it seems thee achieved thy ends. Did many men die in this battle?'

Alan didn't meet my eyes. 'Don't be naïve, brother Mark. Men do die in battle.' He hesitated. 'And in this case, it seems our allies killed some of the wounded too, which is their custom, as you know. But there was never an omelette made without breaking eggs. You spent the last four months in Upper Canada after all, brother Mark, though you knew it not. You shouldn't repine.' He was delving in his haversack. 'And here's something else. A letter for you, brother.'

I took the letter, which was sealed with a wafer. I could just read the direction in the half dark. It was written in a firm flowing hand and the sender's address was written over the seal: *C. Armitage, Yonge Street, by York, Upper Canada*. I hesitated to rip the seal. Alan was still talking. I caught the one word.

'York?' I repeated, looking up. 'What about York?'

'Listen, will you, for God's sake! Even you must care! So many things have happened! York is taken! The Yankees have burned York!'

I stared at him, clutching my letter in my hand. 'The Americans . . . they're in Yonge Street? Why didn't thee say so at once?'

'I was telling you about Michigan, which surely concerns us the most. This news came through today: York is taken. And, God help us, Brock is dead!'

'He died defending York?'

'No, Mark. He was killed at Queenston last October. The Americans tried to cross the Niagara and invade Upper Canada. We beat them back. We had the victory, but at what a cost! And this was last October! Since then Sheaffe's been making a mull of the whole business, as you might expect. How could that man succeed Brock? We've been away too bloody long.' Alan laid his shoulder against the door and shoved it open savagely.

'Thee can hardly wish now thee'd come home sooner,' I pointed out mildly as I followed him inside.

He ignored that. He was pacing up and down, his stick tapping on the floor. I crouched down to mend the fire. 'Where's Rachel?' I asked. Alan looked round vaguely. Clearly he'd forgotten all about her. I answered my own question. 'She'll have taken the bairn to bed, seemingly.'

'So while I was lying on my back in that bloody wigwam, our troops beat the Yankees back at Frenchtown on the Raisin River,' went on Alan. 'That's south of Detroit – way south of here.'

'I thought Detroit was taken months ago?'

'It was. The Americans brought this new army up from

Kentucky. It was the same old plan – to cross the Niagara and invade Upper Canada. Winchester bungled it. Instead of pressing on they put up a fort to over-winter – only they were short of rations – no winter clothing – their case was a good deal worse than ours. Even so, they beat Procter at first. But when it came to a pitched battle we made short work of them.'

'Thee means they were all killed?'

'No . . . not exactly.'

'Not exactly killed?'

'I mean, mostly they were taken prisoner – they were induced to surrender, for fear of reprisals from our Indian allies. In fact, brother Mark, Michigan is ours!'

'Thee means thy Indian allies killed them after they'd surrendered?'

'Not all of them, brother Mark, not all of them.' I was intimate enough with Alan to know when he was being evasive. 'If it had been Brock now . . . But then if it had been Tecumseh leading the Indians . . . It's true; I didn't like what I heard. The worst of it is, it gives the Yankees fuel for libel, and by God you can be sure they'll use it.'

'If they speak the plain truth, Alan, there's no libel in that.'

He ignored me. 'But we kept them out of Upper Canada! Brock saw to that at Queenston. But Brock's dead. What's the good of a victory if you don't follow it up? Our Indian allies are still coming in. The worst of it is, now we've lost Brock we don't have a decent general to our name. God knows what'll happen this season.' He knocked against the table, and a stoneware bowl went crashing to the floor, where it broke into two pieces. 'Damn!'

'Sit down,' I said. 'Thee's taken Michigan; thee doesn't need to break up the house as well. Has thee eaten?' Oddly enough, Alan's anxieties over a war that meant nothing to me had the effect of soothing my own mind. Two hours ago I'd been beyond hunger, caught up in my own small whirlwind of loss and pain. Now I was dragged back into this world of strife and conflict, my senses were unaccountably restored to me. I picked up the flinders from under Alan's feet. 'It wants but half a dozen rivets to be almost as good as it was,' I said, examining them.

'Is that all you can say? Is that all you care about?'

'No. But small things must still be thought on, or where would we be?' As I spoke I was rummaging in the bread crock and dresser cupboards. 'Is this all the food in the house?' I asked, as I set out bread and water and a little of our own dried meat on the table.

'There's no food in Mackinac, brother Mark,' said Alan irritably. 'Does nothing interest you but your own empty stomach? Obviously not, or you might realise by now what kind of winter it's been here. The garrison's been on basic rations since September. The first supplies came through from Montreal a week ago. Captain Roberts lies at death's door. The troops had no winter supplies at all. Roberts ordered coats for the soldiers to be made out of trade blankets – that's one thing we did have here – piles of them, in fact. And then the whooping cough broke out in the village – never been heard of in these parts before – and a score of children died of that. There's still a war on, brother Mark. It may not make any difference to you, but this is still the front line. If we don't hold on, that's the end of Upper Canada. If we do hold on it's probably the end anyway. York is fallen. Brock is dead. We're still waiting to see if more Indian allies come in from the west. Some of our Indians did come in from northern Michigan. Askin fitted them out and sent them down to Detroit. I don't know how many came because of me. I guess I'll never know.' Alan aimed a kick at the kindling basket with his good foot. 'I should have been with them! You and Loic would've come back here, and I'd have rallied the Indians myself and gone south with them. Those were Brock's orders, and now he's dead, and I've done nothing! It'd be just the same if I'd never come here. I might as well have stayed with the North West all the time. I wish I bloody had!'

'Perhaps my sister wishes thee had too.' The words were no sooner out than I wished them unsaid. Inwardly I was furious at what he'd just disclosed. Of course I should have guessed it long ago. It wasn't just the betrayal to me, but the unspoken admission that Rachel's recovery had never figured in his plan at all. When we set out, I now saw, privately he wasn't even admitting it as a possibility. It was all I could do to master my own temper, without tramping up and down the room like a caged bear the way Alan was doing. I could have told him too – indeed, I often had – that wars could lead to no good end. He seemed to think, too, that I had no worries of my own, and in an access of self-pity I thought that wrong in him.

As if on cue, the door of Alan's room opened, and Rachel came out, looking sleepy and tousled. 'Alan, can thee stop shouting? Thee'll wake the bairn.'

I could think of no words more calculated to put a man out of temper, but I was quite wrong. Alan looked from one of us to the other, and suddenly grinned at me. 'I beg your pardon, brother. What can a man do with such a family but behave righteously under all conditions? To hell with the war and all our prospects. Put my want of temper down to hunger.' He sat down at the table, and pulled the loaf towards him. 'Rachel, will you eat?'

'I'll be back shortly,' I said. Outside it was quite dark. I walked past the fort to Market Street, where I heard a babble of voices from the tavern where we'd dined my first evening in Mackinac, and over them the thin strains of a fiddle. Above the black rectangles of the houses the stars were out. A new moon had risen over Bois Blanc. I could see the circle of the old moon inside the shining crescent. I watched it for a while, while the heat of rage within me slowly subsided. When I went home Alan and Rachel were sitting opposite one another at the table, eating bread and meat in apparent harmony. They glanced at me as I sat down to join them.

'' Tis the shock, too,' I remarked presently. They looked at me enquiringly. 'Coming back,' I explained, as I took out my knife and cut myself a hunk of meat. 'Coming back to all this. It's a shock.' I looked up and caught Rachel looking at me scathingly. I didn't need to be told that compared to her I had nothing to complain of. I braced myself for a setdown, but she didn't speak. She tossed her head instead, and pulled the mangled loaf towards her.

Alan said presently with his mouth full, 'One thing, though. We hold the lakes. The Yankees can't take us on at sea.'

'It appears they don't need to,' snapped Rachel. 'They can get to York anyway.'

At the thought of this filthy war carried into Yonge Street my heart seemed to lurch within my breast. Under cover of my end of the table, I cleaned my knife on my bread, and slit open my letter. My hands were trembling. I was afraid Rachel would ask me what I was at, but I could wait no longer. I held the paper on my knee hidden by the table, and read by candlelight.

3rd Day of Eleventh Month, 1812
To our Friend in Christ Jesus, Mark,

It was kind in thee to write me a letter. It was a gift to us all to have thee with us last winter. My good-sister Sarah was brought to bed of a fine boy on the 29th Day of Fifth Month last. His name is John, for he hath been indeed a gift from God to this small family. The house is the less sorrowful for his presence, and yet it grieves me when I think how my father and mother and Hannah and Elizabeth would also have delighted in him. Thomas and I think he hath a look of my father, particularly when he smiles, which he hath been able to do since he was two months old.

We have thought of thee and prayed for thee and Rachel each day. Perhaps even as I write thee has found her. Pray God it may be so. 'For the Lord is merciful and gracious, slow to anger, and plenteous in mercy.' But if it be not so, then his will be done. The thoughts of our hearts are with thee, Mark, and we look ever for news of thee, and of our beloved Rachel, and hope always to hear good tidings.

The times have not been easy. The rumours of war, and the depredations made upon our community by the war tax, and the persecution of our young men for the militia, hath been compounded by a lack of harmony within our Meeting, which hath been very grievous to us. I ask thee to hold us all at Yonge Street in the light, and to pray that our differences may be speedily resolved. It is one thing to have war raging without, and another to suffer conflict within. When I say within, I mean both within the Meeting and within our own hearts also, for who cannot be stirred by the winds of controversy that blow upon us from every side, it now seemeth, even from the midst of our own Meeting?

The Declaration of War, though long expected, wrought sadly upon us. The whole world seems plunged into an outward conflict that hath no reasonable prospect of coming to an end. When the news of war came, there was Ministry in Meeting from the twelfth chapter of Revelation, about the woman clothed with the sun, and the moon under her feet, and upon her head a crown with twelve stars, and about the Dragon, which is war, being thrown down from heaven. I cannot say I understand the passage, but the words which stay in my mind are these: And

I heard a loud voice saying in heaven, 'Now is come Salvation, and Strength, and the Kingdom of our God.' I hope and pray it may be so: that out of the calamitous events of our time a Kingdom of Peace may truly come, even on earth as it is in heaven.

David Willson is no longer in unity with us, but holds meetings at his own house on First Day and Fifth Day. For this he was disowned three weeks ago, and this hath made much turmoil amongst us, as thee may well imagine. He left us because he thought us not passionate enough in our desire for peace, nor courageous enough to act upon the visions of that Kingdom of Mercy which God hath opened to us. I think David Willson over-given to a histrionic style of ministry, which is not seemly, but I am concerned that we may not reject the substance of enlightenment because we like not its style. For if ever a flock required a sign from its loving shepherd, this is that flock. We wander in a wilderness of our own making, and the wolves howl at the door.

Meanwhile several among us have joined with David Willson at Gwilimbury and proclaim themselves the Children of Peace, subject not to the letter of the scriptures nor to the oppressions of a violent world, but guided only by the Light that illuminates every man in his own heart.

Friend Mark, we think of thee often, and hold thee in our hearts and prayers. The God of Peace be with thee.

In Friendship
Clemency Armitage

'What is thee doing, Mark?'

I folded the paper and looked my sister in the face. Clemency had said nothing I could not share. 'I'm reading a letter from Yonge Street. Thee can see it after supper.' I put the folded sheet on the table, and addressed her plainly. 'There are no Friends here but thee and me, Rachel. There is none else in Mackinac to witness to our Testimonies. Tomorrow is First Day. Will thee and me have our Meeting for Worship here in McGulpin's house? We can put up a notice on the door, to say that any who wish may attend. 'Twould not be alone' – I said this to reassure myself as much as her – 'for they'll be meeting at Yonge Street too, and at Mosedale, and everywhere else where there are Friends. Will thee join me in that?'

I saw her colour rise and the tears come to her eyes. It was the first time since I'd found her – the first time, perhaps, in the annals of our joint lives – that she looked at me as though she saw me clearly: not just her brother Mark, but the man that I am, myself. 'I'm disowned, Mark,' she said quietly.

'No matter. Is not Meeting for Worship open to any who desire to come?'

'Ay,' she said, still looking at me as if the scales had fallen from her eyes at last. 'Ay, if that's what thee wishes. I will come.'

CHAPTER 26

NONE CAME TO OUR FIRST DAY MEETING BUT OURSELVES, but the news of our advertisement soon spread about the place, and as a result we were visited on the Second Day following by none other than Madeleine La Framboise. Rachel and I were sitting together on the bench behind the house, while the bairn played with the neighbour's cat, which was rolling in the grass at our feet. It was a good-natured tabby that had been used to come into our kitchen begging for scraps when Alan and I had lived at McGulpin's house before.

Our visitor, finding no one in the house, came round to the back to find us. As soon as she saw her, Rachel ran to meet her, and greeted her in the Ottawa tongue. That made me uneasy, especially when they spoke together so rapidly that I couldn't catch the words. Presently Madeleine La Framboise walked over to me. 'So, Mr Greenhow, you found your sister after all.'

'Ay,' I said. A new thought occurred to me. 'Thee knew!' I stated, and looked her in the eyes.

'You did very well, Mr Greenhow,' she said, ignoring me. 'I congratulate you.'

'Thee *knew*!' I repeated, for I would not let it go so lightly.

'Mr Greenhow,' she said to me. 'You know nothing of this country. Who has suffered most, do you think? Your sister is restored to you, and I give thanks to God for all his mercies.' She turned away from me, and smiled at the bairn, who'd sat up in the grass and was staring at her, wide-eyed.

'This is my daughter, Zhawenjigewin,' said Rachel, her chin up.

Before Madeleine could speak again, someone called from the front of the house. 'Alan! Mark! Is anyone there?'

'It's Loic!' I left the two women to each other, and fairly ran round the house.

Loic smiled when he saw me, then embraced me. I didn't recoil; I was just as pleased to see him though had not the same way of showing it. 'Loic! I'm glad to see thee. Come thy ways in.'

After three days of trying to read my sister's unpredictable silences, it was a relief to be able to speak plainly. They were all well on Bois Blanc, Loic told me. It would be better, however, if I stayed away. Waase'aaban's mother had insisted on taking her younger daughter back to the village. Pakané's brother had arrived, but no one had told him anything, and with luck no one ever would. Waase'aaban was sad. 'But she will live,' said Loic. 'And you, Mark? I am sorry it has ended in such a way. You will be all right, though, I think?'

'Ay,' I said. Then I thought Loic deserved a little more. 'I would have married her,' I told him. 'I would be with her now, if I could. And yet when I think it over I understand what Beedaubun said. Perhaps I come from too far away. Perhaps we could not have understood each other enough. I don't know.'

'*Oui,*' said Loic, 'and perhaps also you are a little relieved that you are still free? If that is so – and I think you cannot deny it – I would not think too hardly of your-self. There is no man alive who has not thought that, or wished that, however much he loves his woman, or how-ever sad he is to lose her. For now you may go your ways, and not worry about it any more. And perhaps for a while it was very good, and so you have no cause to be sorry.'

'I did wrong,' I said sombrely.

'Bah! What is *wrong*? It pleased you. You pleased Waase'aaban – of that I am very sure – and now you are free, you will make love all the better to the next woman. In this I see no cause for sorrow.'

'And what of Waase'aaban?'

'Waase'aaban? She is among her own people. She is loved. What more would you? If you say that it was bad to make love to her, you insult her, I think. If you would speak of her with respect, you must admit now that it was good. Isn't that so?'

'Ay,' I said, half convinced.

I walked over to the Company Office with Loic, but Alan wasn't there. We eventually ran him to earth coming out of the rear gate of the fort. There was a note from Rachel when we got back to McGulpin's house which said, *Gone to la maison de Mme La Framboise*. I don't know if Alan or Loic shared my relief, but I was glad we had that last afternoon to ourselves, just the three of us. Alan paid Loic double for all the extra months we'd been away. He said the Company had just paid him, so he could make himself all the richer by giving the excess away.[1] Otherwise we just sat and talked, and when Anne

---

[1] Alan and Loic shared this strange kind of logic about money, which made no sense to me then. Now perhaps I understand it better. It has been my experience that men who give easily often live very well, though they may not grow richer than a life of simplicity requires. Certainly this turned out to be true of both Alan and Loic. Alan also gave me twelve guineas from his pay, for I had no money left, and I still had to make my way home.

appeared to cook the meal we moved outside, until the sun sank behind the house next door. Then Loic and I carried his father's little canoe down to the shore, so he could tow it home. I helped him get both canoes afloat. Before he got in he turned to me, where we stood in calf-deep water.

'*Adieu*, Mark.'

I was prepared this time, and didn't shrink away when he kissed me on both cheeks in the French fashion. 'Farewell, Loic,' I said steadily.

He climbed neatly aboard, and I watched him paddle away into the gathering dusk.

The next morning Alan and I went to the barber. When the fellow had done trimming me, I looked in his mirror, and saw my skin all white where my beard had been, and under the shaggy locks of hair that had grown almost over my eyes, for all that I'd hacked them off myself with my hunting knife from time to time. I used Alan's money to buy two trade shirts and two pairs of grey stockings at the Company store, but I could no longer conceive of wearing my boots in a canoe, so I had on the summer moccasins that Waase'aaban made for me. My squirrel-skin winter cap I'd laid aside – I'd lost the voyageur hat somewhere in my travels – and I bought a broad-brimmed beaver at the trade store. I was loath to do it, thinking how the beaver pelts had been carried all the way to London, and the hat all the way back to Mackinac again, which seemed to me not consonant with simplicity, but I wanted to restore at least a small part of my former self. It was a process that must be faced, along the miles that lay ahead of me, and I thought I might as well begin now.

Rachel was spending much of her time with Madeleine

La Framboise. When she was with me and Alan she scarcely spoke. She looked after Clemency well enough, but it alarmed me when I overheard her talking to the child, for she spoke in the Ottawa tongue, which could not sound natural in my own sister. In fact it made me furious. 'She'll have to grow up speaking English,' I said roughly. '*Thee* speaks English. What does thee think thee's about? The child – and thee should thank God for it – will never be in Michigan again.'

Rachel cast me a look of scorn and horror, seized the baby, who instantly began to wail, and fled the house.

I watched her from the door. Her skirts flying, she ran straight to the garden of Madeleine La Framboise and rushed up to the door. I could hear her sobbing noisily as she went. That was more like the old Rachel. There seemed little point in following her, but an hour or so later I did go round, and knocked at the door. The black maid answered me, as she'd done when I came here a year ago. She offered to take my hat, but I said no, at which she shrugged, and showed me into the parlour.

Madame La Framboise was alone. She greeted me ceremoniously. 'You have come to find your sister?'

'Ay.'

'She is laid down upon my bed.' Madeleine La Framboise gestured for me to be seated, and I sat down gingerly on the edge of a little armchair upholstered in chintz. 'Your sister is not well, Mr Greenhorn.'

'Isn't she?' I was dismayed. 'She's always been healthy enough before. What ails her?' A horrid thought struck me. 'Thee doesn't mean to tell me she's pregnant again?'

For a moment I thought she smiled, but it must have been a trick of the light. 'I am speaking of her mind,' said Madame La Framboise. 'She suffers, I think, more than you know.'

I shook my head firmly. 'Rachel's not mad,' I assured her. 'Not in the least. Sometimes' – I didn't wish to be disloyal, but I was feart we were getting into deep waters – 'she makes folk anxious, with her tantrums and such-like, but there's nothing in it. Why, when she was a little lass, she even found a way to make herself faint – one of the other lasses showed her how to do it – and she'd make play with that. But my mother said take no notice, and she soon got out of it, when it got her nowhere.'

'I don't think you understand,' said Madeleine La Framboise.

'So Rachel tells me,' I said ruefully, and sighed. There was nothing for it but to grasp the bull by the horns. 'Tell me then, if thee pleases, what it is I have not understood, and what it is that we must do.'

'I think you have not properly understood what it means for your sister to have lived among my people for three years, and how it makes it difficult for her to be with her family now.'

'Thee means she didn't want to be rescued?'

'Mr Greenhow,' she said, and there was a pause. Whatever she had been going to say, I am fairly sure she did not say it. Instead she told me, 'I think you have done the best you could, and before long your sister may thank you for it. For the rest of her life she will be grateful to you, I make no doubt. But for now . . .' She looked at me speculatively for a moment. 'I think it would be well if Rachel stays here for a little. Will you explain that to her husband, please? I think it will not be for long. In any case, I go to Grand River quite soon. But for now, I think this is best.'

Explaining it to Alan was not so easy. Since he was never at home, I thought Rachel's absence for a few days would make very little difference to him. I was wrong, but I felt I'd done enough dealing with my sister's crotchets, without having to pander to Alan's. 'If thee doesn't like it,' I said irritably, when I'd listened to him rant for close on ten minutes. 'Thee can go next door and fetch her back. But I'll have naught to do with it.'

Naturally he didn't go. Over the next few days I saw Rachel and Madeleine La Framboise in the garden, or out walking. I missed my little niece – each day that passed marked a lost opportunity with her that would never come again – but I kept my distance. I was rewarded; within a week Rachel came back to us, walking in one evening as if nothing had happened. I never heard her speak Ottawa to the child again – but then I was not always by. The little girl now wore an amulet of some kind round her neck on a leather cord, which I could not like, but I held my peace, and Rachel was similarly restrained with me.

Now that my mission was accomplished, I was anxious to get back to Yonge Street, and render our Friends there any assistance I could. There was no reason for me to stay longer at Mackinac, and every reason for me to go. Alan and I went down to the South West Company office to see if I might get a passage across Lake Huron with the supply boats, which were plying to and fro in spite of the Americans, now that the lakes were open. At the factory we found the clerks passing round an *Upper Canada Gazette* barely two weeks old, printed in York. The existence of the paper spoke for itself, and within its pages the good news was confirmed: the Americans, having raided and burned the Parliament Buildings at York, were unable to sustain a military presence across the lake, and had retired to the New York shore. The worst losses had been the stores in the military depot, and the destruction of a half-built vessel in the shipyard. Both had been fired on General Sheaffe's orders, rather than allow them to fall into American hands.

'So you needn't hurry after all,' said Alan. 'Your friends will have suffered no hurt; the Yankees were only in York six days and never went inland. Stay a few more weeks. I have to be busy, and it's good for Rachel to have you here, just for a little while.'

I let him persuade me. As far as I know Rachel confided in no one but Madeleine La Framboise, and I dared not begin to imagine what they said to one another. But that must soon end, for Madeleine La Framboise was preparing to go to her trading post on Grand River, just as if there were no war on at all. Alan was hardly with us in the daytime. I wondered if Rachel was used to his neglect, as I was. Of course they were closeted together at night. I know not if she told him then any more than she told me. She gave away nothing of the relations between them, but seeing the way that Alan's eyes rested upon her – he was perfectly unconscious of it, I think – I was quite sure his love for her was not only rekindled, but requited too. I prayed that they might not again be separated, for I judged Alan's memory to be none of the longest, in terms of faithfulness, but now that he had Rachel back again, at bed and board, it was as if he'd never been parted from her. He had her measure, too, and I was glad of that. He never seemed in the least discomposed by her sharp ways. I could only wish him joy of her, but still they didn't wish me to take my leave.

Sixth Month came and went. At first the news was all bad. The Americans took Fort George on the Niagara River, and then the British abandoned Fort Erie and withdrew from the Niagara shore. An American army, as Alan had predicted, crossed over by boat and followed the

British into Upper Canada. What the Americans had they failed to hold, however, for less than two weeks later Fort Erie was won back, and on 5th day of Sixth Month seven hundred British troops of the 8th and 49th Regiments beat back an American army numbering three thousand at Stoney Creek. The two American commanding officers were captured, and Upper Canada was again saved from invasion.

At Mackinac all was quiet. The British garrison and the American civilians co-existed in an uneasy alliance against the threat of hunger. Supplies were coming in fairly regularly now that the lakes were open. We were starved more for news. For all that that the Michigan Territory was supposedly part of Upper Canada, it supplied little of our wants at Mackinac. The local Indians brought in fresh fish, which was a welcome addition to our diet, but corn was at a premium, and would remain so until after harvest. Only the Lord knew what would have happened by then.

Meanwhile Rachel and I walked out most days, taking the child, up to Dousman's farm, where the bairn liked to look at the animals, or along the shore, sometimes as far as the beach where the British had landed. Away from the fort and the village the island basked in midsummer quiet. We walked along well-trodden paths in the dappled shade of the woods, and sometimes, when no one was about, I swam in the lake, which was still chill but getting warmer, while Rachel and the bairn paddled in the shallows. We explored the strange rock formations, and climbed up and down the little hill. The islanders at the outlying farms grew used to seeing us. At Dousman's farm we sometimes went in for a glass of milk, but usually we passed the time of day with folk and went our ways.

Thus we created a little pool of peace of our own

in the very eye of the storm. The war raged without, and we heeded it not. We were both well aware of the parting that was to come, and on one occasion we spoke the knowledge that we shared: that this time, when we said farewell, we would most likely never see one another more, at least, not in this world. Never did I feel so much in charity with Rachel, nor had peace between us ever lasted unbroken for so long. The weather was kind, and its benign warmth was reflected in our hearts. I thanked God for this brief blessing vouchsafed to us, and while it was given I was content to turn my back upon the wide world, and live within our little Eden as if we were still children together back at Highside. The bairn thrived, and began to say English words, including my own name. When Rachel and I talked, it was often to talk about old times. At first I was reluctant, thinking that such memories would be hurtful, but Rachel persisted, and I think we came to a better understanding than we'd ever known. She told me a little about her travels with Judith, and once she talked – and wept – about the child that died, and the early months of her marriage.

'I was lonelier then than I've ever been in my life, Mark. I'd cast myself off, by my own act. I'd only myself to blame. That made it worse. One gets to a certain point of loneliness where the outside world no longer matters. Anything can happen. There seems no point in resisting. The strange thing is, by not resisting, one finds a way back into the world. But to lose oneself so far – it's dangerous, Mark. There are no limits to what can happen to thee then.'

I supposed her to be talking about her sojourn among the Indians, and I said, 'Thee's safe home now. Thee can forget about thy captivity, in good time.'

'No!' Clearly I'd said the wrong thing, as usual. 'No,

never! What's "safe" to me? What's "home"? There's no such thing any more! Thee tells me to forget, Mark, as if I were a bairn waking from a bad dream. I tell thee, I'll never forget! I'd never wish to! It's a terrible burden, but it's a gift too, to become two people in the space of one life. It's not a captivity. I think it might be a strength, if only I have the courage to make it so. One thing I know: I can never look at anyone wholly from the outside ever again.'

'Thee thinks about it too much.' I wished I understood better what she was talking about, but I tried to reassure her. 'Thee must go on with thy life, not always be looking back.' I looked at her. 'But if thee can't forget, wouldn't it help thee to tell me what happened?'

'I can never tell thee,' said Rachel with finality, but then she softened suddenly – her moods changed as fast as Alan's did – and she laid her hand on my knee, where I sat beside her on a grassy bank above the shore. 'I love thee well, Mark. I'll never forget what thee's done for me. I wish I could talk about it ... I know thee wants me to explain ... I can't. Has thee never noticed, the more thee and I talk to one another, the less we agree? I think it was always so, and now more than ever, perhaps. I'm sorry, have I hurt thee, saying that? I don't mean to; I have much to thank thee for.'

'I'm not likely to judge thee,' I said, not answering her last question. She had hurt me, and not for the first time. No one else ever seemed to think my understanding so deficient.

'I *have* hurt thee.' She was watching me more closely than I liked. 'And thee hurts me, sometimes, more than thee knows. I wish ... When thee gets home, I'd like thee to remember ...'

'Ay?'

'When I was little, I liked to be with thee more than anything,' said Rachel suddenly. 'Thee wouldn't always let me come with thee. Less and less, in fact. I was hurt. I would have liked above all things to be thy brother. Will thee remember that?'

'Ay.' My own memory of the past was that the older she'd got, the more impatient she'd been with me. Often she'd say things that made no sense, and made me feel stupid and humiliated, though I did my best to hide it. I don't think we were made to understand each other. Very soon we'd be parted. There was nothing I need explain; I wanted the last days to be good ones. 'Ay,' I said again. 'I'll remember that.'

On First Days we put up our notice of Meeting for Worship at McGulpin's house, and after that first time when it was just the two of us, four or five people usually came. They were nearly all women. I think mostly they were curious, but I believe the silence may have spoken to them in some degree. I didn't ask: their inward lives were no business of mine, but I like to believe they found a little space of peace among Friends in that time of war. It was a small pebble cast into a whirlpool, and the ripples from it were swallowed up at once. But there is no knowing who was touched a little, and in that I put my faith, as ever.

The time came when we had to think of the future. Alan was to go to Fort William in Seventh Month, when the brigades would come through from Montreal for the North West Company rendezvous. He had to see the agents, he said. The future of the South West Company, and the relations between the North West and the American Fur Company would remain in doubt so long as there was war. There'd been no news from the Pacific.

'That's where the issue will be decided,' said Alan. 'I have to find out.'

'And what will thee do then?'

'I don't know. I'd like to go back to the North West. When I get to Fort William I'll talk to Sim and Tomas. I'm sick of this bloody war. You could say I've made a mull of it, for my own part. I'll do what I have to do for my country, but I'll be damn glad when it's over.'

'I thought thee enjoyed it? I didn't know thee fought for England?'

'I don't enjoy it,' said Alan shortly. 'Whatever I thought at the beginning, I don't enjoy it now. And I'm not English. This isn't an English war, Mark. Do you see Napoleon at Mackinac? I don't.'

'So what is thy country then? Great Britain?' I'd never seen him disillusioned before, and I was curious.

Alan shrugged. 'How should I know? I knew once, but I don't now. Where I live, I suppose. I don't want the Yankees in Canada. I'll go on fighting for that if I have to. But I wish it were all over.'

'So thee will fight, or go back to the North West. And what of Rachel? And the bairn?'

'If I get Montreal leave this winter, I can get them settled there. I'm hoping that's what the agents will say. By next spring this leg should be as good as ever. If they'll take me back to the North West, I can keep your sister in clover, brother Mark, whatever the Yankees may do. The fact is we'll win this war – you don't need to worry about that – and I'll look after her, better than I did before. That I promise you.' He looked sideways at me – we were sitting on the bench outside in the cool of the evening – 'I'm serious, Mark. I will look after her, you know.'

I came out of Mackinac a hybrid creature, in patched

grey breeches and a deerskin tunic (my plain coat was tattered beyond redemption, and suitable cloth was short in Mackinac). Alan, Rachel, the bairn and I left for the Sault in a South West Company canoe. I'd forgotten how fast eight voyageurs in a *canot du nord* could speed through the water. I wasn't required to paddle, so I was able to look about me. I'd never done this journey in daylight. We crossed St Martin's Bay, and followed the shoreline east, skirting several small islands, and finally rounding the point and heading north-west past St Joseph's Island and into the Straits of St Mary's. There was no border to worry about now. We kept our eyes open, for although the British held the Lakes, and the Indians hereabouts were friendly, there was no knowing whether American ships might be lurking among so many islands. The lake breathed around us in a gentle rise and fall, so smooth that when I looked back I could see a line of little eddies where the paddles had dipped. We hugged the left shore close enough to see each tree along the forest's edge. The islands on our right lay in a blue haze, sometimes close and sometimes so far off they could have been a bank of cloud. I watched the long line of St Joseph's Island and thought of the time I'd talked to Alan in John Askin's house, less than a year ago.

The moon was waxing full, so after we'd crossed a bay – about a mile or so of open water – we went ashore so the voyageurs could eat and rest, and then pressed on into the night. I was reminded all the more of that first moonlit journey on this river. The water shone like glass, until it fell within the shade of the forest, where all was pitch-black and impenetrable. So the long miles passed, until at last we saw white water gleaming ahead of us, which was the rapids at the Sault. We crossed the river, and beached among half a dozen other canoes below the North West jetty. There we camped for the remainder of the night. In spite of the thoughts and memories that crowded in upon me, I slept sound.

When we walked up to Charles Ermatinger's house next morning, the Sault appeared unchanged, except that there were more militia about the place, and that made me all the more aware of the changes in myself. I could not rest; the sands were running out fast, and I would feel easier now, I thought, when all was over. When I accompanied Alan to the Company offices, I saw a two-masted schooner on the river, its mainsail being slowly furled. While I was waiting for Alan I watched while the other sails were lowered, and the ship drifted neatly in alongside. I read the name on the bow: *Nancy.* Even as the men were tying the moorings, I was walking down to see if there was anyone I could speak to. But I'd barely set foot on the jetty when I heard a shout from the shore path. 'Monsieur Greenhorn! By all that's wonderful, Mark Greenhorn!'

I spun round. '*Hugh!* Hugh Chisholm!'

We shook hands heartily. ''Tis you indeed, Greenhow! I thought it was one of the old *coureurs de bois* come to haunt our Factory. But no, 'tis a Quaker dressed in skins, which is even more remarkable. But you have a new broad-brim, I see! I thought the red cap suited you right well.' All the while he was still staring at me in clear amazement and shaking my hand, pumping it up and down as if he were genuinely glad to lay eyes on me again.

He told me his brigade of canoes had arrived in the Sault barely half an hour ago. The canal was busy today, for everyone was on the way to Fort William. They were waiting their turn to go up into Superior.

'Is Marc with thee?' I asked him. 'And Jean-Pierre? And Jacques?'

'Marc is here. Jacques went for a soldier a year ago. Jean-Pierre – I know not. Young Alban is with us. But what of you, Mark? You did search for your sister?'

'Ay, and found her too.' I grinned at his astonishment. 'She's here at Charles Ermatinger's house. And Alan is here too – he's in the Company office right behind thee.'

After that everything happened so fast I could barely take it in. Perhaps God in his mercy disposed it so, for a drawn-out parting would have served no good purpose. The canoes could not wait. The rendezvous at Fort William was more pressing than any private business. Alan and Hugh had it all fixed in minutes. Then Alan went quickly back to Ermatinger's house to say goodbye to Rachel. Hugh sent Alban with him to carry his things. I watched them go. When Alan was walking fast the limp was still evident. A year ago he would have run. I hoped with all my heart that I had set the leg right, and next year he would be as hale as ever.[2] Hugh and I walked up the canal path, while I told him all that had happened. We found Hugh's brigade still waiting in the queue of canoes to go into Lake Superior through the lock. When Marc saw me he leapt ashore, and, schooled by Loic, I submitted to his enthusiastic greetings. *'Mais regardez-vous, mon brave! Quel homme vous êtes devenu! Je suis fier de vous, mon voyageur!'*

The three of us stood by the canal, talking fast, for there was little time to tell all the news we had, while the canoes floated offshore beside us. Hugh asked me, 'And what will you do, Monsieur Greenhorn, now that

[2] I did get Alan to tell me eventually, when I pointed out I'd set the bone myself, and naturally had an interest in my handiwork. He said the bone was as strong as ever, but he was troubled with a limp until the surgeon in Montreal said this could be cured by making the sole of one boot quarter of an inch thicker than the other, and that, wrote Alan, had pretty much done the trick.

your task is done? Will you take your sister back to Montreal?'

'No. She'll wait for Alan to come back. Charlotte Ermatinger invited her to stay with them until that happens. There's nothing more for me to do. I can go home.'

'So you'll go straight back to England?'

'First I must see my friends in Yonge Street. Then I'll go back.'

The last canoe of the previous brigade had left the lock. Marc ran back to his canoe. The water level in the lock fell slowly, came level, and the lower gate was raised. Hugh and I strolled over as the first of Hugh's brigade paddled into the narrow space. One by one we watched the loaded canoes go through. The gates were just opening for the last one when we heard quick irregular footsteps on the boarded towpath behind us.

'Just in time,' said Hugh cheerfully. 'We'll let them go through and get aboard from the bank. All right, Alan?'

'Ay,' said Alan shortly. I wondered how Rachel had taken this sudden departure. I didn't ask, but quietly followed the others past the lock. The *canot du maître* – it seemed so large to me now, after my long acquaintance with Loic's canoe – slid through the gate, and came in close to the bank, which shelved steeply enough for the three men to be able to step aboard. Alan's small chest was lifted over, and Alban stepped aboard after it. He held out a steadying hand to Hugh, who took his place in front of Marc. Hugh shifted his haversack over to make room for Alan beside him. Alan held out his hand to me. '*Au revoir*, brother Mark. I have much to thank thee for.'

I took his hand. 'Fare thee well, Alan.'

Suddenly he let go my hand and hugged me hard. '*Sòraidh slàn leat, a bhràthair. Turas math dhut!*'

This time I made no attempt to follow the canoes along the shore path. I stood still where they'd left me until they'd disappeared into the haze that hung over the lake. I thought I saw a flash of white, which might have been Hugh waving his handkerchief, but the lake was very misty, and I may have been mistaken.

Before I went back to Rachel I finished my interrupted errand, and found the captain of the schooner. They were busy unloading the supplies and trade goods they'd brought in, and as soon as that was done they were leaving again for Penetanguishine. I was welcome to take passage with them – the ship was going back almost empty, the captain said – but I must be aboard before dawn, for the wind was favourable, and they intended to leave at first light.

'So,' said Rachel, when we stood on the jetty that evening, my knapsack and basket of provisions at my feet. 'This is it. If I'd known when I woke this morning what one day would bring ... It's a mercy I didn't, I suppose.' Suddenly she took my hand, and held it between both of hers. 'I wish Clemency were old enough to remember thee.'

'Ay,' I said. 'I wish that too. Thee'll tell her about me, though.'

'Ay,' said Rachel.

I wondered what she would tell the child, and what would lie hidden until all who'd been part of the tale were dead, and the truth was gone for ever. It was likely I'd never see the bairn again, nor Rachel either. The sands had almost run. There were things I had never said, the sort of things no man says for so long as there is always tomorrow. I tried, awkward as I was, to say them now. 'I love thee, Rachel. Thy mother and father love thee. To us thee can never be disowned.'

'Ay, Mark, thee's shown me that.'

My sister was never one to hug and kiss. When we were children she dealt out a slap more easily than a caress, and, knowing I'd be chastised for hitting back, I mostly kept out of range. For the first and last time in our lives we fairly clung to one another. The moments passed, and vanished. When she let me go I shouldered my knapsack. She brushed her tears away, reached up, and briefly touched my cheek. By the time I'd reached the gangplank she'd left the jetty. The last I saw of her, she was striding away along the shore path, back to Ermatinger's house where her little girl lay sleeping. I waited, in case she looked back, but she never turned. I picked up my basket of food, walked up the gangplank, and stepped aboard.[3]

[3] I have never seen my niece or my sister since. At Fort William Alan was interviewed by the North West Company agents, and as a result he was re-employed, as a senior clerk, by the North West Company. They gave him Montreal leave that winter, so that his leg might heal. Alan arrived in Montreal with his wife and child in Ninth Month, about four weeks after I'd left the city. He never told me how he was employed in the last year of the war, but after the peace in '14 he was back in Montreal. He bought a house near Mount Royal – he sent me a neatly penned sketch of it – in which he installed his little family. The last letter I have from Rachel is dated Twelfth Month, 1814. I think she was happy when she wrote it. I have it in front of me now. She speaks lovingly of her little girl, and says, *I think thee will be happy for me, Mark, when I tell thee that we are to be blessed with another little one in Seventh Month. Truly the Lord hath been good to us, after our long travail. I think it will be good for Clemency; the bairn is in a fair way to becoming spoilt, between the two of us, and will profit by the addition* . . .

It was late in 1815 when Alan's letter came. The baby was a difficult cross-birth. My sister Rachel was in labour two days. The bairn died with her, unborn. Alan went back to *le pays d'en haut* the following year. My niece Clemency grew up in her father's house in Montreal, cared for by her nurse and governess. Alan had her educated at a Convent, which I could not like, but the nuns taught her to write a dutiful letter: that at least I can vouch for. In the folds of Rachel's last letter I found just now an embossed invitation card, which arrived at Highside early in 1833: *Alan Mackenzie requests the pleasure of your company at the marriage of his daughter Clemency* . . . When it came, I wrote back and told him plainly that even if the letter had arrived in time, I could not have met such a request, the distance being too great, and it being contrary to the Principles of our Society to attend a marriage made before a priest. I wrote to my niece and told her we would, as always, hold her in the Light, and that her husband Georges Camelon would henceforward share her place in our prayers and hearts. I expressed as well as I could the affection I bore to her for her mother's sake. She wrote back very prettily; I have since heard from her twice more; there are two children now, or is it three?

As for my brother Alan, he became an agent of the North West Company when the war was over, and after '15 he over-wintered in *le pays d'en haut* for several years. When the North West merged with Hudson's Bay in '21 he was more often in Montreal, but he'd still be away in the wild country for months at a time. I know he made money. What his domestic arrangements were – or are – I have never asked, and he has never told me. He is a faithful correspondent. We were born in the same year, so I can very well imagine what it is like for him to grow old. I can't imagine that either of us will ever cross the ocean that lies between us, and as for that other crossing we must make, I believe with all my heart in the mercy of the God who created us, but whether we rise again at the last so as to know one another again, that I do not know, nor do I find it my heart to believe it, however much I may wish it might be so.

CHAPTER 27

I'D LEFT YONGE STREET FIFTEEN MONTHS AGO JUST as the snow was melting. I returned in the drowsy heat of a summer evening, while the shadows lengthened across the dusty track before me. It was a long day's walk south from Penetanguishine. The swell of the lake was still with me, so all the time the forest seemed to be gently rocking. Occasionally I drank from a shrunken creek, but otherwise I never stopped walking, while the day-long heat waxed and waned, and the sun glared relentlessly on the white road ahead of me. My mind was still full of images of chasing clouds and open water, and a myriad islands that grew wilder and rockier as we'd sailed into Georgian Bay, reminding me more and more of my own hill country far away. When I got to Yonge Street I was not prepared for the little farms with their neat fences. The settled land seemed so small and tame. I'd meant to think things over while I was on the road, so I'd be ready, but the present had turned too quickly into the past. When I stood in the stern of the *Nancy*, watching the Sault disappear from my sight, although the ship was quickly caught by the current and borne away, and myself with it, my sad heart refused to follow, and it hadn't caught up yet. So I was arriving unprepared, and I felt a little pang of fear because of that.

Presently I met a man walking along the road towards me. He wore a broad-brimmed hat and a plain grey coat of old-fashioned cut. I had not worn such a coat myself for over a year.

'Good evening, friend,' he said, as he passed me.

'Good evening,' I replied, but I didn't call him Friend, for I didn't wish him to know me, though I vaguely recalled his face from Meeting.

I felt his eyes on my back as I walked away, but I didn't look round.

I saw Amos Armitage's place by the roadside and turned right along the farm track before I reached it. The potholes were baked hard and full of little stones. I walked slowly, feeling parched and sticky. My boots were coated in white dust. I felt a strange fluttering under my ribs. When I reached the door of Thomas's house it was open, and – I looked twice – a little child was sitting on the clean step, clutching the remains of a jam tart. Its face and its short frock were liberally spread with jam. Its fat cheeks bulged. Tendrils of red hair had escaped from under its starched cap.

'Good evening, Friend,' I said gently. The baby stopped chewing and stared at me with round blue eyes as I reached over its head to knock at the door.

My throat was so dry that my voice came out as a feeble sort of croak. But someone heard, for a voice cried, 'Come in, Friend! Who is there?'

She was standing at the kitchen table in an apron that was too big for her, rolling out dough. With the heat of the cooking fire the room was like a furnace. I stared at her, unable to believe my eyes. Her mouth fell open when she saw me; she was as amazed as I was, but after the first second she recognised me. Whatever I had expected, it was not this. 'Aunt Judith!'

'Mark!' She dropped her rolling pin, and the next thing

I knew her floury arms were round my neck, and she was hugging me. 'Mark! Our little Mark!'

'Not so much of the little, Friend.' I extricated myself as politely as I could – my aunt had never embraced me before – and looked into her face. 'Judith, how came thee here?'

'Mark, lad, I could ask thee the same.' She wiped away two tears with the corner of her apron, and left a streak of flour across her cheek. 'I feared thee was dead!' With a touch of her old manner she added, 'Could thee not have written, Mark?'

'I did write. Did Clemency not say?' I added, although truly there was no need to justify myself. 'I couldn't write to thee. Thee left no address.'

'Ay,' said Judith. 'Clemency had a letter. But that was dated Seventh Month last year! Where has thee been, Mark? Thee never found her, then?'

'Ay. I found her.'

'Then where is she?' she flashed, as if I'd carelessly left Rachel in the yard. Some things never change.

'I'll tell thee,' I said. 'All is well. But I've walked a long way, and I'm hungry. I'll tell thee all. But where is Cl . . . Thomas? And Sarah?'

'Thee *found* her!' She was only just beginning to take it in. 'Oh, Mark, lad! Does thee mean it? Thee doesn't just hope to spare me?'

'Judith,' I said sternly. 'Would thee doubt my word?'

'No, no!' she cried. ''Tis just that . . . I never thought . . . Thee *found* her!' Her face grew sharp in sudden fear. 'Dead, Mark? Is she dead?'

'No. Alive and very well.'

'Ah!' Judith made a sound that might have been a sob. '*She was dead and is alive again, she was lost and is found.*'

'Ay,' I said.

I saw her face begin to work, and then all of a sudden she cast herself upon my chest and hugged me as she had never done before. 'Oh, Mark, lad! Oh, Mark!' I tried to think of her as my mother's little sister – as indeed she was – and not as my formidable aunt Judith, and I did my best to soothe her, as it might have been my own mother. Presently I got her to sit down and be a little more rational.

'Oh, Mark, lad, may the Lord be thanked. For God is indeed merciful to us! Thanks be to God ...' We were silent together for a little space, and then Judith said. *'For his mercy is on them that fear him, Throughout all generations* ... Thanks be to God! Now, Mark, tell me ...'

There was a wail from the doorstep.

'Johnnie! Here I am, sweetheart.' Judith hurried away. She came back with the sticky infant on her hip, and began rubbing its face with a piece of flannel. I winced in sympathy; I could remember having the same thing done to me, possibly by the same efficient hand.

'This is Thomas's baby?'

'Of course. This is John Armitage. Is he not a fine lad?' John was jerking his head to and fro, trying to avoid the wet cloth. 'That's my good lad!' cooed Judith, and set him on his legs. He clung to her skirts, and watched me. I met his gaze. I had forgotten until this moment that when I was a little lad Judith had not irritated me in the least. I'd forgotten that when she baked she used to make us pastry people and our own special jam tarts out of the bits of dough left over. I found myself smiling at her. 'Truly, Judith, all is well. Rachel is safe. I'll tell thee the whole story. But I never thought to find thee here. Clemency said thee was going home.'

'Ah, Mark, I thought to go! But when it came to crossing that ocean again – and this without my companion. I thought of that terrible sea, and the truth is, Mark, lad – cowardly though it be – for would I not have been in the hand of the Lord as well as if it were on dry land? –

I could not face it. And when I laid this before the Lord, he put it into my mind, as plainly as thee spoke to me just now, that this particular cup was not mine to drink. For there is work for me here. Also, Mark, I could not leave, knowing that thee, and Rachel, had vanished into the pathless wilderness, and I the only kin thee had in this land to pray for thee and watch for thee. Sometimes I could not keep faith in my heart – I thought we would hear no more of either of ye ever again – but I knew what I must do. I have not so much life left that I should grudge spending the rest of it in waiting.'

I was touched. 'That was kind of thee, Judith.'

While I ate the jam tarts that were put in front of me, I told her nearly all that had happened. Judith exclaimed, and wept a little more, and altogether behaved more harmoniously to me than she had done since I was out of short coats. I gave her time, and then, when still no one of the family had appeared, I asked her casually, 'Is Clemency not here, then?'

'Clemency? She went to pick raspberries – we're making preserves, Mark. In fact – 'tis pity thee didn't know. Thee could have brought more jars from York with thee.'

'Where?'

'Mark, lad, I don't know. They have glass enough in York, I've no doubt. Now round here there's not a glass jar to be got for love or money, not at this time of year, and everyone coming round here trying to borrow the jelly pan, which I bought myself in Philadelphia, for I noted the lack of it before.'

'Aunt Judith, I meant, where is Clemency?'

'Gone to pick raspberries, as I told thee.'

'But *where* . . .' I caught her eyes, and reddened. Aunt Judith is as shrewd as they make them, and this wasn't the first time in my life I'd been taken in by her. It dawned on me too, that this was her way of expressing her joy and thankfulness that Rachel was restored to the world.

'The far side of the hayfield, as if thee was going to the Indians' lodge. Just before thee gets to the forest.'

I turned to go, but just as I reached the door she came over to me and gave my arm a little squeeze. 'Thee truly has come back,' she whispered, as if still trying to convince herself. 'Oh, Mark, lad, thee truly *has!*'

I crossed the shorn field slowly, for I had much to think on. I was already resolved, and yet uncertain. I knew the thoughts of my own heart, or thought I did, but no man can ever be sure of the thoughts of another. The hot sun beat upon my back. The smell of ripe hay still lingered, and I could still see the marks of the scythe in the new-cut grass. I reached the fence, and followed a well-beaten path towards the forest gate. A tangle of nettles and brambles half hid the rail fence. There were raspberry stems among the thickets, all picked bare. Someone had lifted down the gap rail. I came to the opening, and saw a young woman in a grey gown with a basket on her arm. She had her back to me. I came close enough to see the red curls escaping from under her cap. Then she heard me, and swung round.

I'd forgotten the pockmarks. Since I saw her last I'd looked upon much beauty, and I'd forgotten how scarred she was. Tendrils of red hair had fallen across her forehead. She must have been so pretty once. Her body – the way she held herself – was young and full of grace, but not so graceful as one that I remembered.

'*Mark?*' It was a question, not an exclamation, as if she couldn't quite believe that it was I.

'Judith told me I'd find thee here.'

Perhaps in that first instant I'd given away more of my thoughts than I knew, because she hung back, as if she were afraid I had come so far only to hurt her.

'Thee saw Judith? She sent thee? Did thee find out . . . Did thee find anything about Rachel?'

'I found her,' I told her. 'She is back with her husband now. She has a little lass, about the age of thy nephew, John.'

She gazed at me, and slowly I saw a great light dawn in her face. Her smile was as generous as I remembered it. 'Oh, Mark! God has shown thee his mercy! I am so thankful for thee. How came it about?'

I began to tell my story again as we walked slowly back across the hayfield with the basket of raspberries scarcely half-filled. It made me blithe to see Clemency so happy that her friend was safe and well. But before we came to the yard I stopped her going in.

'There is one other thing I must tell thee.'

'What?' she said quickly. 'Is it something bad?'

'Bad? Why should it be bad?' I took my courage in my hands. 'Clemency, I want to marry thee. Here. Soon. Amongst our Friends in Yonge Street. I'd like to take thee back with me.' She looked as if she didn't understand, so I stumbled on. 'To England, I mean. To be my wife. I mean that my home will be thine, and everything I have I'll share with thee.'

She gave a little half smile, as if that pleased her. Then – the ways of women are ever strange to me – she frowned, and was silent. 'Why does thee want to marry me, Friend?' she asked at last.

'Because I love thee.' That was true, as far as it went, and I had every faith that it would grow.

She gave me a considering look. Never had a silence seemed so long. Then she said, 'I too have somewhat to tell thee.'

I felt a sudden chill, as if the sun had set before its time and left me in icy shadow. I was not the only man in Yonge Street . . . I might have guessed it. Never did she seem to me so desirable as now. I had to ask her, though. 'Ay?'

'Did Judith tell thee anything about what's happened here since thee's been gone? No? She didn't mention the Children of Peace?'

'Who?' I felt the sun rise again silently in my heart. 'The Children of Peace? Who are they?'

'I told thee in my letter how David Willson was no longer in unity with Friends in Yonge Street, didn't I?'

'Ay, thee did.'

'He had visions,' said Clemency. I cared not a whit for David Willson's visions, but clearly Clemency did, so I gave the matter my serious attention. 'I have to tell thee, Mark! It was like this: Peace may walk through the world, but we see her not. She is a woman robed in red – red for all the blood that is shed on earth, for all the killing of men by men, all who have died in war and bloody conflict since the world began. Peace walks among us, but wherever she goes men turn upon her and revile her and try to kill her. Whenever she bears a child, wild beasts devour it as soon as it is born. She can never be fruitful and multiply, for the hounds of war forever swallow up the fruits of peace. But in David Willson's vision she comes to earth again, and she carries two children in her arms, the Children of Peace, and through them peace may come to earth at last.'

'Ay,' I said. 'Ay, well.'

'Mark, thee must understand me! We're so close to each other here in Yonge Street, and so few! I knew not what to think. And now thee asks me to decide another thing! I used to trust myself, and now I cannot! Does thee – I mean thee, Mark – never think it possible that thee may be mistaken?'

'Friend, I've made a mort of mistakes in my time. But this that I ask thee – no, I'm not mistaken about that.'

'Thee doesn't believe in visions?'

'I wouldn't say that,' I said cautiously. 'George Fox had visions enough. I've thought about such matters quite a lot since last I saw thee. If we were all Children of Peace it would be no bad thing. I'm not sure about David Willson, though, I must admit. I trust him not.'

''Tis not just David Willson. 'Tis the Doans, and . . . Even some of our elders, Mark – even Amos and Martha Armitage – oh, several very weighty Friends – have left Yonge Street and gone over to David Willson's Meeting for Worship – for so they call it. They call themselves the Children of Peace, and we are no longer in unity with any of them.'

'I can see why thee's troubled.'

'Friend, I was more than troubled!' She was suddenly vehement. 'I was tempted – oh, more tempted than thee can imagine. It wasn't just that I was lonely, and full of grief. It wasn't just that I thought to be alone for evermore. Not just my own hurt – all that I feel, all that's happened to me – it's only a part of something larger that happens to everybody. And every time we compromise, every time we let the world be as it will, and depart from the principles of our Society – even by the least little bit – then we bring more strife into the world, and more sorrow. Among the Children of Peace . . . at least perhaps they have a clear vision of a better world. At least things become simple – some sort of simplicity is possible.'

'Simplicity is not the same as turning thy back on the world.'

'I didn't say that!'

'No, and thee hasn't joined the Children of Peace, has thee?'

'No, but what I'm saying to thee, Mark, is that I've been sorely tempted. There's such strife and turmoil every-where. Sometimes I think I might join them yet. Has thee never found thyself – even in thy heart – out of unity with Friends on any matter?'

'Ay.' The question struck home. My thoughts were in turmoil but I tried not to show it. 'Ay, but the principles of our Society must be more reliable than the promptings of our hearts. Sometimes it may be hard to see that, but it must be so. Thee – I mean we – we make mistakes sometimes, and then we have to put them behind us, and let them be gone.'

'If it were only that simple!'

'Lass,' I said. 'There's naught so simple as what I'm asking thee.'

'I don't think so,' said Clemency, but at least I'd made her smile, though I couldn't think why.

She hadn't given me her answer, but for the time being I forbore to press her. When we went in we found everyone at home, and a good smell of stew from the pot simmering over the fire. There was much rejoicing that night over our lost sheep that was found. There was sadness too, because Rachel could never come back to us, but great joy and thanksgiving that she lived, and was safe and well, though she could never again be in unity with Friends.

The next day was First Day, and we went to Meeting. I found it much depleted. I was told that above thirty members had departed from the Meetings round about and joined the Children of Peace at Gwilimbury. It seemed to me that the Meeting at Yonge Street was much beleaguered, by strife within and war without, and I feared for it. They had the stalwart presence of my aunt Judith, to be sure, and they gave me a good welcome. I had no great desire to help them in their affliction, I must admit. I wanted nothing more than to go home, but I still had not got what I came for, and so I bided my time for seven days. I was kept busy helping with the hay harvest. It was the custom in Yonge Street for everyone to turn out to help their neighbours, reaping at each farm by turn. So it was that I met everyone I'd known before, and was taken back into their midst as if I'd never been away.

There were certain things I had to watch in myself. I had unwittingly departed from our manner of plain speech – indeed I have not quite regained it to this day. I had talked over-much to those who were not in unity with us, and who had a very different manner of expressing themselves. I had also read too much of a secular nature, and now that habit was formed it was never to be undone, though naturally I didn't mention this to the Friends at Yonge Street. A literary habit was better understood by Friends in my own country, for here we're used to poets and such-like, even in our own dales. I'd grown used to my deerskin tunic, and when the Friends kindly supplied me with a new plain coat, I put my wilderness accoutrements aside with a suppressed pang of regret. I kept quiet also about some of the items in my knapsack, particularly the string of bears' claws, and my quill-embroidered moccasins.[1] I was not afraid to bring out my hunting knife, though, because Thomas wanted to know all about the bear, and how we had survived by hunting through the winter far beyond the frontier in the Michigan Territory. He admired my sundial compass too. I never mentioned to him that I'd learned to smoke tobacco, but while I was at Yonge Street I began to feel the want of it as never before, so

---

[1] These claws now hang from the mirror over the washstand in our bedroom, which I use each day to shave by. The moccasins were the warmest house-slippers I ever had. My wife patched them for me many times, until at last they fell apart. I sent a bale of furs, including the bearskin, by North West Company canoe to Montreal, where I found it waiting for me at William Mackenzie's house, as directed. The furs are pretty well-worn now, but the hearthrug in here I will not change. Alan and Caleb wouldn't wish me to: they have lain on it as babies, played rough games with it as lads, and read their way through my library while stretched out on it, and neither they nor I would have anything in this room changed one whit.

much so that one afternoon I walked away into the forest, and took the path to Mesquacosy's wigwam.

But of course it was still high summer, so the winter camp was deserted. I looked at the bare frame of the wigwam, and the empty hearth, and to my surprise I came close to shedding tears. It came home to me there, I think, that what was past would never come again.

On the eighth day I went back to the stubble field with a rake after supper, for I could not rest, and occupied myself in a desultory way gleaning some of the leftover stalks. The treetops to the west of me were tipped with gold, but down in the field creeping shadows crossed the shaven grass, softly sprinkling it with dew. I could smell the cool of the evening in the air. I ached for my own home, and for something more tangible as well. I wished I had some tobacco, even though the mosquitoes weren't troubling me tonight. I reached the end of a long row, and looked up, leaning on my rake.

Clemency was sitting on the rail fence watching me, her feet up on the rail like a boy, and her chin in her hands. The unshorn grass beneath the fence was thick with buttercups and vetch. Clemency's cap was awry, as usual, and a lock of thick red hair curled over her shoulder.

'Thy cap's crooked.'

'Ay,' she sighed. 'It always is.' She put her hands up to straighten it.

I dropped the rake, walked over to her, and took the cap off her head entirely. It was as I thought: a cloud of wild hair flew up all around her head. She gaped at me, and through the scars I saw her blush. 'What is thee *doing*, Mark?'

'What is *thee* doing, watching me like that and saying naught? How long has thee been there?'

'Give me back my cap!'

'Thee came to find me?'

'Give me back my cap!'

'No.' I pulled her down off the fence and held her arms above her elbows. 'Will thee marry me?'

She looked me in the eyes, and I could see her own were troubled. 'I love thee,' she said simply. 'But thee . . . I don't know. I never thought to see thee more.'

An image flashed through my mind, faster than the twinkling of an eye, of the shore at Bois Blanc. This was no different, only it couldn't be done that way, not this time. With Clemency it must be after the manner of Friends. 'I love thee,' I said. 'I told thee that. I'd like to sail from Quebec before the winter comes. My parents are waiting for me, and I want to be home. They'll welcome thee, I know, as if thee were their own daughter. So I need to know from thee now, is it yea or nay?'

'Yea,' she said, and so the matter was settled between us, for all time.

The whole of Yonge Street Meeting came to bear witness to our marriage, and in their ministry they spoke of the unity that would ever be between themselves and us as Friends, for all that the great ocean would soon divide us, never to meet in this world more.[2]

---

[2] While Judith remained at Yonge Street we got news of the Meeting there at least once a year. She also informed us of the subsequent history of the Children of Peace. In '25 they began to build their great Temple at Gwilimbury, which was decorated with banners representing the visions of David Willson, and within which edifice, Judith said, they had music and chantings, all far removed from the principles of the Religious Society from which they sprang. Since Judith left Yonge Street seven years ago, and went to live with Friends in Philadelphia, we seldom hear from Yonge Street Meeting. Thomas is a poor correspondent, and on the rare occasions he does write to his sister he has little to tell us, other than the state of the weather and the harvest. It would be kinder to Clemency if he were to say more about his growing family, and the Friends in Meeting, but a man is as he is, and I'm sure if we were ever to see Thomas again, it would be as if we had but parted yesterday.

Editor's afterword

I TURNED THE LAST PAGE. IN FRONT OF ME THERE
was nothing but a blank sheet. It had a few brown spots
at the edges. I couldn't – wouldn't – believe it. I turned
over every page until I reached the end of the foolscap
notebook. Eleven pages. Every single one was completely,
maddeningly blank. Mark had cheated me at the last.
There had still been the deceptive thickness of pages
under my hand as I turned the last sheet. How could
he leave me like that, without one word of warning or
farewell to the reader who'd followed him every step of
the way? He didn't even tell me how he and Clemency
got home. Right up to the foot of his very last page his
script was as close-written as ever, with no indication that
he had plenty of room to spare for all he wished to say.

I've done all I could to find out more. I don't know
if the rest of Mark's life was uneventful. I can only say
that, so far as either archives or local tales can tell us,
it was unrecorded. There is nothing left of him but the
grudging record of birth, marriage and death. (I'd known
Mark's death date for weeks: he attained his threescore and
ten, and a few more years besides. Clemency outlived him
by two years.) Being a Quaker, not even his tombstone
is marked. Presumably he was buried in the graveyard at

Mosedale, which is just across the road from the Meeting House. In life he must always have been taciturn in public. I came upon his private history as an eavesdropper, like a thief in the night, and only within its stolen pages can I hear his voice. I find myself thinking about all the other stories that have vanished into the silence, all the voices that will never be heard any more.

As I sit at my desk I can hear a hammering from the loft, where the builders are at work (they didn't come at all yesterday, or the day before) on my new study. In a few weeks I'll have moved the computer and all these papers into my new workspace. Right now I have a temporary desk at the sitting-room window. I look out towards the head of Derwentwater, and between the showers I can see Grasmoor washed in mist, like a pale ghost. I climbed to the summit of Grasmoor last week. I've been up Blencathra too: you can go straight out of our back gate on to its eastern slopes. I'll miss this view when I move upstairs. This is where Mark sat. *Here*. He actually sat *here*, in what seemed to him to be the present, as this seems to me to be now.

The thing I'd like to know more than anything else – this is irrational, I realise – is, did he achieve the one ambition he ever expresses? Did he indeed walk every ridge in Lakeland, from Swarthmoor to Caldbeck, from Gosforth to Shap? In all my researches I have done my best to stick with the things that I know for certain, but my inmost thoughts are my own to do what I like with: I choose to believe that he did.